"SO YOU WANT TO KISS ME."

"Surely that doesn't surprise you." He tilted his head, his gaze lowering to her lips. "You've been kissed before, perhaps?"

Her lips felt dry, and she resisted the impulse to lick them. "Innumerable times."

"But not by me."

His mouth closed over hers.

Pulsing heat coursed through her. She was used to being in control, but as his lips molded to hers, teasing and consuming, she felt anything but in control. Her mind, her heart, all her senses were spinning wildly.

Slowly he bent her back against the tree. Warm, sure fingers slid down her shoulders, caressing her waist and hips, then drifting lower. A distant, dreamy part of her became aware of the rustling of her skirt and the cool breeze that brushed across her legs.

"*Victoria!*"

Tearing her mouth from Althorpe's, she drew in a gasping breath. "Yes, Father?"

Avon Books by
Suzanne Enoch

Suzanne Enoch

With This Ring

Meet Me At Midnight

AVON BOOKS
An Imprint of HarperCollinsPublishers

This is a work of fiction. Names, characters, places, and incidents are products of the author's imagination or are used fictitiously and are not to be construed as real. Any resemblance to actual events, locales, organizations, or persons, living or dead, is entirely coincidental.

AVON BOOKS
An Imprint of HarperCollins*Publishers*
10 East 53rd Street
New York, New York 10022-5299

Copyright © 2000 by Suzanne Enoch
ISBN: 0-380-80917-6
www.avonromance.com

First Avon Books paperback printing: October 2000

Avon Trademark Reg. U.S. Pat. Off. and in Other Countries, Marca Registrada, Hecho en U.S.A.
HarperCollins® is a trademark of HarperCollins Publishers Inc.

Printed in the U.S.A.

10 9 8 7 6

For Cheryl and Mark—
Hugs and kisses.

Chapter 1

⌒⌒⌒○⌒○⌒⌒⌒

Lady Victoria Fontaine threw back her head and laughed. "Faster, Marley!"

Below her, Viscount Marley tightened his grip around her legs and began spinning around even more recklessly. The other dancers fled to the edges of the ballroom despite the beckoning notes of the quadrille, their glares and envious whispers just a whirling blur. This would be the *last* time her parents kept her housebound for three days. Teach her restraint—ha! Chuckling breathlessly, she flung out her arms.

"Faster!"

"I'm getting dizzy, Vixen," Marley panted, his words muffled in her gown's rumpled green silk. He hefted her higher in the air.

"Then spin the other way!"

"Vix . . . damnation!" Marley lurched sideways, tottered, and dumped them both to the polished ballroom floor.

"Oops!" Vixen laughed again as her herd of admirers swooped forward to assist her to her feet. Poor Marley had to scramble out of the way to avoid being trampled. "Gadzooks, that was fun." She staggered

1

sideways, blinking as the room continued to swirl and
dip.

"Whoa, Vixen," Lionel Parrish crooned, catching
her up against him. "You nearly showed off your unmentionables to the Duke of Hawling. We can't have
you falling again and giving him an apoplexy."

"I feel like a whirligig, Lionel. Please help me to a
seat."

With Vixen back on her feet, several of her herd
took pity on Marley and pulled him upright, as well.
He dropped into the chair beside her as they found
seats at one side of the room. "Dash it, Vixen, now
you've made me seasick."

"You need a steadier constitution," she said, laughing and out of breath. "Someone fetch me a punch, if
you please."

Immediately half the herd scattered for the refreshment table, while the other half moved in to take their
vacated places. The musicians rallied to begin a country dance. As the ballroom floor refilled, Lucy Havers
escaped from her mother's view and hurried over to
sit on Victoria's other side.

"My goodness! Are you unhurt?" she exclaimed,
grabbing Vixen's hand.

Victoria squeezed her fingers. "Quite. Marley broke
my fall."

He sent her a glare. "If you were a large woman,
Vix, I'd be dead right now."

"If I'd been a large woman, you wouldn't have
lifted me into the air like a victory flag." Grinning, she
returned her attention to Lucy. "Is my hair at all sal-
vageable?"

"Mostly. You've lost a comb."

"I have it, Vixen," Lord William Landry announced,

holding up the delicate ivory piece. "I'll return it to you . . . in exchange for a kiss."

My, that's a surprise. Trying to straighten her midnight ringlets, which did have a definite droop on one side, Victoria favored the Duke of Fenshire's third son with a speculative smile. "Only a kiss? That is my favorite comb, you know."

"Perhaps we might negotiate for more later, but for the moment a kiss will suffice."

"Very well. Lionel, kiss Lord William for me."

"Not for five hundred quid."

Everyone laughed, while inwardly Victoria sighed. The longer she put it off, the more he would gloat about it and insinuate she owed him—and dash it all, that *was* her favorite comb. She stood, straightening her skirt, and stepped up to William Landry. On tiptoes, she brushed her lips against his cheek before he could intercept her for a sounder kiss. He reeked of brandy, but that was no great surprise.

"My comb, please," she said, holding out her hand and unable to keep the smug look off her face. He should have known by now; no one bested the Vixen.

"That hardly counts," William protested, scowling, while the rest of the herd guffawed at him.

"It looked like a kiss to me," Marley said helpfully.

"Hush," Lucy said. "Lady Franton's glaring at us again."

"The old witch," William muttered, and handed over the comb. "If she were any more stiff, she'd be six feet under."

"Perhaps she needs to be spun," Lucy suggested, giggling.

"I could suggest several things she needs," Marley

added darkly. "Though I'd have to be six feet under before I'd give any of it to her."

Lucy turned crimson. Victoria didn't mind frank speech, but neither did she want her few civilized friends driven away. She rapped Marley across the knuckles with her fan. "Stop that."

"Ouch! Defending the downtrodden again, are you?" He rubbed his knuckles. "Lady Franton's more elevated than your usual charity cases."

"You're a bad influence, Marley," she said, beginning to become annoyed. She was used to the flirtations and the insults to her civic-mindedness, but her herd never seemed to come up with anything new to discuss. "I don't think I'm going to speak to you any longer."

"Hm. Bad luck for you, Marley," Lionel Parrish said. "Make way for the next fellow."

Immediately the herd began jostling for position, and Victoria wasn't quite certain whether they were joking or were utterly serious. They expected her to be flattered by the attention, but in truth, it was becoming very, very old. Being behind locked doors at Fontaine House almost seemed attractive in comparison. Almost. "I've decided to make a vow," she stated.

"Not of chastity, I hope," Lord William returned with another guffaw.

Lionel Parrish frowned through the laughter, taking a step closer to Lucy. "This is hardly the place for that sort of talk."

"Watch your knuckles, William," Marley agreed, removing his own hands from Victoria's reach.

"My vow is just as bad for you, Lord William," Victoria retorted. Thank goodness her parents were in Lord Franton's portrait gallery admiring his new acquisitions. William's was only one of several remarks this evening that would help convince them to send her to a convent. "From now on, I intend to converse only with nice men."

Shocked looks greeted her pronouncement, until Stewart Haddington began laughing. "But who else do you know besides us scoundrels, Vixen?"

"Hmm," she mused, trying to regain her equilibrium and her sense of humor. Perhaps Marley had spun her right out of her usual self. "That *is* a problem. Marley, you must be acquainted with a few nice gentlemen. You know—the ones you're always avoiding."

"Certainly I know a moldering corpse or two. But they'd bore you to tears in an instant."

He moved closer, obviously trying to reclaim his usual place at her side, but she made a show of looking for Lucy and stepped aside. She didn't know why, but tonight she couldn't seem to shake the feeling that she'd done all of this before, and that it hadn't been very amusing even then. "How do you know I'd be bored?"

"Nice men are dull, my dear. That's why you're here with me."

"With us," Lord William corrected.

Victoria scowled at the lot of them. Unfortunately, Marley was correct. Nice men *were* dull—and stuffy, constrained, and narrow-minded. And their repertoire of compliments to her looks and insults to her thoughts was the same as anyone else's. At least rogues agreed to spin her. "I only tolerate you gentlemen because you obviously have nowhere else to go," she said haughtily.

"Sad, but true." Lionel nodded, unrepentant. "We're to be pitied."

"I know I pity you," Lucy said with a giggle, blushing again.

He kissed her knuckles. "Thank you, my dear."

"We . . . good God," Marley hissed, his gaze on something at the far end of the ballroom. "I don't bloody believe it."

Victoria started to censure him on his language again, until she spied what—or rather, who—had caught his attention. "Who is that?" she breathed, suddenly conscious of her heart beating fast and hard against her ribs.

Lucy turned to look, as well. "Who is . . . oh, my. Vixen, he's looking right at you, isn't he?"

"I don't think so." Her pulse thudded. "Do you?"

"The bastard," Marley growled under his breath.

He seemed familiar, yet she knew she'd never set eyes on him before. She had the forceful sensation that a Greek god had strolled into Lady Franton's stuffy old ballroom. His elegant dark gray clothing and confident stride as he moved through the crowd proclaimed him a noble; the way he kept his attention on her while greeting acquaintances proclaimed him a rake. But she knew every rake in London—and none of them had ever made her nerves hum with restless anticipation, or made her feel the blood rushing through her veins.

"Sin personified," Lord William grumbled.

"Althorpe," Lionel echoed.

Surprise jolted through her. "Althorpe? Thomas's brother?"

"I'd heard the prodigal son had returned," Marley added, intercepting a footman for a glass of Madeira. "He must have run out of blunt."

"Or they ran him out of Italy." Lord William

watched Lord Althorpe darkly as he made his way unwaveringly toward them.

"I thought it was Spain he was ravaging."

"I heard Prussia."

"Can one be asked to leave an entire continent?" William mused.

All around them, Victoria heard similar speculation, tense and breathless murmurings that mingled with the strains of the country dance. She only half listened; she felt poised on the brink of something—though of course that was ridiculous. Rakes stared at her all the time. "He looks very like his brother," she said in a low voice, trying to regain her uncertain balance. "Thomas's coloring was lighter, though."

"Thomas's soul was lighter," Lord William countered, and stepped forward as the dark male disruption reached them. "Althorpe. Surprised to see you in London."

The Marquis of Althorpe inclined his head. "I like surprises."

Victoria couldn't pull her attention from him. No doubt every female in the room had her eyes glued helplessly to his lean, rangy form. With all the rakes she'd encountered, she'd never seen one who seemed quite as . . . dangerous. His superfine gray coat hugged his broad shoulders and emphasized his narrow hips; black breeches clung to his muscular thighs. The new marquis projected a strength and power that were almost animally attractive.

His eyes, the golden amber of fine whiskey, didn't smile at all as he gazed at her herd of male admirers. She'd half-thought he meant to stride right up to her, throw her over his shoulder, and make away with her,

but he stopped in a civil enough manner to greet the
gentlemen surrounding Lucy and her.

The low drawl of his voice resonated down her
spine, and she tried to ignore the sensation—without
success. A lock of black hair had strayed across his
brow, and her fingers itched with the abrupt desire to
brush it back from his tanned face. His sensuous lips
curved in a slight, jaded smile, and she didn't think it
was her earlier spinning that now made her feel light-
headed.

"Vixen, Lucy, allow me to introduce Sinclair Graf-
ton, the Marquis of Althorpe," William was saying.
"Althorpe, Lady Victoria Fontaine and Miss Lucy
Havers."

The amber gaze returned to her face, studying and
assessing. He took her gloved hand and bowed over
it. "Lady Victoria."

Althorpe then turned away, greeting Lucy in the
same manner, and unexpected, unaccustomed jealousy
stabbed through Victoria. It was ridiculous, but she
didn't want to share her new discovery. With anyone.
"Lord Althorpe. My condolences about your brother,"
she said, deliberately interrupting him.

He returned his attention to her. "My thanks, Lady
Victoria. Had you heard, Marley, that—"

"You're welcome. I would have expressed my condolences earlier, of course, but you weren't available."

Althorpe's gaze traveled the length of her. "If I'd
known you waited in London to comfort me, I would
have returned much sooner," he murmured.

"What does bring you to London?" Marley asked.

The viscount's tone didn't seem particularly
friendly, but no doubt he didn't appreciate the additional competition. Her herd had developed an internal

hierarchy over the course of the last Season or two, one that left Marley with the greatest privileges toward her. She didn't particularly appreciate that, but as none of the others held any more interest for her than he did and it kept the arguing to a minimum, she'd let it go.

The marquis shrugged dismissively. "It's been a while since I've visited, and now that I'm titled, my position has improved. So, tell me, Marl—"

"You've been titled for two years, as I recall," Victoria interrupted again, ignoring Lucy's surprised look. Damn it all, she didn't want him wandering off with Marley to drink and talk about women and wagering.

Again he looked at her. She wished she weren't so petite, so that she didn't have to look up at the towering nobleman standing before her. The top of her head barely came to his shoulder.

"So I have." Something flickered in his amber gaze, though it was gone so swiftly that she couldn't be certain she'd seen anything at all. "Do you have a personal interest in the Althorpe title, my lady?" he continued in his deep drawl.

"Your brother was a friend of mine."

This time she was certain something sharpened his expression. "How unique. I didn't think my stuffy old brother knew anyone who walked without the assistance of a cane."

That seemed callous in the extreme, and she wondered whether he was intentionally baiting her. Why, she had no idea, but she wouldn't stand for such nonsense—not even from the late marquis's own brother. "Thomas was not—"

"Perhaps we might discuss this during the waltz,"

he said, glancing across the room as the orchestra began playing one.

A thrill ran along her nerves again, and she began to suspect that she'd become demented. "This dance belongs to Mr. Parrish," she said. Devilishly handsome or not, Sinclair Grafton was obviously just another self-centered rake—and she had enough of those about already.

Althorpe didn't bother looking at Lionel. "You don't mind, do you, Parrish?"

"Ahem. Not if Vixen doesn't," Lionel answered diplomatically.

"I mind," Marley broke in.

"It's not your waltz." Althorpe held out his hand. The gesture wasn't a suggestion, but a command. "Lady Victoria?"

His manners were turning out to be less promising than his looks. But since she'd already made one scene that evening, Victoria settled for clenching her jaw as he took her around the waist and swept her into the dance.

Touching him, the magnetic sensation was even more powerful. She wondered if he felt it as well. "That was rude, to cut Lionel out like that," she chastised, to have something to do besides stare up into his enigmatic eyes.

"Was it?" The hand around her waist pulled her slowly closer to him. "I prefer to think of it as simply taking advantage."

"To what purpose?"

"You," he answered without hesitation. "Do I need another purpose?"

She sighed, disappointed. Just another rake with the same old well-worn lines. "So out of all the ladies present," she returned, half wondering why she bothered, "you decided to waltz with me."

"I have impeccable taste."

"Or everyone else knows your reputation and turned you down," she countered.

The fleeting something touched his gaze again. "Yet you know my reputation and are dancing with me."

"You didn't give me any choice."

"That would have been unproductive. As you see, I am a successful rake."

She pursed her lips. "How productive is a waltz?"

A considering look touched his face. "For me, the waltz is only the beginning."

Her body swayed against his, their hips brushing, and the heady, dizzy sensation she'd experienced on first seeing him returned, even stronger. Perhaps Marley had twirled her too vigorously—something had shaken up her insides.

But it would take all of her fingers and toes to tally the number of times an experienced rake had attempted to seduce her, and failed. She knew all the lines of that play, and yet with Lord Althorpe she hadn't the least desire to exit. "You have further plans for me, my lord?"

"I'd be a fool or three months dead if I didn't have further plans for you, Lady Victoria." His voice was almost a growl, sensuous and very sure of itself.

Despite herself, a small shiver of anticipation ran down her spine. "You can't shock me, you know."

Humor lit his amber gaze. "I'd wager that I probably could. Twirling is hardly the depth of scandalous behavior. And they don't call me Sin for nothing."

She hadn't been aware that he'd been present at the Franton ball for so long—and she felt like she should have known. She should have sensed his heady, dangerous presence the moment he'd entered the room. "So shock me, Lord Althorpe."

His gaze lowered to her mouth. "We'll start with kisses, then. Deep, slow ones that last forever, that melt you inside."

Heavens, he was good—but he wasn't the only one who had wits. "Perhaps you should begin with *why* you want to kiss me, Lord Althorpe, considering that five minutes ago you were more interested in speaking with Marley than in dancing with me."

Abruptly she sensed that she had his full attention. Nothing changed; not his expression nor his hold on her nor his graceful steps, but she suddenly knew why he had caught her notice from all the way across Lady Franton's ballroom. And why she hadn't felt his presence before. He hadn't wanted her to.

"You must allow me to make amends for giving you the impression that I overlooked you, then," he said in a low, intimate tone, and glanced around the crowded room. "Do you know of anywhere more . . . private where I might apologize to you?"

She wasn't about to flee at his implication and let him think he'd cowed Vixen Fontaine; no one had ever accomplished that. Besides, she wasn't ready to allow him to escape just yet. "Undoubtedly Lady Franton has locked the doors to anywhere secluded."

"Damnation." He cast a scowling glance toward her herd. "We'll have to make do h—"

"Except for her famous garden," she finished. There. She'd called his bluff. Now he could be the one to back down from the challenge.

Instead of conjuring an excuse to remain safely in public, though, he smiled—the least friendly, most dangerous smile she'd ever seen. "The garden. Might I apologize to you in the garden, then, Lady Victoria?"

Uh-oh. Declining now was out of the question, since she'd suggested it. "I don't require an apology," she returned airily, hoping she didn't sound completely demented, "but you may render me an explanation there, if you wish."

They had already neared that side of the ballroom, and it was a simple matter to slip through one of the half-open windows lining the east wall. Lady Franton's exotic garden had won prize ribbons for years, and if not for her familiarity with the grounds in daylight, Victoria would have been hopelessly lost twenty feet from the main house. A scattering of torches dimly lit the flagstone pathways that wound through the flora, rejoining into a circular path around the small pond at the garden's center.

Now that they had escaped the ballroom, she expected Althorpe to conjure a distraction. In all likelihood he'd never expected her to join him, and his flirtation had merely been a tease. One did not publicly remove earls' daughters from a ballroom in order to seduce them.

Part of her, though, wished that weren't so. Her boredom had abruptly vanished; she wanted to sink into him, to have his touch envelop her as his words and his voice had enveloped her senses already.

"Your explanation, my lord?" she prompted. If he intended on retreating, she wished he would get on with it and quit tantalizing her with his presence.

"We're not private enough yet." The marquis slid his hand beneath her elbow, keeping her close beside him, and guided her along the path winding around to the pond.

Uncertain anticipation ran hot just beneath her skin. Light as Lord Althorpe's touch was, she sensed the strength underneath, a hint enough to know that she couldn't pull free from his grip if she wanted to. Far from frightening her, he aroused her in a way no other man had ever managed. She wondered what his lips would taste like, how they would feel pressed against hers.

They stopped beneath the purple overhanging blossoms of a wisteria, the scent of the flowers drifting about and encircling them in heavy summer sweetness. "Now," he murmured, facing her, his palm still cupping her elbow, "where were we? Ah, yes. I was rendering you . . . an explanation."

Victoria met his gaze, golden and catlike in the torchlight. She was very aware of the steel beneath the velvet of his grip; the isolated quiet broken only by the muted chatter of voices and violins and the rustle of the wind, and even the way he had positioned her between the heavy wisteria branches and his lean, hard body—two equally immovable objects.

Whatever it was, he wanted something. Something from her. "I was wrong earlier," she said, trying to sound nonchalant. Sin was a powerful temptation, indeed.

His gaze drifted down the length of her gown and returned to her face. "Wrong about what?"

"When I first saw you, I thought you resembled your brother. You don't."

With one long finger he reached out and brushed a straying lock of hair from her face. "How well did you know old wooden head?"

A tremble ran down Victoria's spine at the feather-light touch. Her involuntary response bothered her, since his callousness offended her. "The Marquis of Althorpe was well respected."

The finger traced her cheekbone. "And I'm not? That's hardly a revelation."

Good God, he was making her shiver. "I don't comprehend why you speak so poorly of your own brother," she countered, trying to keep her voice steady, "particularly when everyone else admired him."

He studied her face in the flickering torchlight, and she had the sense that something besides flirtation had his interest. "Apparently not everyone admired him," he countered. "Someone did put a ball through his head."

Victoria stiffened. "Don't you care at all that he's dead?"

Althorpe shrugged. "Dead is dead." His fingers traced the curve of her ear. "Did I hear Marley call you the Vixen?"

Suddenly things made sense. "Was this entire conversation an attempt to get Vixen Fontaine into the garden, so you could brag about it to all your friends?"

The marquis froze for a heartbeat, then softly caressed the corner of her mouth with his thumb. "What if it was?" His sensuous mouth curved into a slow smile that stopped her breath. "But I don't have any friends. Only rivals."

"So you want to kiss me."

"Surely that doesn't surprise you." He tilted his head, his gaze lowering to her lips. "You've been kissed before, no doubt. By Marley, perhaps?"

Her lips felt dry, and she resisted the impulse to lick them. "Innumerable times. And not just by Marley."

"But not by me."

Then his mouth closed over hers.

Pulsing heat coursed through her. She was used to being in control—of both her emotions and her encounters with men. Yet as his lips molded to hers, teasing and pulling and consuming, she felt anything but in control. Her mind, her heart, all her senses were spinning—more wildly than they ever had in Marley's arms.

Althorpe's hands cupped her face as he tasted her. With a breathless sigh that didn't sound at all like her, Victoria slid her arms up around his shoulders, pulling herself closer against him.

He slowly bent her back until she leaned against the gnarled trunk of the tree. Warm, sure fingers slid down her shoulders, pausing to caress her waist, then her hips, then drifting lower. She tangled her fingers into his hair, trying to guide the heated pressure of his mouth against hers. All she could hear was their ragged breathing and the flying roar of blood through her veins. She'd never felt so hot and dazed and wanton.

A distant, dreamy part of her became aware of the cool breeze that brushed across her legs, hardly enough to cool the heat between them. She was glad for the tree; without it, she wouldn't have been able to stand upright.

"Victoria!"

From the fury in the voice, that might have been the fifth time the Earl of Stiveton had shouted her name, but it was the first time she heard it. Tearing her mouth from Althorpe's, she drew in a gasping breath. "Yes, Father?"

Basil Fontaine stood at the edge of the fish pond and glared at her. His fist clenched a glass of Madeira so tightly that Victoria was surprised he hadn't shattered it. "What in God's name are you doing? And get your hands off her, Althorpe!"

Sometime during their kiss, the marquis had gathered her skirt past her knees and her thighs, exposing her stockings and her silk unmentionables to the moonlight. His kneading, caressing hands had pulled her nearly naked form to the hard length of his body while she'd clung to him helplessly. Slowly, as though he hadn't a care in the world other than kissing her, he lowered his hands from her. Where he had been touching her felt hot.

She wanted to look up at him but resisted the temptation as she straightened. Flustered and discomposed as she was, she couldn't bear to see it if their kiss hadn't affected him as it had affected her. She was the one who made men swoon at will; it wasn't supposed to be the other way around.

"You must be Lord Stiveton," the marquis drawled.

"I don't intend to introduce myself to you under these circumstances, you blackguard! Move away from my daughter!"

Victoria frowned, rational thought beginning to penetrate the warm, rosy cloud. Father hated scenes, particularly the ones that involved her. He certainly wouldn't shout and stomp and draw attention to one—unless it was too late to hide it, and he was trying to salvage what he could of his own good name. She glanced beyond the fish pond, and her heart missed a beat.

"Fiend seize it." Her voice was barely a whisper.

"Not quite the ending I'd envisioned," Althorpe murmured, apparently still unconcerned.

Lady Franton's entire guest list stood on the far side of the fish pond, tittering and whispering and pointing.

At least it seemed like the entire multitude had appeared to witness her latest and worst scandal.

"How dare you carry on with my daughter in that manner!"

Her mother emerged from the crowd to join her father. "Victoria, how could you? Do as your father says, and come away from that awful man!"

Victoria tried to force her brain to function again. She felt sluggish, as though even now she would rather be standing beneath the wisteria kissing the tall rake beside her. "It was just a kiss, Mama," she said in as calm a tone as she could muster.

"Just a kiss?" Lady Franton, their hostess, repeated in her shrill voice. "He was practically inhaling you!"

"No, he—"

Lord Franton stepped into the torchlight. "This is beyond the pale," he announced, as half a dozen of his burliest footmen pounded up behind him. "I let you join us tonight out of respect for your late brother, Althorpe. Obviously, though, you cannot be trusted to conduct yourself in a manner befitting your st—"

"Might I make a suggestion?" the marquis said, his voice as calm as if he were discussing the weather.

No doubt he faced angry crowds all the time. Victoria, though, felt mortified. High spirits were one thing; being caught kissing—being inhaled by—a notorious rake was something else entirely. And now everyone had practically seen her bare bottom!

" 'A suggestion?' " Lord Franton echoed scornfully. "There's only one thing that could put this right, and it's not clever jests and making fun of—"

"Before you continue your tirade," Althorpe interrupted, "I returned to England with the intention of assuming the duties of my title."

Victoria risked a glance at him as the garden abruptly quieted.

"I have no wish to cause offense to either Lady Victoria or to you for our slight indiscretion," he continued, his tone dismissive. "I will therefore 'do the right thing' as you so eloquently put it, Lord Franton: Lady Victoria and I shall marry. Does that satisfy your requirements for propriety?"

Victoria felt the ground drop out from beneath her feet. *"What?"* she gasped.

He nodded, his eyes and expression unreadable as he glanced down at her. "We both stepped too far. It is the only logical solution."

She scowled. "The only 'logical solution,' " she snapped, "is to forget this entire incident. It was a kiss, for heaven's sake! It's not as though we set off for Gretna Green!"

"With his hand halfway up her . . . you-know-what? That was no first kiss," the Duke of Hawling blustered from the crowd of onlookers, while dozens of others echoed the statement in more graphic detail. "With Althorpe's—and the Vixen's—reputations, no doubt he's already well on his way to an heir."

"You were practically . . . fornicating! And in *my* garden!" Lady Franton fainted artistically into her husband's arms.

The accompanying titters and mutterings of agreement were simply too much to bear. "I have never set eyes on him before tonight!" Vix yelled.

"It's not where your eyes have been that we're concerned about, Daughter," her father growled, white-faced. "You'll call on me tomorrow, Althorpe, or I'll see you jailed—or hanged."

The marquis sketched a short bow. "Until tomorrow." He took her hand in his, bending over her knuckles and brushing them softly with his lips. "My lady." With that he turned on his heel and strolled back in the direction of the house.

The rat. Victoria wanted to join him in fleeing, but her father stalked forward to grab her by the arm. "Come along, girl."

"I am not marrying Sin Grafton," she spat out.

"Yes, you are," he hissed. "You've gone too far this time, Victoria. I kept warning you, but you couldn't be bothered to listen. If you don't marry him, none of us will ever be able to show our faces in London again. Half of your fellows have seen your unmentionables—twice in one night, from what Lady Franton told me!"

"But—"

"Enough!" he roared. "We will make the arrangements tomorrow."

Victoria opened her mouth again, but at her father's furious glare she humphed and subsided. Tomorrow was still a good distance away. She would have ample time to explain things when her parents had calmed down enough to listen. One thing was certain, though: she was *not* going to marry Sinclair Grafton, the Marquis of Althorpe, under any circumstances. And certainly not just because he'd swooped in like a dark, seductive demon and said so.

Chapter 2

That damned bastard Marley was still managing to make a wreck of his life.

It had been a close decision: stealing the viscount's female companion, or his last breath. Given the consequences of last evening, Sinclair wasn't certain which would ultimately prove more satisfying.

Someone scratched at the master bedchamber door. Sin ignored it and continued shaving. His valet, though, straightened and glanced at the entry.

"No," Sinclair said before Roman could suggest anything.

"It might be important. Your bride-to-be may have fled England."

"Or one of her other suitors may have arrived to shoot me." One in particular he wouldn't mind seeing. He had a lovely ivory-handled pistol in his pocket for just such an occasion.

The scratch repeated, louder.

"Master Sin, you—"

"Stop being so damned jumpy."

The valet glared at him for another moment, then

pushed away from the wall and stalked over to yank open the door. "It's Milo, my lord."

Not the least bit surprised that his valet had defied him, nor at the identity of his visitor, Sinclair went to work on his chin. "Thank you, Roman. Why don't you see what he wants?"

"I would, my lord, but he still isn't speaking to me."

Somehow, whenever Roman said "my lord," it sounded like a euphemism for "halfwit." With a sigh, Sin dropped his razor into the shaving bowl. Picking up a towel, he climbed to his feet and faced the doorway. "Yes, Milo?"

The butler stepped past Roman, making a point of not looking at the stocky gargoyle of a valet. "The post just delivered a letter for you, my lord. From a Lady Stanton."

Milo's tone wasn't much friendlier than the absolute silence with which he favored Roman. Sin wiped the remaining shaving soap from his face. "Thank you." The butler handed over the missive, and his employer pocketed the folded paper without looking at it. "Milo, did you often interrupt my brother's toilette to bring him insignificant correspondence?"

The butler flushed. "No, my lord." He lifted his pointed chin. "But I do not yet know your routine. Nor was I aware that the letter was insignificant. I apologize if I was in error."

"Apology accepted. Please send Lady Stanton a bouquet of red roses, with my compliments. And inform Mrs. Twaddle that I will not be taking my dinner here this evening."

Milo nodded. "Very good, my lord."

"Milo."

The butler turned around. "Yes, my lord?"

Sinclair granted him a dark smile. "Never mind about Lady Stanton. I'll see to her myself."

"I . . . yes. As you wish, my lord."

As soon as the butler's heels passed over the threshold, Roman shut the door on him. "You should hand that Mr. Highboots his papers."

Sin shrugged as he returned to his dressing table. "Milo's a competent enough butler."

"Well, I don't like the idea of you keeping your brother's staff on. One of 'em might just put a ball through *your* head some night."

"I don't want them out of my sight—or my reach." Dropping back into his chair, Sinclair gestured at a jacket laid out on the large, rumpled bed. "And I am not wearing that blue monstrosity to call on my future father-in-law."

"It's conservative."

"Exactly. He might approve it, and then where would I be? Get me the beige and cream."

"You'll look like a rake."

"I am a rake, you idiot. And I have no intention of letting Stiveton forget that for one damned minute."

He pulled out the letter and opened it, stifling a grin as he caught the valet's disgruntled expression in the dressing mirror. Swiftly he perused the contents and then sank back, scowling. First the *ton* was trying to foist a surprise wedding on him, and now this. When bad news came to call, it always seemed to bring company.

"Fine. Call me an idiot if you want," the valet grumbled from the dressing closet. "But you're the one got trapped into marrying Vixen Fontaine, on his first proper jaunt back in London."

"I didn't get trapped into anything. I made a point

with Marley." He couldn't even say the bastard's name without growling.

"And the marriage?"

"That was just my way of avoiding being stoned and run out of London."

"Ah."

" 'Ah' yourself. No father in his right mind would allow his daughter to marry me. Everyone's simply laboring under the misconception that I'd be safer if I were leg-shackled to some poor female." Sinclair read the letter once more, looking for any hopeful sign. "Bates sends his greetings, by the by."

"He'd better. He owes me ten quid, that lad does." Finally the proper clothes appeared on the bed, and the valet sauntered back to the dressing table. "Who's Lady Stanton, anyway?"

"Some dowager living in Scotland. Wally's great great twice removed or something."

"Sounds safe enough."

Sinclair eyed him. "I'd like to think I'm not completely incompetent. And your ten quid is on the way to London, since you asked."

The valet sobered. "Bates didn't find anything?"

"No. I didn't expect him to, but one can always hope, I suppose. Wally and Crispin are meeting up with him. We'll regroup here. They're letting a house on Weigh House Street. Or Lady Stanton is, rather."

He handed the missive to the valet, who scanned through it much as Sinclair had.

"Well, I'm glad Crispin's coming, anyway," Roman said. "Maybe he can talk some sense into you before you do end up married."

"I'm the Marquis of Althorpe now. I will need to marry eventually, if only for Thomas's sake." And whatever he decided, the thought of having Vixen Fontaine in his bed was considerably arousing. Given Marley's taste in females, he'd expected a hoyden—not a goddess. Those long, curling eyelashes . . .

"I know, I know. But everyone in London thinks you're . . . you know . . . *him*. And *him* shouldn't be taking a bride—not even a wild one like the Vixen."

With a snort, Sinclair recaptured the letter and crumpled it, tossing it into the dying embers of the fireplace. "I am him, and there isn't going to be a marriage right now. Don't complicate things."

The valet folded his arms across his chest and glowered. "You're the one complicating things, Sin. You can't even live in your own house without the servants thinking you're—"

Sinclair glared back at him. "For the last time, Roman, I *am* him. Nothing has changed since France or Prussia or Italy except the target *du jour*. Stop making me defend my poor character."

"But that is not—"

"Leave be."

"All right, my lord." Roman grabbed up the shaving bowl and dumped the contents into the chamber pot. "If you want everyone to think you're a blasted blackguard instead of a hero, and you want to marry an earl's high-flying daughter to keep your disguise, that's your affair. If—"

Sin pushed to his feet. "I am here to find my brother's murderer, Roman. The damned Crown may have kept me lurking about the Continent for the past five years, but Bonaparte's finished now, and so am I. I will keep the disguise, though, for as long as it serves me. Is that clear?"

The valet heaved a breath. "Clear as glass."

"Good." Sinclair favored him with a slight grin. "And don't go about calling me a hero. You'll ruin everything."

Roman folded his arms across his chest. "Well, I'd hate to do that now, wouldn't I?"

"You cannot be serious!"

"I have never been more serious, Victoria." The Earl of Stiveton paced around and around the couch in the middle of the library, his footsteps so heavy that they rattled the glass doors of the display cabinet at the far end of the room. "How many escapades were we supposed to overlook? How much outrageous behavior did you think we could ignore?"

"More than this."

"Victoria!"

Victoria lay supine on the couch, one arm flung across her brow in her best dramatic pose of helpless vulnerability. "It was just a stupid kiss! For heaven's sake, Father."

"You kissed Sinclair Grafton in a completely . . . intimate manner. You let him put his hands all over you. *In public*. I cannot—I will not—tolerate this any longer."

Hmm, she'd used the same vulnerable pose last week. It hadn't worked then, either, and she'd ended up housebound for three long days. Victoria sat up. "So you're making me *marry* him? That seems a bit severe. I've kissed other men, and you haven't—"

"Enough!" Stiveton clapped his hands over his ears. "You shouldn't have kissed anyone. But this time, Victoria, you were caught—in the arms of a complete scapegrace, and in the presence of a crowd."

"An exceptionally stodgy crowd."

"Victoria!"

"But—"

"No more explanations, and no more excuses. Unless he's fled the country by now, you *will* marry Lord Althorpe, and you *will* face the consequences of your actions."

"Haven't you ever done anything just for fun?" she pleaded.

"Fun is for children," he said stiffly. "You are twenty years old. It's time you became a wife—and it now becomes a question of who else would have you."

He stalked out of the room, heading straight for his office. There he would wait until Althorpe arrived, and then he would bargain her off to the infamous blackguard, just so he wouldn't have to put up with her high spirits any longer.

Victoria sighed and flopped back down on the couch again. Ten hours should have been more than enough time to convince him of how unwise he was being, and of what a ridiculous match this would be for everyone concerned. Of course she'd stepped too far; she was always doing that. Her parents should expect it by now.

"I am not getting married!" she yelled at the ceiling.

It didn't reply.

Of all the punishments her parents could devise, this was the absolute worst. In one more year she would come into her majority and be able to travel and aid whatever cause she saw fit. Once she married, that money would go to Sinclair Grafton, and he would no doubt lose every blasted bit at the gaming tables before she could do anything useful with it at all.

Yes, he was handsome, and yes, he'd made her pulse fly when he kissed her. That, though, was no reason for her to marry him. She didn't even know anything about him, except for the rumors of his terrible reputation. Her parents couldn't want her to be leg-shackled to someone like that. They *couldn't* think she deserved someone like that.

Victoria pounded the soft cushions of the couch in frustration. Her only hope was that the idea of marriage horrified Althorpe as much as it did her. Perhaps he had already left for Europe or parts unknown. She shut her eyes, then realized she was slowly tracing her lips with one finger. With an oath, she shot to her feet. One did *not* marry a man simply because he kissed with the skill of Eros. One married a man because he was kind and intelligent and understanding and supportive, and didn't expect his wife to be nothing but a pretty picture who embroidered and had tea parties all day long. She wasn't that kind of woman, and she couldn't—wouldn't—be that kind of wife.

Sinclair hopped down from his phaeton and climbed the shallow marble front steps of Fontaine House. He'd debated whether to call on Lord Stiveton or not, and decided that the Sin Grafton everyone knew would have—with some excuse as to why the marriage was impossible.

From what he knew, the earl was as dull and plodding as a wet sheep, but no fool. While Stiveton's coming to his senses and whisking his daughter away would solve one problem, though, it would leave at least two more.

First, he'd gone too far last night. Lady Vixen Fontaine had seemed likely to know something of Marley's possible involvement in a murder, but he hadn't exactly gotten around to questioning her about it. He'd been too busy ogling the splendid black-haired chit and enjoying the fact that he'd stolen her from her beau. Beaux, actually. If he had behaved that carelessly in France, he would never have survived Bonaparte.

Whatever the Vixen's reputation, though, his was worse—and if he hadn't stepped in with his marriage offer, the Franton soiree would have been both the first and the last gathering to which anyone invited him. And whatever he thought of proper society, he had to have access to it—at least long enough to prove whether Marley or one of the rest of them had killed his brother.

Of course Stiveton wouldn't agree to the marriage. But the earl had to accept an apology sincere enough that it would keep Sinclair in the *ton*'s good graces until he didn't need them any longer.

The second problem was nearly as troubling. Last night he had gone completely insane. Vixen Fontaine had batted her lovely violet eyes at him, and he had forgotten not only his suspicions about Marley, but also those about Lord William Landry and every other possible suspect lurking among her gaggle of admirers.

He hadn't maneuvered her out to the gardens so he could question her; he'd done it so he could kiss her. And if her father and the rest of the gawkers hadn't discovered them, he wouldn't have stopped with kisses. He'd been in low company for too long. And, damn it all, he wanted to kiss her again, and to complete the intimate little interlude they'd begun.

Sinclair took a deep breath and swung the brass knocker against the door. Less than a heartbeat later, the heavy oak barrier swung open.

"Lord Althorpe?" the short, round butler queried, taking in his choice of attire with the expected degree of disdain.

Sinclair ignored it. "Where might I find Lord Stiveton?"

The butler stepped backward. "In the study, my lord. This way."

He followed the butler's clicking heels down the short hallway to a small office tucked under the staircase. The Fontaine family was an old, wealthy, and well-respected one, and he could imagine how deep an offense he'd shown them by manhandling their daughter. Better the likes of him than a cold-blooded murderer like Marley, though. If it had been Marley who shot Thomas. His life seemed to have become a series of "ifs" and "hows" over the past two years, and he was damned tired of not having the answers.

The earl was seated behind a mahogany desk, looking more like a banker than a nobleman. A ledger lay open in front of him, but despite his appearance Sin doubted he'd been doing much accounting this morning. Stiveton looked up as the two men stepped into the room.

"Althorpe. I thought you might have fled the country by now."

"Good morning, Lord Stiveton. Sorry to disappoint you."

The earl narrowed his eyes. "Timms, we are not to be disturbed."

The butler bowed as he pulled the door shut. "Yes, my lord."

"Acting contrite now doesn't excuse your actions last night, Althorpe." Stiveton laid his hands flat against the desktop.

Sinclair shrugged. "My actions last night cannot be excused."

"Agreeing with me won't do you any good, either. How many times have you behaved in some disreputable manner and then escaped without censure?"

Sin lifted an eyebrow. "Do you want an exact count?"

"Whatever liberties you may have taken on the Continent, we do not tolerate such behavior here."

"With all due respect, Lord Stiveton, I may have led, but your daughter followed willingly enough."

The earl slammed to his feet. "This is how you beg for forgiveness?"

Sinclair flicked an imaginary speck of dust from his sleeve. "I'm not begging for anything, Lord Stiveton. I am at your service. I have a suggestion, but do what you will."

Still glaring, Stiveton slowly seated himself again. "Were you expecting me to challenge you to a duel, so I could defend Victoria's honor?"

"Of course not. That would mean my killing you. I was thinking more of your demanding a public apology, and me rendering one."

"That might bandage your reputation, but it wouldn't do anything for my daughter's."

As the mantel clock struck the quarter hour, the earl continued to gaze at him speculatively. Sinclair didn't like the thoughtful expression nor the direction the conversation seemed to be headed, but kept his silence. Stiveton obviously had some solution in mind.

Finally the earl leaned forward, folding his hands over the ledger. "As much as I would like to state otherwise, the events of last night were not entirely your fault."

That sounded promising. "We agree, then, that an apology would suff—"

"Just a moment, Althorpe. I'm not finished. My daughter has an unfortunate lack of self-control. I had hoped proper schooling and discipline would cure her of her impulsiveness, but as you . . . experienced, this is not the case."

Sin dropped unbidden into the uncomfortable gilded chair that faced the desk. At this point he'd thought to hear Vixen's reputation defended and his own further besmirched. That wasn't the case, and, uncharacteristically, he had to stop himself from coming to her defense. After all, for the past five years he'd been luring people into saying and doing things they'd rather not. She hadn't had much of a chance; he hadn't given her one. Abruptly Sinclair realized Stiveton was glaring at him again, so he assumed an intrigued expression. "And?" he prompted.

"And so if I cannot curb her behavior, I will take steps to see that the scandal resulting from it is diverted away from my household. To be blunt, she is now *your* problem."

Sinclair blinked. "You don't actually want her to marry . . . *me*."

"I told you, I do not condone this reprehensible lack of propriety, even in members of my own family. Especially in members of my own family." Stiveton picked up a pencil. "I'll settle ten thousand pounds on her now, and three thousand a year for another year, when she turns twenty-one and comes into her grandmother's inheritance. I imagine now that you're back in London, you'll be going through your family's fortune in no time."

Sin's mind raced. Obviously he'd miscalculated.

The earl didn't seem to realize how sordid his reputation was if he actually intended the marriage. "I continue to be astounded by your generosity. Your daughter *and* ten thousand pounds."

"And all scandal gone from my house. That is what I'm paying for."

"Lord Stiveton, whatever you may say now, you must be aware that any bachelor peer in London would consider your daughter an acceptable bride, once I apologize. Are you certain you—"

"Perhaps they would, but she won't have any of them. This, she has no choice in. The wedding will take place one week from Saturday. I've already sent a note to Prince George. We'll have Westminster Cathedral."

Apparently the earl didn't want to risk giving either of the wedding participants time to make an escape. "The Regent will be attending then, I presume?"

"Given the importance of the two families involved, I assure you that he will be."

"And your daughter is in agreement about this?" Sin asked skeptically.

"Of course she isn't in agreement. But she should have thought of that before she . . . fell into your embrace in such a public setting."

"I—"

"Understand this, Althorpe." The earl tapped the pencil on his desk. "Over the past three years I have suggested at least two dozen possible husbands to her, and I have given her ample time to 'fall in love' with any one of them, which was her stipulation before making a marriage. Instead of making a choice, she has gadded about London breaking hearts, ruining her own and my reputation, and swearing that she will have nothing to do with the idea of marriage. They call her the Vixen, you know."

"I'd heard something about that."

The earl leaned forward again. "Don't mistake me, Althorpe; I find your behavior deplorable."

"You've made your opinion quite clear." Sinclair felt as though he'd just lost his last bishop and his queen in a chess match he hadn't even realized he'd been playing. And now he was about to be mated— literally. He'd been badly outmaneuvered, but surprisingly, he wasn't quite as horrified as he'd thought to be. All he had to do was concede defeat, and bedding Lady Vixen Fontaine would be his consolation prize. Beyond that—well, he'd never had much faith in tomorrows; he'd always left that to Thomas.

"However," Stiveton continued, "you have provided me with the opportunity to see Victoria married into an old, well-regarded family, your own black behavior notwithstanding."

"So glad to be of service," Sin replied sardonically.

"Wait here." Stiveton pushed to his feet. "I'll send your bride in to see you."

Sin wasn't all that certain he wanted to see her. As attractive as his prize was, he didn't like being cornered. But, short of leaving England and abandoning his search, he was going to have to marry Lady Vixen Fontaine. He slouched in the straight-backed chair.

It was his own bloody fault, really. He scowled. He'd been a damned fool, and now Stiveton was using his momentary lapse of sanity to rid the Fontaines of their own scapegrace.

For his family's sake he had meant to marry, after he'd found Thomas's murderer and dealt with him. Not now, though, and not to someone he didn't know and didn't trust. This was going to complicate things, and he didn't need any more blasted complications right now. "Damnation."

"I said the same thing when my father informed me that you were here."

Lady Victoria Fontaine strolled into her father's office, her expression as calm as if she were discussing the weather. Sinclair stood. He'd meant to remain in his arrogant slouch, but as he had noticed last night, he tended to become erect in her presence.

Coming around the back of the chair, he took her hand and brought it to his lips. "Good morning, Lady Victoria."

He liked touching her. When she didn't pull her hand away, he brushed his lips across her knuckles again. She continued gazing at him, her violet eyes the only part of her that didn't look completely composed. Even in a muted gray-and-green muslin gown she drew his eyes, his attention, and—even more strongly than last night—his desire. Finally she freed her hand and turned to the window, and his blood stirred as he watched the silken sway of her hips.

"My father says you accepted his terms for the marriage," she said, leaning against the deep sill.

"They were generous."

Victoria nodded. "He has never been one to quarrel over details."

Sinclair looked at her for a long moment, absorbed by the fast-beating pulse at the soft curve of her throat, until he abruptly remembered that he was Sin Grafton, dedicated rake and hedonist. "You seem to make up your mind fairly quickly, as well."

"I wanted you to drag me off to the garden," she

admitted, blushing, "but I didn't know you were going to attempt to render me naked."

She had wanted him. "You didn't seem unduly disturbed by it—until your father arrived."

The pretty color in her cheeks deepened. "I'll admit, my lord, that you kiss well—but I imagine you've had a great deal of practice."

Amused at the supposed insult, Sinclair swept a bow. "I'm pleased all my hard work's gone to good use."

"Too good, according to my parents."

"I'll apologize for the public setting of our embrace, but I won't apologize for kissing you." He stepped closer, as drawn to her this morning as he'd been last night, despite the marriage noose. "You're delicious."

She cocked her head at him. "Are you still trying to seduce me?" Victoria pushed away from the window, and walked toward the door, saying in a raised voice, "That's hardly necessary, Lord Althorpe; you've already won my hand in marriage."

Curious, Sinclair watched as she softly closed the door and faced him. "If you want to continue what we began last night, my lady," he murmured, "I am a willing participant. Exceedingly willing."

"The only thing I want to participate in is getting us out of trouble," she countered, lowering her voice again. "You can hardly want this marriage any more than I do."

"What do you propose—pardon the pun—to do about it, then?"

She clapped her hands together, abruptly all business. "You've spent the past five years on the Continent. No one would think twice if you decided to return there."

So the little spitfire thought she could dictate terms. Her father was right about one thing, anyway: she was definitely trouble. "Probably not."

"If money is a problem, I do have an independent income at my disposal. Surely you could live comfortably in Paris on, say, a thousand pounds a year?"

Sin couldn't quite believe what he was hearing. "You want me to return to Paris."

"Yes. The sooner, the better."

"And you would pay for my meals, rent, clothing, and general upkeep if I were to do so," he continued, counting the points off on his fingers.

Her expression became a little dubious. "Well, yes."

"All that's lacking, then, is for you to promise to come visit me from time to time and bring me chocolates."

Victoria's eyes narrowed. "I am not proposing keeping you, or some other sordid arrangement. Only keeping you away from me."

"It amounts to about the same thing. Do you have any other almost-husbands lurking about the countryside?"

"I am completely serious!"

Unsure whether he was more annoyed or amused, Sinclair closed the distance between them. "But I don't want to return to Paris. I like it here."

She backed into the wall. "Ouch. I'm certain you'd be much happier with all your high-flying lady friends in Paris. It's quite lovely there this time of year, anyway."

"It's lovely here. Nearly as lovely as you."

"But no one in London even likes you!" she burst out, then blanched.

And no one in London knew he had damned near

died for them more than a dozen times over the past five years. His chest tightening, he turned away so she wouldn't see the sudden anger in his eyes. "They haven't realized how charming I am," he said smoothly, pretending to examine the view out the window.

Surprisingly, she put a hand on his arm. "I'm sorry," she said quietly. "That was cruel."

Brushing her hand away, he faced her again. Pity was another item for which he had nothing but contempt. "I think London will like me considerably more when I am in *your* company, my lady."

"But—"

"You're very popular—quite society's darling." And that could work to his advantage, he realized as he studied her smooth, cream-colored complexion. Why, he was a bloody genius! Not only would their marriage keep him in society's good graces but it would also gain him access to places his tattered reputation would otherwise have denied him. And given her own wildness, she wouldn't cling on his arm every moment and get in his way.

"But I am not going to get married—and certainly not to you!"

He smiled. "Then you shouldn't have kissed me."

Victoria flushed. "Don't you think marriage will interfere with your womanizing and wagering and drinking?"

She sounded desperate. Sin leaned forward, trapping her between the wall and his arms. "Not any more than it would interfere with your flirting and socializing and shopping and whatever else it is that you do."

"It won't!" she shot back at him.

He looked her in the eyes and was surprised when

she looked straight back at him. Most people didn't do that; they had too much to hide. "Apparently," he murmured, "we are perfect for one another." With that, he leaned down and kissed her.

With a surprised sound that came from deep in her chest, Victoria returned the embrace, curving her neck to meet his mouth more fully with hers. Her instant, heated response aroused him, as it had last night in Lady Franton's garden. He wanted to dislike her—to dismiss her as one of the faceless nobility who hadn't bothered to discover who had killed his brother. But while he was reasonably sure she hadn't murdered anyone, he did know one thing for certain: he had kissed a hundred women and never felt this way before.

Slowly and reluctantly he broke the kiss. Her long, curling lashes fluttered open, and her violet eyes looked into his. "If I marry you," she whispered, "it would only be for my family's sake."

Sin chuckled. More likely it would be to escape her family. "May I take you for a picnic tomorrow?"

Victoria cleared her throat, lowering her hands from where she'd draped them over his shoulders. "I'm going shopping tomorrow with Lucy Havers and Marguerite Porter."

"A drive in Hyde Park on Saturday, then."

"I have an engagement." She ducked out from under his arms, making a show of straightening her hair.

He lifted an eyebrow, wondering whether the engagement was with Lord Marley. "I am getting the distinct impression that you don't want to be seen with me."

Hesitation glinted in her eyes. "I still think we may be taking this too seriously," she offered. "Perhaps everyone will come to their senses in the next week, and we won't have to go through with this silly business."

"Perhaps they will. But you will go driving with me on Saturday morning."

She lifted her chin. "Or you'll do what?"

An unbidden smile touched his mouth. Challenging him wasn't exactly the best way to be rid of him, but she would discover that soon enough. "As I told you last night, a kiss is only the beginning of a seduction. The next step is much more . . . interesting."

Before she could comment on that, he swept a bow and pulled the door open again. "I'd best inform my family that I'm getting married. Until Saturday, my lady."

Chapter 3

"Ha, ha! Sin!"
Christopher Grafton bolted down the stairs of Drewsbury House and flung his arms around his brother. Sinclair returned the embrace, holding his younger brother tightly for a long moment before he released him again. A knot he hadn't realized he carried loosened in his chest. He'd lost one brother, but he'd been able to return before anything happened to Christopher. And nothing would happen to him now.

"It's good to see you, Kit," he said, grinning as he stepped backward. "You've grown a foot."

"At least a foot. I'd been hoping I was taller than you now, blast it."

"Christopher has your grandfather's height," a female voice said from the morning room doorway. "I'm surprised you recognized him after five years."

Sinclair's heart jolted, and his sense that he was dreaming left. Now it was real. Now he was home. Slowly Sinclair turned to face the voice. "You haven't changed a bit, Grandmama Augusta. I would recognize you anywhere," he drawled.

Augusta, Lady Drewsbury sipped the cup of tea she

41

held in her hands and eyed him over the rim. "Of course I've changed. I've lost a grandson."

"Grandmama," Christopher chided, flushing to the roots of his dark brown hair. "He's just come back. Give him a moment to breathe before you pounce."

Her slender shoulders rose and fell with the breath she took, while her keen blue eyes remained on Sinclair, assessing him. He wondered what he saw. This was what he had dreaded on returning to London—not the mess he'd been forced to make of his reputation, or even the prospect of ferreting out Thomas's murderer with the trail two years old, and well-covered to begin with.

No, more than anything else he had dreaded facing his grandmother with no explanation he was free to give her for his god-awful behavior over the past five years, and especially for the past two. "No worries, Kit," he said smoothly, those same five years the only thing that kept his voice steady. "Don't spoil our grandmother's fun. No doubt she's been plotting her speech for ages."

"Sin," his brother murmured.

"I did have a speech," she agreed, her tone as calm as if she were discussing the color of his coat. "Now that you're finally here, though, I can't see that it would make any difference. You disappointed me, Sinclair. I have since lowered my standards for judging your behavior. As Christopher said, you've returned. Come and have some tea."

He bit back his cynical response to the insult as unfair. Sin shook his head. Of all the yelling and weeping and name-calling with which Augusta might have greeted him, her quiet acceptance was worse. He had disappointed her; he'd been less than she'd hoped and expected, so she now appeared to expect nothing of him. "I can't stay."

She nodded, apparently expecting that, too. "Very well."

"You can't leave already!" Kit protested. "You only just got here. Are you at least going to be in London for a while?"

"Don't pester your brother, Christopher. No doubt his social calendar is full of invitations and gatherings."

Finally, a little acid. It felt better than the cool nothingness of her earlier tone, but not by much. "Actually, I came to invite you to an event," he said slowly. "On the fifteenth."

Augusta's expression hardened. "You are family, Sinclair, but neither your brother nor I will ever participate in some farce you and your . . . cronies devise."

"Grandmam—"

"It may very well be a farce," Sin agreed, "and I understand if you choose not to attend. I'm not entirely certain I'll be there myself—at least not sober. The event is a wedding. Mine. Prince George—"

"What?" Christopher yelped. "A wedding? *Your* wedding? You've only just returned! Did you bring her back with you from the Continent? Is she Italian?"

"More importantly," his grandmother broke in, "is she carrying your child?"

Augusta's expectations of him seemed to lower each time he opened his mouth. "No. She isn't. And she's English. I met her . . . quite recently." *Good God, had it really only been yesterday?* Sinclair shook himself. "I've been back in London a few days. I've just been somewhat . . . busy."

"It would appear so," Augusta said dryly. "Who is she?"

"Lady Victoria Fontaine."

"The Vixen? You've caught the Vixen?"

Finally Augusta looked surprised. "Hush, Christopher. You mentioned Prince George. He is attending?"

"Yes. He has made Westminster Cathedral available to us."

"Then we shall attend. It is a matter of family honor."

Sinclair bowed. "Thank you, Grandmama." When he straightened, though, she had already vanished back into the morning room. "So much for the family reunion," he muttered.

"What did you expect?" Kit asked. "You've written, what, a dozen times over the past five years? When you couldn't be bothered to appear for Thomas's funeral . . . well, we—she—"

"I didn't know he'd been killed," Sinclair lied, returning to the foyer for his hat and cane. Silently he cursed himself. The lying had become so effortless—easier than the truth.

With the war over, he should have been free to tell his family where he'd been and what he'd been doing since he left—but Thomas had known, and Thomas was dead. As soon as he'd learned of the murder, when he could think again at all, he had vowed to tell them nothing until he was absolutely certain there would be no reprisals against his family for his actions in Europe. That was what mattered—that they remain safe, his reputation be damned.

"Sin," Christopher continued, pursuing him to the front door, "will you call on us again?"

"I don't know. I'm at Grafton House. Come and see

me if you like. If Grandmama will allow it."

Kit scowled. "I'm twenty years old. I do as I please."

Taking a breath, Sinclair put a hand on his younger brother's shoulder. They didn't need two disappointments in the family. "Don't desert her. You're all she has."

"I know *my* duty," his brother said darkly. "She'd only like to see you do yours."

"Wouldn't we all," he returned with a cynical smile. "Wouldn't we all."

Lucy nibbled on another tea cake. "What do you mean, 'What do I know about him?' I don't know anything other than what everyone knows."

Victoria sat back on the comfortable morning room couch and fiddled with her cup of tea. "I meant, have you heard anything over the past few days?" She glanced at the tall grandfather clock in the corner. He'd set this morning as their next meeting; in another five minutes it would be afternoon, and he would be late.

She wasn't nervous or anxious about his arrival, of course. She'd merely invited her friends to call in anticipation of his failure to appear. Her hands folded and unfolded of their own accord, and she scowled down at the silly things. She wasn't nervous at all.

Daintily, Lucy blotted crumbs off her gown with the tip of her finger. "The only thing I've heard is that Marley went out and got completely sluiced after the Franton soiree, and that he hasn't sobered up yet."

That wasn't much of a surprise. Drinking and wagering seemed to be Marley's favorite activities. Lucy's comment at least explained why he hadn't called on her, when previously he had appeared on her parents' doorstep almost daily.

Marguerite Porter, on Victoria's other side, picked at the pink lace sleeve of her day muslin. "Diane Addington was dying to join us today, only her mother absolutely forbade it. She says you're a bad influence, Vixen."

"Hush, Marguerite. It was just bad circumstances." Lucy giggled. "Heavens, if I could have stolen a kiss from Lord Sin, I would have done it, too."

"Is that what they're calling him?" Victoria asked. "See, you did know something I didn't."

"Well, they mostly called him plain Sin, before. It's not much of a change."

"I think it qualifies as a promotion, don't you?" Victoria sighed—and realized she'd been doing a great deal of that lately. "Whatever Diane's mother says, Marguerite, the Addingtons have already accepted the invitation to the wedding." She rose, strolling over to look out the window. Still no sign of Lord Sin.

"Well, no one wants to miss the wedding. It's a pity you didn't go to Almack's last night. Everyone's talking about it."

Her gaze still on Brook Street outside, Victoria took another sip of tea. "I'm not allowed to go anywhere unless accompanied by my parents or my betrothed— as if that would help anything. Father must think I intend to flee or something."

"You don't, do you?" Lucy gave her a distressed look. "That would be horrid, if you left London."

"Of course not. What would I do, flitting about in some foreign country with no money?" The idea had crossed her mind more than once, but it seemed utterly selfish and unproductive. Whatever her father might think, she had as much family pride as he did. And living her life in exile was not something she felt ready to face. Some other solution was bound to arise without resorting to anything that drastic—or permanent.

Marguerite shuddered. "I'm so glad it wasn't me that he ruined," she breathed. "Of course, he's absolutely stunning, but I heard he actually *lived* in a Paris brothel for six months."

"You're not helping anything, Marguerite," Lucy chided.

A phaeton turned up the short, curving drive outside, and Victoria missed whatever Marguerite replied. A tall figure in tanned buckskins, black coat and waistcoat, a brown beaver hat, and gleaming Hessian boots vaulted to the ground and strolled toward the front steps as though he weren't precisely seven minutes late. Her fingers began shaking, and she set the teacup down in the windowsill before she dropped it.

This was ridiculous. Sinclair Grafton was ruining her life—with her own unfortunate assistance, of course—and she was actually anticipating spending time in his company. The man was only concerned with his own situation, and she became shivery and nervous whenever he came into view.

A moment later, Timms scratched at the morning room door and then cracked it open. "Lady Victoria, Lord Althorpe is here to see you."

"Yes, thank y—" she began, but stopped as Althorpe brushed by the butler and strode into the morning room as though he owned it.

"Good morning, my lady," he said, ignoring the room's other occupants to approach her.

"Good afternoon, my lord," she replied, and gestured at her friends. "You remember Miss Lucy Havers, and this is Miss Porter. Mar—"

The marquis intercepted her hand and brought it to his lips. "You noticed," he murmured.

"Noticed what?"

A sensuous smile curved his mouth. "That I'm late."

Victoria blushed. She'd only meant to censure him, not somehow give the impression that she'd been anticipating his arrival. Extracting her fingers from his grip, she gestured again at her guests. "And you noticed, but took no steps to remedy your shortcoming. Marguer—"

"My latecoming, you mean."

She cleared her throat. "Stop interrupting. Marguerite, Lord Althorpe."

The young ladies curtsied in near unison. "My lord."

He kept his gaze on Victoria for another breath, then greeted her companions. "Miss Lucy, Miss Porter. I apologize, but there is only seating for two in my phaeton."

"I didn't think you were going to make an appearance," Victoria cut in before he could do something as ungentlemanly as asking her friends to leave. Despite all his interruptions, he'd noted her friends' names, and in fact, everything she'd said. "They came to save me from spending the day in complete solitude. I am a prisoner, you know."

Althorpe's quicksilver expression altered for just a moment, and then he flashed a rakish smile. "Then I propose a change of plans to set you free—we'll all go for a stroll."

"All of us?" Marguerite squeaked.

"Why not?" He shrugged. "It's a lovely day, and I

would hate to deprive Lady Victoria of her companions."

"Perhaps they don't wish anyone to see them in *your* company," Victoria suggested, frowning. He was supposed to go driving with *her*.

"Vix, that's not nice," Lucy muttered, flushing.

"Well, he's already ruined me, and he can't very well marry all of us," she stated airily.

"Hm. Three to one sounds about right to me," he murmured, the wicked smile touching his eyes.

Victoria had to wrench her mind away from the contemplation of how very attractive that smile was. "Yes, but that means you'll need to find eight more gentlemen to accompany us." With a sniff she faced her friends, trying to ignore the subsequent outburst of laughter that emanated from somewhere deep in his chest. "Don't feel obligated to go walking with us," she said. "He was late, so any of this is his fault."

"Oh, no, I think it'll be fun," Lucy chuckled. "The four of us will make quite a stir."

"That's the spirit." The marquis applauded.

"I . . . I have to . . . to go meet my dressmaker," Marguerite stammered, backing away as though she expected the marquis to turn into a panther and leap on her. "I regret not being able to accompany you."

"Give my regards to your mother," Victoria called as her friend vanished through the morning room door.

"Shall we, ladies? Though I imagine we could squeeze three into the carriage if we got cozy enough."

Lucy stifled another giggle. "Oh, my."

With a sigh, Victoria took Lucy's arm and ushered her toward the door. "Let's get this over with, then."

She and Lucy collected their bonnets and parasols from Timms, and the three of them headed down the

street in the direction of Hyde Park. Althorpe seemed
content to stroll behind the two ladies, but Victoria
kept hold of Lucy just in case he should try to come
between them.

"Shouldn't you be walking with him?" Lucy whispered. "You are betrothed, after all."

"This is close enough," Victoria answered, loud
enough for him to hear. "I'm still hoping my father
will come to his senses and halt this insanity."

In truth, she wanted to walk beside him; to have her
arm in his; to lean into his tall strength, and have him
pay attention and say scandalous things to no one but
her. And that was precisely why she refused to even
turn around and look at him.

When she thought about it, his invitation to the
other two ladies had been rude to her. Apparently the
company of any woman was completely the same to
him—and as stupidly attracted to him as she felt, she
intensely disliked his attitude. If she did have to go
through with marrying him, that was one thing she was
absolutely not going to put up with.

Luckily for Sinclair, he had no idea she was already
making plans for his reformation. He stayed a few feet
behind the two ladies as they entered Hyde Park, his
attention divided between their amusing conversation
and the crowds of vehicles and pedestrians also enjoying the afternoon. He needed access to these people,
and the lovely young lady pretending to ignore him
was his best method of entry. At the moment, though,
Victoria didn't seem to want to be alone with him.

He wished Marguerite Porter had decided to join
them. Her uncle was Viscount Benston, and Benston
had been acquainted with Thomas. Miss Porter was

obviously shy of scandal, but he could wait. If he'd learned one thing working for His Majesty's government, it was patience. Marguerite and the Vixen were friends, and so as long as his relationship with Victoria continued, he would see Miss Porter again.

"You're being very quiet back there," Victoria said, her parasol shielding her face from his view.

"I'm enjoying the sights," he answered, lowering his gaze to contemplate her slender, rounded backside.

Lucy turned to face him. "Have things changed much since you were last in London?"

"A few more locks on the doors, perhaps, though that may be solely in my honor." Seizing the opportunity, Sin increased his pace and caught Lucy's free arm around his. "So tell me, Miss Havers, how many hearts has my betrothed broken?"

"Oh, hundreds."

"Lucy! Don't gossip with him!"

He leaned around Lucy. With one finger he pushed Victoria's parasol down so he could look her in the eye. "It's only fair. You've been trumpeting my foul reputation, and I know nothing of yours."

She narrowed her lovely violet eyes. "Then perhaps you shouldn't have kissed me."

"But I wanted to kiss you." At the sight of her blush, he drew a breath. Good God. "And after we're married, we will pursue the next steps in a seduction. In fact, we shall—"

"Excuse me," Lucy said, blushing crimson as she slipped out from between the two of them, "but are you certain this is only the third time you've . . . conversed?"

Sinclair used her escape to close the gap between

himself and the Vixen. "Tell me, my lady, am I being too familiar?"

"Yes. And if we have any chance of escaping this dreadful trap, your looming over me like this is not going to help."

" 'Looming'?" he repeated, wondering whether she was conscious of her flirtation, or whether she just naturally attracted men to her like bees to a beautiful flower. "I don't believe anyone has ever accused me of looming before."

She pointed the parasol at his chest and shoved. "Yes, looming."

As her lips formed the soft sound, he was aware of just how much he desired to taste them again. Whether a deliberate actress or not, she was irresistible. Almost without thinking, he leaned down toward her.

"Don't you dare," she hissed, lifting the parasol between them again.

He disarmed her, snatching the parasol from her fingers before she could blink. "Why not?"

"Give that back!"

"Why shouldn't I kiss you?"

She stomped her foot. "Because we're trying to get out of this marriage—not make escape impossible."

With only a few days left before half of London witnessed their wedding, he needed to let her know he intended to go through with it. He owed her that. At least that. "*You're* trying to escape this marriage," he said slowly. "I like the idea."

"You what?" She blanched.

"Um, perhaps we should continue our walk," Lucy suggested, glancing past Victoria.

He followed her gaze to the assemblage of pedestrians and carriages, which were beginning to face in their direction. "We seem to have attracted an audience," he murmured, annoyed—not because of the attention, but because he truly had wanted to kiss her.

"I don't care who's watching," Victoria snapped. "Why in the world do you want to be forced into marriage with me?"

"Why should I not?" He smiled, grateful he'd deprived her of the parasol before she could try disemboweling him with it. "As I said, I intended to marry soon, anyway. You're of good family, you're astoundingly lovely, and I've already secured your father's permission. A fairly painless prospect, as I see it."

She didn't look flattered, or amused, or agreeable. In fact, she looked furious.

"The night of the Franton soiree," she ground out, "I made a vow to speak only to nice men. I wish I'd kept it." She turned on her heel, dragging Lucy along with her. "Good day, Lord Althorpe."

"And your parasol, my lady?"

"Keep it."

He tipped his hat. "I'll see you next Saturday, then. For the wedding."

Staying a fair distance behind them, Sinclair made certain they returned safely to Fontaine House. What bothered him the most about marrying Victoria was that if he was somehow the reason Thomas had died, then she had possibly become a target now, as well.

A moment after the two ladies entered the house, his phaeton left the drive and turned up Brook Street toward him. As Sin climbed up into the seat, tossing the umbrella down beside him, Roman handed over the reins and swung over to sit on the narrow perch at the rear of the vehicle. Sin clucked to the team, and they clattered off again.

"Well?" he prompted, once they'd rounded the corner.

"It's possible you're not as insane as I thought," the valet said grudgingly. "You're still a fool, but she's . . . she's . . ."

"Astonishingly attractive," Sin finished, giving a slight grin.

"Much too fine for a blackguard like you're pretending to be. That's what I was going to say."

"And you talk too much for a valet, or a groom, or whatever it is you're pretending to be. I'm not going to have this argument with you again."

"How about this argument, Sin? You could be putting her in d—"

"Danger. I know. Which is why, after Saturday, *you* are going to become her invisible guardian angel."

He felt the valet's frown boring into the back of his skull. It needed to be done, though, and Roman was one of the few people he trusted to do it.

"And who's going to be your guardian angel, while I'm watching her?"

"The devil doesn't need an angel, Roman."

The valet snorted. "Tell that to the killer."

"I hope to, very soon."

By Saturday morning, Victoria would have agreed to marry nearly anyone just so she could escape the house and the frowning silence of her parents. She hated being housebound, and she hated the fact that no one except Lucy would come to call on her, though even her friend had been absent for the past two days. Lady Stiveton kept insisting that everything would be fine after this week, as though having the Marquis of Althorpe put a ring on her finger would render her acceptable again. And the idiotic thing was, it probably would.

"This is ridiculous," she muttered into her dressing mirror.

"Yes, my lady," Jenny agreed, her voice strained as she pulled the laces of the wedding gown tight around Victoria's rib cage.

"Tighter, Jenny," she instructed her maid, gripping the table to keep from being yanked over backward. "If I can't breathe, I'll faint, and then I can't get married."

"A fair last-minute plan, if you hide all the smelling salts first," a new voice replied.

Victoria spun to face the doorway. "Lex!" she shrieked, hurrying forward.

Alexandra Balfour, the Countess of Kilcairn Abbey, returned her warm embrace. "So it's true." She released Victoria and fluffed one of the lace sleeves she'd crushed. "You might have given us a bit more notice. Lucien nearly had to run his team to the ground to get us to London in time. Our coach won't even arrive until tomorrow."

"If this were up to me, it wouldn't be happening at all," Victoria returned, plunking herself down on the edge of the bed.

"My lady, your gown," Jenny protested.

"Excuse us for a few moments, won't you, Jenny?" Alexandra asked, glancing from the maid to Victoria.

The maid bobbed a curtsy. "Lady Victoria is to be at the Cathedral by eleven."

"And she will be."

As Jenny left the room, Alexandra took a seat beside her friend. She was wearing her "I told you so" look, and Victoria scowled. "I don't need a lecture,

Lex. At least no one had to lock me in a cellar to get me to cooperate."

Her friend chuckled. "Point taken. So what happened?"

"Everything—nothing. Take your pick. I kissed the Marquis of Althorpe at the Franton soiree, and everyone saw, and my father decided I had to marry him."

"So why did you kiss him in such a public setting?"

Victoria flopped backward on the bed. "I don't know! He's handsome, and—"

"You've had handsome men begging at your feet since you turned twelve. You never kissed any of them at Lady Franton's party."

"He kissed me first."

"Hmm."

"All right, I'm an idiot. That's why I kissed him." She beat her fist against the mattress. "I make trouble without meaning to. I always have."

"You leap before you think."

Victoria glowered at her friend, not feeling the least bit comforted. "Is this your way of telling me that I deserve this? Because I've had quite enough of that over the past week, thank you very much."

"Actually, I was going to say that in all the time I've known you, including when you attended Miss Grenville's Academy, and after that when I tutored you, you led. You never followed, and you never did anything you didn't want to."

"So you think I want to marry Althorpe? Lord Sin? Well, I don't. He's impossible. His reputation is worse than mine, and he does it on purpose. He *wants* to marry me—but only because it's saved him from the inconvenience of actually looking for a bride."

"He told you that?" Alexandra eyed her skeptically.

"Yes. In those words."

Slowly Alexandra stood. "Then he doesn't deserve you, Vix. But it seems a bit late to stop anything."

"I've tried to stop it. I can't, unless I'm willing to flee and become a fugitive actress or something."

"Well, I can't see that." Her expression rueful, Alexandra fluffed the skirts of Victoria's gown again.

"Neither can I."

"All I can tell you is that I would never have married Lucien on first meeting him. I fell in love with what lay underneath. If you feel compelled to go through with this, all I can advise is that you give yourself some time before you decide to dislike Lord Althorpe. He must have some intelligence, or he would never have survived five years in Europe with Bonaparte racketing about."

"He lived in a brothel for six months." Victoria sighed. "I'll marry him, Lex, because otherwise Father—and the rest of London—will think I care nothing for our family's standing. But I won't have anything further to do with Sin Grafton. Not unless he proves to be something more than what he appears."

Alexandra kissed her on the cheek. "Don't give up hope, Victoria. You constantly surprise me; perhaps he'll surprise you."

"I hope so."

"Are you insane?" John Bates hissed.

"That's a possibility," Sinclair admitted, and turned to view the set of his cravat in the dressing table mirror. "Splendid, Roman. You've outdone yourself."

"Aye," the valet grunted. "Have to make you look pretty for the executioner."

"Sin, you *can't* get married! What happened to avoiding all attachments until—"

"I need her."

"You need her? Or is it that you want her?"

"That too, but—"

"Then just get her on her back and—"

"Stop right there, Bates," Sinclair snapped. "You're talking about my future wife."

"Your wife in twenty minutes," Roman amended. "Bates, where's Crispin? That lad could talk him out of this nonsense."

"You're right. I'll go get him, right now. Don't leave until I get back."

Sin scowled. He was going to marry Victoria Fontaine. He wanted to marry her, and not just because their union would help him catch a murderer. He couldn't figure out what it was about her that compelled him so, but he couldn't deny it, either.

"Bates," Sinclair said, forcing himself to calm down. No one was going to stop him. He simply wouldn't let it happen. "It's likely that Thomas knew whoever killed him. In all probability that makes the murderer one of Lady Vixen Fontaine's acquaintances."

"And what if she gets hurt?"

Sin shrugged into his coat. "I won't let that happen. She knows her way through the dregs of the London *ton* better than I do. Don't worry. When this is over, if she wants an annulment, I'll give her one."

Even as he said it, Sinclair realized that he didn't like the idea at all. He wanted Victoria Fontaine, and oddly enough, the less certain she seemed of him, the stronger his desire for her seemed to become.

The most dangerous part of this insanity was that

he wanted her to desire him—and not just physically. No, he wanted her to *like* him; a blatantly impossible wish, unless he was willing to tell her who he really was. Since that would likely get her—and himself— killed, he seemed to have mired himself into the deepest hole he'd yet managed to dig.

"Unless you've decided to come to your senses, we'd best get you to Westminster Cathedral," Roman said brusquely.

Sinclair stifled his sudden burst of nervous anticipation under years of practiced cynicism. "I keep thinking it'd be a better show if I were drunk for this. Should I be?"

"I would be," Bates muttered.

"I'd say no, Sin," the valet countered. "This is to get you into the nobles' good graces without you looking like a threat. If you embarrass 'em, you're a threat. And then this whole play will be for nothing."

Sinclair nodded. "Good point."

"Besides," Bates added, "you want to be good and sober for this—a clear-eyed witness to the biggest mistake of your life."

Pure, cold nervousness ran through him. Bates was probably right. He'd begun this, though, and he needed to see it through. Sin forced a chuckle. "Only one of many. And if all my mistakes looked like Vixen Fontaine, I wouldn't mind making them." He picked up his kid gloves. "Roman, Lord Stiveton will be sending over his daughter's things during the ceremony. Have them put in the bedchamber adjoining mine, and the spare sitting room."

"You going to tell Milo, too? Because he won't listen to me."

"I already have. I want you to keep an eye out here, though."

The valet sighed. "Aye. It would be nice if you had more than four damned people in the world you trusted, you know."

With another grin, Sin slapped him on the back. "Who says I trust you?"

Roman scowled. "I'll pack a bag for you, just in case you change your mind." He continued grumbling as he straightened the dressing table. "Bringing a vixen into a house that's already full of snakes. That makes as much damned sense as anything."

Chapter 4

❧

All Victoria remembered later of her wedding was that it glittered. Beading and pearls and precious gems reflected the light from the glowing stained glass windows and the hundreds of candles flickering down the long aisles. She didn't faint, though it wouldn't have taken much more than a gentle breeze to send her to the floor.

Everyone was there, from Prince George to the Duke of Wellington to the Duke of Monmouth, most of them smiling benevolently as she numbly repeated the archbishop's words. The whole event seemed such a fraud. The guests didn't all have to be so jolly about it, and they certainly didn't have to celebrate the catastrophe.

When the archbishop pronounced them husband and wife, and Sinclair Grafton lifted her veil, his amber eyes were dancing. This, of all things, apparently amused him. It shook her out of her stupor, and she scowled.

"Don't frown," he murmured, caressing her cheek as he straightened the veil. "I won't disappoint you."

He leaned down and, feather-soft, touched his lips to hers.

It didn't seem like something a rake would say, and she wondered about it all during the reception and dancing at Fontaine House. If that was his way of apologizing, it was far too little, and much too late.

"You make a beautiful bride."

She turned at the sound of the low, masculine drawl, dreading yet another round of stupid congratulations and good wishes. As she met the light gray eyes looking at her, though, and took in the lean, strong figure dressed all in black, she relaxed enough to smile. "Lucien."

The Earl of Kilcairn Abbey took her hand and bowed over it. "Whatever you told Alexandra, no one outfoxes the Vixen. What's your game?"

She sighed, noting that her husband was across the room talking and laughing with some rather inebriated-looking young men. "I think I was outfoxed. It was bound to happen eventually, I suppose."

"Hm. Well, you're not out of options yet, my lady."

"What do you mean by that?"

Kilcairn shrugged. "If you don't like him, shoot him."

Laughter burst from her lips. "Hardly conventional, but I'll keep it in mind."

He nodded, smiling briefly, then stepped closer. "I consider you a friend, Victoria," he continued in a lower voice. "If you have need of anything, you let me know."

Victoria tilted her head at him. "Did Lex put you up to this?"

"No. She said you were less than pleased with this

nonsense. Any and all offers to do violence come from me alone."

Kilcairn didn't make such offers lightly, nor did he do anything without thought. "Thank you, Lucien," she said quietly, lifting her chin, "but I shall manage."

"I don't believe we've been introduced."

Moving so silently that Victoria hadn't even heard him approach, Sinclair took her fingers and placed them on his arm. His attention, though, was on Kilcairn. If Victoria thought he had any reason in the world for the emotion, she would have called him jealous.

"Lord Althorpe, this is the Earl of Kilcairn Abbey. Lucien, Lord Althorpe."

The two tall men were nearly dark-haired mirrors of one another, amber eyes assessing gray ones. Lucien, though, had come to grips with his demons already, and he nodded. "Althorpe. You've backed into a fine marriage."

"I'd like to think so," Sinclair replied, so cool that icicles might have formed from his breath.

Kilcairn, of course, was made of ice. "Just so you appreciate that—and her."

Sinclair's eyes narrowed. Before they could begin pummeling one another, Victoria stepped between them. "That is quite enough stomping and snorting," she announced.

His gray eyes amused, Lucien inclined his head. "Very well. No bloodshed at your reception. Good afternoon, Althorpe."

To his credit, Sin waited until the earl strolled through the door connecting the ballroom to the upstairs sitting room. "Who was that?" he demanded, turning on her.

"I told you," she said, surprised at his vehemence. "Lord Kilcairn. Lucien Balfour."

"One of your conquests?"

"You *are* jealous."

He blinked. "I'm merely trying to sort out the players."

"Well, Lucien isn't one of them." Victoria stepped away from him. "It's good to know, however, that you expect me to begin an affair on our wedding day, my lord."

"You sh—"

"Thank you for thinking so highly of me," she continued, angrier and more frustrated by the moment. "No doubt, though, you are merely judging me by your own standard of behavior."

Althorpe waited calmly. "Finished?"

"Yes. Quite."

"Then I think you should call me Sinclair. Or Sin, if you prefer."

"I would prefer," she said, her jaw clenched, "that you didn't insult me and then change the subject, my lord."

Another barely noticeable pause. "So noted. Will you dance with me, my bride?"

She would have preferred not to; her nerves fairly hummed with agitation already, and she felt torn between wanting to knock him senseless and flee, and wanting to fall into his arms and make him live up to his promises of seduction and ecstasy. "I suppose I should," she answered, and took his proffered hand.

Of course the orchestra began a waltz, and as he drew her into the dance she felt the same magnetic attraction of the night they had met. "Are you nervous?" he asked, pulling her close.

"Why should I be? Waltzing is easy."

"You're trembling," he murmured back. "Do you anticipate tonight?"

She admired self-confidence. Unmitigated arrogance was something else entirely. Victoria clenched her jaw. "Don't you, of all people, try to make this marriage into something other than the farce it is. There will be no 'tonight.' Not in the way you mean."

For a long moment he held her in silence as they glided across the room. "Do you dislike me that much? You didn't just a week ago."

"Wanting to kiss you and wanting to converse with you are two completely different things."

He had no trouble at all grasping the significance of that comment. "You want to kiss me. You want me to kiss you. In that case, conversation can always wait."

She colored again. Goodness, she hadn't blushed so much in ages. "I believe women as a rule do like your attentions. You did say you were a *successful* rake. Otherwise, you would merely be a fool."

Sinclair didn't like that; she could see it in the way his eyes glittered. "I'm not a fool, Victoria. The fools are the ones who held you and then let you go. I want you in my bed."

Victoria favored him with a smile. "You've paid a high enough price for the opportunity, no doubt, but it's *not* going to happen, Sinclair."

His return smile didn't comfort her at all. In fact, it began a delicious cascade of shivers down her spine. And from the way his amber eyes watched her so closely, he knew it, damn it all. "I think you know that it will, sooner or later," he said. "And I think it frightens you a little."

"You most certainly do not frighten me, my lord."

"Sinclair," he corrected softly.

"Sinclair," she repeated. The name felt right on her lips, and she had the odd sense that she was losing some sort of argument she hadn't even realized she was waging with herself. "It's easy to converse with men, anyway," she said, hoping the sudden edge of desperation running through her didn't show in her voice. "All one need do is flatter them."

"But I don't require flattery. That's why I make you nervous. I only want to know about you."

"Yes—how I react to *you*."

"You don't know as much as you think you do."

The waltz ended and she began to pull away, practically trembling with relief. "That is your opinion."

That should have succeeded in silencing him—but he didn't release his warm, sure grip on her waist. Instead, he merely looked at the orchestra and lifted a sardonic eyebrow. Before she could inform him that they would never play two waltzes in a row, they struck up another one.

"You can't dance with me again."

"I *am* dancing with you again. No one will stop us; we've just been married, remember? Besides—you threw me a challenge."

"I did not."

"You said I only wanted to know about you in ways that related to me."

"No, I—"

"In a sense you're correct," he mused, "because knowing about you is one of my desires. So indulge me. Tell me something about yourself."

She managed to summon enough indignation to answer him. "I don't like you."

His soft chuckle reached all the way down to her

toes. "Something that isn't about me, my darling."

Now he was simply gloating. Victoria clenched her jaw. They might agree that he wasn't a fool, but she was certainly acting like one. "Then I suggest *you* pick a topic."

"All right." He glanced around the room, his expression thoughtful. "Ah. Your friends. Tell me about your friends." Gesturing with the hand at her waist, he indicated the stocky, square-jawed man who waltzed with Diane Addington. "Him. Why is he at your wedding?"

She followed his gaze. "I don't know. I don't like him, either."

"Why not?"

"That gentleman is Viscount Perington. He drowns kittens."

"It won't get him sainthood, but it's also not criminal."

"It doesn't seem to matter whose kittens they are. And he keeps a count."

"Then how did he manage to get an invitation?"

"My parents. He asked to marry me last Season, and my refusal deeply offended him."

Lord Althorpe's expression darkened. "I assume, then, that this is your parents' attempt to demonstrate that there are no hard feelings?"

"No. They wanted to show him what a poor match I've made so he'll be amused, and won't refuse my father's bid to add Stiveton factory-fired ceramic pottery to the products he exports. Shall I go on?"

Far from showing the boredom she expected, his eyes seemed to smoulder with that same intensity she'd seen in him the last time they waltzed. "Yes. I'm fascinated. Continue—who is that scarecrow with the high shirt-points over by the refreshment table?"

Unlikely as his interest seemed, something compelled her to believe him. That magnetic energy between them didn't lessen her anxiety, but it did cause a breathless anticipation she'd never felt before to rise in her. "Ramsey DuPont. He proposed to me last year, too."

"I hope he wasn't wearing that same coat."

"Actually, he might have been. Lime green is his favorite color. It improves the tone of his skin, he says."

"And you rejected him because of his poor fashion sense?"

"I rejected him because I don't like him."

"Might you be more specific?"

A smile curved her lips. "Looking for pitfalls to avoid?"

"No, that would relate this conversation back to me," he said smoothly. "I'm just curious."

"I can't be more specific. It was just something about the way he assumed I would accept."

"How did he take your answer, then?"

Unlike his heated reaction to Lucien Balfour, Sinclair's queries about Ramsey didn't seem to have any jealousy motivating them. Victoria decided to probe a little further. "Not well. I'm surprised he's here, unless he means to make a scene."

Sin's expression didn't change. "That would be interesting. Nothing more subversive, though? Just shouting and flailing about?"

"Mostly. Why, were you hoping for something worse?"

His dark smile appeared again. "I just like to be prepared."

So did she. While he was learning several insignificant facts about her, however, she still knew nothing
about him. "Your grandmother is very charming. And
so is your brother. Christopher, isn't it?"

The waltz ended but again he kept hold of her, taking one arm and drawing her toward the refreshment
table. "Yes. I'm surprised you'd never met them,
though, being that you and Thomas were friends."

The jealous note was back again. Apparently he
considered Lucien and Thomas to be serious threats,
but not Perington or Ramsey. Interesting, that. It made
her wonder whether he *was* jealous—and whether or
not he looked at any other females with that intense
amber gaze. In all likelihood he did, and, given his
reputation, he would continue to do so. "I saw them
at the funeral, and offered my condolences. Chatting
didn't seem appropriate."

His gaze sharpened again. "You attended the funeral?"

"Most of the *ton* did. Why didn't you?"

Before he could answer, Lucy Havers swooped in
to kiss her on both cheeks. "You are the most beautiful
bride I've ever seen," she gushed. "I heard Diane tell
her mama she wants the same dress when she marries.
I told her it would be old-fashioned by then."

"That explains the large quantity of Madeira she's
been drinking," Sinclair said dryly.

Victoria hadn't realized he'd noticed—or even that
he knew who Diane Addington was. "Thank you,
Lucy."

"She shouldn't have abandoned you last week. I
have no sympathy for her at all."

"Not everyone has parents as understanding as
yours," Victoria countered feelingly, looking to where

hers stood glowing at the scores of congratulations they'd been receiving all afternoon.

"Where are you going on your honeymoon?" her friend continued. "I forgot to ask you before."

"We're not going," Sinclair said, taking a glass of punch from a footman. "Since I'm just back in town, I am afraid I have some things to take care of first."

Victoria missed a step and would have stumbled if not for her grip on Sinclair's arm. She wasn't surprised, really. Disappointed—that was how she felt. Disappointed.

"Drat. I told Diane I thought you were going to Spain."

"We'll be sure to visit there, then, when we do go," Victoria offered weakly.

Lucy's smile dimpled her cheeks. "Fair enough."

When her friend hurried off to further antagonize Diane Addington, Victoria freed her hand from Althorpe's arm. "You might have said something to me."

"About what?"

"About our travel plans. Or lack thereof."

His wary expression grew more defensive. "You're the one who said I shouldn't pretend this marriage is anything but a farce."

So she had, dash it all. "That was between us."

"Ah. So the world at large is to believe we fell madly in love at first sight."

If nothing else, he had considerable skill at sarcasm. "Yes. Something like that."

"Then give me your arm again."

"You don't have to fall all over me to make everyone think we're fond of one another."

"I'm not very good at doe-eyed, love-struck looks from across the room, my lady."

She was about to retort in kind when she spied Lord
William Landry approaching, a cynical sneer on his
inebriated countenance. "How long do we have to remain here?" she asked tightly.

"I thought we were becoming acquainted."

"I'm acquainted enough for one day."

He hesitated. "Then we'll go home."

Home, of course, meant Grafton House, with him.
Perhaps she would stay longer at the reception, after
all. Victoria drew a breath. Her things were already
gone from this house, and her parents had had ample
time to arrange for her to stay if they had cared to do
so.

"Home is fine with me."

He took her hand again, and they evaded Landry
with little effort. Instead of going to her parents and
formally taking their leave, Sin guided her around the
fringes of the ballroom to the main door.

"Timms," he said in a low voice, "have the groom
bring around my coach."

The butler hesitated. "Of course, my lord. But
don't—"

"Now."

The tall servant bowed. "At once, my lord."

They followed Timms downstairs and waited in the
foyer while he summoned the groom. Music echoed
from the ballroom upstairs; no doubt the guests hadn't
yet realized that the bride and groom were no longer
present.

Both Alexandra and Lucien had claimed that she
wouldn't have allowed this marriage to take place if
she hadn't somehow wanted it. Victoria studied Sinclair's profile. True, she had been bored and restless

and dissatisfied, but marrying an unrepentant hedonist hardly seemed the solution for that.

A part of her, though, wanted to know what would happen next. Something about Sin Grafton had lured her out to the garden that night, and that same something had kept her from fleeing the impending wedding. Now, though, she wondered whether that something—that rampaging physical lust, she supposed it must be—was enough to compensate for the dreams of freedom and independence she had lost.

Viscount Perington, Ramsey DuPont, and Lucien Balfour. The first two were already suspects, and he was more than happy to include the third. The Vixen knew all of them, knew things about them that he hadn't known, and nothing she'd said had inclined him to remove them from his list. Just the opposite. Sinclair gazed at his bride, seated as far from him as the confines of the coach would allow.

For once in his life, he wasn't certain how to proceed. In the past, the people he'd guided into traps and confessions had occasionally earned his pity, but never his compassion. Yet he had a hard time convincing himself that Victoria Fontaine—Grafton, now—deserved this.

"Your father had the rest of your things sent over during the reception," he said, unused to seeing her quiet and reserved.

"Yes, I know. Where am I to sleep?"

He didn't suppose she'd forgotten there would be no "tonight" tonight, but for a few moments he had held out hope that she might change her mind. Until he'd announced to all and sundry that he had no intention of indulging in a honeymoon, he might have had a chance.

Sin scowled in the dimness, then wiped the expression from his face as she glanced at him and then back out the window. Because he needed to stay in London, they were going to stay in London. He hadn't even considered that she might at least want to be consulted about their travel plans. He was becoming more of a boor every time he turned around. Not surprising, he supposed, but another disappointment for everyone concerned.

"I can't convince you to join me, I suppose?" he offered because she would expect it.

She faced him. "No. You could force me, of c—"

"I won't," he interrupted flatly. "Goes against my morals, such as they are." He'd thought to reassure her, but at the abruptly curious look she gave him, he realized he'd given something away. "What?"

"Given your haste to marry and to assume the duties of your title, I would have assumed you intended on starting a family. You said this marriage was 'convenient' for you, after all."

"I like a challenge."

She smiled. "I'm happy to oblige you."

"Good God," he muttered, impressed despite the considerable trouble he foresaw for himself. "I can be very persuasive, Victoria. I want you. I want to taste your lips again."

Victoria blushed. "You won't be tasting them any time soon, my lord."

"Sin," he murmured. "I shall anticipate the future, then." He sat back. "I've put you in the bedchamber adjoining mine. The door locks from either side. I'll give you the key."

"And will you have a key?"

He shook his head. "You'll be inviting me in soon enough."

The coach rocked to a halt. Ordinarily it would have been only a second or two before a footman pulled the door open, but Sinclair imagined their early arrival had caused substantial chaos in the household. Indeed, nearly thirty seconds passed before a panting Orser yanked open the door and flipped down the steps.

"We didn't expect you yet, my lord," he said.

"So I gathered."

He had instructed the staff to assemble out front to welcome the new mistress of the house when she arrived. As he stepped to the ground and turned to take Victoria's hand, he was gratified to see all twenty-two of his London employees hurrying out of the house and lining up along the short drive.

"I'm causing turmoil already," Vixen murmured.

He smiled, guiding her toward the head of the line. "We thrive on turmoil. I do, anyway."

"That remains to be seen, my lord," she said, releasing his hand to advance on her own.

He'd thought the mass of curious servants ogling her would make his bride nervous, but she merely nodded politely and stopped before Milo. Her composure made sense, though; she would be more used to the hubbub of elite London life than he was.

"Milo," he said, and the butler stepped forward. "Victoria, our butler, Milo. Milo, I am pleased to present the Marchioness of Althorpe."

The butler bowed. "Lady Althorpe."

Sinclair hung back, watching, as Milo introduced Victoria to the head servants. He had met them in much the same way a few weeks earlier. Today,

though, and despite the rush, they seemed less non-
plussed. But Victoria wasn't replacing a beloved master or mistress, as he had; she had no one else's
sterling reputation to greet her with a slap in the face
at the front door. He was relieved; she would be facing
enough from him without the servants to add insult to
injury.

Roman, of course, hadn't joined the rest of the servants, he would be lurking inside, watching and waiting to see if any other lurkers appeared. Of course, he
might also be making the acquaintance of Victoria's
maid, who also seemed to be absent.

"Thank you, Milo," he said, stepping forward as the
litany ended.

"Very good, my lord. May I assume that you and
Lady Althorpe will be dining at home this evening?"

He supposed it would be pushing things too far,
even for him, if he spent the evening reviewing the
latest list of suspects and information with his compatriots. They were probably still at the reception
searching for any crumbs of information anyway.
"Yes." They arrived up the shallow steps at the front
door, and he stopped, looking at his petite bride. "Shall
I carry you over the threshold, my lady?"

Color touched her cheeks, though he wasn't certain
whether it was nerves or annoyance. "No. I don't think
so."

"After you, then." Hiding his disappointment, he
gestured her into the house. Admittedly she had little
reason to want his attentions, and in fact that would
make things easier on him. But damn it all, tonight
was his wedding night, and he wanted her—more
badly with each passing moment.

With a hesitation so slight he might have imagined

it, she stepped into Grafton House. As she took in the dark, polished floor and deep-grained mahogany wood of the foyer, it occurred to him that his brother had expensive, if very conservative, taste. In Grafton House he had indulged it fully.

"The morning room is there to your right," he said, gesturing at the nearest door, "and the downstairs sitting room, which has an ample supply of Thomas's very good brandy, adjoins it. Across—"

"I think I would like to go to my room and rest," she interrupted.

The mob of servants behind them increased the volume of their muttering. So much for presenting a unified front to the household. "This way, then." Stifling a sigh, Sinclair led the way to the curving staircase. "What happened to only the two of us knowing this marriage is a sham?" he murmured.

"I only said I was tired, which I am."

"You're certain you're not going into hiding? You said I couldn't shock you."

"You haven't." She stopped at the top of the stairs, and he turned around. "Hiding," she said crisply, "would imply that I am frightened of you, which I am not."

He took a step closer. "Good. We'll sit for dinner at eight, unless you can think of something more . . . enjoyable for us to be doing."

"Hm. My mind's a blank. You'll have to occupy yourself." Victoria held out her hand, the gesture more vulnerable-looking than defiant as she stood there in her delicate silk-and-lace wedding gown. He wanted to take the clips from her dark hair and let it spill over his hands.

"The key," she said.

Sinclair blinked. "You're serious."

"Did I say something to make you doubt that?"

He shook his head, amused. The master spy had been outmaneuvered by a wisp of a female who barely came to his shoulder. "No." Digging into his pocket, he produced the key. Reluctantly he placed it into her palm, curling her fingers closed with his. "I won't hurt you, Victoria," he said softly, hoping he was telling the truth. "I'm not quite that awful."

For a long moment she looked at him in silence, while he gave her his best harmless expression. "I hope not," she said finally, her voice catching.

He resumed the tour down the hallway. "Your rooms are here. My bedchamber is the door just beyond."

"Very well. Thank you, my lord. Sinclair."

"You're welcome. And don't think you're confined to your private rooms. This house is yours now."

"You don't think I'll run away?"

He smiled. "You haven't so far."

He seemed willing to stand in the hallway all afternoon chatting with her. Part of Victoria—the part that tried to convince her this wasn't a sham and a nightmare, but something that deep down she wanted for herself—was willing to stay as well. Rational thinking, sleeplessness, and nerves won out, though, and with a half smile that hopefully looked more sincere than it felt, Victoria slipped into her bedchamber and closed the door. And gasped as something rubbed against her ankles.

"Lord Baggles," she cooed, kneeling, "you nearly frightened me out of my wits. What are you doing here?"

"He wouldn't go into the cage, my lady," Jenny said, stepping into the bedchamber from an adjoining dressing room. "I thought perhaps Lady Kilcairn might look after him while you and Lord Althorpe are away."

"With her icky dog Shakespeare determined to pull my sweetum's pretty little ears off?" Victoria gathered the gray-and-black ball of fur known as Lord Baggles into her arms and stood. "It's not necessary to banish my pretty little kitty, anyway."

"Will that snooty Milo keep an eye on him, then? Or maybe Miss Lucy would," Jenny continued. "I left the two trunks packed as you said, but I didn't know which traveling dress to put out."

Victoria glanced at the two large trunks standing beneath the window. "Don't put any of them out. We're going to be staying in London."

"But—"

"He's just returned to England, Jenny. Why would he want to go dragging about the Continent again, and with a wife he barely knows?" Lord Baggles jumped from her loose grip onto the large bed.

"Because he just got married, I would guess."

"I hardly think that will interfere with his social schedule." She heaved a breath, knowing she must sound forlorn. "Or mine."

"Shall I send for the rest of your babies, then, my lady?"

"Please do. Father and Mother will be relieved to see them gone from the house." She scratched Lord Baggles behind the ears, and he purred. "And I could use a few more friends."

Jenny cleared her throat. "Well, at least Lord Althorpe is generous with his rooms," she said. "For once we'll have enough space for all your clothes, I think." She paused, considering. "I hope."

"That seems as sound a reason to marry as anything else I've come up with. So show me my new rooms then, Jenny."

Her maid was correct; the marquis had allotted her not just the bedchamber and dressing room but also an adjoining private sitting room, and beyond that a small conservatory complete with a balcony with floor-length windows. The delicate plants looked terribly unkempt, but no doubt they had only been sparsely tended since Thomas's death. She wasn't a very keen gardener herself, but puttering around in the airy, well-lighted room might be rather nice on occasion.

The doorway between the greenhouse and the sitting room looked new; and the best thing about her private chambers was that she could go all the way from bed to balcony without setting foot in the upstairs hallway. Lord Althorpe had given her space and privacy, which would have been both splendid and thoughtful if she'd enjoyed spending time alone. Unfortunately, as her father often lamented, she seemed to be the most social creature in London.

She returned with Jenny to the bedchamber to change out of her wedding gown. Through the dressing room another door stood, and she stopped, gazing at it. *His* dressing room and bedchamber would be through there. She was tempted to try the door just to see if it was locked, but it might not be, and he might be inside, and she didn't quite feel ready to face him again so soon. She couldn't even seem to converse when he was present—and if there was one thing at which she excelled, it was conversation.

Slowly she pulled out the key and looked at it. He hadn't wanted to give it to her, but he'd done so anyway. Of course, he'd also claimed that she wouldn't want to use it for long. With a sniff, Victoria put the key into the lock and turned it. The click wasn't as satisfying as she'd hoped, but it did make a point.

"The blue muslin, or the green silk, my lady?"

She started. "Hm? Oh, the green silk, I think. I'm not certain how formal one is supposed to be for a first meal with one's spouse, but I'd rather be overdressed than undressed."

The maid looked at her. "Underdressed you mean, don't you, my lady?"

Victoria scowled and returned to the bedchamber, flopping onto the bed. "For heaven's sake. Of course I do. Underdressed."

"Though since you are married to a very handsome gentleman," the maid mused as she laid the dress across a chair, "the other seems sure to arise, as well."

"Jenny!"

The maid blushed. "Well, it's true, my lady."

"This is not a real marriage, Jenny. Not as far as I'm concerned."

"I wonder what his lordship thinks about that?"

"I'm sure I have no idea. And even less concern."

Despite her pronouncements, by eight o'clock that evening she had spent an inordinate amount of time considering the delicious, heady quality of her groom's kisses. Though she was used to the layout of London's largest town houses, she still managed to get lost on her way to dinner, detouring into the library and the music room before she found the main dining room. He'd said the house was hers now, but that wasn't quite true; legally, she had just become an additional piece of his property, and he owned her as much as he owned Grafton House.

She arrived at the dining room before Sinclair did. Half a dozen footmen and the butler stood ranged in the room, waiting for someone to wait upon. "Good evening," she said, moving to the seat at the foot of the table.

"Good evening, my lady," Milo responded, hurrying forward to hold her chair for her.

"This must be very odd for all of you," she continued in her friendliest tone, as she sat down. "First a new marquis and now his wife, all in less than a month. Have you been in the Graftons' employ long, Milo?"

"Yes, my lady. More than half the staff remains from the previous Lord Althorpe's residence."

"He was a good man."

"A very kind man," Milo stated, so emphatically that she smiled up at him.

"Lord Althorpe must be pleased to see such loyalty to his family. How long did you serve Thomas?"

"Five years, my lady. And if I may say so, the . . . bastard who killed him deserves a good hanging."

The other servants nodded their heads in agreement. Victoria had to wonder, though, whether they more regretted losing their old employer or gaining a new one.

"There you are," came from the doorway.

The slight, familiar shiver tingled down her spine at the sound of his low drawl.

"Good evening, Sinclair," she said, his name on her lips sounding foreign and familiar all at the same time. She wondered if she would ever grow used to saying it.

"You look stunning," he said, circling around behind her before he took his seat at the opposite end of the long, formal table.

"Thank you."

He inclined his head. "I went to fetch you, but you seem able to navigate on your own."

"One house is very like another." She knew she sounded arch, but with the way her tongue seized up in his presence, she was relieved just to be able to utter a coherent sentence.

"I suppose they are. I haven't visited many since my return. I should pay more attention, I imagine."

"It hardly signifies. There's always a servant about to guide an infrequent visitor, and the frequent ones have already visited enough to know where they're going."

His expression grew intent for the length of a heartbeat, and then he was Sin, the rake with the dark, sensual smile again. "I seem to fall under the category of infrequent visitor."

He also seemed to have completely forgotten that she was a first-time visitor to Grafton House. "I feel that way, myself," she said, just to remind him that he should have been making supportive comments to her—not the other way around.

"We'll have to remedy that. I think I've become familiar enough with the place to give you a tour. Whenever you'd like. Tomorrow, perhaps."

"Perhaps. I do have a charity luncheon to attend tomorrow."

He lifted an eyebrow, jaded and cynical again. "I was under the impression that you thought we were going to be out of town tomorrow."

Drat. "So I was. But the luncheon has been set for months—and I agreed to participate long before I met you. If I'm in London, I have to attend. You said I shouldn't alter my social calendar." She looked down at her plate as Milo served a very delectable-smelling roast pheasant. "You may accompany me, if you wish."

Sinclair snorted. "Me—at a charity luncheon? I'm surprised you let yourself be pulled into it, but I'm not that daft."

That was just about enough of that. "I didn't get pulled into anything, my lord," she retorted, clenching her fork. "I volunteered. That's what charity is, you know. Giving of yourself."

"If that's the definition," he said around a mouthful of pheasant, "then this bird committed charity. It's certainly given of itself. And damned tastily, too."

She glanced at the assembled servants. If he wasn't concerned about the impression he made in front of them, then she didn't care about how oafish he looked, either. "If you confuse eating a bird with charitable works, I can see how your loyalties became so confused in Europe."

He froze, then slowly set down his utensils, his gaze all the while on her face. "My loyalties?"

"Yes. Why else would you gad about France when the rest of England was at war with it?"

For a long moment he said nothing. Then, his shoulders perceivably relaxing, he resumed eating. "My loyalties in Europe were never unclear. They were always to myself."

"And that is even more sad than if you'd chosen the wrong side." Angry and disappointed, she pushed away from the table and stood. "Excuse me, but I think I'll retire early this evening."

This time he didn't look up at all. "Good night then, Victoria."

"Sinclair."

Chapter 5

S inclair paced his bedchamber, pausing each time before the dressing room door and then resuming his stalking again. He'd be damned if he would try the door, or if he would enter her room—not until she begged him to.

So she questioned his loyalties. *She*, a frivolous, flirtatious, and spoiled London beauty, had questioned *his* loyalties. Of course, that had been the idea: to give everyone—especially Bonaparte—the impression that he was too self-absorbed to care about politics, and that he would do anything so long as it amused and benefitted him. Those same qualities were supposed to give him equally free rein in London, to find Thomas's killer.

Obviously, he was becoming demented. Victoria was supposed to think him a boor, but now that she did, he didn't like it. "Idiot," he muttered. "Jackass."

The clock downstairs chimed twice. With another oath at his inattention, he grabbed his discarded coat and slipped out to the dark hallway. Swiftly he made his way downstairs, avoiding the step with the nasty creak, and slipped into the first-floor office. Even in the dark it took only a second to unhook the latch and swing open the window. It moved silently; he'd made certain of that the day he'd returned to London.

Once over the casement, he dropped to the ground and, hugging the deep shadows close by the house, crept out to the stable. "Bates," he whispered.

" 'Bout time," a lower, more guttural voice answered from behind him.

Sin swung around, in the same fluid movement pulling the pistol from his pocket and aiming it.

"Jesus!"

Sin froze, the muzzle of his pistol pressed against the man's forehead. "Don't move."

"Not likely to, with that cannon pointing at me. For God's sake, Sin, it was a joke."

Sinclair slowly lowered the pistol and pocketed it again. "Doing poor impressions of dead assassins really isn't that amusing, Wally."

"I told you," Bates said, coming around the corner of the building with a tall, muscular man beside him. "Not funny."

Wally ran a hand through his thinning blond hair. "Well, if you hadn't been late coming out here, I wouldn't have had time to think it up."

Sinclair nodded. "I lost track of the time."

"That's expected," Bates said, his teeth glinting in the moonlight as he grinned. "It being your wedding night and all."

"I'm surprised you left that warm, soft bed at all," Wally contributed.

As he had no intention of informing them that he and his bride had spent their first night of matrimonial bliss in separate bedchambers, Sinclair merely shrugged. "Just tell me it was worth it."

The tawny-haired giant with Bates stepped forward. "That supposed witness we tracked down turned out to be an old, drunk squire with no more sense than pence."

The soft Scottish accent didn't make the news any more palatable. "Nothing at all?"

"Nae. He heard that I was offering money for information, but I don't think he knew your brother from Prince George."

"I didn't think offering a reward would work," Sin acknowledged softly, "but we had to try."

Wally was shaking his head. "If money was the key, somebody would have flushed the bastard out two years ago."

"I know. We're just going to have to do it the old-fashioned way. We can't eliminate any of our suspects without proof to the contrary."

"That could take a very long time, Sin."

He looked at Bates. "You're not obligated to join me."

The younger man scowled. "Don't start with that damned nonsense again."

"Where d'you want to begin?" Crispin added.

The little quip Victoria had shot at him stuck in his mind. He'd thought of it before, but in a more nebulous way. "We have two extremes to choose from," he said slowly. "Most of the servants were gone, and none of the ones working that night remember seeing or hearing anything unusual. So—we have either a complete stranger who sneaked into that huge house and managed to find, surprise, and kill Thomas without running into anyone else; or, we have someone familiar enough with the house and its inhabitants to do the deed and escape unnoticed."

"With a thunderstorm for cover, I can't think why either one couldn't be plausible," Bates said thoughtfully.

"We've had this conversation before," Wally grumbled, hunching his shoulders against the cool night breeze.

"And we'll continue to have it until we find the damned murderer." Sinclair glared at him. "I measured: the study desk is twelve feet from the door. It's closer to the window, but one casement is painted shut, and until a few days ago, the other had a squeak loud enough to raise the dead."

"Plenty of warning for your brother, whichever direction the gunman came from," Crispin said with his usual astuteness, "but he didnae see the need to stand up or to reach for a weapon."

"Exactly. I'm willing to wager that Thomas was well acquainted with his killer. And I think we have to proceed from there."

"No changes to the list, then?"

"Not by much. I want a sound alibi with witnesses before we dismiss any of them. Wally, you take Mr. Ramsey DuPont. I doubt he's our man, but he seems to have a mean streak. Bates, you luck into Lord Perington, who likes to drown cats and has a successful export business. And Crispin, the Earl of Kilcairn Abbey is yours."

"Lucky me," the big Scot muttered. "Lucifer Balfour himself. Ye didnae suspect him before."

"I do now." That wasn't quite true, but he couldn't forget Victoria's delighted reaction to Kilcairn's presence. He'd be more than pleased to discover anything unpleasant about Lucien Balfour.

"We'll keep communicating through Lady Stanton,"

he continued. "If I don't hear from you before Thursday, we'll meet at Jezebel's Harem at midnight."

Bates narrowed one eye. "Uh, Sin, are you certain about that?"

"Yes. Why?"

"A married gentleman at Jezebel's might raise a few eyebrows, you know."

Sinclair cursed. "You're right. Damnation. Boodles', then. Are you still in good standing there, Crispin?"

"Aye. A bit proper for us, but we'll manage it."

"I'll see you then. And be careful."

"Take your own advice, Sin," Crispin said. "You've done some mad things in your life, but getting married because you need a sound list of suspects—that's daft, even for you."

"Or it just might be my most brilliant strategy yet," Sinclair countered.

"Aye. Or it might be for some other reason entirely."

Sinclair scowled. "Like what?"

Crispin just smiled. "G'night, Sin." A moment later, the three men vanished into the darkness.

Sinclair stood where he was for a moment, then turned back to the house and the open study window. Whether Victoria wanted to share his bed yet or not, she'd already answered some questions about three of their suspects and a logical method of entry. On one route, at least, the path looked nicely clear.

Victoria stepped back from the window and let the curtain fall closed again. She hadn't seen them all that well, but she was fairly certain those three gentlemen were the same ones Sinclair had conversed with at their reception. Funny, they had seemed hopelessly silly and drunk then, but out in the Grafton stable yard they all looked as sober as she was. It had been several hours, of course, but it still seemed odd.

She sat on the edge of her bed and absently stroked Lord Baggles. She wasn't aware of any rakes who went lurking about their own stable yards in the middle of the night, armed and apparently quite proficient with their weaponry. And that wasn't all. The straight, attentive line of his body, the spare way he spoke and gestured—they reminded her of a different Sinclair Grafton, the one whose kiss had sent her headlong into marriage.

Victoria sighed, tired down to her bones. It was his fault she was spying on him, though, because she'd only been looking out at the moonlight. He'd been the one providing something for her to see.

In all likelihood he had a perfectly logical explanation for his odd little meeting. Asking, though, would mean admitting that she'd been watching him out the window. She didn't feel ready to hear or render explanations just yet, not when she hadn't even sorted out how she'd ended up married.

Sin had already left to go riding the next morning when she went downstairs to the breakfast room. Generally, by the time she made her appearance at Fontaine House, two or three young men would already have gathered in the morning room with invitations for picnics and carriage rides, just on the chance she might have a spare moment during the day.

Grafton House seemed completely devoid of young, admiring men, including her husband. Except for the edge of annoyance at being ignored and disregarded, she rather liked it. There was no one to be clever for, no one to converse with about the same things she'd discussed a hundred times before.

"Milo," she said as she buttered her toast, "I am expecting a few more things this morning. How does Lord Althorpe feel about animals?"

"Animals, my lady?"

She smiled at his puzzled look. "Yes. Animals."

"I don't know, my lady. He has purchased several horses since his arrival, if that helps."

Victoria paused, the toast halfway to her lips. "You said 'arrival.' Not 'return.' Didn't you know Lord Althorpe before he came to assume the title?"

The butler intercepted the teapot from a footman, signaled the servant to leave, and refilled her cup himself. "I met him on one prior occasion, my lady, shortly after I began my employment here. His visit, however, was quite . . . brief, and quite correctly Lord Althorpe did not introduce us."

Hmmm. That was exceedingly interesting. Though the butler hadn't said anything definitive, nor would he if he had any intelligence, she had the distinct feeling that he didn't like his new employer. Since Sinclair didn't seem inclined to tell her anything about himself, she would simply have to find an alternative means of learning.

"That's a shame, considering the present circumstance," she continued, spooning sugar into her tea. "Was the late marquis fond of his brother?"

"I wasn't privy to his private ruminations, of course, but I can say that they quarreled that one time, and that afterwards the former Lord Althorpe rarely spoke of his brother—except when he read the morning newspaper."

"The newspaper?"

"Yes. Several times as he took his breakfast, I heard him exclaim about the foolish chances Sinclair took." He cleared his throat. "Those were his words, of course. I would never pass judgment on either Lord Althorpe."

"Oh, no. What a pity, though, that the brothers didn't get along. I often wished I had had a sister with whom to chat."

"Well, there is young Christopher. Lord Althorpe—the former Lord Althorpe—doted on him."

She favored him with a warm look. Men were so easy to deal with. "You seem fond of young Christopher, yourself."

"He is a fine young man."

"I met him yesterday. He seemed quite charming to me, as well. I was surprised that . . . my husband hadn't mentioned him before." Calling Sin her husband seemed so odd, but constantly referring to him as "the marquis" and "Lord Althorpe" was wearing thin.

"It's my understanding that the grandmother, Lady Drewsbury, didn't approve of the new marquis's long delay in assuming the title. That is mere speculation, of course."

Victoria put a hand on Milo's arm. "Of course. I appreciate your assistance." She chuckled. "I'm afraid I have a great deal of catching up to do. I think I've found my tutor."

A movement at the edge of her vision caught her eye, but when she looked toward the hall doorway, no one was there. She fleetingly hoped Jenny hadn't allowed Lord Baggles to escape. A moment later the front door rattled and opened, and she jumped.

"If you'll excuse me, my lady," the butler said hurriedly, exiting.

He nearly slammed into the marquis as Sinclair strolled into the room. "There you are, Milo," he exclaimed, handing over his hat and black greatcoat. "See that Diable is put up, won't you?"

"Yes, my lord."

"And good morning, Victoria." Althorpe sidestepped the butler and sank into the chair beside her, ignoring the place that had been laid at the head of the table. The servants rushed to move the place settings.

"Good morning."

A wave of shivers cascaded along her skin as he leaned his chin in one hand to gaze at her. The sensation wasn't at all unpleasant, and neither was the sight of his deceptively lazy amber eyes taking her in.

" 'Diable'?" she repeated, mainly to turn his disconcerting attention away from her.

"Seemed the fashionable thing to name the beast. His real name's Frederick the Dependable. Hardly awe-inspiring at all."

She chuckled, relieved that he seemed willing to forget their poor parting last night. "I'd have to agree."

His return smile made her heart race. "Did you sleep well?" he asked softly as a footman poured him a cup of coffee.

He didn't seem to be making any attempt to dissemble about their relationship in front of the servants. The most likely reason, though, was that the household already knew. She hadn't exactly been tactful, either, last evening.

"Yes, I did. And my rooms are lovely. I should have told you that before. Thank you."

"I'm glad you like them, but you certainly don't need to thank me for them."

"Even so, it was thoughtful."

He straightened. "Well, it's my understanding that females like to have a private area where they can escape from the bustle of the household."

And there he was again, categorizing her when he didn't even know the first thing about her. If it wasn't for those occasional compelling looks and words, she was certain that she wouldn't like him at all. "Well, if a man's home is his castle, it follows that a woman needs at least a room or two," she said, sipping her tea and watching him over the rim of the delicate porcelain cup.

He lifted an eyebrow. "I can't quite tell, but I almost think you're arguing with me about something."

"You're mistaken. I don't know you well enough to argue with you."

"Back to that again, are we? You are persistent."

"It's one of my finest qualities."

"What time is your luncheon today?"

Victoria blinked at the swift change of topic. Apparently he didn't wish to argue with her; she didn't know quite what to make of it. "I need to be at Lady Nofton's no later than one o'clock. The luncheon begins at half past."

"Females only, I suppose?"

"A few civic-minded gentlemen attend," she answered, wondering what he was after. "Mostly the more liberal set, and the occasional clergyman."

"Pretty chits like you, or toothless old spinsters?"

"I don't pay all that much attention to the outer casements of my friends," she said stiffly. "And if you intend on having affairs, don't expect me to make the introductions for you."

His slight smile stopped the next insult in her throat. In all likelihood, he was quite aware that he had that effect on her and used it on purpose.

Sin took a strawberry from her plate, contemplated it for a moment, and then popped it into his mouth. "I apologize," he said, after he'd swallowed. "I was only curious as to what you would say. I'm afraid I've acquired coarse manners."

"My old instructor, Miss Grenville, used to say that the only thing better than a fine apology was avoiding the need to make one in the first place."

"I'll remember that. And I didn't mean to offend you—really."

"I accept your apology, my . . . Sinclair."

"So men are permitted to attend your luncheon?"

"Yes, we welcome it." She sipped her tea again, but he remained silent. "Why?"

"I thought I might accompany you today."

Victoria stared at him. "At the risk of repeating myself—why?"

Sinclair leaned closer. "I'm trying to become acquainted with you. You've turned me away from the most pleasurable route, so I'm forced to attend charitable luncheons with clergymen and Tories."

Victoria blushed. "Your subtle method of reminding me of what you want isn't likely to sway me, either."

"Then I'll have to try a different method." Before she could react to that, he put his hand over hers. "Might I accompany you?"

With a deeper flush, she extracted her hand. "You'll be bored silly, but it might do you some good."

Sinclair stood. "Excellent. I have an errand, but I'll be back shortly."

Still trying to figure out why in the world Lord Sin wanted to attend a charity luncheon, Victoria nodded. "Well, the afternoon looks to be interesting, anyway," she said into her teacup. Milo cleared his throat sympathetically—or so she imagined, anyway.

Milo hadn't killed anyone.

Sinclair leaned against the counter of Hoby's boot-making establishment, barely paying attention to the clerk who shuffled through a stack of musty invoices. In one morning, over toasted bread and strawberries, Victoria had discovered more information than he'd coerced from the damned butler in nearly a month.

True, the butler had reason to dislike him and none to resent Victoria, but it was more than that. She'd had the stuffy rascal gabbing like an old fishmonger just back from the docks. And though Milo might not have an alibi and corroborating witnesses, Sinclair knew enough. The butler had genuinely liked Thomas.

Thank God he'd decided to slip into the house to see what mood his bride was in, and thank Lucifer he'd done it in time to overhear the conversation. Roman would be disappointed to learn of the butler's innocence, but Sin was relieved. It would help him sleep a bit more soundly at night, anyway.

"Here we are. Thomas Grafton, Lord Althorpe. Is this what you wanted, my lord?"

The clerk began to pull an invoice from the middle of the stack. Straightening, Sinclair reached for the paper and knocked his elbow into the top of the stack. With a whoosh, a hundred invoices slid off the counter and onto the floor.

"Bloody hell," he growled. "Sorry about that."

With a stifled sigh the clerk squatted down to gather the papers. "No worries, my lord."

As soon as the fellow looked away, Sin lifted the edge of the remaining stack and flipped through the dozen papers before and after the one left sticking out from the pile. Hoby's had had five other customers the day Thomas had come to pick up his new boots—five nobles who'd been in town, and in Thomas's vicinity, at the time of the murder. That had been the last day of his brother's life, and the boots were the ones in which they'd buried him.

He recognized two of the names and memorized the others, letting the stack go as the clerk straightened again. "Gadzooks, what a mess," he said sympathetically.

"It's all right. They're all numbered." The fellow dumped the disheveled pile onto the counter and pulled out the invoice in question. "His lordship paid at the time of delivery. No amount is owing, as I thought."

"Well, that's good news. The fewer debts the better, I always say."

The clerk nodded and began reorganizing invoices. "Yes, my lord."

That taken care of, Sinclair returned to his phaeton and headed back toward Berkeley Square. For once he'd stumbled onto a bit of luck. He hadn't realized that Astin Hovarth had been in London that week. Being able to talk freely with a good friend of Thomas's, someone who knew his other acquaintances and his habits well, would be a boon. Before the damned charity luncheon, he should have time to scrawl out a letter to the Earl of Kingsfeld. It seemed a good time for a reunion with Astin, and he needed another hint of a direction before he sent out his bloodhounds.

Milo opened the front door for him, but the odd look on the butler's face stopped Sinclair on the front steps. "What is it?"

"Nothing, my lord."

"You look as though you've swallowed a canary."

The butler made a choking sound. "Lady Althorpe just received a few additional . . . items from Fontaine House."

"Oh, really?" That was better than hearing she'd fled the country, anyway.

"I believe she is in the conservatory, my lord."

"Very good."

Giving the butler a backward glance, Sinclair climbed the curving staircase to the second floor. As he neared his spouse's rooms, he passed a pair of footmen carrying what looked like the remains of several exotic plants and flowers.

The conservatory door was closed, and Sinclair rapped his knuckles against the hard wood.

"Just a moment."

That moment and several more passed before the door opened. Victoria's maid, Jenny, gave him a startled look, then turned toward the interior of the room.

"It's Lord Althorpe, my lady."

"Have him come—Jenny, stop Henrietta!"

Before she finished speaking, a small white streak dashed between the maid's feet and sprang for the open doorway. Almost without thinking, Sin crouched and scooped it into his arms. And scowled down at it.

"What the dev—"

Victoria swept around her maid and slammed full into him. "Oh!"

He was already off balance from snagging the creature, and he staggered backward. His bride tottered, then tumbled onto her backside.

"Are you all right?" he asked, trying to decide whether to burst into laughter or flee downstairs in terror.

She put a hand to her collapsing cascade of black hair. "Yes. Quite."

Sinclair squatted down beside her, presenting her with the captured thing. "I presume you were after this?"

"Thank goodness. Come here, sweetums," she cooed, gathering it against her lovely bosom.

"What is it, precisely?" he asked, scratching it behind what looked like an ear, mostly so he could have the excuse of brushing his fingers against his wife's soft skin.

"She's a poodle."

"That's not a poodle."

"Yes, she is!" Victoria said indignantly. "Mostly, anyway. We're almost certain of it. Aren't you, Henrietta, my little one?"

"It's a mop. A mop with legs."

She chuckled, her eyes sparkling as she looked up at him. "Don't tease her. She's very shy."

Damnation, he wanted to kiss her. "Perhaps if she had a trim so that she actually looked like a dog, she might be a bit more confident."

The humor faded from her violet gaze. "No, we don't trim Henrietta."

Sinclair's legs were cramping, so he bent his knees further and sat backward onto the floor beside her. "Why is that?"

"I found her in Covent Garden, shivering in a gutter.

Someone had set her fur on fire." A single tear ran down her smooth, soft cheek. "Thank goodness it had been raining."

He brushed her tear away with his thumb. "Maybe she's not so silly-looking, after all."

"I prefer to think of her as endearing." Victoria smiled again, and his heart gave an odd flip-flop in his chest.

"Exceedingly endearing," he murmured.

Her eyes met his, and then she blushed and turned her attention to the little dog. "Yes, aren't you, sweetie? She gets skittish in new places. That's why she ran."

Finding the sudden shyness of Henrietta's owner endearing as well, Sin rocked forward onto his feet and stood. "She'll come to like it here before she knows it," he said, holding down his hand.

The smile remained on her face as she grasped his fingers and allowed him to pull her to her feet. How long they would have stood there in the hallway, gazing at one another, he had no idea. Just as he leaned down to taste her lips, an earsplitting yowl came from the conservatory.

"Good God! What was—"

"Sheba!"

Victoria thrust Henrietta into his arms and dashed back into the room. Feeling distinctly addled, and not a little frustrated, Sin followed. A row of some dozen cages stood in the center of the room. The oddest menagerie of little beasties he'd ever seen stood and sat and slept and pecked and yowled from inside them.

His bride knelt before the furthest cage and gently extracted an orange feline from it. With a stream of the same cooing murmurs she'd used on Henrietta, she gathered the cat into her arms. For a moment Sinclair reflected that he wouldn't mind at all being one of the Vixen's pets.

"So that would be Sheba."

She started, as though she had forgotten he was there. "Yes. She's just hungry, I think." Splitting her attention between him and the row of cages, Victoria flushed again. "I . . . hope you don't mind, but Mama and Papa would never look after them, and they are my responsibility, and you said Grafton House was mine now, too, and I couldn't give them—"

"I don't mind," he said firmly.

"Oh. Good. Because they're staying."

"So I gathered." He couldn't help the cynicism that touched his voice, though in truth he was amused—and intrigued.

"And what is that supposed to mean?" she asked defensively. "You certainly won't have to worry about them, or pay a shilling toward their care. They are my responsibility, and you'll hardly even know they're h—"

"I was surprised," he interrupted. "Somehow I didn't envision the Vixen mothering a gaggle of strays and misfits."

She held his gaze. "If I didn't, who would?"

He wasn't about to begin an argument with her right before her luncheon, especially when her unexpected compassion had him feeling like a wobbly-kneed schoolboy. "This does explain your dislike of Lord Perington. Which feline did you rescue from him?"

"Lord Baggles. He's in my bedchamber, napping."

"I had no idea so many sadists populated London."

Victoria shrugged, still absently stroking Sheba.

"Weak men have to prove their superiority on creatures weaker than themselves."

After only one day, the woman he had thought he married was turning out to be someone else entirely. He already knew he wanted to make love to her—but he hadn't realized until now that her lovely features might not even be the best part of her.

Victoria kept catching herself looking at Lord Althorpe as they left their carriage and made their way into Lady Nofton's substantial garden just outside of London for the charity luncheon. He hadn't batted an eye about her menagerie, and in fact had seemed to understand and agree with her motives for taking them in. She didn't know quite what she'd expected from him, but it certainly hadn't been that.

"You're being waved at," he murmured from beside her.

She blinked, belatedly noticing the substantial woman trundling across the grass toward them. "It's Lady Nofton. Be nice."

His arm beneath her hand tensed, then relaxed again. "I'm not one of your pets," he drawled. "And neither am I twelve years old."

"I didn't mean to imply that you were," she returned, glancing sideways at him as he released her arm. "I just don't want anything to go wrong today."

"Ah. I see. I'm worse than a twelve-year-old. I'm Sin Grafton."

"You've made your own reputation."

"And so have you."

She wanted to stick her tongue out at him. As the person who usually said something too direct and thereby made a muck of things, Victoria reflected that it might be a nice change to have someone around who was ten times worse. And whatever his feelings about being present today, he hadn't made any fuss about her attending one of her charitable causes. Another surprise—though everything she discovered about him seemed to be one.

"Victoria," the large blond woman said, taking both of her hands. "I'm so glad you were able to attend. I'm having a terrible time with the place settings."

Victoria smiled. "Show me your list, and we'll have a look. Sinclair, may I introduce Lady Nofton? Estelle, my husband, Lord Althorpe."

Estelle's brown eyes grew round as she offered a belated curtsy. "My lord. I'm . . . pleased you decided to attend our humble little function."

Sin smiled, the charming one that didn't touch his eyes. "I'm always ready for a good gathering. What are we supporting, anyway?"

Victoria cleared her throat. He might have asked that earlier, for heaven's sake. "We support limiting the number of hours children work each day," she said, "and increasing the amount of schooling they receive."

"Splendid. Where might I find some port to toast your efforts? I'll be happy to participate—as long as you charity ladies have provided something stronger than punch to drink."

"Oh," Lady Nofton stammered, her dismay almost palpable, "Hollins, my butler, can assist you. My husband is absent today, but he keeps a generous supply of liquor in his study."

Althorpe nodded. "I'm off, then. Lady Nofton, Victoria."

"You actually did marry him, then," Estelle said as they watched him round the corner of the house. "I'd heard, but then when you arrived today, I thought perhaps I'd been mistaken."

"No mistake." Victoria sighed.

"Sin Grafton, himself. Oh, my. He's quite . . . delectable-looking, isn't he?" Lady Nofton's substantial frame shook with her tittering laughter.

"I suppose he is. Never mind that, though. Let's have a look at your seating arrangements before the guests arrive."

By the time they decided that Lady Dash would sit beside Lady Hargrove but not her sister-in-law Lady Magston, the carriages began to arrive. Victoria had just begun to wonder where her husband had vanished to, when he materialized beside her.

"I had no idea you knew so many stodgy people," he said, nodding as the Count and Countess of Magston passed by them and nearly tripped over a border fence as they turned to stare at him.

"Hush."

He chuckled, and she leaned closer to him, sniffing and abruptly suspicious.

Victoria cursed under her breath. "You're drunk? You can't be drunk. You've only been gone for twenty minutes."

"I try not to waste time. But don't worry, I'll let everyone know the cause has my full support. Is that Lord Dash? The marksman?" He started forward.

She grabbed him by the arm to hold him back. "Please don't support anything on my account," she whispered urgently. "Some of the people here actually believe the law needs to be changed."

"And some of them are here for the roast chicken. They might support you with their stomachs, but how many back it up with their purses?"

"Enough to make the luncheon worthwhile," she snapped. "Not everyone here thinks of nothing but themselves."

His lazy amber eyes glinted. "Indeed," he drawled softly. "I'm learning something new every day."

She stood on her tiptoes, trying to look him in the eye and demand that he leave before he offended one of their patrons, but she abruptly noticed something. His clothes reeked of whiskey, but his soft breath on her cheek still carried the tang of the peppermint candy he'd snagged from a bowl on their way out of Grafton House.

Victoria narrowed her eyes, remembering the three supposedly intoxicated strangers at their wedding and their sober midnight rendezvous last evening. "I'm learning new things, as well."

He tilted his head at her. "And what might you be learning, Victoria?"

"I'm not sure yet. But I am beginning to learn what you're not, Sinclair Grafton."

"Enlighten me. What am I not?"

"You're not drunk, for one thing."

At that moment Estelle summoned Victoria to the front table, and she walked away. Let him think about that for awhile.

Chapter 6

"**W**ho was that nasty fellow with the large nose? The one who ate all the Brazilian cashews."

"You ate your share of them," Victoria returned airily, apparently fascinated by the hordes of pedestrians outside the carriage.

Sinclair crossed his ankles. "Yes, but I didn't snatch a platter of them from a neighboring table when no one was looking."

"Apparently at least one person was looking."

He scowled. Whatever he'd done wrong at the charity luncheon, his bride was hanging onto it like a dog on a ham bone. "So I noticed him stuffing himself. Who the devil was the fat ox?"

Finally she looked at him. "Why were you pretending to be drunk? Was it because I asked you to behave yourself? Was it just to embarrass me?"

She'd left him a way out, though any answer would make him look like a cad. "I'm not used to being told what to do," he returned, sidestepping. "Especially by someone five stone lighter and eight years younger than I am."

"And a female."

"Yes. And a female."

She folded her arms across her lovely bosom, her expression as warm as icicles. "Fine. I won't tell you what to do. But don't you dare tell me what to do or who to speak to or how to conduct myself."

"I'm not your damned parent. I haven't given you any orders. But don't you throw any tantrums in my direction, Vixen. I went to your useless charity luncheon and watched some fat man whose name you won't tell me eat cashews. You got your way."

To his surprise, a tear ran down her cheek. "It was not useless." She swiped the tear away with her fingers. "And that fat, stupid man is a vicar in Cheapside. If it takes a few Brazilian cashews to convince him to talk to his parishioners about setting up another local school, then I would happily give him a thousand of them."

He'd begun to think her invulnerable. How pleasant to know that he could wound her with such little effort. "Oh. Point taken," he muttered.

"What?"

"I said, 'Point taken,' " he repeated more loudly. "You were doing something worthwhile, and I was . . . being myself." The self he'd become over the past few years, anyway. The one who'd seen holy vicars sell out a loyal parishioner for a bottle of whiskey—when he'd been the one to provide the bottle.

"I don't think you were being yourself."

Damnation. "For God's sake, Victoria, I was trying to have a bit of fun with you and it misfired," he said, hoping volume and conviction would carry some weight with her.

She jabbed a well-manicured finger into his knee. "So you're nothing but a boor?"

"Apparently. I did compromise you horribly in Lady Franton's garden."

"And then you offered to marry me, thereby saving my reputation."

"And my own."

Victoria began another jab, and he caught her hand in his.

"Make your point verbally, if you please."

"Aha!"

She didn't try to withdraw her fingers from his grip. Her skin was so smooth, and her hand so delicate that he could scarcely remember what they'd been talking about. "Aha, what?"

"That *was* my point."

Shifting his grip, he tugged her out of her seat and yanked her across the small space of the coach to sit her down beside him. "I seem to have suffered an apoplexy. What point did you make?"

She lifted her face to him. "You didn't let me poke you again. You don't repeat mistakes."

"What?"

"So you're being a boor on purpose. Why?"

He looked at her. "That's a very weak argument."

"Nevertheless, I asked you a question. Please do me the courtesy of answering it."

Obviously, words had failed. Sin met her mouth with his. It was a ragged, desperate kiss, solely meant to distract her from her very troublesome line of questions. And it sent a jolt of electricity through him. She shifted closer to him, deepening the kiss of her own volition. He was ready—more than ready—to follow, however far she wanted to go.

Her soft lips parted at his teasing, her arms draped over his shoulders, and Sinclair had to stifle a triumphant groan. Good God, he wanted to make love to her. He reached for his walking cane to rap on the roof and signal Roman to make another circuit—or two—around Hyde Park.

"Sinclair," she murmured against his mouth.

"Hm?"

"Answer the question."

He sat up, letting the cane fall back against the seat. Her lips and cheeks were flushed, and she still clung to his neck as though she intended never to let go. Yet distraction obviously wasn't going to work, either. He wanted to trust her, but he couldn't be certain which part of his body was telling him that.

"The question," he repeated thickly. "You've missed the straightest path. I'm being a boor because I am a boor. Just because I don't want you drawing blood with your damned nails doesn't mean I'm playing games or hiding things."

She studied his face while he gazed back at her evenly and waited for a lightning bolt from heaven to strike him dead. He'd told lies as blatant before, but never to anyone to whom he'd wanted to tell the truth.

"All right," she said quietly, withdrawing her arms. "If that's how you want it. But if you won't trust me, don't expect me to trust you."

"I don't believe I asked you to."

"No, you didn't." Victoria turned away again to resume gazing out the window. Hurt and disappointment showed in every line of her slender body.

Seeing her disappointed, though, was far better than seeing her—or himself—dead. And so, though he wanted to apologize, to assure her that if she would just be patient he would try to make things right for them both, he kept silent.

The coach turned up the drive and stopped. As a footman pulled open the door and flipped down the step, Victoria glanced at him again. "I have a dinner engagement this evening."

He followed her to the ground. "Anyone I know?"

"I didn't ask them."

Well, this wasn't going to be very productive. He needed access to her friends. If she'd decided to ignore his existence, that was going to become considerably more difficult. So, he had two choices. He could tell her another lie that would hopefully leave her feeling more charitable toward him, or he could tell her the truth. A little bit of the truth—enough to regain her cooperation, but not to put her or his friends in any danger.

Milo pulled open the front door as they reached it. "Good afternoon, Lord and Lady Althorpe. How was your luncheon?"

In the four weeks Sinclair had known the butler, Milo had never asked him how any part of his day or evening had gone. Obviously, the question wasn't for his benefit. "Quite well," he answered anyway, when Victoria kept walking. "It was very enlightening."

"Ha," she said to the air, heading for the stairs and, undoubtedly, her private rooms above. And she still had the damned key.

"Victoria, may I have a word with you?" he asked.

"You've had several already."

Sinclair strode forward and scooped her into his arms before she could so much as gasp. "I require several more," he stated grimly, continuing up the staircase with her in his arms.

"Put me down! At once!"

"No."

His rooms began at one end of the hall, and hers at the other. After a few seconds' debate he decided on neutral territory, and pushed open the library door opposite the master bedchamber. Once inside, he kicked the door shut and then plunked his bride down on the sofa beneath the window.

"You are worse than a boor!" she snapped, shooting to her feet again. "No one has ever treated me in such a disrespectful manner, and I certainly won't tolerate it from you!"

"Sit," he ordered.

She folded her arms across her chest. "No."

He took a step closer. "If you won't sit down, it will be my pleasure to convince you to do so, Vixen."

Victoria's expression could have frozen the sun, but after a moment's defiance she sank gracefully onto the cushions again. "As you wish, my lord," she said, her jaw clenched.

"Thank you." Now that he had her attention, though, he wasn't quite certain where to begin. He'd kept his own counsel and his own secrets for so damned long that he had no idea how to part with any of them, or how to sort out which ones might be safe for her to know and which ones wouldn't be. From the expression on her face, growing grimmer by the moment, he'd best think of something.

"I haven't been entirely honest with you," he said slowly.

"Don't expect me to act surprised." She leaned over to pick up a book and open it. "In fact, I no longer care."

Hoping that wasn't true, that after only two days he

hadn't alienated her beyond repair, Sinclair paced from the door to the window and back again. "I did return to London with a purpose other than assuming the marquisdom."

"Yes. You mentioned something about finding a spouse." Licking her forefinger, she began flipping pages, slowly and noisily. "I was there."

"I intend to find the man—or woman—who murdered my brother."

Victoria slammed the book closed. "I knew it!"

"Yes, well," he continued, trying to ignore the sudden dryness of his mouth and the hard pounding of his heart, "don't make more of it than there is."

Her violet eyes were still suspicious as he faced her again. "Why not just say that's what you're doing, for heaven's sake? And why did you wait so long to come back to London if you wanted to see justice done?"

At least she still seemed interested. "I was . . . obliged to remain where I was," he said slowly. "And obviously whoever killed Thomas thinks he's gotten away with the murder. I don't want to disabuse him of that fact until after I've caught him."

"So what does that have to do with your pretending to be drunk? Or with those three men lurking in the stable yard?"

He froze, then fixed a puzzled look on his face. "What three men lurking in the stable yard?"

She sighed. "The three men I saw you out there talking with last night; the same three who were at our wedding pretending to be drunk—or so I presume. I have some reason to doubt that now, as you know."

Good God. She was astounding. He and the lads weren't sloppy; they would have died a long time ago if they had been. Yet she had noticed them and in two days figured out part of their play. No wonder she'd become so immediately suspicious of him. He hadn't realized how intelligent she was, and it didn't leave him feeling any better about including her.

Sinclair cleared his throat. "I know those gentlemen from my excursions in Europe. They offered to help me out."

"And the supposed drunkenness?"

"People talk more freely when they think you're inebriated. It's a habit, I suppose."

As he finished speaking, he realized he'd said too much. Thankfully, she seemed too absorbed by the rest of the information to realize that he'd stumbled.

For a long moment Victoria sat in silence, looking down at her hands. "Might I ask you a question?"

"Yes."

"How many of the stories about your escapades in Europe are true?"

He relaxed a little. "Most of them." On the surface, anyway.

Slowly she stood again. "Very well, Sinclair. You've given me something to think about."

Any answer was better than outright rejection. "And might I ask you the same question? How many of your supposed exploits in London are true?"

She strolled to the door and opened it. "Most of them," she said airily, and turned up the hallway to her rooms.

Sin resumed pacing. Victoria wasn't precisely an ally; he wasn't willing to tell her enough to make her one. But she wasn't an enemy, either, and that felt like a victory—or at least the beginnings of a truce.

*   *   *

"A shilling for your thoughts, dear."

Victoria started, realizing she'd been shoving her potatoes back and forth across her plate for the past five minutes. "They'll cost you at least a pound, Lex."

Alexandra Balfour smiled. "Done."

"But we demand the thought in advance of payment," Lucien Balfour said from her other side. "And considering that I have received permission to play faro at White's tonight, it'd better be an astonishing thought."

His wife scowled at him. "Don't be silly, Lucien. Obviously she came here to talk."

"No, actually I came here because I told Sinclair I had a dinner engagement. I needed . . . a moment to recover my wits." She glanced at her friend. "I probably chose the wrong location for that, now that I think about it." Witlessness was not a weakness to suffer from in the Balfours' formidable presence.

"Nonsense," Alexandra countered. "Don't say anything, then, if you don't wish to. I'm just glad to see you." She shot another look at the earl.

Victoria couldn't read it, but apparently Lucien could. He pushed back from the table and stood. "I'm off to White's, then."

"Oh, no, you don't need to go because of—"

"I'm not." He nodded in Alexandra's direction. "I'm going because of her."

"He's terrified of me," Lex said dryly.

"Only when she has slicing apparatus to hand." Lord Kilcairn strolled over to his wife's chair and leaned over the back of it. Alexandra tilted up her face and touched her lips to Lucien's.

Victoria fidgeted. That was what being married was supposed to be like. Sinclair could use a few hundred lessons in that. And so could she, no doubt, since she'd arranged to spend the second night of her marriage dining without her husband.

"All right, Vix," Alexandra continued when Lucien vanished. "What's troubling you?"

"I really didn't come here to complain. Sinclair made me angry, and so I said I had a dinner engagement." She shrugged. "So here I am, abusing your friendship."

"You never could, with what you've done for me. What made you angry?"

"Lex, don't. You're not my governess any longer."

"But I am still your friend."

"You're also the one who said if I didn't learn to behave, I'd end up married to some incorrigible scoundrel."

Lex grinned. "No, it was Miss Grenville who said that. I told you you'd end up with a poor reputation."

Victoria pushed her plate away. "Well, you were both right, I suppose."

"Is he incorrigible?"

"Oh, I don't know." Cursing, Victoria stood to pace around the table. "I can't even be in the same room with him without us arguing." And without her thinking about his delicious kisses and his warm, sure touch—which made his boorishness even more annoying.

Alexandra cleared her throat. "So. How did Lord Althorpe react to your menagerie?"

"I think they amused him. He didn't seem to mind, anyway."

"That's something, isn't it? I tend to think that any man who can accept Henrietta and Mungo Park can't be all bad."

"I haven't actually introduced him to Mungo yet."

"Uh-oh. That could be the deciding factor in any relationship."

Alexandra was merely trying to raise her spirits, of course, but she appreciated the gesture nonetheless. "You have a point. But how can someone be so attractive and so . . . aggravating at the same time?"

"Well, h—"

"And don't say I should ask myself that question, Alexandra."

Her friend chuckled. "Then I won't say anything at all—except that you're not a coward or a quitter."

"And I also suppose I should try being married for more than one day before I turn my nose up at it completely."

"I think that's fair enough."

"I'll let you know."

Sin was gone when she returned to Grafton House, and Victoria went to feed and visit with her pets in the conservatory. The cats especially seemed to enjoy the overgrown plants scattered throughout the room, while Henrietta and the foxhound, Grosvenor, had commandeered the old couch she'd purchased for them. Mungo Park was still pretending to be part of the ornate cornice work above the window, but the pile of nuts she'd left for him on the mantel had shrunk by half.

She would love to give them the run of the house once they became used to their new setting, but she wasn't certain how Sinclair would feel about that. Her parents had insisted that the useless beasts stay in the room adjacent to her bedchamber, with even Lord Baggles only allowed out at night and only as far as her closed doors permitted. Lord and Lady Stiveton would have been happy to keep her enclosed in the same space.

For a long time after she retired for the evening, she stood looking out the window, but no shadowy figures appeared tonight. No doubt Sinclair had picked a different place for his rendezvous—somewhere she would never know about.

He had said that he pretended drunkenness out of habit, to loosen the tongues of those around him. That implied he'd used such tactics before, and often. And apparently his cronies used them as well. The question was, why? What information had he been looking for, precisely? Did it all relate to his brother's murder? She didn't think so—he'd said he'd returned to England for the purpose of finding the killer. So apparently he'd been up to something else in Europe.

And if he admitted to feigning drunkenness, were there other habits he merely pretended to? She kept thinking of that other Sinclair—the sharp, focused, and very sensual one who made an occasional appearance, apparently just to confuse and torture her.

Victoria smiled as she slipped beneath the warm, soft covers. They'd been married only a day, and she'd already discovered one secret. It was only a matter of time before she learned the others.

"You told her?"

Bates's jaw dropped, while Wally sprayed ale across the floor. Crispin Harding managed to look smug, as though he'd expected nothing less.

"I didn't have much choice," Sin said defensively. "She saw you clods out in my stable yard the other night." She'd seen him, too, but he left out that fact.

"So you told her the truth?" Bates hissed. "You? The master of misdirection?"

"I didn't tell her *everything*, for God's sake. Just enough to keep her from asking sticky questions." He hoped the tale he'd told would suffice; his bride seemed to have an uncanny ability to see more than she was supposed to.

She'd been avoiding him for the past three days, either going out with her friends or staying in her rooms with her menagerie. He'd made a point several times of encountering her, both to determine whether she'd decided to give him a chance, and because he seemed to have developed an odd need to see her. He wanted more, of course—he wanted to touch her and kiss her and hold her—but he could wait for that. For a little while longer. He was patient, but he wasn't a eunuch, for God's sake.

"You're going soft. A pair of pretty blue eyes looks at you, and you tell her all our secrets." Wally signaled for another tankard of ale.

"Violet eyes," Sin corrected. "They're quite remarkable, really. And all I told her was that I wanted to find Thomas's killer."

"And how did you explain us?"

"Just to say that you were helping. And keep your voice down." Crispin continued to gaze at Sinclair knowingly, and he scowled. "Speak, giant."

"I was just wondering when you were going t'ask us whether we'd found out anything interesting."

Sin kept his silence while a footman provided them with fresh drinks. He didn't like what the Scotsman implied: that he'd become so involved with Vixen that he'd forgotten his brother's murder. "I assumed you would tell me if you'd learned anything."

"Nothing from me," Wally muttered. "The cat drowner also kicks dogs and growls at small children. Our next saint, I suppose. Exports whatever he gets a good price on. Not much else, though, and nothing I could find that seemed illegal enough to warrant a murder. He attended Parliament yesterday, but you know that."

Sinclair nodded. "I saw him. And Kilcairn, who seems to be rabidly anti-Bonaparte."

"Aye," Crispin agreed. "His cousin was killed in Belgium. Hate t'say it, Sin, but I don't think he's your man."

As little liking as he had for the earl, he'd already come to that conclusion himself. "Why would I hate to hear that we've eliminated a suspect?"

"Because you practically breathed fire at 'im at your wedding. I figured you might want a chance t'make worms' meat of 'im."

"Right."

"Let flights of angels sing him to his rest."

"Crisp—"

"Let all your yesterdays light his way to dusty death."

"I get your meaning. Quit quoting Shakespeare," Sinclair grumbled. "Someone might mistake you for a gentleman."

Crispin grinned. "Only the nephew of one, m'boy. Only the nephew of one."

"Aye," Wally mimicked, "only the nephew of the bloody Duke of Argyle."

"The fav'rite nephew, Wallace. And be thankful— without my blue-blooded relations, ye'd likely never see the inside of a fine gentleman's club like this one."

"Don't forget I'm a duchess's grandson, Scot."

Bates snorted. "If you lot are finished discussing the blueness of your blood, I don't have any news, either. That sot Ramsey DuPont couldn't manage a murder if someone loaded a pistol and aimed it for him."

"Are all three of our fine gentlemen innocent enough that we can cross them off the list, then?"

Crispin nodded. "Aye. If Kilcairn had killed your brother, it would've been in a fair fight. Not a murder."

Sinclair narrowed his eyes. "You're not making me any more fond of him."

The Scotsman had the temerity to grin. "I know."

"DuPont is clear, too. He might do a murder, but not one clever enough to fool anybody."

"Wally?"

"Oh, fiend seize it. Give me another few days for the cat drowner. I don't have anything near a motive yet, but I wouldn't put it past the bastard."

Sinclair wasn't surprised. To find the murderer among the first three suspects on his list would have been too much to expect, but he wasn't willing to discount anything—including luck. "Well then, we may as well move on to the next three n—"

"Excuse me, Althorpe."

Sinclair turned in his chair. Part of him still expected to hear his brother's soft voice answering the summons. "Lord William," he drawled.

William Landry was drunk—which, if the rumors were accurate, wasn't any surprise. The hostility on his pretty face was unexpected, however, until Sin remembered that the Duke of Fenshire's son had been one of the wolves circling Vixen the night he'd whisked her out to the garden. It was just what he needed for the evening: a former, drunken suitor who had probably been more intimate with his new wife than he had.

"I think you should know," Lord William continued darkly, "that just because you managed the easiest path to the Vixen's bed doesn't mean the rest of us are about to pretend we like having you here."

"I really don't care what you like or dislike," Sinclair said. "Was there anything else?"

"Well," Lord William drawled, looking over his shoulder at his equally inebriated table mates, "I—that is, we—were wondering, is the Vixen as wild in bed as she is when she's upright?"

Sin launched out of his chair and slammed his fist into Landry's face. Dimly he heard his own companions cursing and clearing furniture out of the way, but he ignored them as he knocked the buffoon backward over a chair.

Landry hadn't been with her—but the revelation didn't comfort him any. Someone Victoria had accepted as her friend and admirer would *not* utter such things in public. Not while he had anything to say about it. Snarling, he yanked the reeling Landry back to his feet and then leveled him again with a solid punch to the jaw.

Before he could dive in for more, a pair of arms wrapped around his waist and hoisted him off the ground. "Damn it, Crispin, put me down!" he growled.

"You plannin' on finishing 'im off, Sin?"

He looked down at Lord William, wheezing and curled up on the floor. Killing someone now would definitely complicate his own investigation. "No."

The big Scotsman let go, and he dropped to his feet. Eyeing the milling footmen and guests surrounding them, Sin squatted down at Landry's shoulder. "Don't ever insult my wife again," he said softly, "or I'll finish the job."

Landry moaned, but otherwise didn't acknowledge his warning. It didn't seem likely, though, that he would forget the lesson. Sinclair straightened, ignoring Wally's proffered handkerchief for the blood and brandy staining his cravat, and strolled to the door.

"I don't think you have to worry about anyone thinking you've become too respectable," Bates offered as they stopped in the street outside.

"No doubt." He rubbed his knuckles. Wise or not, it had felt good to pummel the weasel; he hadn't been in a decent brawl since they'd left Europe. "As I was about to say, I confirmed three more of our suspects, all of whom were in town and all of whom possibly saw Thomas the day he was killed." He extracted the Hoby's list from his pocket and handed it to Bates.

"Anything on Marley?"

"Nothing so far," Sinclair replied. The viscount had made himself scarce since the Franton soiree. And since Marley had been the one peer Thomas had mentioned in his letters as having "troublesome notions," he was first on Sinclair's personal list. "You just leave him to me."

"I'm not about to get between the two of you," Bates muttered.

"Do you have anything else going?" Wally asked, eyeing the list from over Bates's shoulder.

"I'm trying to get hold of the voting records for the House of Lords. If nothing else, it'll tell us who wasn't in London that week."

"That'd make things a bit easier," Crispin agreed.

"If it was actually a peer." Bates sighed as he handed the list to the Scotsman.

After two years, that was only one of the many "ifs" they'd faced on returning to London. The task hadn't seemed that daunting from the distance of Paris and a hundred triumphant missions at least as sticky and dangerous as this one. They'd never had to follow a trail that had been cold for so long, though, or one that involved so many supposedly respectable people.

"I'm tracking down someone who might be able to give us some help with that." He glanced back toward Boodle's. "Considering the gossip I've managed to stir up, I think we should correspond through Lady Stanton for the next few days instead of meeting face to face."

With their usual grumbling, Wally and Bates agreed, then headed off east toward Covent Garden and the less reputable part of London. Crispin, though, remained where he was.

"What now?" Sin asked resignedly.

"Go home," his friend said. "When this is over she'll still be there, and you'll still have to deal with her."

"Hmm. Wise words, coming from a confirmed bachelor."

"Aye. You were one o' those too, until you set eyes on Vixen Fontaine."

"I'm not some love-struck halfwit, Harding. Believe me."

"Tell that to William Landry. That wasn't the most subtle thing you've ever done, Sin."

Sinclair bristled, then clamped an iron fist over his anger. He was going insane, obviously. "Every day I think of Thomas and how if I'd been here he might be alive," he said slowly. "*Every day.* I haven't forgotten why I came back to this pit. And I will find out who killed him—no matter what it takes, and even if I have to do it alone."

"And no matter who ye hurt."

"Vixen Fontaine is the most valuable resource we've been able to get our hands on. She's not the first woman I've used."

"She's the first woman ye've married."

"Oh, shut up."

"Eventually you're going to have t'ask yourself why you're doing this, ye know."

"Good night, Crispin."

By the time he returned to Grafton House, Victoria was asleep. In fact, the entire household had retired for the evening. Used to the darkness, Sinclair made his way down the long hallway and the maze of rooms into Thomas's old office. Slowly he sank into the seat behind the mahogany desk. Fairly early in the evening, with the lamps lit, there could be no doubt: Thomas had seen his killer nearly as soon as he or she had entered the room. And still he had made no apparent effort to defend himself.

One of these pleasant, bland-faced nobles had killed him—had murdered him—in cold blood. Sinclair didn't trust any of them, after some of the hidden foibles he'd discovered about their kind in Europe. And what tore at him the most was that the whole thing could be his fault, if he had learned the wrong information and someone thought he had passed it on to Thomas.

"Are you all right?"

He started, grabbing for his pistol even as his brain registered that it was Vixen who had spoken. She stood in the doorway, a lighter shadow against the black of the hallway. With an effort, he relaxed his shoulders and leaned back in the chair. "I'm fine. What are you doing up?"

"I heard you come in." Tentatively she stepped into the moonlit room. "This is where Thomas was killed, isn't it?"

"Yes." Her black hair hung loose and curling down her shoulders, and his fingers twitched with the sudden desire to touch it. To touch her.

"Wasn't he seated at his desk when . . . it . . . happened?"

"Right again."

She tilted her head at him. "I'm sorry I misjudged you, Sinclair."

"You probably didn't."

Victoria glided up to him and held out one hand. "Don't sit there. It makes my skin crawl."

Sin let her wrap her small, slender hand around his and pull him to his feet. "How well did you know Thomas, really?" he asked.

"He was quite a bit older than you, wasn't he?"

Since she didn't seem in any hurry to leave, or to relinquish her grip on his hand, he tugged her closer. Then he leaned down slowly, to give her time to object if she chose. When she didn't, he kissed her softly, savoring the warm, supple play of her mouth against his.

"Yes. He was nearly forty—a good ten years my senior. He and my grandmother practically raised Kit and me." Sinclair ran his fingers along the line of her jaw. "You didn't answer my question: were you and Thomas well acquainted?"

"Hm?" she said, her voice dreamy. "Oh. No, I didn't know him that well. I think my set was too loud for him."

"Anything you could tell me about him might help."

"Well, he was kind, and quiet—he admired Gainsborough's paintings, as I recall. In fact, he mentioned to me that he sketched, himself."

"Did he now?" Sinclair murmured, feeling his brother's loss even more keenly. "I didn't know that."

"He said he wasn't any good at it, but I remember thinking that he probably was. Have you found any of his work?"

"I haven't had time yet to look for much besides incriminating letters. My grandmother may have them, though."

"You should ask her."

"Perhaps I will." He gazed down at her upturned face. "Why so friendly tonight?"

"I'm not sure. I just keep thinking how awful it would be to lose a family member like that, and then I saw you sitting in that chair, with that look on your face, and—"

"What look?"

"That . . . intense look you have sometimes. And seeing that, I keep wondering what could possibly have kept you away from here for two years."

No one had ever mentioned that he had "a look." A telltale change of expression could have gotten him killed. Hopefully, if he did have one, it was something he'd developed since his return to England. More likely, though, it was something no one else would notice except for Victoria. "If I'd known you were here, I wouldn't have stayed away so long," he murmured.

Abruptly she wedged a hand against his chest and shoved. "Stop trying to use my compassion for your situation to seduce me."

He took a step back. "You were the one who came to find me, Victoria. And you're the one who uses Thomas as an excuse every time we kiss. Why do I make you so nervous?" She unsettled him at least as much, but he had no intention of letting her know that.

"You do not make me nervous," she stated. "I told you before, you are *not* the first man to kiss me, or to murmur sweet, flattering nothings to gain my favor."

He narrowed his eyes, a vision of Marley twirling her in the air crossing his mind. "You didn't marry any of them, though."

"None of them managed to be so clumsy as to attempt a seduction in front of my father and half of London." She turned on her heel. "Good night, my lord."

His argument had been a weak one, he knew, and he had been clumsy that night—but only because in everything he'd expected to find when he returned to London, he hadn't expected *her*. After several days together he still had little idea of what moved her and motivated her, when he could usually assess someone's character in a matter of minutes. And it wasn't her fault she kept advancing and withdrawing—he kept changing the battlefield rules.

"Who do you think killed Thomas?" he asked quietly, reminding himself that he asked the question because he needed her cooperation—not because he didn't like himself when he made her angry.

Halfway out the door, she stopped. "I don't know." She faced him again. "Who do you think did it?"

Sin released a breath he hadn't realized he'd been holding. Victoria was right about one thing; he did use her compassion every chance he got. "Everyone."

"Everyone?"

He shrugged. "I'm not about to eliminate anyone. Anyone's capable. What I need is a motive."

"Like what?"

Sinclair leaned back against the edge of the desk. "That's the difficult part. I don't know with what—or whom—Thomas was involved. He corresponded when he could, but the letters didn't always reach me, and when they did, they weren't very informative." Thomas had been far too careful to let slip that his brother was anything but a roué. His own return correspondence had been equally uninformative. Something, though, had gone wrong.

"Why were you in Europe—in Paris, even—when it was so dangerous? What kept you there, Sinclair?"

He wanted to tell her. She spoke with him in the same guileless, interested way she spoke with Milo, and, like the butler, he wanted to tell her everything. But until he knew why Thomas had died, he didn't dare. "It was . . . entertaining. Wagering, drinking, women, all day and all night. Bonaparte's new world order may have sounded conservative, but his nobles and most of his officers didn't think it applied to them."

"Someone told me you lived in a brothel for six months. Is that true?"

He was going to hate himself for this later. "Madame Hebiere's. Prettiest chits in Paris." And visited by some of the most influential members of Bonaparte's government. "Come now, Vixen, you like your amusements, too, don't you?"

"Sometimes. They keep me occupied."

Victoria was looking at him again, a half-wary, half-curious expression on her face. He waited, wondering what she thought she had seen this time.

"Last month," she said slowly, "Lord Liverpool announced that the last of Bonaparte's known conspirators had been arrested."

Uh-oh. "Did he?"

"Yes. And if you were so friendly with that maniac's officers and nobles, how did you manage to avoid arrest?"

"I suggest you tread very carefully, Victoria. Are you implying that I'm a traitor?"

"No. I'm implying that you're not one." She backed out of the room and turned for the stairs. "Good night, Sinclair."

For a long moment he remained where he was, torn between admiration and dismay. Perhaps he needed to rethink this telling her everything business, in case she figured out the entire knotted mess on her own.

Chapter 7

Bold as she liked to think herself, Victoria still had to fight a flock of butterflies banging about in her stomach as she stepped down from the Althorpe carriage. She sensed that the cause of her unexpected trepidation was a very basic one; this morning, she cared about the outcome of her adventure, and she cared about what the person she was about to visit might think of her. Taking a deep breath, she climbed the shallow steps and swung the brass knocker against the white door.

It swung open. "Yes, miss?" An elderly, kind-looking man in fashionable black livery looked at her curiously.

"Is Lady Drewsbury home?"

"I shall inquire. May I say who is calling?"

She hadn't yet made up any calling cards that reflected her new name. It still seemed somewhat . . . premature. "Lady Althorpe," she replied, the words strange on her tongue.

Immediately the butler stepped to one side. "Excuse me for not recognizing you, my lady. If I may direct you to the drawing room?"

130

"Thank you."

The butler led her upstairs to a small, light room on the east side of the house. Decorated with embroidery and overstuffed pillows, it was obviously a woman's room, in a woman's household.

She sat in one of the chairs that overlooked the small garden adjoining the house, and she fidgeted. If Lady Drewsbury didn't like her, didn't wish to speak to her, she didn't know what she should do next. Finally she knew which questions to ask, but not who would have the answers. And she wanted the answers with a need that startled her in its fierce intensity.

"Lady Althorpe."

Victoria bolted back to her feet and curtsied as Lady Drewsbury entered the room. Technically she outranked Baron Drewsbury's widow, but she didn't have the tiniest desire to slight her. "Lady Drewsbury."

"Please, sit. And call me Augusta."

"Augusta. Thank you. And please call me Victoria, or Vixen, if you prefer."

The baroness took the seat opposite her and signaled to the waiting butler for tea. "I would have suggested that you call me Grandmama, but I have the feeling that will take a little getting used to—for both of us."

Victoria smiled, a little more at ease. So far, so good. "I suppose you're wondering what's brought me here."

"I can guess. Sinclair?"

Her heart began to flutter again. "Yes."

"Grandmama, I thought I made it clear that I was to be informed immediately if any attractive ladies entered the house." Christopher Grafton strode into the room, a handful of obviously hastily picked daisies clutched in one hand. "Even if they crossed the street in front of the house."

"My apologies, Christopher. I thought you meant single ladies."

"Normally, yes. But I'm desperate." With an engaging grin, the youngest Grafton brother presented the bouquet to Victoria. "For you, my lady," he announced, and swept her an elegant bow.

"Vixen, please," she said, chuckling. "And thank you."

"Vixen it is. Is my brother with you? Oh, no, of course not. Parliament's in session today, isn't it? Since it's Wednesday, it—"

"Christopher," Lady Drewsbury interrupted, "since you seem to be carrying on an adequate conversation with yourself, please do it elsewhere."

"Oh, bother. Yes, Grandmama. Vixen." With another easy grin, he left the room.

"I'm not sure whether he's keeping me young or making me old," Augusta said with a smile. "Taft, please put Lady Althorpe's flowers in water."

The butler approached and relieved Victoria of the disheveled daisies. When he'd gone as well, Lady Drewsbury poured them both tea and sat back to sip hers.

"Now," she continued, "where were we? Ah, the fellow who's definitely making me old. Sinclair."

Victoria spooned sugar into her tea. "I'm not really sure why I'm here," she began, "except that I had a few questions Sinclair can't—or won't—answer, and I thought perhaps you might be able to assist me."

"I would have to hear the questions first. I'm afraid I don't know Sinclair nearly as well as I used to."

Bitterness and regret tightened the baroness's tone.

Still, it seemed like the best invitation Victoria was likely to get. "First, I . . . need to ask for your word that this conversation won't go beyond the two of us."

Augusta's gaze sharpened. "Is Sinclair in some sort of trouble? Or should I ask whether he is in more trouble than usual?"

"Not trouble—not the way you're thinking, anyway."

The two women looked at one another. Victoria, at least, wondered what the dowager baroness saw.

"You have my word," Augusta said finally.

"Thank you. When Sinclair left for Europe, had he and Thomas quarreled?"

"They argued incessantly," their grandmother confirmed. "Which isn't that surprising, considering that Thomas was so conservative, and Sinclair was even wilder than Christopher is now. When I think about it, Christopher is about the age Sinclair was when he went off to begin his adventures. Thank goodness Christopher doesn't seem so inclined. I couldn't stand to lose the last of them."

"Have you lost Sinclair?"

"That, my dear, I don't intend to answer."

Sometimes she just didn't know when to shut her mouth. "I'm sorry. I don't mean to intrude."

"Of course you do. And I mean to answer you, where I can. I find myself curious as to why he chose you—and you, him."

"I'm not sure it was a choice, so much as a mistake." Victoria flushed. "I didn't mean that to be an insult. I'm just very . . . confused."

To Victoria's relief, Lady Drewsbury smiled. "Then ask your next question, Victoria, and we'll see if we can remedy that."

"Oh. Yes. Was Sinclair ever in the military?"

"Heavens, no. Thomas even offered to purchase him a captain's commission, and Sinclair turned him down."

That didn't quite fit. Victoria sipped her tea, remembering the swift, efficient way Sin had drawn his pistol at one of the men in the stable yard, and how he hadn't done it last night when she had surprised him in the office. "I'm not quite certain how to ask this," she said slowly, "but do you have any idea what might have kept him in Europe for the last two years? Especially when he seems to have wanted so badly to return to London."

"If he'd wanted it badly, he would have done it." The older woman sighed. "I have no idea. Sinclair and Thomas, despite the difference in their ages, were very close."

"He told me he was 'prevented' from returning."

"I can't think of anything that would keep him away—not even Bonaparte and the war."

"He wouldn't tell me, except to say that he enjoyed the wagering and the drinking and the women." Victoria scowled, then wiped the expression from her face as Augusta looked at her curiously. She was *not* jealous. It was just so frustrating trying to figure him out, like trying to look at a painting with a veil thrown over it. "Since he fakes his drinking, though, I'm not certain I believe—"

Lady Drewsbury straightened. "What do you mean?"

"He and his three friends—the ones who are trying to help him investigate the murder—he said they pretended to be drunk to encourage people to talk more freely. He said it had gotten to be a habit. Why or how, I'm not sure."

"He's investigating?"

Victoria nodded. "He's very serious about it. Almost obsessed, I think."

For a moment the two women sat looking at one another. Then Augusta set down her cup of tea. "*You* think he was somehow involved with the war, don't you? He never told me he was investigating anything—much less Thomas's death."

"I could be completely wrong, but—"

"No. I don't think you are."

Slowly Victoria smiled. "Neither do I." She set her own cup aside. "He said he corresponded with Thomas. Do you have any of his letters?"

"I have them all." Lady Drewsbury stood, looking more robust than she had upon entering the room. "Come with me, Victoria."

When Victoria returned to Grafton House, she was armed with both Thomas's old sketches and some very interesting letters Sinclair had written to his brother. She carried them up to her private sitting room herself, refusing even Jenny's assistance with the bulky package.

She thought she had uncovered the truth, and now she needed to decide how to confront Sinclair with it—and with the fact that his grandmother and brother would be joining them for dinner.

A heady anticipation made her pulse race. Despite his reputation, she hadn't quite thought she'd married a blackguard. Discovering that Sinclair Grafton was, in fact, a hero—even better, a hero in disguise—left her with warm, tingling skin and the desire to throw herself on him as soon as he returned home.

The door burst open. "Vixen, did you hear?"

Victoria started, then finished tucking the parcel behind a chair. "Lucy? What are you—"

"Never mind that!" Her eyes wide with suppressed excitement, Lucy Havers hurried across the room to grab Victoria's hands. "You didn't hear, did you?" She giggled, her cheeks glowing.

For once she was less than pleased to see her friend; Lucy hadn't figured in her daydream of waylaying Sin. "No, I didn't hear. What in the world is it?"

"Your husband floored Lord William!"

Victoria frowned. That didn't quite fit her view of Lord Althorpe either. "William Landry?"

"Yes! Drew his cork! Lionel said William's nose bled for twenty minutes!"

"But why in the world would Sinclair hit Lord William? He knows we're friends."

Lucy flushed a deeper scarlet. "I think William said something," she whispered, though the only one close enough to hear was Lord Baggles, who had gone back to sleep in the windowsill after the initial outburst.

"Said something about what?" Victoria eyed her friend, who abruptly began to stammer. "He said something about me, didn't he?"

The younger woman nodded.

"And Sinclair hit him?"

"Several times. A big, blond-haired man had to pull him off William before Sinclair killed him."

That would have been the well-built gentleman from the stable yard, no doubt. Perhaps William had interrupted another secret—or not so secret—meeting. "When did this happen?"

"Last night, at Boodle's. Lionel said Lord William

was drunk, but that Lord Sin couldn't have been—not with the way he moved."

She'd seen that briefly before—that lithe, dangerous way he had when he forgot himself. "Or perhaps Sinclair is just more used to being drunk than William is," she offered, trying to ignore the additional acceleration of her pulse. She was going to combust if he didn't arrive soon. Sinclair had slipped, defending her honor. And then he'd come home and she'd quarreled with him, dash it all. "Lucy, he'll be home any minute. I don't want him to know that I know."

Her friend smiled. "But are you pleased?"

Victoria grinned like a madwoman. "Yes. I'm pleased."

"It's *so* romantic. Tell me what he says."

"I will."

After Lucy left, Victoria rose and paced. *His actions last night didn't change anything,* she kept telling herself. If he was what she suspected, he was used to putting himself in harm's way. But this time he had risked doing it for her.

A confident hand knocked at the door.

Victoria jumped. "Come in."

Sinclair pushed open the door and leaned into the room. "Milo said you wanted to see me?"

"Yes. I . . . ah . . . I wanted—could you close the door?"

He complied, then followed her as she edged toward the window. Her heart beat so hard and fast that she thought he must be able to hear it.

"What's wrong?"

"Nothing." Oh, she was being ridiculous. Just because he had surprised her about himself was no reason for her knees to get wobbly. Just because the attraction she'd felt for him from the beginning was a candle compared with the burst of sunlight she felt now was no reason for her carefully thought-out words to become all tangled in her mind.

Humor touched his amber gaze. "Are you sure you're all right? You haven't adopted an elephant or something, have you?"

A laugh escaped her throat, nervous and giddy and not sounding at all like her. "No. I just wanted to apologize . . . for being so short with you last night."

He lifted an eyebrow. "Why? I had it coming to me. I told you I was nasty and cruel."

"No. I interrupted your private thoughts about your brother, and took advantage of your raw emotional state."

To her growing agitation, Sinclair took another step toward her, a panther stalking a gazelle. She couldn't back away any farther without falling through the window—which didn't matter, since she was a gazelle who very much wanted to be caught. In fact, she was feeling rather like a panther herself. But she wanted to tell him that she'd uncovered his secret, if she could manage it before she completely lost the ability to speak.

"You couldn't take advantage of me if you tried, Victoria."

That did it. At the sight of his knowing, teasing smile, she couldn't help herself any longer. Taking a deep, unsteady breath, Victoria strode up to her husband, twined her fingers into his black, wavy hair, pulled his face down toward hers, and kissed him. His lips, hard and soft at the same time, molded with hers, pulling and teasing until she quite lost track of who was kissing whom.

Finally he lifted his head to take a breath. "I like the way you apologize," he murmured, his amber eyes glinting.

She rose on her tiptoes, catching his mouth again. "It's not just an apology," she managed shakily. "It's also a thank you."

His hands slowly slid down her back to her hips, and he pulled her closer against him. "You're welcome, whatever the hell I did." As her heart skittered again, his mouth skimmed her chin and trailed down the base of her jaw and her throat.

Victoria groaned. "Lucy . . . told me you were at Boodle's last night."

Sin's mouth found hers again. If it hadn't been for his strong arms around her, she thought she would fall to the floor. His tongue teased her lips open, and then pushed inside to explore and plunder her. She liked this, with a fierceness she hadn't expected. Men had wanted her, and had tempted her before, but Sinclair was different. If what she suspected was true, Sinclair wasn't some idle nobleman with no ambition other than netting a wealthy heiress.

"What did William say that made you hit him?"

He lifted his face from hers. "Do you really want to know? Is it important?"

"I don't want to know because of William," she murmured, sliding her hands down his chest, feeling the hard muscles there. "I want to know because of you."

A half-smile touched his sensuous mouth. "You want to know what made me react."

She nodded. "Yes."

Sin drew a breath, studying her with that intensity he usually kept hidden. And she abruptly realized what it was. Desire. Desire he concealed behind his cynicism and his jaded quips, and that he couldn't hide from her now. "He wanted to know what you were like. In . . . intimate circumstances."

"And?"

"And I was angry—because you had obviously considered him a friend."

"I've never expected much of my male friends. They all seem to have the same curiosities."

"Well, I have those curiosities, too, Victoria." Moving his hands in small, caressing circles down to her hips and her buttocks, he pulled her more closely against him. "Do you feel my curiosity?"

Her mouth abruptly dry, she nodded again. "I've been aware of your . . . curiosity for several minutes now." His growing hardness against her hip made her curious, too, and intensely aware.

"That's why I hit him, Victoria—because I didn't know the answer to his damned question."

It would have been easier if he had just pushed her to the floor and thrown himself on her. "To be perfectly honest, my lord, I don't know the answer either." Her hands shaking, she tugged his shirt loose from his breeches. "Men have such expectations, you know."

Sinclair caught her hands in his and held them up against his chest. "You said you'd kissed men before. By the dozens."

"Yes I have." She gave a bitter smile. "I even kissed Lord William once. Obviously a mistake."

"But not more than kissing?"

His question was sharp, his voice a deep growl. He demanded an answer, and he was jealous, even after guessing what she was going to say. Victoria wanted to melt into him. "Never more than kissing."

"Until now."

She pulled her hands free to run them up his chest again, this time under his shirt, against his warm skin. "Not until you."

Sinclair rested his forehead against hers, his lips relentless as they teased hers and then backed away, until she wanted to grab him and hold him still so she could kiss him again and again. "Victoria," he murmured, "as I recall, last night you didn't like me very much."

"Today I think maybe I know who you are."

He opened his mouth again, but this time she put her palm over it. "Are you going to stand there and ask questions all afternoon long? I might change my mind, you know."

He pulled her hand away from his face. "No, you won't," he said.

Still holding her hand, he backed toward the door of her bedchamber. She had no choice but to follow— not that she had the least objection to that. There was steel beneath the velvet of his grip but only passion and desire in his gaze. She could still say no if she wanted to, and that was why she didn't. This was the Sinclair she'd kissed in the garden that first night— the one she'd desired, and the one she burned for now.

"You have some expectations to live up to yourself, you know," she said shakily. "Living in a brothel for six months—"

"I'll attempt not to disappoint you."

Lord Baggles rose from the windowsill to follow them, but Sin shut the door before he could do so, leaving the startled feline in the sitting room. His short, disgusted yowl made Victoria chuckle.

"You're not earning any commendations from my cat."

"I'm not going to make love to your cat," he said dryly and pulled her forward, into the circle of his arms.

She expected him to kiss her again, but he merely looked into her eyes for a long moment. "What?"

"I'm becoming acquainted with you," he murmured. "I've wanted you since the damned Frantons' garden. Even before that." Then he dipped his head and claimed her mouth again.

Lust. That's what it was; lust. She'd wanted him from the beginning, too. . . . Victoria moaned.

Most men assumed that she was more worldly than she was. As a consequence, and because she'd never bothered correcting their misinformation, she'd heard a great deal about sexual activities. Some of it had been interesting, and even arousing, but much of it—especially the ardent reactions of the nameless females involved—had sounded completely comical. She also suspected that some of the escapades had been fabricated.

It was with some surprise, then, that she realized how affected she was by him. Pulling the coat from Sinclair's shoulders and dropping it to the floor was simple, even with her hands shaking. The small buttons of his waistcoat, though, were completely beyond her. "Drat it all," she hissed. "I'm sorry."

With a low chuckle, he covered her hands, tightened his grip on the sides of his waistcoat, and pulled. In quick succession, the buttons flew off and plunked to the floor. "Don't be. You excite me, too."

He treated the buttons running down the back of her gown with more respect, though she almost wished he wouldn't. Having him stand behind her, his lips caressing her shoulders and the back of her neck, nearly made her insane. She wanted to touch him, to hold him, but she was faced in the wrong direction. "Just rip them, Sinclair," she ordered in a voice so husky with desire that she barely recognized it.

"I like this dress," he protested, his murmur rumbling against her shoulder and going through her down to her toes. "Be patient."

If she was patient, she might come to her senses. Victoria whipped around to kiss him again, hot and open-mouthed. "I don't want to be patient. I want to be with you. Now."

He'd released the buttons far enough to slide the violet gown forward off her shoulders. It fell in a lavender-scented heap around her ankles, leaving her in her shift and her shoes. Sin sank to his knees, fitting his hands around her right ankle. A slight tug and her shoe was untied.

She put her hands on his shoulders for balance, mesmerized by the play of muscles beneath his shirt as he slipped the shoe from her foot. He repeated the process with her left shoe, then, still kneeling, ran his fingers slowly up her legs, gathering the shift in his hands as he went.

"You have done this before."

He lifted his face to look up at her. "Never with you."

He stood and slowly drew the shift up past her hips, over her waist, above her breasts, and over her head. Her first instinct was to cover herself, but seeing the hungry, devouring look in his eyes excited her more than even his intoxicating kisses. His hands slipped around her waist, his warm, sure grip setting her afire.

"My God, Victoria," he murmured, trailing his gaze down her length and up to her face again, "you are . . . the word beyond beautiful that hasn't been invented yet."

Victoria chuckled, more willing to let him take his time now that things were proceeding. "You wax poetical."

"You are poetry."

She shivered, her breathing ragged, as he slowly circled first one breast, then the other, with his thumbs. Closer and closer he circled, until with agonizing gentleness he brushed across her nipples.

She gasped, arching her back as the sensitive buds hardened in response to his touch. Something new awakened inside her, secret and hot and yearning. "Sinclair," she breathed, and reached for his loose shirt.

He helped her remove it and his cravat, and she ran her hands along the hard, smooth planes of his chest once more. "I think my legs are going to give way." She leaned against him for support, and the feel of her bare breasts crushed against his chest increased her light-headedness.

"Perhaps you should lie down," he suggested, his own voice a low, sensuous growl.

He swept her up in his arms with no noticeable effort at all and carried her to her bed. The bed was covered with an artistic profusion of green and gold pillows, and he set her down among them.

Sitting on the edge of the bed beside her, Sin pulled off his boots and tossed them over his shoulder with a flourish.

"Now, where was I?" His gaze drifted along the length of her body again. "Ah, yes. Right there." Leaning over her, he ran his lips feather-light along the sensitive skin of her round, full breast, tracing the path his thumb had made.

As he reached her nipple and drew it into his mouth, she gasped again. Victoria twined her fingers into his hair, arching her back as he caressed and suckled first one breast, and then the other. Nothing had ever felt like this, so fulfilling and yet so full of hints that much more was to come.

She slid her hands down his back to his waist. He still wore his breeches—it was completely unfair that he should be clothed while she was naked, and it must have been terribly uncomfortable for him as well.

She found the top fastening of his breeches and opened it. Sin stopped his delectable trail of kisses and lifted his head.

"Did I do something wrong?" she asked unevenly, barely able to keep her thoughts straight, much less speak them aloud.

He grinned. "Absolutely not. Surprising, yes—proceed at will, Victoria."

She wanted him to keep calling her Victoria. Being known as the Vixen was fun and wicked, but Sinclair made her name sound so intimate that she couldn't imagine him calling her anything else. Not here, and not now.

"Kiss me again," she said, lifting her head to meet him. At the same time, she managed to open the second button.

He chuckled against her mouth, a sound of pure delight and lustful passion that made her grin, as well. He propped himself up on one elbow, and his free hand drifted down her stomach to the dark curls below.

"My goodness," she groaned as his finger slid down between her legs.

"Fair is fair."

She yanked the third button open. One more to go, and it didn't stand a chance. He shifted his hips to make himself more accessible, and the last button gave way. She hesitated, not quite certain what to do next, but then a second finger joined the first, and she knew exactly what she wanted from him.

Sin settled his weight closer along her body. Slipping her hands beneath his waistband, she inched the tight breeches down. She felt him come free, the hard length of him brushing the inside of her thigh. Victoria drew a ragged breath, instinctively lifting her hips and parting her legs at the sensation of his hand intimately moving at the very edge of her secret place.

"Sinclair," she gasped again, and he took her left breast into his mouth and suckled, thrusting his tongue against her nipple in the same rhythm his fingers were adopting.

She arched again, on fire everywhere he touched her. With a desperate keening sound, she kneaded her hands into his hard, muscled buttocks and pulled him over her.

"Now!" she demanded.

His breathing was as unsteady as hers as he shifted atop her. "Victoria," he murmured, and entered her.

Victoria would have screamed at the intense flood of sensations, but his mouth over hers muffled the sound. She clutched his shoulders convulsively while he held very still, most of his weight on his arms.

"Shh," he whispered. "Give it a moment."

The low, melodious voice shook, and she realized how difficult it was for him to be patient right now.

She eased her grip a little, hoping she hadn't drawn blood, and smiled up at him. "Proceed."

He chuckled breathlessly, and she felt his laugh all the way through her being. Then he began to move his hips against her, and she moaned again, closing her eyes.

"Look at me," he commanded. "I want to see your eyes."

Her eyes flew open again, watching the lustful passion in his amber gaze. She arched her hips to meet each thrust of his, and her breath caught. Deep inside she began to pulse, and then, with a rush unlike anything she'd ever imagined, she exploded. Sinclair tucked his face against her shoulder, moving hard and fast against her, and then shuddered as he planted his seed deep inside her.

"Now," he whispered, lowering himself slowly on top of her as she welcomed his strong, warm weight, "now we're married."

Chapter 8

Sinclair couldn't help feeling satisfied that he was the first man to have had Vixen Fontaine. And the only man, if he had anything to say about it. The chance for an annulment no longer existed, unless they cared to tell a very tall tale, but it didn't matter. He was beginning to think he didn't want to let her go. "I should have begun pummeling William Landry weeks ago," he murmured into her hair.

She chuckled. "I wish you had. I would have liked to have done this with you before we were married."

He lifted his head. "That's somewhat frowned upon."

She looked like a disheveled angel, and her smile would put sunlight to shame. "I know. It would have been very wicked."

Chuckling as well, Sinclair shifted off of her and onto the cool coverlet. "Is there anyone else I can clobber for you?"

To his surprise, the light in her eyes dimmed a little. "Just the man who killed your brother."

Sin sighed, twining her long, curling hair around his fingers, distracted by the thought of lying with her like this every morning for the rest of their lives. "Eventually. Not today, though, I'm afraid."

"I've been thinking. About what you're trying to do."

"And?"

"I want to help you."

His breath stopped. "No. Absolutely not." A little information here and there was one thing; her active participation . . . he didn't even want to think about what might happen to her.

She sat up, naked and beautiful in the afternoon sunlight that shone through the window. "It makes sense. I know these people far better than you do, and I'm good at finding things out."

"Things like what?" he asked skeptically.

Her gaze traveled from his nether regions up to his face again. "Well, for example, I know you're a spy for the War Office."

He sat bolt upright. *"What?"* He forced out a belated, incredulous laugh. "Good God, what gave you that idea?"

Victoria nodded. "I also know that you couldn't return to England when Thomas was killed because you were pretending to be smitten with Marshal Pierre Augereau's daughter, and that you were about to find out from her where Bonaparte's forces were massing."

Someone was talking too damned much. "Just who told you that nonsense?" he asked slowly, anger curling down his spine to replace the sated lust he'd enjoyed only a moment ago.

She looked at him evenly. "You did, Sinclair."

"I don't think so," he said hotly. Seeing the wariness in her eyes, though, he stopped. Being too insistent would only confirm her suspicions. He leaned closer, trying a different tack. "Don't you realize that this could be the clue I've b—"

"I'll show you," she said and scooted off the bed.

Moving fast, Sin lunged after her and grabbed her wrist. "Victoria, this is not—"

"Sinclair, I'm telling you the truth," she replied in a calm voice, obviously assumed for his benefit. "The proof is in the sitting room. Come with me if you want."

He wasn't about to let her out of his sight now. While she pulled on her shift, he grabbed his breeches and yanked them on. The cat stalked into the room as soon as Victoria opened the door, but Sin ignored Lord Baggles's expression of wounded annoyance as he followed his wife back into the sitting room. Something had gone damned wrong. Someone had talked—and until he found out who'd done it, he couldn't determine how to protect her.

She headed for the chair nearest the fireplace, then abruptly stopped, her shoulders heaving with the deep breath she took. In her bare feet she came just to the top of his shoulder, but when she turned to face him, he refused to be softened by the hesitant, almost apologetic look in her eyes.

"What is it?" he demanded instead.

"It's just that I realized you're going to be angry with me, and I was rather hoping for more of"—she gestured toward her bedchamber—"that."

Good God. No wonder they called her the Vixen. "I'm not likely to deny you that, whether I'm angry or not," he said dryly, surprised out of the worst of his annoyance.

"Can you do that when you're angry?" she asked curiously, tilting her head at him.

"Yes, though I wouldn't recommend it. Don't change the subject."

"Very well, then."

She bent down and dragged a bulky package from behind the chair. About the size and shape of an end table without legs, it was wrapped in what looked like her green visiting shawl.

"Here, let me get it," he grumbled, stepping forward.

"I can manage," she retorted, heaving the bundle onto the couch and plunking herself down beside it. "I carried it up here on my own."

"Why?"

His wife flushed. "Because I didn't want anyone else to see what it was. Now sit down, and please, try to remain calm."

This was sounding worse and worse. He sat in the chair facing her and the package. "All right, I'm sitting. Now, what in the world led you to believe I'm a spy, of all things?"

With a half-annoyed look at him, she lifted a corner of the shawl, dug through what sounded like papers, and then extracted a handful of them. "This leads me to believe you're a spy." She opened one of the papers and perused it. "Ah. Here we go. 'Though I appreciate your regaling me with your misadventures picnicking with Miss Hampstead, Thomas,' " she read, " 'in your next correspondence please refrain from any further mention of fine wines. Despite their lovely coloring, I find myself overly saturated with references to them— this being Paris, after all.' "

Sinclair stared at her, the blood draining from his face. It took two tries before he could force himself to speak. "Two questions, Victoria: first, how does that make me a spy? And second, where in damnation did you get that letter?"

"You probably don't know," she began in a matter-of-fact tone, despite the wariness in her eyes, "that before my debut I was tutored by Alexandra Gallant, who—"

"Is this pertinent?" he snapped, wanting to snatch the letters and the parcel from her and demand an explanation.

"Yes, it is. You know Alexandra as the Countess of Kilcairn Abbey."

Kilcairn again, damn him. "And?" he prompted.

"Lex followed the Peninsular War very closely, and insisted that I do so as well. I read the *London Times* every day. I remember in particular reading about how, in the spring of 1814, Le Compte de Chenerre, arrested by Bonaparte's supporters, vanished from a Paris prison and reappeared two weeks later in Hampstead together with several documents pertaining to France's alliance with Prussia. And before you ask, the Chenerre estate boasted one of France's finest vineyards."

To give himself a moment to compose his thoughts, Sinclair stood and stalked to the window. "So. To clarify, because I happened to mention wine and Miss Hampstead in the same—"

"And Paris," she interrupted.

"—and Paris in the same correspondence, I had . . . something to do with Le Compte de Chenerre and his misadventures."

For several seconds she sat quietly, while he forced himself to keep breathing. She couldn't possibly know how much it hurt to hear her read those words, penned to his brother in utter ignorance of the fact that a year later Thomas would be dead.

"You date your letter to Thomas the ninth of May, 1814, a week after Chenerre's reappearance; and your brother never went on a picnic with any female named Miss Hampstead."

"This is ridic—"

"I have five more of your letters which, if one reads them carefully, in some way refer to events in France and elsewhere in Europe where England had an unexplainable turn of good fortune. Sinclair, I understand your need for secrecy and discretion. But please, don't treat me like an idiot. Please."

He kept his gaze fixed out the window, though the curtains might have been closed for all the attention he paid to the view. "Where did you find those letters?"

"Your grandmother had them."

He whipped around to face her. *"What?"*

"She also had your brother's sketches." Moving aside her shawl, she lifted a large, flattened wooden box onto her lap. "Come look at them."

Clenching both fists, he remained by the window. "Don't think you can distract me, Vixen. You went—"

"—behind your back? Snooped? You left me no choice. And don't say you trusted me, because obviously you didn't. You still don't."

"I don't trust anyone. I've found it to be dangerous, both for me and for everyone else concerned."

"Because your brother knew?"

"Because my brother knew—and now he's dead." He gazed at the box in her lap. "I suppose you gabbed all about it to my grandmother. You had no right to do that, Victoria." The thought of losing someone else to their unknown assassin had haunted him for the past two years. He should have known better. He should have gotten the hell away from Lady Victoria Fontaine the moment he realized how attracted he was to her.

"I know that now. Honestly, I didn't know what I would find out about you until I found it. Would you have expected me to do nothing if I discovered you were a traitor or something?"

"No," he said grudgingly, making himself return to the couch and seat himself beside her, close enough that his thigh brushed against the thin material of her shift.

She put her hand, shaking a little, over his clenched fist. "Your secret is safe with me."

"I've heard that before."

"Not from me. I won't tell anyone, Sinclair. And I think you already know that your grandmother won't either."

The difficult part was, somewhere deep down, he did trust her. He'd trusted her the moment he set eyes on her, with no logical explanation for it at all, especially considering whose company she'd been keeping. "Obviously, you're not going to let this go. But you have to remember, Vixen; it's not just a secret. It's a dangerous secret."

"I'm not five years old. I know that. And I still want to help. I *need* to help, Sinclair."

Forcing himself to relax, he touched her cheek. "You're far too lovely to risk at a game like this. And I have enough to live down already. I don't want to add your death to that list."

Her violet eyes narrowed. "And what am I not 'far too lovely' for? Parties? Dances? Sharing your bed? That leaves me with a great deal of unoccupied time."

"Victoria, y—"

She stood, dropping the box onto the couch. "Don't try to humor me. I found you out, Sinclair. What makes you think you can keep me from finding the killer?"

This was getting out of hand. People did not argue with his decisions—especially not the petite, fearless sprite who had for some reason married him. "Tying you to the bedpost would keep you from just about everything. I won't risk it."

"That is so typical!" Victoria snapped. "Just because you're some huge, looming . . . male, you think you can tell me what to do. I won't—"

Someone scratched at the sitting room door. "Lady Althorpe?"

"Drat," she fumed. "Milo. I can't answer the door looking like this."

Sinclair stood. "I can."

"But you—we—"

Despite his frustration and anger, he enjoyed seeing her flustered. It didn't happen very often. "We're married. It's allowed."

As he strode over and pulled open the door, he had to admit that seeing the butler's startled expression was rather satisfying. With bare feet and breeches, the rest of his wardrobe nowhere to be seen, few could doubt what he and Vixen had been up to.

"What is it?"

"Er, the—that is, Lady Althorpe's dinner guests have arrived."

"What dinner guests?" Sin asked.

"Oh, no!" Victoria squeaked, and fled in a blur of white back into her bedchamber.

Sinclair looked after her, then back at the butler.

"I'll inform the marchioness," he said, and closed the door in Milo's face.

His wife hadn't closed the bedchamber door, which was good news for the door. He could hear her rustling about in the dressing room, and he followed her in.

"Whom did you invite for dinner?"

She jumped. "I was going to sit down with you and explain everything in a calm and rational manner," she shot, throwing gowns and stockings over her shoulder with reckless abandon. "And then I found out that you hit Lord William, and that was so . . . romantic, and now it's too late, and oh, I've just made a muck of everything again!"

She looked like a miniature whirlwind. Obviously her guest list was not going to be welcome news, but even so, the part of him that enjoyed thinking on his feet was in heaven when Victoria was present.

"Victoria," he repeated, with admirable calm he thought, "who is downstairs?"

Victoria squeezed her eyes shut, then peeked one open again. "Your grandmother and your brother."

Sinclair blinked. "I must be losing my hearing," he said slowly. "I thought I heard you say you've invited my family over for dinner, without informing me, and certainly without my permission."

"Yes, I did. And I'm glad. You should have seen your grandmother's face today, when she realized that you . . ."

"That I wasn't the hopeless scapegrace she thought I was?" he finished. "I would rather have her disappointed in me than dead." He grabbed one of her stray shoes off a cushioned seat and hurled it into the bedchamber. It hit the wall with a satisfying thud. "Damnation, Victoria!"

She snatched a pretty gray evening gown off the floor and left the dressing room. "Then don't come downstairs," she shot, and stalked off in the direction of her wildlife preserve.

They were halfway through their potato stew when the dining room door opened. Victoria looked up, hoping it would be Sinclair, but was still surprised when he strolled into the room. She could tell he remained agitated, yet he had joined them. She had to see that as a good sign; otherwise she was just flailing about with no clue how to help him, or how even to get through to him.

She had no idea when she'd become so obsessed with figuring him out, but obviously Sinclair Grafton had become her latest project—and she was determined to save him. From himself, from the wall he'd built to protect his family, and from the unknown assassin who'd taken his brother away. Making love with him had only intensified her determination tenfold.

"Good evening." He strolled up to his grandmother's chair and leaned over to kiss her on the cheek. Augusta reached up to cup his face, but he evaded the caress and straightened again.

"Do you want a kiss, too, Kit?" he drawled.

His brother grinned, perceptibly relaxing. "A handshake will do."

Sin complied, then took the seat at the opposite end of the table from Victoria. She'd been hoping for the offer of a kiss for herself, but on the other hand, she'd rather he be angry with her right now than with his family.

"I see you've kept most of the old staff," Augusta

commented, nodding in Milo's direction.

"It made sense. They know the house better than I do."

"The boat races on the Thames are tomorrow," his brother said around a mouthful of baked ham. "I've twenty quid on Dash's team, because he's recruited that Greek brute, Stephano. Are you going to attend?"

"I hadn't planned on it," Sin said, the look he sent his wife telling her very clearly that one dinner was not going to reconcile him to his family.

"Oh. Jolly good, though. No matter," Christopher stumbled, shoveling in another mouthful and clearly disappointed.

"But I don't see why not," Sinclair continued smoothly. "It'll give me a chance to catch up on Oxford gossip."

His brother grinned. "Excellent. Don't wager on Dash, though. You'll frighten all my potential victims away and ruin the odds." Christopher leaned down the table toward Victoria. "Grandmama refuses to attend, but will you accompany us, Vixen? It'll be a smashing lot of fun."

Sinclair continued eating, giving her no clue whether he wanted her to join them or not. That in itself was all the hint she needed. "Thank you, Christopher, but I'm having luncheon with some friends."

His face lit up. "Kit, please. Would they be female friends, by chance?"

She laughed. "Almost exclusively. Is there anyone in particular you wish to meet? I'm sure I could arrange something."

"That's a splendid idea, my dear," Augusta said.

They all looked at Lady Drewsbury. "It is?" Kit asked dubiously.

"Yes. Your joining our family, Victoria, together with Sinclair's return to London, both need to be celebrated. I believe I shall hold a ball at Drewsbury House."

Christopher whooped. "You are the absolute top of the trees, Grandmama!"

"It's been my lifelong goal to achieve such status," Augusta said dryly, though her eyes danced.

From Sinclair's expression, he wasn't nearly as pleased with the idea as his brother. Seeing Augusta's plans for a family reunion about to collapse, Victoria clapped, forcing a delighted smile. "What a splendid idea, Augusta. May I help you with the guest list, at least?"

"Of course. If we're to make Christopher happy, we must include your friends. Mine are positively fossilized."

"And do we have a date for this illustrious gathering?" Sinclair asked.

"How about the fifteenth? That gives us four days to do the invitations, and ten days for preparation and responses."

Well, he hadn't said no, but the more he thought about it, the more likely he was to do so. Victoria rose and made her way around the table to his side. "Is that agreeable to you, Sinclair?" she asked softly, taking his free hand and bringing it to her lips.

She caught the surprised look that passed between Augusta and Kit, but ignored it as Sin smiled up at her. The expression didn't touch his eyes. "I think it's a grand idea," he said warmly. "And it'll keep you busy."

Her fleetingly pleased surprise turned to annoyance. Damnation—she should have realized. While she was planning a glorious family reunion, he was plotting how to keep her away from the murder investigation.

Victoria smiled brightly at him. "Thank you." She whirled around to face Christopher. "I'll invite all of my unmarried friends. You are going to be *very* sought after."

Kit chuckled. "I think I'm about to faint from happiness."

Sin gave her a darker look. "Mm. So am I."

Despite his obvious annoyance with her, he was pleasant and charming with his family, so at least the evening wasn't a complete waste. Sin saw Kit and Augusta out to their carriage, then returned to the foyer, where Victoria waited and tried not to pace.

"I like your family," she said as Milo closed the front door.

Sinclair glanced at the butler. "Thank you, Milo. We're through for the evening."

The butler bowed. "Very good, my lord. Good night."

"Good night, Milo," Victoria said, smiling.

Milo hesitated, but when neither of his employers showed an inclination to leave the entryway, he bowed again and backed down the hall toward the servants' quarters. When he vanished around the corner, Sinclair faced her.

"Come with me," he said, and turned for the stairs.

She stuck her tongue out at his back. "I was helping you."

He stopped and faced her again. "I know. Come with me."

"But are you angry, or not?"

"Yes, I am—extremely. You've started more trou-

ble than you realize, Victoria. Now come with me, or
I'll carry you upstairs again."

The threat wasn't very effective, because she liked
it when he lifted her up and carried her about. Her
pulse stirred. Making love would just distract the both
of them, though, and she needed to know what he
wanted. "I'm coming."

To her surprise he led her past the library, past her
own rooms, to his bedchamber door. When he opened
it and stepped aside for her to enter, she hesitated.

"Nervous?" he asked in his low voice.

She shivered. "Not a bit," she snapped, and walked
past him into the room.

He closed the door behind them, then caught her
arm and turned her to face him. Before she could protest, he bent his head and kissed her.

Victoria felt it down to her toes. It was different
than it had been before; more possessive, and more
sure. And more intoxicating, though she hadn't be-
lieved that possible. "Sinclair," she murmured, sliding
her arms around his shoulders and raising up on her
toes. Distraction did have its merits.

"Should I leave, then?" a gruff voice said.

She squawked, banging Sin on the chin as she
jumped at the strange voice.

"Damn," her husband grumbled, not seeming at all
put out, and rubbed where her forehead had thwacked
him. "Victoria, this is Roman."

A small, compact man emerged from an overstuffed
chair and sketched a bow. He looked like a dock-
worker or a sailor who'd seen too many seasons of
rough weather. A terrible scar ran down the left side
of his face, pulling the corner of his mouth up in a

perpetual grin, while two of the fingers of his left hand seemed to be permanently hooked.

"Hello," she said tentatively. "I thought you were a groom."

"Among other things," he answered, scratching his head.

"Roman's my valet . . . mostly." Her husband gazed at her coolly. "He's a spy, too. Or he was, I should say."

"Sin! What in—"

"Well, that makes sense," she interrupted, and strode forward to shake his hand. "How do you do, Roman?"

"I'm daft, my lady," the valet grunted, glaring at Sinclair, "because I'm hearing things."

The marquis waved a hand at the valet. "She guessed. She deduced, actually. Have a seat, Roman. I want the two of you to become acquainted."

"You do?" they both asked at the same time.

"Yes."

Victoria looked at the valet, who looked back at her. Sinclair had strolled over to the far side of the fireplace. Angry with her or not, Sin was giving her exactly what she wanted—access to that hidden part of his life he'd guarded from everyone else. She sat. A moment later, the valet seated himself opposite her.

"Brandy?" Sin asked jovially, and handed a full snifter to Roman. "And one for you, Victoria."

Beginning to wonder whether she'd fallen asleep and stumbled into an exceedingly odd dream, she took the second glass. He poured one for himself and sat on the wide arm of her chair, close enough to touch but not doing so.

"Roman," he began, "Lady Althorpe would like to

help us with our investigation. I would appreciate if
you would tell her why that is a very bad idea."

"So that's what this is about?" Victoria set her snifter aside and stood, anger and disappointment replacing her wary optimism. "I'm not a child, Sinclair,
and I'm not stupid. Don't think you can frighten me
with—"

"Sit," he ordered and grabbed the edge of her skirt
to pull her back into the chair.

Victoria plunked down on her bottom. She had
never liked being told what to do, especially when she
was certain for one of the few times in her life that
the task she had set for herself was the right one. "I
don't care what tales of blood and horror you mean to
have him tell me," she said. "You can't order me
about."

"Actually, I can."

"Such things ain't fit for a lady to hear, Sin," the
valet grumbled, eyeing the fine brandy like it was
about to bite him.

"And that is exactly my point. It's not fit for a lady
to hear, much less for a lady to be involved with."

"If you lived in a brothel, Sinclair, you must have
had females assisting you—to some degree, anyway."

"Whores and thieves," he answered promptly, obviously anticipating the question. "Neither of which
describes you."

"And they had more right to assist you than I do,
apparently."

Sin swore under his breath. "It's not that, Vixen,
and you know it. You're a lady of gentle breeding.
You have no idea what it's like, looking for wolves in
your own flock of sheep. I don't want to see you hurt."

Obviously he wasn't going to give in, and just as

obviously he thought her utterly incapable of making a meaningful contribution. Well, she could maneuver as well as he could. She'd managed the gentlemen of the *ton* for nearly three years, since she turned eighteen. And even before that.

"I think you're making a mistake," she said haughtily, unable to keep the injured tone from her voice, "but if you won't include me in your life, then so be it." She rose again, and this time he didn't try to prevent it. "Just don't expect me to include you in mine. Now, if you'll excuse me, gentlemen, I have a soiree to help your grandmother plan. Good evening."

"My lady."

Sinclair watched her exit through his dressing room into her own bedchamber. He flinched as the lock clicked shut. If spending another night alone was the price for keeping her out of harm's way, though, he would pay it.

"I thought you wanted her help." Roman gulped down his brandy.

"I did. I do. I just didn't want her to know about it."

"Oh. Seems a bit late for that."

Sin slid sideways to drop into the chair she'd vacated. "I'm aware of that, thank you."

"So what comes next?"

"You get the hell out of my bedchamber and leave me in peace. I need to think."

"Fine." The valet stood and walked to the door. "Seems to me, Sin, that you've leg-shackled yourself to a female you can't control. That's not good for a spy, and it's surely not good for a husband."

"Good night, Roman."

The valet was correct, of course, which didn't make

the situation any more palatable. Sin prided himself on knowing just how far he could trust an ally—or an enemy—and just how they would react to any given circumstance. Victoria played by another set of rules entirely, and she'd begun playing havoc with him, as well.

He sipped his brandy. Or maybe the problem was that she wasn't playing. They were married, which had begun to seem like one of his better ideas. Unless he wanted the marriage to end when he found Thomas's murderer, he needed to figure her out, figure out what she wanted, and decide if that was what he was prepared to give her—and himself.

Most importantly, though, he needed to acknowledge that he was becoming quite fond of Victoria Fontaine-Grafton. He had known that he wanted her; he still wanted her, even more now that he'd tasted her passion. Given her frivolous, flirtatious reputation, he'd thought to use her only to gain access to her society. What he hadn't expected was to *like* her—to admire her bright wit and very sincere warmth and compassion, which apparently even extended to include him.

He finished his brandy and then hers, then poured himself another, and then decided he'd be damned if he was going to lie awake all night just because his wife declined to join him in his bedchamber. Digging through his wardrobe, he found an elegant and suitably dark evening coat, slipped it on, and went hunting.

His prime target was playing cards at the Society Club, and after a cold glare at the doorman, he was allowed into the chandelier-lit parlor as well. Thomas had helped him in more ways than his brother could have realized; without the former Lord Althorpe's sterling reputation to speak in his defense, the current Lord Althorpe would very likely have found himself banned from half of the gentlemen's clubs of London.

"Mind if I join you?" he drawled, dropping into an empty seat without waiting for an answer.

"Well, if it isn't that damned female-stealing bastard, Althorpe. Join us, by all means."

John Madsen, Lord Marley, snatched up the table's bottle of port before Sinclair could reach for it and pointedly emptied it into his own glass and those of his four companions. Undaunted, Sin signaled for another bottle, which looked to be the table's fourth. "What's been played?" he asked coolly, feeling the brandy burning through his veins and knowing his lads would be appalled to see him going hunting in his present mood, and in his current condition.

"We'll start a new round," Marley answered. "Wouldn't want you to miss anything."

"That's kind of you."

Lionel Parrish, seated beside Marley, glanced uneasily between the two of them. "You play faro then, Althorpe? I thought vingt-et-un was the preferred game on the Continent."

Sin kept his gaze on Marley. "I'm known to wager on just about anything. And to win more than I lose."

Marley signaled the dealer to lay out the suit of hearts. "Most winnings can be lost again," he said, dropping two quid by the seven.

So he wanted to talk about Vixen. That was fine by Sinclair. "Losing would take forever, with the pittance you're wagering." Glad he'd dumped money into his pockets before he left the house, Sin folded a twenty-pound note into the shape of a lady's bonnet and placed it by the queen.

"Nothing's been played," Parrish protested. "Beginning a set with a twenty quid wager? That's too rich for my blood."

A fourth player, Viscount Whyling, eyed the table and the wagers. "Nice hat," he said.

"My thanks. I can do a full-breasted woman with a hundred-pound note."

"I can do one for two shillings, in Charing Cross," Whyling replied, grinning.

The table's fifth occupant chortled drunkenly. "Two shillings. That's splendid, Whyling."

It was fairly clever, but it was also distracting Marley. "Yes, but if I win, I keep the hundred quid," Sinclair retorted. "In fact, now that I consider it, that is the most economical part of marriage, gentlemen."

Marley looked at him balefully. "What's so economical about marriage?" he growled.

Sinclair just smiled at him.

Parrish cleared his throat. "I believe it's been well documented that there's no such thing as *gratis* where sexual relations are concerned."

"Good point, Parrish. In my exper—"

"Shut up, Althorpe!" Marley bellowed. "We all know you've had the Vixen. You don't need to give us the details."

Sin scowled. "I was speaking in general terms, my boy. I don't believe I mentioned my wife." He realized he really was far too drunk and far too frustrated with Victoria to be engaging in this particular conversation. Still, if it drew Marley out, he would face Vixen with the consequences of his idiocy—if he couldn't avoid it.

"No, you didn't," Parrish said forcefully. "It's my wager, isn't it? I'll put five on the queen. At least if I go down, I'll be taking your golden ship with me."

Vaguely grateful to Marley's companion for aiding his escape, Sinclair decided to head them all toward other ground. "I wish my brother had had the stomach for wagering. I might have been able to begin enjoying my inheritance pre-posthumously."

"Perhaps your brother was just selective in who he wagered with," Marley drawled, the angry red color in his face fading. "We spent many pleasant evenings together."

Clenching his jaw, Sin hardly noticed as he and Parrish won the round. "I'm sorry, I didn't quite hear that. Did you mention 'Thomas' and 'pleasant' in the same breath?"

Whyling laughed again, and Sinclair decided he didn't like the viscount all that much, after all. The fifth player, whom he remembered only as a Mr. Henning, managed a halfhearted chuckle. "Didn't really know Althorpe, but he seemed a good sort."

"He was," Marley said, sneering at Sin. "Had a good head on his shoulders, even if he occasionally faced it in the wrong direction."

Aha. "Excuse me," Sin drawled. "You may disparage my late, lamented brother's character at will, but not his sexual preferences. That's rather below the belt."

"I wasn't talking about that, you nitwit. He kept telling me to divest myself of all my shares in French companies. Noble, I'll admit, but I would have lost a fortune if I'd done it."

"You lost it anyway, didn't you?" Whyling commented. "Partially to me, and in this very room, as I recall."

"Now, now," Parrish said, pushing down on Marley's shoulder as he began to lurch to his feet. "No use wasting good port to lament bad debts. I'm here to play faro."

Sinclair nodded, deciding he would ask some very pointed questions of Victoria about her former beau in the morning. "As am I."

Chapter 9

"Are you sure we should all be here?" Lucy asked. "After hearing about Lord William I'm fairly certain I don't want to make Lord Althorpe angry."

"Nonsense," Victoria answered warmly. "He keeps insisting that this is my home as much as it's his. My half wants to visit with my friends."

"You promised you'd tell me what happened when you asked him about Lord William," Lucy whispered.

Nothing in the world could have prevented Victoria from turning crimson. Swallowing, she took her friend's arm and led the way into the huge Grafton ballroom. "Oh, nothing much," she said flippantly. "You know how men are."

"No, I d—"

"It's a shame you won't have the ball here," Venetia Hilston tittered with the best timing she'd ever exhibited. "You could fit half of London in this ballroom."

"You could," Lionel Parrish agreed, seizing Lucy's other hand and sweeping her into a waltz, "but that would leave us no room to dance."

"It would be awfully warm, as well, with so many people," Venetia said earnestly.

"She really has no sense of humor, does she?" Lord Geoffrey Tremont murmured in Victoria's ear.

He'd been buzzing about her all afternoon, like a bee after a flower. With a chuckle Victoria scraped him off against Nora Jeffrie's rotund form. "Marguerite, you should play for us," she suggested, "and then we could all dance."

"Yes, please play, Marguerite," Lucy called, as Parrish continued swirling her around the huge ballroom.

Miss Porter didn't need any more encouragement than that, and she hurried to the pianoforte in the corner, beneath the large picture windows. In a moment she launched into a waltz.

Gathering her friends at Grafton House had been a superb idea, if Victoria said so herself. The day was too windy for riding or strolling in Hyde Park, and if she'd still been living at Fontaine House her parents would have collapsed from mortification at having such a wild set of young people about. Besides, she wanted to find out if anyone knew who the previous Lord Althorpe might have been courting. A wealthy, respectable, single gentleman with a prestigious title couldn't have been completely without female hangers-on.

"May I have this dance?" Lord Geoffrey murmured, having somehow escaped Nora.

Victoria stifled her annoyed frown and smiled instead. "Of course, Lord Geoffrey."

The dandy had endlessly pursued her, stealing her away from Marley whenever he could manage it and then spending the entire time gloating over how he'd won her—as though she'd been a prize sow at a country fair. If he hadn't stumbled on their circle at lunch-eon, she would never have invited him to join them at Grafton House.

He was a fair dancer, at least, and she had learned that a few well-placed nods and exclamations satisfied her portion of the conversation quite well. While he prattled on about how clever he'd been to find them, she watched Lucy and Lionel waltz.

Parrish had begun last Season as one of her admir-ers, but after a few subtle pushes in the right direction, he had become Lucy Havers's staunch protector and companion. Victoria smiled. She'd never been one for matchmaking, but that particular pairing of sweet souls had been so obvious that she couldn't help herself.

Halfway through the second waltz, Marguerite's nimble fingers stumbled over part of a simple phrase. That was unusual enough that Victoria looked over at her friend—and nearly stumbled over Lord Geoffrey's feet. Sin leaned against the pianoforte, chatting with Miss Porter as though he'd known her for years.

Annoyed with him or not, the first emotion that hit her was thrilled anticipation. Whatever she thought of his stupid snobbery about not allowing her to assist with his investigation, he continually surprised her—and in her experience, that was something both rare and treasured.

He didn't interrupt or attempt to cut in, as she'd expected, but remained leaning against the pianoforte until the waltz concluded. His presence of course caused a stir, and Victoria was glad that Marley had declined to join them today. She would not invite Lord William again.

"He doesn't seem to mind us," Lord Geoffrey murmured, as they continued circling the room.

"Why should he?" Victoria returned, halfway to wishing Sinclair would cut in. "You're my friends."

"I actually meant *us*, my dear. You and I."

"I see. It's a dance, my dear—not a Bacchanalian ceremony."

"Well, it's just that I heard he bloodied William Landry's nose, and that he and Marley nearly came to blows last night. I wouldn't have expected someone like him to be the jealous type, especially with the way you . . . met, but one can never know, I suppose. And I have no desire to have my teeth handed me, despite the pleasure of dancing with a female as lovely as you are."

Victoria glanced at her husband again. First he'd gone after Lord William, and now Marley. As far as she knew, Parrish had been out with his friend last evening, but Lionel hadn't mentioned anything about running into Sinclair. She'd thought Sin had gone to bed after she stalked out of his little conference. Apparently he hadn't gotten his fill of fighting with just herself as an adversary.

When the waltz ended, she freed herself from Lord Geoffrey's grip and strolled over to the pianoforte. "Good afternoon," she said, giving a tentative smile.

She expected the same selfish arrogance he'd shown last night. Instead, Sin leaned down to softly brush his lips against her cheek. "Good afternoon."

As usual when he touched her or kissed her, she wanted to sink into his embrace and start pulling his clothes off. It wouldn't be very ladylike, but she had more than a hunch that it would be immensely satisfying. It was dashed confusing, being angry with and distrustful of someone and at the same time helplessly attracted to him.

"Althorpe," Parrish said as he approached, Lucy on his arm. His demeanor seemed a little cool, especially for him, and especially now that she knew something unpleasant had occurred last evening.

Sinclair likewise assumed his aloof, rakish guise and returned Lionel's greeting with a brief handshake. "Mr. Parrish."

Victoria cleared her throat, wondering what in the world had happened last night, and why no one had bothered to tell her about it. "Sinclair, have you met everyone?"

"No. I don't believe I have."

Victoria made introductions all around, while with calculated efficiency Sin charmed everyone present— except for Lionel Parrish, who kept his distance.

Growing more curious by the moment, Victoria finally cornered Parrish herself. "All right, what's going on?" she whispered.

"Hm? Nothing, Vixen."

"Why didn't you mention that Sinclair and Marley fought last night?"

He drew a breath. "They didn't fight; they exchanged words."

"About me?"

"Ask your husband. Marley's a friend of mine, Vix. Not a close friend, but I have no wish to be pummeled by him, or by Althorpe."

"Fine. I'll ask Sinclair, then."

She turned away, but stopped when Lionel touched her shoulder. "I worry about you," he murmured. "Are you certain you're all right with him?"

"You don't need to worry about—"

"Is there any more dancing planned for this afternoon?" Sinclair asked, joining them.

Immediately Parrish lowered his arm. "Actually, I think we need to be going. *The Magic Flute* premieres at the opera house tonight, and it looks to be a sad crush."

"Will you be attending?" Lucy asked, prancing up to take Victoria's hand, obviously unaware of the tension flowing between the two men.

"I . . . don't know," she stumbled, forcing herself not to look at Sinclair like some puppy begging for a bone. "We hadn't discussed it."

"Would you like to attend?" Sin asked, his tone intimate, as though a dozen other people weren't in the room to overhear.

"I would like to," she admitted, blushing, "but it's not necess—"

"Yes, we'll be attending," he interrupted, smiling at Lucy.

"Good luck finding seats," Lord Geoffrey grumbled. "I couldn't, and I even offered fifty quid to Harris to give me his box."

"My grandmother has a box."

Victoria tried not to stare at him as though he'd just solved the riddle of the Sphinx. Another surprise, and another kindness to her. It was difficult to keep her balance when the ground kept shifting.

She saw her friends to the door, while Sin—either on purpose or by accident—kept himself between her and Parrish. As they left, he looked at her. "What were you and Parrish conversing about?"

"About what happened between you and Marley last night," she answered, glancing pointedly at Milo, still lurking in the foyer.

Sinclair gestured her toward his private office. "What did he tell you, then?"

"He told me to ask you." As she followed him into the room, he closed the door behind her. "I assume the conversation was about my virtues or lack thereof, again," she continued, "but given the way you're acting, I'm not certain how well I came out this time."

"Jesus," he muttered. "Do you miss anything?"

"About as much as you do. So what happened?"

"Nothing you need to concern yourself with."

"Fine." She folded her arms across her chest. "How were the boat races?"

"Two boats sank, and no one drowned." Sinclair strode to the desk and back again, avoiding the chair where his brother had been shot. "Vix—"

"I said you didn't need to tell me. I'll ask Marley."

His expression hardened. "You are not going to ask Marley anything. Is that clear?"

She held his gaze. "As far as I'm aware, you've excluded me from joining your merry little band of spies. You can't order me not to see my friends."

He stalked closer. "I am your husband."

"And so I'm supposed to obey you? Ha!" She turned on her heel. "Make me."

"Just how much do you know about Lord Marley?" he shot back.

"I know more about him than I do about you." Victoria paused in the doorway. "I assume we're still going to the opera tonight, so you can spy on everyone?"

He was silent for a moment. "Yes."

Obviously she didn't mean much to him, if he was more concerned with his little games than with how angry and hurt she felt. She didn't know why she'd expected—or hoped for—anything different. "I'll see you this evening, then," she said quietly, and left the room.

Sinclair had to stalk the length of the room and curse for a good five minutes before he could pull his thoughts together enough to decide his next step. Victoria didn't understand—obviously she would never be able to understand—that these people she called her friends and invited to visit her house weren't what they seemed. At least one of them was a killer; from what he'd uncovered in Europe, another good half of them were liars, adulterers, cheaters, traitors, and profiteers.

Not her, though—she was none of those things, and he didn't want her anywhere near them. He would find his own clues from now on, if she would just agree to stay out of this misery.

Still cursing under his breath, Sinclair sat behind the desk and pulled out a stack of paper to write some letters. The first was simple—Lady Stanton sent a note to her nephew, Wally Jerrison, currently lodging with several friends on Weigh House Street, reporting that Lord Marley had disagreed with Thomas Grafton's views on French trade and Bonaparte.

The second note was equally brief, but it took him five times as long to compose. Finally he settled for, "Grandmama, if you have any extra chairs available, Victoria and I would very much like to join you at the opera this evening. Sinclair."

The "very much" part had exited in the first draft. However, he meant it, so at the last moment he added it again onto the final copy. Being seen in his company could be dangerous, yet those well-acquainted with Thomas would know that all three brothers adored their grandmother. Avoiding her could potentially be as damaging as anything else. And in truth, after spending dinner with her the other day, he'd realized how very much he'd missed her—and Christopher.

The second reason for the extra plea was even more complicated. He'd lied again—to Victoria. They were attending the opera not so he could spy on everyone but because she wanted to go. He simply wanted to spend time with his wife in a place they could be together without arguing or lying. He'd begun to think of her more than he had any right to.

The response to the second missive came not twenty minutes after he sent it out. Despite the simple "Christopher and I would be delighted to have you join us. Augusta," he could almost hear the surprise in his grandmother's writing. Kit would no doubt be less than delighted to attend an opera, but the way Victoria's female friends seemed to materialize out of thin air whenever she appeared in public, his younger brother would no doubt be adequately compensated for his suffering.

He sent Milo to inform Victoria that they definitely would be attending the opera, and then went into the library. Victoria had left Thomas's box of sketches there. Several times he'd gone to the door and then decided he had something more pressing to do, but obviously he couldn't put it off indefinitely.

Sitting at the table that occupied the middle of the large, airy room, he pulled the wooden box to him, unfastened the leather straps binding it, and carefully lifted it open. The first sketch was of Christopher, when he must have been sixteen or seventeen, his hair its usual disheveled riot, and an easy, open grin on his face.

Victoria had been right; even to Sin's untrained eye, Thomas's sketches were excellent. The next few were of Althorpe—the trees at the edge of the lake, the stables, and the grand old manor itself. The sketches told him nothing about who might have killed his brother, but everything about quiet, thoughtful Thomas.

The last drawings looked slightly more helpful, if no less painful to view. Thomas had obviously made a hobby of sketching his peers. Since Sin hadn't heard anyone but Victoria mention the former Lord Althorpe's fondness for drawing, Thomas had probably done it from memory rather than using actual models.

His good friend Astin Hovarth, the Earl of Kingsfeld, appeared on several pages—at White's club, on horseback, and wearing his hunting attire. Lady Grayson, Grandmama Augusta, Lord Hodgiss, Miss Pickering—had all fallen victim to Thomas's talents, as well.

As he gingerly lifted the next sketch from the box, Sinclair paused. Sitting in what looked like a ballroom, vague faceless forms surrounding her and no doubt representing her multitude of suitors and admirers, was Lady Victoria Fontaine. Even her image had the power to make his heart pound.

Their lovemaking hadn't quenched his urge for her at all, and neither had any of their arguments or her obvious disappointment in him as a husband. But at the moment that wasn't his priority, and he couldn't allow it to become so. He wasn't certain he knew how to become any sort of proper husband, anyway.

In the portrait, a wisp of curling dark hair had strayed across her brow. The expression on her smooth, oval face bespoke her humor and intelligence, while the twinkle in her eyes said that she knew exactly what the men surrounding her wanted. Sinclair ran his finger across her brow, but the lock of hair remained elegantly out of place.

Thomas had chosen to sketch her. Had he been one of her admirers? Sinclair didn't think so—not a serious one, anyway, or he wouldn't have seen the knowing humor in her gaze. She'd said she and Thomas had been friends, but not close ones; given her natural compassion and the way she seemed to inspire everyone's confidences, it wasn't surprising that Thomas had told her that he drew. Had he told her anything else, perhaps something she hadn't even realized?

When he'd finished gazing at the sketches, he carefully returned them to their box and fastened it closed again. They were the last and most personal items he had of his brother, and he decided to have most of them framed and added to the portrait hall at Althorpe. Thomas would no doubt have been embarrassed to see his private sketches so prominently displayed, but Sinclair wanted them there, wanted the reminder of his brother's life in something other than accounting ledgers and official papers.

He was debating whether to make a late afternoon visit to Pall Mall and the clubs or to continue the enormous task of sifting through the items in the attic, which he'd begun shortly after he arrived and discontinued when Victoria had joined the household. Now that she knew what he was doing and why, attempting to keep it a secret didn't make much sense any longer. The attic seemed more likely to bear fruit, and he pushed away from the table, only to feel something rubbing against his ankles.

Startled, he looked down to see a large white and

gray feline twining about his legs, purring hard enough
to make the round, plump body shake. "Well, hello
there, Lord Baggles," he said, reaching down to
scratch it behind the ears. "You've forgiven me, I see."

By way of answer, the cat leapt onto his lap and
curled into a large ball of soft fuzz, his purring gaining
strength until it sounded like the grinding stones of a
flour mill. Sin continued scratching the feline, willing
to delay climbing about the attic for another few
minutes if it put him in good graces with Lord Baggles, and thereby his mistress. Dimly he heard shouting out in the street, but it sounded like a vendor's
argument, and he ignored it.

The library door slammed open. "Trouble, Sin," Roman said and vanished again.

"Damnation. Sorry, old boy." Sinclair lifted the un-
protesting cat over to the couch to continue his nap in
peace.

He could hear Roman's heavy footsteps clunking
down the stairs, and he followed the valet to the first
floor. Half the household's servants milled about in
the foyer and the front rooms that overlooked the
street. As he neared the entry, Milo turned and saw
him.

"Oh, thank goodness, my lord. Lady Al—"

Vixen. Sin pushed past him and strode out to the
front steps. Out in the street his petite wife stood, her
arms folded, directly in the path of a rickety milk cart.
At the front of the cart was quite possibly the most
dilapidated, underfed pony he'd ever set eyes on. And
sitting in the driver's perch, an equally squalid-looking
man sat glaring at Victoria.

"I said, get outta the way, miss!" he bellowed. "I've
deliveries to make."

"I don't care what you have to do," she retorted. "You have no right to beat that animal in that awful manner."

"You try making old Joe go, miss. You'd be encouragin' him, too."

"I would not! I do not beat animals."

Sin clearly saw the angry, defiant gleam in the cart driver's eyes, and he saw the hand tightening on the whip. With an oath, he vaulted down the shallow steps. Before the driver could do more than give him a surprised look, he jumped up onto the nearest wheel, reached over, and grabbed the whip. "As much as she dislikes seeing animals hurt," he said in a low, taut voice, dark anger coursing through him, "you can't begin to imagine what I would do to you if you injured her."

The driver swallowed nervously, his dirty Adam's apple bobbing. "I wasn't . . . I'm just trying to make a living here, m'lord, and she won't get out of the way."

Sinclair hopped back to the ground. "I believe Lady Althorpe's objection is to your method of handling your animal, not to the way you make your living."

"But—"

"How much, then?" He sensed Victoria moving up to stand beside him, but he kept his attention on the driver.

" 'How much?' " the man repeated.

"For the horse, cart, and milk."

"A . . . a lord with a milk cart? You've gone mad."

"I've been meaning to take up a hobby. How much?" Sinclair said crisply.

"I couldn't part with old Joe and the rest for less than ten quid," the driver said, folding his own arms.

The price was outrageous, but Sin wasn't in the

mood to argue, or to let Victoria be disappointed in him yet again today. "I'll give you twenty quid so you can get a decent animal you won't have to beat. Is that fair enough?"

"Aye, m'lord."

"Then get down from there. Roman, pay the man, and send him on his way. Grimsby, take the beast around back and unharness and feed him. Orser, put the milk into one of my carriages and take it to the nearest orphanage, with Lady Althorpe's compliments."

A chorus of "Aye, my lord" greeted the orders, and he turned to face Victoria. She wore a surprised look on her face, her stance hesitant and defiant at the same time. No doubt she expected a lecture on the idiocy of facing down a large, burly man carrying a whip— no doubt she'd heard such lectures before.

"Old Joe," Sin said slowly, "does not get to live in the conservatory with the rest of your menagerie."

She stared at him, then her violet eyes began to dance. "Fair enough. Shall we go in?"

"By all means. And Lord Baggles is snoring in the library, by the way."

"I'll remove him at once."

"Why?"

She stopped on the bottom step, looking him in the eye from her elevated perch. "Are you doing this just so I won't be angry with you?"

"Of course I am. Is it working?"

Victoria grinned. "I'll let you know."

Seizing the opportunity, he closed the last few inches separating them and kissed her. Victoria froze for the space of a heartbeat. He half thought her next action would be to kick him in his sensitive parts, but he decided it was worth the risk. To his relief, though, her hands slid up over his shoulders and her lips deepened their embrace with his.

Delight and arousal coursed through him at her passionate response. Before she could come to her senses and remember what a boor he was, he swept her up into his arms and climbed the remaining steps into the house.

"Sinclair, what are you doing?" she murmured against his mouth, chuckling breathlessly.

"Taking you upstairs."

"But the servants are watching."

"Are you shocked, my dear?"

She shook her head, snuggling closer against his chest. One-handed, she began untying the intricate knots of his cravat. Sinclair was beginning to think the morning room was a viable alternative when a loud, masculine laugh stopped him cold.

Victoria still in his arms, he whipped around to see a tall, muscular figure silhouetted in the front doorway. "Kingsfeld," he said, relaxing as much as his aroused body would allow. Thank God for Victoria's long skirts.

"Sin Grafton, as I live and breathe. Weren't you doing the same thing the last time I saw you?"

Victoria lifted an eyebrow. "Really."

Pleased as he was to see the Earl of Kingsfeld, at the moment Sinclair wouldn't have wept a tear if he fell down the steps and broke his neck. "I'm afraid I don't remember," he said smoothly. "That was quite a while ago, when I was very young and stupid."

"Your taste in females, though, remains intact, boy. Introduce me to this goddess."

"Right. Kingsfeld, my wife Victoria, Lady Althorpe.

She twisted her ankle. Victoria, Astin Hovarth, the Earl of Kingsfeld. A friend of my brother's."

"Lord Kingsfeld," the Vixen said in her most charming voice, smiling. "I'm certain we've seen one another before. I'm glad we've finally been introduced."

The large earl swept a bow that lowered his head to the level of his knees. "The pleasure is mine, my lady."

At the moment Victoria was inclined to agree with him, because obviously she and Sinclair weren't going to have any. She ached for Sin; she had since she'd met him. One time in his arms was not nearly enough to cure her of her need to be near him, and she was loathe to lose this opportunity.

Victoria glanced again at Kingsfeld and inwardly sighed. If he had been a friend of Thomas's, then no doubt Sinclair would want to speak to him. "I think I should rest my ankle in the morning room," she announced.

"Of course," her husband said promptly.

While Kingsfeld relinquished his hat and gloves to Milo, Sinclair carried her into the morning room and set her gently on the couch. Before he could completely escape, she grabbed him by the lapels and pulled him down for another slow, deep kiss. He sank onto the edge of the couch, her face cupped between his long-fingered hands.

"So, Sin," the earl said, entering the room, "I received your note. What was it that you wanted to discuss with me?"

Frustrated humor in his whiskey-colored eyes, Sinclair straightened. "Comfortable?" he asked her solicitously.

"No."

Sin cleared his throat. "I'll fetch your shawl. Be with you in a moment, Kingsfeld." With that, he bolted past the earl toward the stairs.

"No hurry. I'll just get acquainted with Lady Althorpe."

Trying to focus on something other than how splendidly her husband kissed, Victoria studied Astin Hovarth as he poured himself a glass of port from the decanter beneath the window. He had Sin's height but was bulkier through the shoulders and chest than her husband, more like a draft horse than a thoroughbred. Light blue eyes studied the room briefly before they returned to her, and she remembered that it had likely been better than two years since he had last set foot in Grafton House.

"Does anything seem different?" she asked, as he seated himself in the chair closest to her.

"Well, Thomas never had a lady as lovely as you on his couch. I would have noticed that."

She smiled. "Surely Lord Althorpe wasn't completely celibate."

"Hm? Oh, no. But his taste was obviously much more dull than his brother's." He toasted her with his glass. "You're Vixen Fontaine, aren't you?"

"I was," she said ruefully.

"Once a songbird always a songbird," he said congenially. "Sin always did have an eye for the pretty chits."

"Did he now?" she returned. "He seems very unlike h—"

"I was surprised to see him back in London. Thought by now he'd have set himself up in Paris with some French skirt or other." He chuckled to himself.

"Thomas always used to say he never knew where Sinclair would turn up."

She wondered at that. Thomas seemed to have had a better idea of Sin's location than anyone but his fellow spies. Apparently he hadn't passed the information on to Lord Kingsfeld. "I like unpredict—"

"No doubt he thought that being married to the Vixen, he wouldn't have to settle himself down by much."

The earl continued to chat obliviously, while Victoria tried not to scowl at him. She didn't like being interrupted, but even worse was being ignored. And for him to be speaking about Sin's, well, sins, as though she weren't even present, wasn't at all polite. Finally he wound down his speech about the different hotels and inns found in Paris and looked at her.

"Would you like me to fetch you a nice fluffy pillow for your ankle? You're being very brave not to cry, my dear."

"I'm fine, thank—"

"In my experience, most chits spring leaks at the drop of a flower petal." He took another sip of port. "Indeed they do. Were you saying something?"

Sin strolled back into the room, her green lace shawl bunched in his hands. "Here you go."

"Obviously nothing important," Vixen returned cheerfully, standing and taking the wrap from her husband's surprised fingers.

"What's not important?"

"Anything I say. I shall leave the two of you to chat."

"But your ankle," he said, frowning at her.

"It feels much better now," she said demurely and left the room to go find Lord Baggles, who at least noticed whether or not she was in the room.

Lord Kingsfeld stayed for dinner. Victoria joined the two men, arriving at the table as late as possible. She ate as quickly as she could, determined not to utter an unlistened-to word in the earl's presence.

"Your wife is such a pretty bird," Kingsfeld said, smiling at her as Milo refilled his glass of wine. "Even her voice is like a song."

Victoria dug into her roasted potato to hide her deepening annoyance. Obviously Lord Kingsfeld thought she was an idiot. Like so many men, he saw her face and form, and nothing else. If she had been certain that Sin had all the information he needed from his so-called friend, she would have taken great pleasure in enlightening Kingsfeld about just how much in error he was.

"Have you opened Hovarth House?" Sinclair asked.

"Yes, just this morning. I hadn't intended to spend much time in London this Season, but I couldn't resist your note."

"I'm pleased you've come. You've already been most helpful."

Kingsfeld smiled. "Then I am pleased, as well. And you are to be congratulated. A pretty, proper wife— so difficult to find these days."

Sinclair didn't bat an eyelash, but Victoria wanted to vomit. Instead she set her napkin on the table and rose. "If you'll excuse me, gentlemen, I would like to fix my hair before we leave."

"Leave?"

"The opera," Sinclair explained. For a moment Victoria thought he might ask Kingsfeld to join them, but thankfully he contented himself with giving her an indulgent look. "Vixen loves the opera."

"Yes, I certainly do," she said, her jaw clenched, and curtsied. "Good evening, Lord Kingsfeld."

He stood and bowed to her. "Lady Althorpe. I hope we shall be seeing much more of one another."

She smiled. "Oh, I'm certain we shall." *From as far away as possible.*

Chapter 10

❦❦❦

"**A**ll right, what the devil is going on?" Sinclair sat back in the carriage opposite Victoria and tried not to glare at her.

"Nothing. Did you learn anything interesting from Lord Kingsfeld?"

He blew out his breath. "Yes. Hopefully. Now tell me what's upset you."

The Vixen laughed, though even a deaf man would have heard the annoyance in her voice. Apparently he'd bumbled even worse than he'd thought.

"Well, Sinclair, your friend did arrive at a rather . . . awkward moment," she offered.

"Don't let that concern you. I'll make it up to you." He leaned forward to take her hand, drawing her across the carriage to sit beside him. "Repeatedly, if you'll let me."

Victoria pulled her hand free, though she otherwise made no move to escape. "I have a question for you first."

"I'm listening."

"You received a letter this afternoon."

Sin furrowed his brow. "Yes. I know. What of it?"

190

She folded her arms. "Who is Lady Stanton?"

Good God. He'd never expected that she might be jealous over him. She'd only mentioned his conquests in terms of his experience. This was rather refreshing. "No one you need to concern yourself about," he hedged. All he needed was for her to begin intercepting his correspondence to look for clues.

"I see. Then don't expect me to tell you anything." Victoria started to move back to the opposite seat.

He was *not* going to spend another night alone. Sinclair put out his arm, stopping her escape. "Damnation, Vix. Some things I just can't tell you," he growled. "They aren't my secrets."

Her annoyed expression slowly eased. "That's all I want—for you to be honest with me."

"I shall endeavor. Now, you be honest with me. What happened today?" He took her hand again and kissed her knuckles.

"Don't do that. You'll get me all warm again, and I'll have to sit in the theater and pretend not to notice you for half the night."

"I make you warm?" he repeated, immeasurably pleased to hear that news. He slowly ran his fingers in circles around her palm.

"You know you do. So stop that."

"I will, if you'll tell me what happened." The low neckline of her mauve silk gown tantalized him, and he ran his fingers across the exposed skin of her bosom. "Otherwise, I won't promise anything." Feeling her sudden trembling, he leaned forward, replacing his fingers with his lips.

"Sinclair . . . Oh, don't do that."

"Then talk to me," he murmured, slipping his fingers under the lace neckline. He glanced up at her face to see her eyes closed and her mouth open in an enticing "oh." Sin grinned and resumed his trail of kisses. It was a heady feeling, to realize that he affected Vixen Fontaine so strongly. It was also a helpless feeling, to know how strongly she affected him. He'd never been under anyone's sway like this, and he wasn't certain whether he liked the sensation or not.

She twined her fingers into his hair and pulled him away from her heaving bosom. "All right, all right. Lord Kingsfeld merely . . . said something I didn't appreciate."

He furrowed his brow, half wishing she'd resisted a bit longer. "What did he say?"

Victoria searched his face for a moment. "You didn't notice?"

That didn't sound promising. "Apparently not."

"He said I was a pretty little bird."

"Which you didn't appreciate because . . ."

"Do you think I'm a pretty little bird?" his wife asked instead, tight-lipped.

"Well, I'm not going to answer that. I'm not a complete idiot."

"But am I?"

"Vixen—"

"Nearly everything your friend said to me was an insult. Did you not notice, or do you not care?"

He scowled. "I had other things on my mind."

Victoria opened her mouth, then closed it again, sitting back. "I know that. It's just that . . . I don't see how men as intelligent as you and your brother could have a birdbrained friend like that."

Fortunately, Sinclair knew enough not to come to Astin's defense. Vixen wasn't nearly as self-absorbed as her reputation made her out to be, and yet something had offended her. It bothered him, as well, because she was right: he hadn't paid attention to how Astin had treated her—he'd been concerned only with what the earl knew about Thomas. He'd disappointed her again, and he had the feeling his own shortcomings had hurt her more than any insult by Kingsfeld.

"Sinclair?"

"Hm? Sorry. I'm just—"

"Attempting to figure out why I'm so upset," she finished, thankfully not looking angry. "I don't know. I just didn't expect it, I suppose. I've never even spoken to him before today." To his surprise, she leaned her cheek against his shoulder. "Heaven knows men have assumed I was stupid before," Victoria sighed. "I do have something of a reputation."

A peculiar sensation ran through Sinclair's chest; strange and familiar all at the same time. He held his breath, trying to memorize it before it was gone. It didn't seem to go anywhere, though, but settled, warm and close, somewhere in the vicinity of his heart.

"Victoria," he said softly, reluctant to disturb the peace between them, "having acquired a reputation myself, I know what I'm talking about when I say that no one has the right to assume anyone else's capacity for understanding, or for injury."

She was silent for a full minute. "You know, Sinclair," she finally said, a quaver in her otherwise calm voice, "for a hardheaded scoundrel, you can occasionally be very nice."

"Thank you. Are you certain you don't want to return to Grafton House?"

He felt her soft chuckle against his shoulder. "Not after you told your grandmother we'd be attending. And even if you won't let me help, I won't be the reason you miss an opportunity to go out and spy."

His outspoken wife sounded entirely too docile, but he wasn't about to start an argument in his present addled and ridiculously contented state.

Fortunately the coach stopped before he could begin reciting poetry, since the only ditties he remembered were extremely vulgar and mostly in French. The theater's lobby was so densely packed with glittering nobility that for a moment Sin had the sensation he'd been locked in someone's jewelry box. Despite the fact that no one could even move in a straight line, Victoria's friends and admirers immediately managed to surround them.

"Lionel said it would be a sad crush," Lucy Havers exclaimed. "Sophie L'Anjou is making her London debut tonight. She's supposed to be fabulous."

Sinclair stifled a curse. With all the damned places he could have visited with his wife, it would have to be the same blasted building where Sophie L'Anjou had set up residence.

"Did you see Mademoiselle L'Anjou when she performed in Paris?" Victoria asked, with her usual guileless insight. "She's reputed to be quite popular there."

"Yes," he answered offhandedly. "I saw her on several occasions. She has a lovely voice." And several other lovely parts that he'd become rather familiar with during the course of his duties for the War Office.

"Althorpe!"

Still unused to hearing that name directed at him, Sinclair turned as Kit and Grandmama Augusta reached them. Kit was grinning like a lunatic, and had the Earl of Kingsfeld in tow.

"Look who I found."

His first instinct was to set his supposed friend on

his backside for behaving like a patronizing buffoon to his wife. Before he could begin punching anyone, though, Victoria's hand crept down to entwine with his. He forced himself to relax the tensed muscles across his back. If Victoria wanted to hold his hand, berating Kingsfeld could damned well wait for somewhere more private.

"Thank you so much for allowing us to attend tonight," Victoria said to his grandmother, kissing her on the cheek.

"It's my pleasure, believe me," Augusta replied, giving Sin a meaningful look he pretended to be unable to read. He certainly hadn't done anything to earn her forgiveness; he hadn't explained himself, and for damned certain he hadn't found Thomas's killer. He almost felt easier around her when she was annoyed at him.

"Hello," Kit said to Lucy, taking her hand and bowing over it. "I'm Althorpe's fascinatingly witty brother, Kit Grafton."

Laughing, Victoria made introductions all around, not even hesitating when she came to Kingsfeld. It was for his sake, Sinclair knew, and he wanted to kiss her a thousand times for being more warm and compassionate than he could ever possibly deserve.

"Where are you sitting this evening?" he asked Astin, not feeling nearly as charitable as Vixen.

"Nowhere. I actually came by to talk to you for a moment, if I may."

Ah. Perhaps the berating could begin sooner than he had thought. "Will you excuse me a minute, Victoria, Grandmama?"

Victoria smiled. "Of course. Don't be long."

She hadn't told him to behave, at least not aloud,

but he'd gotten her meaning clearly enough. Together, he and Kingsfeld muscled their way to a fairly secluded corner. "What did you want?"

"After our chat this afternoon, I went through some of my papers. I didn't find anything that struck me as odd, until I saw this." The earl pulled a paper from his pocket and unfolded it.

Something had so badly stained and blurred the single page that Sinclair couldn't begin to decipher what it might say. "All right, what is it?"

"It's part of a paper your brother and I were working on, part of a presentation before the House. This"—he gestured at the substantial stain—"is what resulted when Lord Marley stopped by our table at White's to disagree with certain issues Thomas supported. I had completely forgotten about it, but now that I recall, Marley was quite angry."

"What did your presentation concern?"

"The same topics everything concerned two years ago: Bonaparte and France."

Marley again, and France again. And though Thomas would have opposed Bonaparte anyway, he had become much more militant about it once Sin had joined the War Office. "My thanks, Astin," he said. "Please keep this between us for now."

"Of course."

Kingsfeld nodded but made no move to depart. He'd given what might turn out to be valuable information, so Sinclair stifled his impatience and waited.

Finally the earl cleared his throat. "I fear I owe you an apology, Sin," he said in a low voice.

"For what?"

"This afternoon, I may have been . . . overly enthusiastic in commenting on your wife's lovely appearance."

Sin blinked. "You were?"

"I am deeply sorry if I offended you, and I hope it doesn't damage our friendship. Your brother was a good friend."

"I don't think it's me you need to apologize to, Astin. It wasn't me that you offended."

The earl frowned. "It wasn't?"

"Victoria is quite a bit more than a pretty little bird. You'll come to see that, though, when you become better acquainted."

"Very good." Kingsfeld looked equal parts intrigued and relieved. "I'll keep that in mind."

"Good idea. I'll speak with you later."

"Of course. Good evening."

The news wasn't anything astonishing, but Kingsfeld had only been looking for one afternoon. And Sinclair could put the reported incident at White's down as one more black mark against Marley. Compared with the rest of the field, Marley was pulling ahead by a neck—which was now nearly stuck out far enough for a noose to fit around.

When he returned to his party, they had begun moving for the stairs, heading for the balcony and Augusta's private box. One person, though, was conspicuously absent. "Where's Victoria?" Sin asked, scanning the crowded lobby for her petite, mauve-garbed form.

"She went off with that big fellow over there," his brother said, gesturing. "She said she'd only be a moment."

"Kilcairn," Sinclair growled, his hackles immediately rising. But just then, Victoria nodded and returned to his side. "What did he want?" he asked in as calm a voice as he could manage.

"*I* wanted to inquire whether Alexandra would be attending Susan Maugrie's recital tomorrow. What did Lord Kingsfeld want?"

Sinclair continued glaring over her head at Kilcairn, who lifted an eyebrow at him and turned to follow his wife up the stairs. "Nothing much," he said automatically, then caught her slight frown. "He did want to apologize," he added, reminding himself that he didn't have to be as close-mouthed as he used to be.

Her expression became skeptical. "Oh, really?"

He took her arm, moving closer to her and lowering his voice. "Apparently he thought he was handing you too many compliments, as if that were possible, and that I might have been offended."

"Your friend is an oaf," she replied, obviously not impressed.

"I know. I wasn't particularly moved myself. But he's never been one before, which is why I'm inclined to give him the benefit of the doubt."

"And he gave you some news about Thomas at the same time he was apologizing, didn't he?"

"What does that have to do with anything?"

"Everything."

Sin wasn't quite certain what she meant by that, but odds were it wasn't a compliment. Arguing wouldn't serve much purpose when they both agreed that she was right, though. He'd had an opportunity to inform Kingsfeld that his wife neither appreciated nor deserved inane, patronizing, clichéd compliments, and he hadn't taken it.

On the other hand, he hadn't forgotten she'd been chatting with Kilcairn, and that she'd managed to turn the conversation conveniently away from that little fact. "Whose recital was that tomorrow?"

Victoria was silent for a heartbeat. "Susan Maugrie's."

"And will Alexandra Balfour be attending?"

"Yes."

"Perhaps I'll join you, as well."

"And perhaps one day you'll trust me a little. Not everyone has a hidden reason for everything they do and every conversation they have."

He sighed. "I wish I could believe that."

"I hope someday you'll be able to," she returned in the same tone. "Out of everyone in London, only one person shot your brother."

"That only makes the rest of them not guilty of that particular crime. It doesn't make them innocent."

"What are you two gabbing about?" Kit asked, moving ahead to their box as they reached the top of the stairs, and pulling the curtain aside for Augusta. "You look serious as sinners on Sunday."

"Just a difference of opinion," Sinclair said, maneuvering so he could take a seat at the back of the box, in the shadows.

Augusta stopped beside the same chair he meant to claim for himself. "Nonsense, Sinclair. Sit beside your wife."

"You and Victoria are far more fond of the opera than Kit and I. If I sat in front, I would have to stay awake."

"Then I'll sit in the back, as well," Victoria stated. "Everyone stares at me when I sit in the front anyway, and it's terribly distracting."

"We can't all lurk in the shadows," Kit grumbled. "We'll look like fugitives."

"Quite right," Augusta agreed. "Christopher, sit here beside your grandmother." She plunked herself down in the rear chair.

Sin stifled an oath. Victoria was beginning to look at him suspiciously, so he held one of the front seats for her while she gracefully seated herself. Sending up a fervent prayer that Sophie L'Anjou wouldn't cast her eyes in his direction, he took the chair beside her.

A footman provided them with glasses of port, and Sin resisted the urge to down his at once. Getting drunk and falling over the balcony railing would not be the ideal way to avoid Sophie's notice.

The curtain rose, and he sank a little lower in his chair. The theater was full to the rafters, with even Prinny and his entourage occupying the royal's box on the opposite side of the stage. Prince George, though, seemed more interested in viewing the crowd than the opera. Female patrons, in particular, received an intense scrutiny through his jeweled opera glasses.

The crowd applauded as Sophie L'Anjou glided onto the stage and made a deep curtsy that showed off most of her spectacular bosom to any interested parties in the audience. Slouching still further, Sinclair returned his attention to the Regent.

The jeweled glasses had become fixed on Sophie's bosom as she began her first aria of the evening, and Sinclair stifled a smile. With royalty in the audience, Sophie wasn't likely to waste her time seeking out anyone else. Below the prince on the orchestra level, though, half a dozen young men had their attention aimed in another direction entirely.

Locating the object of their interest was easy, since he was seated beside her. Victoria kept her gaze on the stage, her slender body slightly forward in her chair as she watched and listened. Sinclair felt so drawn to her that his fingers twitched with the desire to pull the clips from her long black hair and let it cascade over his hands. Her lips, painted the same color as her dress for the evening, beckoned him with their soft, supple warmth.

As though sensing the heat of his gaze, she turned her head and looked at him. "What?" she mouthed.

He smiled. "You."

She blushed. "Shh. You're missing the story."

Sin shook his head. "I'm not missing anything," he whispered.

"Vixen?" Christopher whispered, leaning forward and gripping the back of Sin's chair. "That girl—Lucy—she's not serious about anyone, is she?"

"I'm afraid she is, Kit."

"Blast it. Who was that other one? Marguerite? She batted her eyes at me, I think."

"That's because she's half blind," Sin muttered, grinning.

"She is not," Victoria protested. "She's just shy."

"So was she batting her eyes, or not?" Leaning forward as he was, Kit didn't notice Augusta until she reached over and cuffed him on the back of the head. "Dash it, Grandmama," he protested. "It took me an hour to get my hair to look this way. It's the very latest, you know."

"You could've gotten straight out of bed and achieved the same look," Augusta replied calmly. "Now hush."

Victoria opened her fan and lifted it to her face. Her shoulders shook with her silent laughter, and her eyes sparkled as she glanced at Sinclair again. "She may have been batting, Kit," she whispered. "I'll find out for you."

"Splendid," Christopher returned, then had to dodge another swipe from his grandmother. "All right, all right. I'll be quiet. You have no sense of romance, Grandmama."

"And you have no sense at all, Christopher James Grafton. Hush."

They did settle down after that, and the remainder of the opera passed uneventfully. Prinny vanished as soon as the curtain fell, no doubt to introduce himself to Mademoiselle L'Anjou. That was fine with Sinclair.

"Did you enjoy it?" he asked Victoria as she took his arm.

"It was wonderful," she returned, smiling. "My parents rarely let me attend. They thought it was too frivolous, I suppose."

Sinclair made a mental note to purchase the next available box. "If they thought opera was frivolous, I'm surprised anything in the world could have convinced them to let me near you."

Her expression grew more somber. "They thought I was too frivolous, as well."

He put his hand over hers where it rested on his arm. "That is their mistake, and their loss. And my gain."

"Hmm. I continue to be impressed by your better qualities," she mused, her violet eyes dancing.

If she didn't agree to spend the night with him tonight, he was going to break down her door. "I continue to be surprised that I have better qualities."

At the foot of the wide staircase, Augusta paused to wait for them. "Will you come for dinner tomorrow night?" She must have seen the hesitation in his eyes, because she turned to Victoria before he could draw a breath to respond. "The responses to the invitations have begun to arrive, and I hear you have a talent for arranging seating charts, my dear."

"Who told you that?"

"Lady Chilton." Augusta smiled. "I support the orphaned children's fund."

The two of them immediately began chatting about charitable causes, while Kit prattled to his brother about some horse race he wanted to attend, and Sin mentally undressed his wife. When he was finally able to pry them apart, he said a quick good evening to his relations and escorted Victoria to their waiting coach. As he handed her in, the driver leaned over the top to look at him.

"It's a mad crush, my lord. It'll take me a few minutes just to get out of this."

Sin nodded. "Take your time, Gibbs. We're in no hurry."

The accompanying footman and the driver glanced at one another, and he thought he caught their knowing grins as he stepped inside and pulled the door closed. Just in case they hadn't caught his meaning, he closed the flimsy latch on the inside of the door, as well.

"What are you doing?" Victoria asked, unbuttoning her gloves.

"Let me do that," he said, drawing her hand forward. Slowly, he unbuttoned the second delicate button and pulled the soft kid glove from her fingers.

She was staring at him, her color scarlet. *"In the carriage?"*

"Yes. Definitely in the carriage." As the coach rolled forward a few feet, he took her other hand and rendered it naked, as well.

"Sinclair, won't they know?" She gestured toward the driver's perch.

"Probably." Leaning forward, he unfastened the clasp of her cloak and let it slide down the seat behind her.

"But—"

"Kiss me," he interrupted, tugging her forward.

Victoria half fell into his arms, pushing him back in his seat and meeting his mouth with a passion he'd begun to think he'd dreamed.

Hot, unrestrained desire inflamed him. She was his. Even as her mouth molded with his, she was undoing his waistcoat, as hungry for him as he was for her. Moaning, she started to tug at his coat, but he put his hands over hers and returned them to his chest.

"No need for that in here," he murmured, sweeping his arms behind her and swiftly undoing the first few buttons down her back. Tugging the loosened gown forward, he bent his head and claimed her left breast, caressing her nipple with his lips and his tongue.

She arched against him, gasping. He was already hard, and as he repeated his attentions to her other breast he coaxed her up onto her knees, gathering her heavy skirts into his hands and lifting them. She immediately realized what he was doing, and bent forward to unfasten his breeches and free him.

With a low, throaty chuckle she straddled him, and he guided her down onto his lap. He groaned as he entered her, reveling in the hot, tight slide of her flesh around him.

"Like this?" she panted, rising up a little and then sinking down again.

"Just like that," he encouraged, grinning. "You learn fast."

She repeated the rising and sinking motion, watching his face intently with half-closed, glittering eyes. "Are there other ways to . . . do this? Other ways for us to be together?"

Good God, he'd made it to heaven, after all. "Several," he groaned. "Dozens."

She kissed him again, hot and open-mouthed. "I want you to show me all of them," she panted.

"Repeatedly." He groaned again, lifting his hips to meet her and praying that he lived long enough to do so.

Victoria opened her eyes. Her head lay on Sinclair's bare chest, which rose and fell softly with his light breathing. Muffled beneath his ribs, she could hear the slow, steady beat of his heart.

Morning sunlight splintered through the gaps in the master bedchamber's heavy green curtains, falling across the foot of the bed like long, thin bars of precious gold. Their clothes were still piled on the floor where they'd dumped them, and Lord Baggles lay curled and sleeping in the chair by the fireplace. She hadn't even realized he'd slunk into the room.

She felt far too sated and comfortable to move, but by shifting her head just a little she could see that the dressing room door between the two bedchambers stood open.

"What is that?" Sin asked quietly, humor touching his voice.

Victoria lifted her head to look at his face. "What is what?"

He untwined his fingers from hers and pointed upward. "That."

By shifting in his arms, she could turn enough to

see the small gray parrot perched on the headboard and eyeing them. "Oh. That's Mungo Park."

"Mungo Park. After the explorer?"

"Yes. He just flew into the kitchen one day, looking half starved. Cook wanted to make parrot pie of him, but I disagreed. Strongly."

"How long do you think he's been there?"

" 'Oh, Sinclair, that feels so good,' " Mungo Park said, in a passable imitation of his mistress in the throes of passion.

"Oh, no," she squawked, mortified, and buried her face in Sin's broad chest.

Her husband gave a shout of laughter.

"That is not funny," she protested, pulling the sheet over her head.

"Yes it is," he managed, wrapping his strong arms around her and laughing harder.

" 'Oh, Sinclair, that feels so good.' "

"How long do parrots live?" he mused.

"About another five minutes."

He hauled the sheet down again, pulled her further up along his lean, muscular body, and kissed her. "You did say that several times. You can hardly blame Mungo Park for noticing."

"My mother thought it was terrible when I taught him to say 'Dash it all.' She'll drop dead if she hears this."

"She did give birth to you," he countered. "Your parents have had intercourse on at least one occasion."

"Yes, but I doubt they enjoyed it."

He lifted her so he could look into her eyes. "Did you?"

" 'Oh, touch me there again, Sinclair.' "

A grin tugged at her husband's sensuous lips and he glanced up at Mungo. "I wasn't talking to you."

Victoria started to answer him with an enthusiastic affirmative, but with the parrot still perched over their heads, she thought better of it. She twisted free of his loose grip and squirmed closer. "I never imagined," she whispered into his ear. "And I could never imagine being with anyone but you."

Sin gently brushed a lock from her face and searched her gaze for a long moment with his deep, whiskey-colored eyes. "Thank you," he murmured.

Just then Roman rapped on the door, and Henrietta and Grosvenor trotted into the room, barking at the intrusion.

"Stay here," her husband said, and rose. Pulling a blanket off the back of a chair, he wrapped it around his waist and knotted it, then waded through the dogs and cats and opened the door.

Victoria felt like barking at Roman herself. Pulling the blanket up to her neck, she watched Sinclair as he and Roman spoke, her husband dangerous-looking even barefoot and with nothing but a knitted blanket around his waist. He let everyone think he was a scapegrace and a wastrel, but seeing him like that, natural and unguarded and at ease, she didn't know how anyone could mistake him for anything but a patriot who had risked his life for his country more times than he would probably ever tell her.

She was going to help him, whether he wanted her assistance or not. Until he solved this murder, he would never be able to trust anyone—not even her, not completely. And until he had put this behind him, she would never have all of him, as she had for a few moments last night, when he'd been briefly able to forget everything but her. Maybe she was being selfish, but she wanted that Sinclair Grafton. And if it took finding a murderer to have him, then so be it.

Chapter 11

"Lucien, do you have a moment?"

Lord Kilcairn looked up from his billiards table. "Alexandra isn't here," he said, and returned to lining up his shot. "She and cousin Rose went shopping."

Victoria stayed in the doorway. "I wanted to speak to you actually."

"Then grab a stick."

That was as much of an invitation as she was likely to get from him, so she pulled a billiards cue off the rack on the wall and approached the table. "You know all sorts of nefarious people, don't you?"

The earl took his shot, missed, and straightened. "Not as many as I used to, but I can probably find a scalawag or an assassin or two without much difficulty. Why?"

Leaning over the table, Victoria carefully lined up the cue, made her shot, and sank the ball. "Oh, I'm splendid at this, aren't I?"

"Beginner's luck."

She straightened, ready to launch into her speech, but Lucien motioned her to take another shot. "I have something of a problem," she said, sizing up the table again.

"So I gathered. What can I do for you?"

Her shot missed, and she moved out of the way as Lucien walked around the table. "I'm not certain. What did you know of Thomas Grafton?"

"Althorpe? Not much. We didn't socialize." He made his shot. "What is it you want to know? Personal, or professional?"

"Both. I'm . . . assisting Sinclair with a project of sorts."

"A project involving dead relations-in-law."

She blushed. "Something like that."

He leaned on his cue. "I don't know who killed Althorpe, if that's what you're after, but in the months before he died, he didn't make any new friends in Parliament."

Eventually she would learn simply to ask Lucien a direct question instead of leading up to it with polite, roundabout chitchat. "Why is that?"

"A great many of the old titles have holdings in France. He wouldn't acknowledge the difference between keeping a four-hundred-year-old piece of land and actively engaging in commerce with Bonaparte loyalists. Some of them didn't like the implication that they were traitors because they chose not to divest themselves of everything French."

"Did he stop at implications?"

"In public he did. Privately, I don't know." The earl shrugged. "You might ask Kingsfeld or Lady Jane Netherby about that. They socialized."

There *had* been a female involved. "I'll do that. If you think of anything else, will you let me know?"

He nodded and went back to his shot. "I'll do that."

As she turned for the door, though, he straightened again. "Vixen?"

She stopped. "Yes?"

"Just remember what they say about curiosity."

Victoria smiled. "Meow."

She knew exactly where Lady Jane Netherby resided, but it took her a full day to arrange for a casual, coincidental meeting over some new French fabrics at Newton's. Waiting until Lucy and Marguerite were occupied with hair ribbons, she suddenly became interested in calico fabrics, as that was what Lady Jane was looking at.

"The blue definitely complements your eyes," she said, smiling.

Lady Jane, a tall, classically featured lady in her late twenties, lifted the bolt of fabric again. "Do you think so? I thought it might do for a spring walking dress."

Victoria nodded. "That's a fetching idea. You didn't see any gray or violet patterns, did you? I would do the same thing myself."

"Welfield, didn't you say you had some gray in the back?"

The clerk nodded. "I'll fetch it right away, my lady."

"Thank you." Victoria held out her hand. "I'm Victoria, Lady Althorpe."

The auburn-haired woman's smile faltered as she returned the handshake. "Lady Jane Netherby. You married Thomas Grafton's brother."

"Yes, Sinclair. You knew Thomas?"

Lady Jane lifted another bolt of fabric, holding it up to the window's light. "Yes. We were friends."

"I knew him only a little," Victoria returned. "But I did like him. It's so sad, to learn only after someone is gone that they would have been someone you would like to have known better."

The taller woman's wan smile returned. "Indeed. Knowing someone too well, though, has its own drawbacks."

"How so?" Victoria asked, taking the gray calico from the clerk as he returned. Was she being warned off? Or was Sinclair making her paranoid?

"Everyone has faults, Lady Althorpe. While someone lives, their acquaintances see whatever the individual wishes seen. After someone dies, though, their reputation becomes what everyone else chooses to make of it."

"You mean if someone looks for ill they'll find ill, and vice versa."

"Exactly." Lady Jane summoned Welfield again. "I'll take ten yards of the blue one, Welfield. Have it sent to Madame Treveau's dress shop, if you please."

"Yes, my lady."

The older woman offered her hand to Victoria again. "I apologize, but I have an engagement this afternoon. It was very pleasant to meet you."

"And you," Victoria said warmly, watching the lady out of the store and still not certain whether she'd been given a message or whether Lady Jane Netherby was simply odd. Whichever it was, Jane knew something.

She wanted to ask Sinclair his opinion, but then he would know she was still investigating. She hadn't promised to stop, but she knew he assumed she had. He still had secrets himself, though, so keeping this one simply made them even.

Pondering Lady Jane's words, she returned to her friends. "That one's pretty, Marguerite," she said, pointing at one of the dozen hair ribbons her friend had draped over her arm.

"Yes, I thought so, too, if I wear the yellow silk."

"To what?"

"To your ball, of course. Only I wore yellow at the opera last week, so perhaps I should wear the green and ivory instead."

"The yellow silk is prettier," Lucy countered.

"Yes, but I don't want him to think I wear nothing but yellow. He'll begin to call me 'the daffodil' or something."

Victoria frowned. " 'He?' Which 'he' are you talking about?"

"Kit Grafton, I'll wager," Lucy said slyly, giggling.

"Lucy!"

"Well, you've talked about no one else for a week. Who else could it be?"

"Kit? Really?" Marguerite *had* been batting her eyes at Christopher then. He'd be relieved to know that the night at the opera hadn't been a complete waste. "He mentioned to me that he was fond of yellow." Or he would become fond of it, as soon as Victoria informed him of his preference.

"I'm buying the yellow ribbon then," Marguerite announced.

Lucy giggled again. "What are you going to wear, Vixen?"

"I hadn't really thought about it."

"But it's tomorrow night! You always plan what you're going to wear weeks ahead of time."

"Well, this time we'll all be surprised."

As they continued with their shopping along fashionable Bond Street, though, she kept thinking about what Lucy had said. Ever since she'd debuted, she'd been in a frenzy: teas, luncheons, balls, recitals, and soirees, one after the other. She was popular, and she knew the silly things men liked to converse about—that was easy, since their favorite topic was invariably themselves. But even with her days and nights and every waking moment filled with things to do, she'd been utterly and deathly bored.

Now, though, her social calendar had slowed a little, and she'd used the open spaces for more important things. Charity luncheons, bringing clothes and food to the underprivileged, and helping Sinclair all took up the same amount of time she'd spent before, but with one gaping difference: the days did not bore her any longer. If nothing else, she owed Sin for that.

When she returned to Grafton House, Milo informed her that Lord Althorpe was out in the stables. She went to find him, smiling to herself as she decided how she wanted to thank him—though that depended on whether any of the grooms were about.

Thankfully, when she pushed the squeaky door open and stepped into the cool dimness of the stable, he was there alone, leaning over the stall door and feeding Old Joe an apple.

"Good afternoon," she said, her pulse beginning to race as it always did when she was alone with him.

"How was shopping?" he asked, leaving the stall and coming to meet her.

"Very productive. How is Old Joe?"

"Now that he's begun to fatten up a little, someone could almost mistake him for a horse." He slid his arm across her shoulders, tucking her against his side with a familiar possessiveness. "What are you going to do with him?"

"Don't you have a stud herd at Althorpe?"

Sin raised an eyebrow. "I believe I do, but I am not letting him loose with the mares to make little Old Joes everywhere."

Victoria laughed. "I'll think of something then."

He started them toward the door, but she halted, glancing up at the loft. Still no stableboys.

"What is it?"

She ran both hands down his chest, feeling the play of the muscles across his hard, flat stomach, and stopping at his belt. "Where are all your employees?" she asked.

"Errands," he answered promptly. "Mrs. Twaddle is making apple tarts for dinner. I say we go steal them while they're hot."

"You're so domestic," she cooed, and unfastened his belt.

"Jesus," he whispered, clear surprise in his amber eyes. "I've created a monster."

"Kiss me," she murmured, already hot and shivery for his knowing touch.

"Inside the house," he stated, putting his hands on her shoulders and turning her back toward the large double doors.

As she spun back again, she glimpsed something for a moment before it was gone in the deep gloom in the corner. A sleeve of dark superfine, unless she was greatly mistaken. Apparently she'd discovered another of Sinclair's clandestine meetings. Since he'd spent the last eight nights with her, he had to be holding them some other time.

Annoyance flashed. Obviously he still didn't trust her a whit. And obviously she'd become completely befuddled by him if she hadn't realized he was still meeting his mysterious friends directly behind her back.

"Let's go in," he repeated.

Victoria leaned back against him and wriggled her bottom. "What's wrong with the stable?" she asked, just loudly enough so that their unseen audience could hear.

"Straw and dirt," he said. The words sounded clipped, as though he had his jaw clenched. "I'm sure we can find somewhere cleaner and more comfortable. You can tell me all about your day."

She wriggled again. "I don't want to talk." Stifling a grin as she felt his muscles jump, she bent forward at the waist. "Oh, dear, I have a stone in my shoe."

"You little . . ." he began, then stopped. "Inside. Now."

"But you promised me another lesson."

"I think you're learning fast enough on your own, Vixen." His hands encircled her waist, and he drew her upright again. "Inside, where we can take our time," he murmured, pulling her closer and shifting his own hips.

Well, she'd succeeded in arousing him. Now she wasn't certain what to do next. She certainly didn't want him falling on her with his friends watching. Victoria turned in his arms to face him. "There are two things you can show me, Sinclair. One of them is your friends hiding behind those bales of hay."

He scowled. "What are you talking about?"

"Stop playing games," she snapped. "I'm not an idiot." She jabbed her finger toward the corner. "I saw at least one of your friends, over there."

"Just now?"

"Yes, just now."

He let her go and launched himself over the bales of hay. Straw and dust exploded into the air, and someone yelped.

Gasping, Victoria grabbed a rake and charged around the bales. And nearly skewered the stranger Sin flung toward the door.

"No, Victoria!" Sinclair bellowed.

Shrieking, she heaved the rake sideways and managed to turn the pointy end away and just clip the fellow across the shoulder with the stout handle. His solid, off-balance weight against it knocked her over, and the three of them landed in a tangled heap of limbs with her on the bottom.

"Damnation, Wally, get off my wife!" Sinclair snarled, and the constricting weight left her chest.

Victoria sat up, dazed, as Sinclair knelt beside her. "My goodness," she panted.

"Are you all right?" he asked brusquely, brushing straw from her hair and running his hands down her arms.

"Yes, I'm fine. Gadzooks."

"I'm not fine," the stranger said, rolling into a sitting position and holding his right hand with his left. "You dislocated my finger, Sin."

"You're lucky I didn't break it off. I warned you about your damned tricks."

"I was just—"

"Shut up and wait here."

Sinclair scooped Victoria into his arms and stood. Before she could utter another word, he strode out of the stable toward the kitchen entrance at the back of the house.

"I'm fine. Really," she protested.

He didn't answer. His lean face was white, taut with

either anger or worry, or a mixture of both. Without ceremony he kicked open the door and carried her through the kitchen. Mrs. Twaddle and the cook's assistants gaped, and Victoria sent them a small smile and a halfhearted wave.

"Send Jenny up to Lady Althorpe's bedchamber at once," he barked and took her up the servants' back stairs.

"Sinclair, this is ridiculous. I'm a bit dirty, but otherwise I am completely sound. Completely."

Her bedchamber door stood open, which was fortunate since he looked ready to break it down if it wasn't. Gently he set her on the bed, then stepped to the bedstand to fetch the washbasin and cloth lying there. As he wet the cloth and lifted it toward her face, she caught his wrist.

"Stop that. Talk to me."

He shook his head tightly, the muscles of his jaw clenching. Pulling his hand free, he straightened and paced back and forth.

"You might have been hurt," he managed, his voice a low, rumbling growl.

"But I wasn't."

Sin gestured in the direction of the stable yard. "You saw someone lurking in the stable, and you didn't say anything. You *flirted* with me."

"I knew it was one of your—"

"You *thought* it was one of my friends."

Victoria swallowed. She'd seen him angry before, but never like this; never so furious he seemed almost out of control. She was frightened—not of him, but for him. "I'm sorry I've upset you. The next time I see someone lurking, I'll tell you. I promise."

"That is not—" He stopped, then took a deep breath

and knelt at her feet. "That is not the point," he re-peated in a quieter voice. "If that hadn't been damned Wally out there, you might not have had a second chance to make the right choice."

She stared at him. Sinclair wasn't angry that he might have looked foolish, or that he'd caused a scene in front of the servants. He was upset because she might have been hurt. Slowly she reached out to cup his face with hands that had begun to tremble.

"I'm all right," she whispered, an unbidden tear run-ning down her cheek. "I'm sorry. I didn't realize—"

Brushing her hands aside, he rose up and captured her mouth in a fierce, possessive kiss. "I won't lose you," he murmured.

Victoria flung her arms around him, returning his kisses twofold. Slowly Sinclair became aware that Ro-man, Jenny, Milo, and what looked like half the house-hold staff stood crowded in the doorway, but he couldn't seem to let go of his wife. They'd been damned lucky this afternoon; one or both of them might very easily have ended the day dead. He might have lost her to the same murderer who'd taken his brother, and he would have been helpless to stop it.

He felt her lithe body stiffen as she, too, realized they had an audience. Reluctantly he released her and stood. "Jenny, Lady Althorpe took a spill."

The maid hurried forward. "I'll see to her at once, my lord."

"You do that." With a last look at his wife, Sin turned for the door.

"Sin?" Roman muttered as he passed.

"Come with me." His valet's presence was the only thing that would keep him from killing Wally.

To his credit, Wally was still seated on one of the

hay bales, nursing the fingers of his right hand. He
shot to his feet as Sinclair strode inside, Roman on his
heels.

"Sin, I thought you knew I was there," the spy
blurted, flushing. "Really. I only ducked when Vixen
came in, so she wouldn't—"

"Roman, take a look at his finger."

"Aye, Sin."

"But Sin, I didn't—"

"Wally, you'd best have a damned good reason for
being here, because if you don't, I'm going to send
you back to Weigh House Street in pieces."

"Crispin sent me." While Roman took charge of his
right hand, Wally dug into his pocket with his left.
"Here."

Still glaring, Sinclair took the missive and opened
it. He swiftly read it, then slowed down and read it
again. "Fine," he said stiffly, crumpling the note and
shoving it into his own pocket. "Just get going before
anyone else sees you."

"Everything all right, Sin?" Roman asked.

"Yes. Everything's wonderful. Blasted, bloody
wonderful."

No wonder Crispin had declined to deliver the note
himself. They'd cleared Kilcairn, but it was like Crispin to make an extra check or two, just in case. And
it was like Vixen to go and visit the earl for twenty
minutes while his wife was away. They were friends,
after all. It abruptly seemed past time that he became
better acquainted with the Earl of Kilcairn Abbey,
himself.

Arranging to meet him was easier than he'd expected. He knew Kilcairn frequented White's, and

when he strolled into the club at half past ten that evening, the earl was there, seated with Lord Belton, Henning, and a few others.

As Henning saw him approaching, he stood. "Ah, I forgot. Promised I'd introduce Charles Blumton to the Duke of Wycliffe this evening," he stammered, and hurried off.

"Lucky Wycliffe," Lucien murmured, and Lord Belton chuckled.

Sinclair gestured at the vacated seat beside Kilcairn. "Do you mind?"

The earl gazed at him. "Actually, yes, I do."

Out of the corner of his eye, Sin spied Crispin, seated at the opposite end of the room and obviously unhappy to see him in such close proximity to Kilcairn. "Any particular reason?"

Rumblings started around the edges of the room, and inwardly Sinclair sighed. Of all Kilcairn's group, the earl was the only one with whom he would have thought twice about picking a fight, but he wasn't going to leave without finding out what he wanted to know.

"People you sit down to talk with always seem to end up with bloody noses," Kilcairn drawled, sipping his brandy. "I insist on a flag of truce before I allow you anywhere near me."

Sinclair looked at him for a moment, adjusting his opinion of the earl upward. "Fair enough. Any specific boundaries?"

"White's is good enough for me."

"Agreed."

Kilcairn gestured at Henning's empty seat. "Join us, then. Robert's been prattling about his wife and impending offspring, though, so I imagine you'll be bored senseless within minutes."

"You said you were looking forward to the birth," Lord Belton protested.

"Yes, so you'd stop talking about it." His eyes dancing, the earl sat back in his chair and nudged a half-empty box of cigars in Sin's direction.

"What about you, Althorpe?" Belton said. "Are you planning a family?"

"I really hadn't thought about it," Sinclair answered, abruptly struck by the vision of dark-haired little girls with Victoria's eyes playing in the morning room. Sweet Lucifer, he *was* becoming domestic.

"I would say not, with the way you've got the Vixen running every which way," Kilcairn commented. "Eventually she will begin hinting about it, though. They all do."

Sinclair frowned. "What do you mean, 'Vixen running every which way'?"

"Uh-oh," Belton muttered and stood. "I'm going over to see what Bromley's up to."

"I'm with you, Robert," Lord Daubner said, rising as well. In a moment, Sin and Kilcairn were alone at the table.

"Hm," the earl mused. "Cowards." He emptied his glass of brandy and gestured for another. "What're you drinking?"

"Whiskey."

"An odd drink for an Englishman who spends all his time gadding about France."

"And you smoke an American cigar." Sinclair leaned forward. "We can discuss our loyalties when the truce is over. At the moment, I'd like to know what you were talking about in regards to my wife."

The earl looked at him. "She told me she was working on a project for you. If you want to know anything else, you'll have to ask her. I don't gossip about my friends."

Damnation. He knew she'd been entirely too quiet. And now she'd let yet another person in on his secrets—and put him in that person's debt. "Kilcairn, I have to ask you for your discretion in this."

Kilcairn shrugged. "I'd think less of you if you didn't want to find your brother's killer. At least I presume that's what this is about."

"That's none of your affair."

The earl set his snifter down on the table. "I consider Vixen to be a good friend. And she wouldn't have married a fool, whatever she might have been caught doing with him."

"Is that a compliment?"

"Of sorts, I suppose. I don't know exactly what you're about, Althorpe, and I haven't pried into your loyalties because she seems to like you. If you need my help, ask me for it. I won't gossip, as I said, but I will tell you what I know." Stretching again, the earl stood. "Now. My wife's begun hinting, so I'd best go home and take care of matters."

"No, Mungo," Victoria said patiently. " 'Dash it all.' Say it."

" 'Ooh, like a mare and a stallion.' "

She closed her eyes, knowing her cheeks must be scarlet. "You were listening again last night, weren't you, you evil little bird?"

" '*Now*, Sin. I want you ins—' "

"Victoria?" Sinclair called, rapping on her sitting room door.

"Come in," she returned, relieved at the interruption. As Sin stalked into the room, though, relief sagged into concern. Something had made him angry again, and odds were it was her. "How are your mysterious friends?" she asked, in case anything could still distract him.

"I don't know. I went to see your friend."

She fed Mungo Park the last bit of biscuit. "Which friend?"

"Kilcairn."

"Kil—" Victoria snapped her mouth shut. "I thought you didn't like him."

"I didn't. And since he told me you've been carrying on your little investigation behind my back, I'm still not overly fond of him."

Some very colorful profanities danced through her mind, but Mungo Park was still in the room. "I didn't go behind your back." Striding forward, she grabbed his hand and pulled him into her bedchamber, closing the door so the parrot couldn't overhear. "I'm helping you find Thomas's killer."

"I asked you not to do that."

"Because you don't want to see me hurt. Talking to Lucien Balfour is not the least bit dangerous." She couldn't miss his skeptical expression. "Well, maybe it is, a little, but not for me."

"Victoria," he said, abruptly relaxing his shoulders. "I don't want to fight with you." He sank onto the edge of her bed. "But neither am I going to let you continue this investigation. Not only could you be hurt, but you might alert whoever murdered Thomas, and I would never get my hands on him."

The change in tactic surprised her. If he expected her to apologize and become his meek little useless wife, though, he hadn't learned much about her at all.

"How important is finding Thomas's killer to you, Sinclair?" she asked quietly, sitting beside him and lifting Henrietta onto her lap so she could scratch the little disheveled dog behind the ears.

"You know how important it is," he said a little sharply. "Or I thought you did, anyway."

"I do know—very well. So we both agree that it's the most important thing in the world to you."

"Then why do you insist on become entangled with it?"

"*Because* it's the most important thing in the world to you." She looked down, hoping he couldn't hear the hurt in her voice. "It's not a pleasant feeling to be shoved aside. I know you don't want me to get hurt, but it's more than that. And I know we were trapped into this marriage, and that it's been an inconvenience. Nevertheless, I . . ." She stopped.

"You what?" he asked quietly.

She was falling in love with him. But that was not what this conversation was about. "I admire what you're doing," she said instead, "and what you've done already. People think I'm silly and flighty and dim, and maybe you do, too. But I'm acquainted with people you're not, and I can speak with people who would be uncomfortable speaking with you. I can help. I can contribute, and it hurts that you think I can't."

"I don't think you're silly and flighty," he returned in his deep, soft voice—the one that made her tremble. "And you're certainly not dim. And—"

"Then why—"

"Let me finish," he said with more volume. "I know you could help. When we first met, I thought I would want to use your assistance."

She looked up at him. His amber gaze was serious, and surprisingly compassionate, but it didn't leave her feeling any more hopeful about her chances of being included. "What changed your mind, then?"

"Henrietta, and Lord Baggles, and Mungo Park, and the children's charities, the schools, and all the other animals, people, and causes you've adopted." He smiled a little. "You even like me."

"But Sinclair—"

He held up one hand, and she subsided. Whatever his argument was, he'd obviously considered it carefully. Whether she agreed with it or not, she owed him the chance to finish.

"I do have my suspicions about who killed Thomas. You have a warm and compassionate heart, Victoria. As I realized that, I knew I couldn't expect you to help me. Not when the killer might very well turn out to be a friend—a good friend—of yours."

Her heart stopped. "Not Lucien! He would never—"

"No. Not Kilcairn. I could wish you didn't find him quite so admirable, but it's not him. You've proven my point, though. You can't even conceive that a friend of yours might be a killer."

He was right, she realized. And he was wrong. "I admit I could never believe it would be Lucien, or certain other of my friends. I'm not as naive, or as weak-hearted, as you think, though. Try me, Sinclair. Who among my friends do you suspect?"

For a long moment she feared he wouldn't tell her. That meant he would never trust her completely, and they would never have a real, true marriage—the kind that she'd always longed for, and the kind that she had begun to hope she could have with him.

Then he looked at her again. "John Madsen," he said flatly.

"*Marley?*" she blurted, before she could stop herself. He narrowed his eyes, and she pressed on before he could say she'd proved him right. "What . . . are your reasons for suspecting Lord Marley?" she forced out in a calmer voice, setting Henrietta down and folding her hands in her lap.

Sin stood up again and paced back and forth in front of her. "I'll give you the short list, on the condition that you stay out of this from now on."

It was times like this that Victoria wished she were a large, tall man, so she could simply knock her husband on the head and make him listen to reason. "Tell me first," she countered, "and then we can discuss the rest."

Over the next few moments she learned some new profanity, part of it in Portuguese and Italian, she thought, grateful that Mungo was in the other room. Finally Sinclair came to a stop in front of her.

"All right. Marley has shares in several export companies which made quite a tidy profit during the Peninsular War. Thomas opposed any dealings with France while Bonaparte had control."

"I'm sure many people opposed dealings with France then."

"I know that. But Thomas was very vocal about it. He wrote me that Marley had threatened him. And it wasn't just a portion of Marley's money that was tied up in trade, though that's the story he tells. Except for his entitled properties, all of his money was in export stocks."

She'd heard some of Marley's tirades about commerce versus country, and had thought them childish and self-centered. Now they suddenly seemed more sinister. "Marley's not rich as Croesus these days, but he's not quite a pauper either," she said quietly.

He nodded. "I know. He made it through the war fairly intact."

"I still don't see why Marley would single out your bro—"

"They used to be friends," Sinclair interrupted. "From recent comments he's made, Marley pretends their relationship never changed."

"But you know that it did."

"I know that it did." He shrugged. "There's more, as well. Marley and Thomas were both at Hoby's the day he died; Marley had been in Grafton House numerous times and knew Thomas liked to spend the evenings in his office. . . . Are you all right?"

Victoria had begun shaking. She knew Marley. She'd considered him a friend. For God's sake, she'd let him kiss her. "I . . . don't want you to think I'm incapable of believing you if I say you're wrong," she said slowly. "It's not because he's my friend, or anything like that."

"What, then?"

She could have wept from relief. He was still listening. He might think she was in error, but he was still willing to listen to what she had to say. Oh, Lord—she wasn't just falling in love with him. She'd already fallen.

"Marley likes things that are easy. Gambling is easy. Killing someone and getting away with it can't be."

"Greed and self-preservation are good motivators." Sin came forward and sank to his knees before her.

"I'm not absolutely certain—yet. But do you see why I don't want you involved?"

"Did you know that Thomas had been social with Lady Jane Netherby?"

He frowned at her. "You said you didn't know of any acquaintances."

"I didn't. I do now."

Sinclair's amber eyes darkened. "Kilcairn."

"Yes, he tends to know everything about everyone."

He remained silently at her feet, his expression distracted and thoughtful. Her heart leapt. Finally, she'd given him information that he didn't already know.

"Lady Jane Netherby," he repeated. "Are you certain?"

Victoria nodded. "And when I introduced myself to her, she reacted very oddly. In fact—"

"You *introduced* yourself to her?"

"Sinclair, I'm not completely incompetent," Victoria snapped. "I was at the same dress shop, and we were looking at the same calico fabrics. She was friendly—perhaps a little aloof, but I put it to shyness. When I said I was Lady Althorpe, though, she said something cryptic and practically bolted out the door."

He put his hands on her knees. "What did she say?"

"When she mentioned that she and Thomas had been friends, I said that I wished I'd known him better. She replied that knowing someone too well can have its drawbacks. Then she went on about how a person's reputation is theirs to control while they're alive, but after they're dead it rests in the hands of anyone who cares to speak about them."

His grip on her knees tightened. Slowly he raised himself up until their faces were only inches apart. "I knew he'd been seeing someone, but he never mentioned who it was. He kept teasing me with it—and then, of course, his letters stopped."

The pain and regret in his voice hurt to hear. Victoria cupped his face in her hands and kissed him. He leaned into her, plundering her mouth hungrily. Just as the heat skittering through her veins became molten fire, though, he sank back again.

"Get dressed," he said, standing up. "I want to introduce you to someone."

Chapter 12

By the time Sinclair and Victoria left Grafton House it was nearly midnight, and a heavy fog had settled over the streets. They didn't have far to go, so rather than attracting attention with a horse and rig, Sin took Vixen's hand and set out toward Hyde Park.

Quiet as Mayfair was this evening, Sinclair kept a firm grip on his walking cane—and the razor-sharp rapier sheathed inside the ebony wood. He wasn't about to let anything happen to Victoria.

The safest way to keep her under control would be to include her in the plotting—to a degree. He couldn't deny any longer that she'd already helped, and in more ways than her sleuthing. There were moments now, in her presence, when he felt almost human again.

They crossed into the park and Victoria edged closer to him. He resisted the urge to pull her into the protection of his arms, though; he needed to be alert, and the closer she was to him, the less clear his mind seemed to become.

At the nearest grove of oak trees, they stopped. "Lady Stanton," he called in a low voice, and caught

Victoria's surprised look. Again he read jealousy in her violet gaze, and he found it profoundly satisfying.

A wall of fog drifted before them. As it cleared a little, he caught sight of Crispin rounding a tree and making his way toward them. "Are we late?" he asked.

The big Scotsman kept his gaze on Victoria, his expression unreadable. "Nae. I'm early."

"Crispin, my wife, Victoria. Vixen, Crispin Harding."

"*You're* Lady Stanton?"

"Sometimes." Crispin turned his attention to Sinclair. "Do ye have a moment for a private word, Sin?"

Sinclair shook his head. He knew what the private word would be, and he had no desire to hear a lecture on whether he was leading this investigation with his brain or his nether regions. He was the one who usually gave that lecture. "What do you know about Lady Jane Netherby?" he asked instead.

"Netherby? She'd be the daughter of the Earl of Brumley." Harding glanced at Victoria again, obviously uncertain how much he should be saying.

"Thomas was seeing her," Sin supplied. "She seemed a bit skittish about discussing him."

"Not skittish," Victoria contributed in a low voice. "Reluctant to talk, once she realized who I was. Not just about Thomas, but about anything."

"If she was thinkin' she might be the next Lady Althorpe, meeting you might not have been very cheery for her," Crispin returned.

"Crispin, I would—"

"—appreciate if I'd look into her, anyway," the Scot finished. "Aye. Just in case you're still interested, three nobles left London by sunrise the day after the murder." He pulled a note from his pocket and handed it over.

"Who?" Sinclair asked, trying to decipher Crispin's scrawl in the darkness.

"The Duke of Highbarrow, Lord Closter, and . . ." He looked at Victoria again. "And one other," he finished acridly.

"Lord Marley, you mean," she said, holding the big man's gaze as though she discussed murder and murderers all the time.

Crispin's expression eased a little. "Aye. Lord Marley. You have anything more for me, Sin?"

Sin hesitated. The big Scot was looking for a chance to vent his anger, and Sinclair really didn't want Victoria to hear any of it. Neither, though, did he want to leave her alone. "All right. Vixen, wait right here for a moment. Don't move."

"I'm not going anywhere."

Sinclair motioned Crispin to follow him. A few paces away, beyond the shelter of the trees, he stopped. "Don't give me that look, Harding," he whispered. "I can't keep her from helping, but I can use it to our advantage."

"Ye want her to tag along, that's fine. None o' my affair. But if she makes a bad step, all of us could end up dead. Ye might've asked me and the lads before ye gave her all our secrets."

"I'm giving her what she needs to know to help me find a murderer," Sin retorted in a low voice. "When we all returned to London I thought I could just sniff around the fringes of Mayfair, but that wasn't very practical. I need to be right in the middle. I'm a part of this damned society now, and if I keep skulking about and prying, the wrong person *will* notice."

"So she's your armor for a full frontal assault. Does she know that?"

"Probably. And I'm not going to discuss it any further. Are you set for tomorrow night?"

"Aye. We'll be ready. You just go and have a grand time with your new friends." Harding turned on his heel.

"Crispin," Sin muttered at his back. "Be careful."

The big Scot paused. "You're the one who's risking his neck, Sin. I just hope ye know what you're doing."

"So do I."

Victoria jumped as he emerged from the fog. "My goodness. I almost expect Frankenstein's monster out here tonight."

"You'd probably adopt him," Sin said dryly, and was rewarded by her hushed laugh.

"Your Lady Stanton doesn't like my being here, I presume," she said.

Sinclair took her hand again. "Let's get you back inside. It's cold tonight."

"He thinks I'll do something stupid."

"No, he doesn't."

"You're not just humoring me, are you?" Victoria pulled her hand free and stopped. "You're not just pretending that I'm being helpful?"

What had it been like, he suddenly wondered, for this intelligent, beautiful young woman to spend all of her time in the company of men who addressed her perfect breasts rather than her eyes? To have someone court her diamonds and not even notice there might be a diamond beneath?

"No," he said quietly. "I'm not pretending. You'll just have to give us all a bit of time to get used to you. We're—I'm—not used to being able to trust anyone."

She nodded. "I know. There are people you can trust, though." Victoria leaned against his shoulder, both hands wrapped around his arm. "Good, honest people do exist."

"I'm beginning to believe you." He'd found one, it seemed. And he wasn't about to let her go.

Augusta's ball certainly drew an eclectic circle of guests, Victoria reflected. Lady Drewsbury's dignified friends mingled with the young gentlemen Kit had invited down from Oxford. Into the mix was added Victoria's rather wild set, or at least those who hadn't gotten into fights with her husband. Sinclair's choices occupied the fringes—his three allies, who mingled and chatted with various suspects Sin had wanted to encounter in a controlled, yet social, setting.

"This is...unexpected," Lionel Parrish commented, as he approached with a glass of Madeira for her and one for Lucy. "I hope we don't end the evening with a civil war. It would definitely be memorable, but a bit bloody as well, I would imagine."

"It's amazing," Lucy agreed. "I'd never have thought to see Lord Liverpool and Lord Halifax in the same room together without either of them throwing things."

Victoria was rather surprised herself that no one had yet called anyone else outside for a duel. "Lady Augusta is amazing."

"And so are you," Lionel pointed out. "Even your husband looks civilized."

She turned to see Sinclair, standing by the musicians and chatting with Kit and one of his young friends.

He looked more than civilized; he looked delicious. Her pulse jumped and sped. "Yes, he cleans up rather well."

"And you convinced Marley to come," Parrish continued, surprise touching his dry voice. "That was a . . . brave choice on your part."

A shiver of an entirely different sort ran down her spine as she caught sight of Marley, encircled by their usual set of cronies. She'd sent him a personal invitation at Sinclair's request, though it had made her feel dirty and nauseous to do it. Sinclair had called it a compromise of conscience. The offhand statement made her wonder how many times he'd had to compromise parts of himself to accomplish a task.

"May I steal Vixen away for a moment?" Sin's warm hands slid down her shoulders.

Whether he was humoring her or not, over the past day or two she'd begun to feel part of his life instead of apart from it. It was a heady feeling.

"Oh, yes," Lucy said, chuckling. "We have to go tease Marguerite, anyway."

"Tease her about what?" Sinclair asked Victoria, as Lucy and Lionel departed.

"About batting her eyes at your brother, I would imagine," she supplied.

"Kit? What . . . Oh. I don't think he's quite ready for matrimony, yet."

"Hmm. Sometimes it just sneaks up on you when you least expect it."

"I see." Gently he kneaded her shoulders. "And what might one expect if this happens?"

She wanted to lean back against him and have him wrap his strong arms around her. "One never knows," she murmured. "It's very . . . interesting, I hear."

His soft chuckle vibrated deep inside her. This was what being married was supposed to be like: two people with eyes only for one another, the rest of the world and killers and disapproving parents and friends be damned. Smiling, she resisted the urge simply to close her eyes and let the moment sink into her.

A heartbeat later she wished she had closed her eyes, but it was too late. She straightened as reality intruded. "Your Crispin is scowling at us."

Sinclair cleared his throat and released her, stepping around to face her. "Right. Is she here, yet?"

Victoria knew immediately to whom he was referring. They had sent one additional belated invitation, to Lady Jane Netherby. "No. I told you she wouldn't come."

"That's part of the test, too. It all means something."

"I just wish we knew what."

"We will. Eventually."

She nodded. "Whom do you want me to begin with?"

"I thought Lord and Lady Hastor would be a good choice. He and Thomas went hunting together on several occasions."

Victoria looked in their direction and had to stifle her sudden frown. "But they're chatting with my parents."

He smiled, his eyes dancing with cynical humor. "Well, I can't very well speak to them then, can I?"

"I suppose not. What's your plan?"

"If it makes you feel any better, while you're suffering your torture, I thought I might have a little chat with Kilcairn."

"Really?"

"If you trust him that much, I suppose I can trust him a little."

She wanted to throw her arms around him and kiss him. He trusted her. Not only that, but he'd admitted it. "Good luck," she murmured, trying to keep from grinning like a halfwit.

"Let me know if you see Lady Jane." Leaning down, he brushed his lips across her cheek and then went to find Lucien.

Usually, parties like this were beyond easy—they left her bored and restless and feeling like a new dress in a window display. Tonight, though, nervousness and tension sizzled through her as she moved from group to group spread throughout the Drewsbury House ballroom, the drawing room, and an upstairs study. Nothing was the same. Every word she spoke, everything she heard, was sifted through her senses for one purpose: to learn something about Thomas Grafton's murder.

After only an hour she was ready to run screaming into the street. When she looked for deceit and lies, she seemed to see them everywhere. Sinclair had managed to do this all day, every day, for five years. No wonder he regarded everyone with such jaded cynicism.

"Good evening, Lady Althorpe."

She jumped, nearly spilling her glass of Madeira down the front of Lord Hauverton's coat. "Lord Kingsfeld," she said, hanging desperately onto her tired smile. "We'd given up on seeing you this evening."

"I meant to be here earlier." The earl smiled. "I owe you an apology, it seems."

"We began badly," she said, determined to be congenial. "Let us speak no more of it."

He took her hand and bowed over it. "You are a gracious lady. Might I impose on you to guide me to Sin?"

Her annoyance deepened, but she'd never been one to shrink from a challenge. "It's no imposition. Lord and Lady Hauverton, if you'll excuse me?"

"I hope Sin explained my mistake to you," Kingsfeld said as he strolled beside her. "Surely you must be accustomed to the men of your acquaintance reminding you of your beauty."

"As I said, the past is the past. Today, we'll speak of today. Where is Kingsfeld Park? Sinclair never said."

"Staffordshire. A more lovely place you've never seen. It even rivals Althorpe, if I do say so myself."

"Did you spend much time at Althorpe, then? Or Thomas at Kingsfeld? Wiltshire and Staffordshire are quite distant from one another."

"I visited when I could. Thomas never left Althorpe until the Season and his duties with Parliament demanded it, and then he returned to it as quickly as he could."

That made sense, if Thomas was worried about missing one of Sinclair's scattered letters. "I look forward to seeing the estate. Sinclair and Kit both speak very fondly of it. I've seen some of Thomas's sketches, so I have an idea, but there's nothing like seeing a place with one's own eyes."

"Ah, yes, Thomas's doodles." Kingsfeld chuckled. "I'm a firm believer in not keeping anything about that could cause undue embarrassment in the event of one's untimely death."

"Did you ever view any of his sketches? I don't see how they could cause anything but pride in his abilities, and sorrow that he didn't have time to further develop his talents."

He smiled. "So you consider yourself knowledgeable in the arts?"

Her annoyance deepened. Though his continued belief in her dim-wittedness wasn't surprising, it grated considerably. Neither did she feel inclined to be quite as polite toward him as she had been the last time. This time, Sinclair already had whatever information he needed from the patronizing twit. "Knowledgeable? Not so much about pencil and charcoal sketches, but I have advised several of my friends regarding landscapes. I'm a particular fan of Gainsborough's garden portraits."

"I find them highly romanticized and far too softhearted and flattering."

"I thought the object of art was to reflect and capture beauty."

"The *objet d'art*, my dear, is to make the artist money."

"Money might be a product, but art is its own *raison d'etre*. Many things are." She felt like sticking her tongue out at him. Her skill at French could stand against anyone's—except, Sin's, perhaps.

"You sound like Thomas. I believe nothing exists unless it has some use. Conversely, something which is or becomes useless is always discarded."

"Is your argument then that nothing and no one is useful unless they somehow benefit you with a physical, monetary profit?"

"Don't try to understand it, my dear. Women are simply unable to grasp the finer points of economics."

Victoria smiled through clenched teeth. "Which would make women useless, by your own argument. I shall therefore leave you to Sinclair."

Stopping beside her husband, she didn't bother trying to disguise the fury in her eyes. He would notice her annoyance whether she tried to hide it or not, anyway.

"Vixen?" he said, lifting an eyebrow.

"Lord Kingsfeld desires to speak with you," she said flatly, and left them.

Astin Hovarth was a complete ass. She should have ended the conversation by calling him an ape and kicking him very hard in his unmentionables.

"My goodness," Alexandra Balfour murmured, slipping her arm around Victoria's, "were you aware that you have smoke rising from your ears?"

"I'm going to write Emma Grenville before I retire tonight and recommend that she add sword and pistol practice to the Academy's curriculum," Victoria growled. "When the insult calls for it, women should be allowed to defend their own honor."

"In duels?"

"Some *gentlemen*, and I use the term loosely, are so stupid and stubborn that the only thing to change their minds would be a ball in their stupid, unyielding brains."

"Sit!" Lady Kilcairn ordered, her voice alarmed. "I'll fetch you a glass of punch." She propelled Victoria toward a chair.

"Make it a brandy."

"All right, if you wait here for me and promise you'll never repeat what you just said to your husband."

"Why would . . . oh, my." Victoria blanched, shuddering. "I didn't mean it like that."

"I know that. For heaven's sake."

Across the room Sin talked with Kingsfeld and Lucien. Thank goodness he hadn't overheard her advocating murdering someone to alter their point of view. His friend's callous assertions about worth and his definitions of uselessness had just been so aggravating . . .

Victoria sat straight up, the blood draining from her face. It couldn't be. *Not Kingsfeld.* Not Thomas Grafton's closest friend. She stared at him as he stood smiling and at ease, saying something to Sinclair. It didn't make any sense—and yet, in a horrifying, sickening way, it did.

"You look awful," Lex said, handing her a glass and taking the seat beside her. "Drink your brandy."

She drank it in two swallows. The brandy burned her throat, and she sputtered and coughed, her eyes watering.

"Victoria, don't upset yourself so much. You only said it to me, and I know you didn't mean any of it."

The sputtering and choking gave her a moment to gather her thoughts into some sort of order. "I know," she rasped. "My ability to say stupid things just amazes me sometimes." She couldn't say anything about Kingsfeld until she'd thought it through, or had some proof—something more than dislike and wild speculation.

"So now he's got you drinking brandy?" Augusta said, sitting down on her other side. "I knew that boy was a bad influence."

"He'd have to be the most awful creature on earth to be a bad influence on me." Forcing a smile, Victoria rose to her feet. "It's my fault. I need a bit of fresh air, though. Excuse me for a moment."

"Of course, dear."

Ignoring the two ladies' surprised looks, Victoria gathered her skirts and hurried for the balcony overlooking Augusta's small garden. She drew a deep breath, grateful for the chill night air.

"Even married women aren't supposed to venture out to a balcony alone."

Victoria shrieked. Clapping both hands over her mouth, she managed to stifle most of the sound and hoped the orchestra inside had covered the remainder of her squawk. "Marley," she gasped. "You nearly frightened me to death."

The chestnut-haired viscount remained where he was, in the shadows at the near end of the balcony. "So I see."

"What are you doing out here?"

He shrugged. "I'm not drunk enough to go back inside yet. And you?"

"The same."

"Jesus Christ, Vixen. Of all the men you could have picked over me, you chose Sin Grafton?"

Marley was still a suspect, she reminded herself. It still could be him. She edged back toward the doorway. "I wouldn't have married you regardless."

"I know that. I'm not an idiot."

"So w—"

"You weren't going to marry anyone, so that seemed fair enough. Then in he walks, and you change the rules."

"You didn't have to come tonight, if that's how you feel."

"You *asked* me to come, Vixen. And you've spent

better than an hour now ignoring me. So what do you want?"

A *confession*, she thought, though now it seemed that might come from another source entirely. "I wanted to know if we could still be friends," she improvised.

He straightened. "I don't think we ever were friends. You wanted someone you could get into trouble with and who wouldn't mind the damage to his reputation."

She narrowed her eyes. "And what did you want?"

"You."

Lionel Parrish chose that moment to stroll out to the balcony. He looked so surprised to see the two of them that he had to have known they were there. "Beg pardon," he said but made no move to go back inside. "Got too dangerous in the ballroom."

Victoria stepped closer to him. "Dangerous? How?"

"Liverpool mentioned a new trade agreement with the Colonies, and Haverly spewed port all over the floor. A prelude to bloodshed, I'm certain."

"I'd best get back inside, then, and dance with one of them," she said with a swift smile. "Will you guide me in the direction of the battle?"

With a glance at Marley, Parrish offered his arm. "Just keep a watch for barbed tongues and rapier wit. I may faint if challenged."

"I'll protect you."

Purposely not looking back at Marley, Victoria allowed Lionel to escort her back into the ballroom. The viscount hadn't behaved in a particularly dangerous manner, but even so she was relieved to escape unscathed. In the past he'd seemed content just to socialize with her, with occasional kisses. She didn't like that he'd expected something more intimate from her, as though her friendship hadn't been enough.

In the ballroom, despite Lionel's dire description, everything seemed fairly calm. He looked sideways at her. "Hm. Perhaps I exaggerated."

"Thank you, Lionel."

"I saw Marley head out there earlier. I would have intercepted you, but you move quite fast."

She laughed. "I'll move more slowly next time."

Kingsfeld had left Sin and gone on to chat with Lady Augusta. She must be insane, Victoria thought. No one could kill someone and then remain close friends with the victim's family. Marley made more sense. At least he made no secret of disliking Sinclair.

Lady Jane Netherby glided into the ballroom from the direction of the study. The cool, subdued expression she wore faltered and then reformed. Curious, Victoria followed the direction of the woman's gaze— right to Lord Kingsfeld. Her breath caught.

"Lionel, have you seen Sinclair?" she asked, looking around for her husband.

"Last I saw, he was in the drawing room. Is everything all right?"

Blast it, she was going to have to learn not to give so much away. She was a terrible card player, too. "Yes. I need to speak to him, though."

"I'll relinquish you, then. Lucy's been bribing the orchestra for a country dance, anyway."

"Save a waltz for me," she said, releasing his arm.

"I'm your man, unless war's broken out by then."

Halfway to the drawing room Sin appeared in the doorway, Crispin Harding a few steps behind him. Though not obvious, both men had their attention on Lady Jane Netherby. Victoria frowned. Mr. Harding had informed Sin of the woman's presence, then—which was the most important thing, of course. But she had wanted to be the one to tell him.

Sinclair had opted against an introduction, deciding an accidental meeting would be more productive. Now, putting on a guise of slight drunkenness so realistic that Victoria could only watch and admire, he maneuvered close to Lady Jane, executed a clumsy backstep, and collided with her.

Victoria belatedly realized she was staring, and she whirled around to study a potted ivy. As she did so, though, she caught sight of Lord Kingsfeld. He was also watching the conversation between Sinclair and Lady Jane. His expression remained the same mildly bored one he'd worn all evening, but something in his eyes made her shudder.

She was imagining things. She had to be. Had Sinclair told him they were looking for Lady Jane? And what was Lady Jane so reluctant to talk about?

Shaking herself, Victoria went to find Augusta and listen to some calm reassurances of the uprightness of the Earl of Kingfeld's character. Their hostess, though, was in the middle of the ballroom floor, dancing a country dance with Kit. They seemed so happy to have Sinclair back, so completely unaware of the intrigue clinging to the shadows all around them.

Then and there, she made a promise to herself. It would kill Sinclair if anything happened to his grandmother or his younger brother. Whether she decided to confide in Sin about her suspicions of Kingsfeld or not, she would see that *nothing* happened to his family. Nothing.

*   *   *

Sin trailed hot, slow kisses from the nape of Victoria's neck down the length of her spine. She writhed under his ministrations, muffling her moans and throaty laughter in the pillows.

Something was bothering her; she'd been quiet for the entire ride back to Grafton House, and even his teasing questions had only half roused her from her contemplations. He could guess at least part of the problem; she'd spent the evening spying on her friends and acquaintances, and had more than likely discovered one or two things she would rather not have known. That was his fault, and he was determined to draw her out of the doldrums.

"Sinclair," she said, trying to turn over, "I need to tell you something."

He kept her pinned on her stomach. "Tell me."

"I can't . . . think with you . . . kissing me like that."

That was handy to know. Her brain didn't function in close proximity to him, just as he seemed to go witless the moment their eyes met. Slowly he slid his palms over her rounded bottom and down the backs of her legs. "All right." He sighed with mock disappointment, sitting back on his knees.

She squirmed, turning onto her back. "Did you learn anything from Lady Jane?"

Pulling her right foot toward him, he began massaging it with lazy, deep circles. "I thought you had something to tell me."

"I do."

The hesitation in her eyes worried him. What did she think she'd found out now? "And?"

"And I want to hear what you have to say, first— to see if what I have to say still makes sense."

Now his impetuous bride was being cautious. Another worrisome sign. "Lady Jane Netherby knows something. I've sent Bates to see what he can dig up at her parents' country residence, and Wally's about to become enamored of her personal maid."

"Poor Wally."

"He deserves it, after frightening me half to death the other day."

"What did she say to you?"

"Not much. She was friends with Thomas, and was sorry for our loss. Very sorry. Nothing about bringing anyone to justice, or mistakes he might have made, or anyone he might have angered, or that she couldn't understand why this happened." He took a breath, noting the intense interest on Victoria's face. "All of which indicates to me that she might know the answers to those questions already." Fairness made him kiss her ankle and smile. "You did a good job, discovering her."

"I don't think she and Marley know one another. He's never looked in her direction or mentioned her name in the last two years, anyway."

He turned his attentions to her left foot. "Is that what you wanted to tell me?" he asked, trying to keep his tone cool. Every time she defended damned Lord Marley he had the urge to shake her. It hurt, knowing that she liked—had probably even kissed—the man who in all likelihood had murdered Thomas.

"No." She hesitated again, then sat up, pulling her foot free and replacing it with her hands. "What if I told you that I knew of someone who was acquainted with both Lady Jane Netherby and your brother, and that this same person was in town the day Thomas was killed, knew Grafton House quite well, and didn't believe in allowing things useless to him to exist?"

His voice caught. "I would want to know this person's name. At once."

Victoria took a deep breath, holding his gaze almost defiantly. "The Earl of Kingsfeld."

Sin blinked. "Astin? Don't be ridiculous."

"I am not being ridiculous," she retorted. "He said some very coldhearted things about discarding objects—and people—if they became useless."

"And what in the world leads you to believe that he thought his closest friend was useless, or that by 'discard' he meant 'murder'?"

Yanking her hands free, Victoria slid off the edge of the bed and stood. "You've asked me to consider Marley a suspect, and I have. I start . . . shaking whenever I set eyes on him. It just seems to me that someone as suspicious as you wouldn't want to rule out anyone. I'm not saying Kingsfeld did it, I'm just saying . . . don't turn your back on him."

"So now you're the expert? I've known Astin Hovarth for twelve years. He would not—"

"How much have you seen of him over the past five years? I don't like him, and I don't trust him."

He stood as well, shamelessly using his height to force her to look up at him. "You're the one who's been telling me I should be more trusting. Or did you only mean that I should trust *your* friends and *your* judgment, and not my own? This is not a game, Victoria. You can't just pick someone you don't like and accuse them of murder."

Tears filled her eyes. "I know this isn't a game," she snapped, swiping at her wet cheeks. "If it makes a difference, pretend someone whose judgment you trust was warning you." She stalked to the door ad-

joining their bedchambers. "I just don't want anything
to happen to you."

He clamped his jaw shut over his angry retort as
her voice broke and she disappeared through the door,
slamming it closed behind her. Damnation. He'd been
about to make love to a beautiful woman who, despite
his boorishness, had evidently decided she cared for
him at least a little. And he had all but called *her* a
fool.

Perhaps the argument would make her realize,
though, that he hadn't just come up with his list of
suspects overnight. For two years he'd been pondering, and seeking information where he could. Not all
the fingers pointed at Marley; if they did, Marley
would be dead or imprisoned by now. He'd seen
enough, though, to want a much closer look. The evidence wasn't anything like the string of coincidences
Victoria had used to conjure Astin Hovarth, of all people.

Grumbling, he climbed back into his large, empty
bed and yanked up the covers. A squawk made him
look up, to where Mungo Park perched in his favorite
spot at the peak of the headboard.

" 'Now, Sin. I want you inside me,' " the bird mimicked.

"Oh, shut up," Sin returned, and buried his head
beneath the sheets.

First thing in the morning, Victoria sat down and
made a list. The page had two columns: friends she
could trust to keep their silence, and friends who
would carry tales of anything she said to the rest of
London. When she finished it, the list was alarmingly
one-sided. For someone who claimed to dislike gossip,

she'd certainly managed to acquire a great many chatty friends.

As she reread the trustworthy names, she crossed out Sinclair Grafton, his three spy friends, and his valet. They wouldn't carry tales, but based on Sin's reaction last night, neither were they going to allow her to continue her own investigation of the Earl of Kingsfeld.

She then sent a note to her friend Emma Grenville, inquiring if there might be any records at Miss Grenville's Academy that would indicate whether Lady Jane Netherby had attended or not. Emma's aunt, Miss Grenville, had kept meticulous records, including the names of any visitors or unusual occurrences. She knew that because she'd once seen her own file, practically two inches thick. It should appease Sinclair to see that she was investigating in an extremely safe—and useless—manner.

That done, she gave the missive to Milo and strolled into the downstairs office. Sin would be at Parliament this morning, so she didn't have to worry about him discovering her. According to Jenny, Roman had left on an errand as well, so for the moment Grafton House was spy-free. Nearly.

Closing the office door, she slowly took in the room. A slight shiver ran down her spine. A man had died, violently, in this room. If he had known the killer, he might also have known his life was in danger. Why this room? Why that night? Some clue must remain.

Though Sinclair had already looked through the desk for incriminating letters or notes, the killer would have had the first opportunity to do so. And from her experience, people did not necessarily keep private information in public places. Her husband had no doubt considered that already, as well, but it was a large room. He might have missed something—particularly if he was searching for different evidence than she was.

She started with the bookshelf beside the door. No dust clung to the shelves or the books, but she doubted any of the servants had moved or opened anything.

Most of the books were law tomes or listings of property and taxes and trade charters. Thomas had taken his duties in the House of Lords very seriously, but she already knew that about him. One by one she took down the books, flipped through the pages looking for any notes or markings the late Marquis of Althorpe might have made, and then replaced them again.

If his death had surprised Thomas as much as it had his family, he probably wouldn't have hidden anything away. As intelligent as she'd known him to be, though, she couldn't believe that he would have been completely astonished that night. He might have put something aside, just in case.

Two hours later, as she removed Culpeper's *Herbal Guide* from the shelf beside the window and flipped the heavy book open, several sheets of yellowed paper fluttered down to the carpet.

For a long moment she just stood looking at them. Her tired back, smudged fingers, and wounded feelings all ceased to matter. Thomas Grafton had left this for someone to find, and she had found it.

"Steady," she whispered, gathering her skirts and sinking to the floor. "It might be nothing. It's probably nothing."

It wasn't nothing. She realized that almost immediately. Writing filled the three pages, meticulous writing couched in legal terms and accompanied by notations and statistics. Words here and there had been scratched out and replaced with others, while nearly indecipherable notes lined the margins and inched in to overlap the main text.

The office door clicked and opened. "Victoria, what are you—"

Sin stopped, taking in the sight of her seated on the floor with Culpeper open beside her and the pages clutched in her hands. She raised them toward him. "I think I found something," she said, her voice unsteady.

He strode over to her and knelt down. "What is it?" he asked sharply, taking the papers from her.

"I think it's a proposal," she said, watching his intense expression as he scanned through the pages. "Something about trade and France."

Sinclair nodded. "An early draft of one. Where did you find it?"

"In the middle of the Culpeper."

"That doesn't make any sense. Why in the world would Thomas hide a parliamentary treatise in an herbal guide?"

"So no one would find it?" she suggested.

He met her gaze. "Don't read more into it than you see. It is an early draft. He might have been marking his place in the book."

"Mm. Did he have an interest in"—she looked at the open Culpeper—"in figwort, for treating purulent wounds?"

Scowling, Sin read the pages through more slowly. "Not likely."

"Sinclair—"

"This calls for a cessation of trade with France and

a divestiture of all French holdings by the English nobility, to 'set an example for the world, and most especially, for Bonaparte.'" He glanced at her again. "You know, Astin showed me part of a proposal he and Thomas were working on together. He said Marley was none too happy with either of them about it."

Victoria resisted the urge to begin another argument. The object was to find a killer, not to argue over whose acquaintance was less trustworthy. "Was it the same proposal?"

"I don't know. The page had had port spilled on it. By Marley. It was completely illegible."

Pressing her lips together, Victoria debated for several long seconds whether to say anything or not. He'd told her not to read more into something than she saw; neither, though, could she turn a blind eye toward something she did see. "Why did Lord Kingsfeld keep the page, then?" she asked softly.

Sin's jaw ground shut. "What?"

"Lord Kingsfeld told me himself that he discards useless objects," she said quickly, before he could tell her she was stupid and wrong. "Why, then, would he keep a completely illegible piece of paper for more than two years? And why would he know precisely where to find it when he needed to show it to you?"

He opened his mouth to answer, then closed it again. "Before we meander farther along this path," he said flatly, "we have to determine what became of this proposal. We already know that it didn't pass. I'll go through the House records to see when it was defeated by Parliament. That will be the determining factor of its significance."

Standing, he retrieved the Culpeper and returned it

to its place on the bookshelf. Then he held his hand down to her.

She grasped his fingers. "Sinclair, I don't mean to hurt—"

"You made a point," he said gruffly, pulling her effortlessly to her feet. "Just how good a point remains to be seen."

Chapter 13

S he was up to something. Sin looked sideways at Victoria as he drove their phaeton past Rotten Row in Hyde Park.

For three days she'd been calm and quiet, barely speaking of the investigation except to inquire whether he'd learned anything new. And she was sharing his bed again, thank God, with a passion and enthusiasm that left him breathless. If there was one thing Victoria Grafton wasn't, it was shy.

And that was the crux of the problem. It had taken only one conversation to realize that his impetuous bride didn't shirk from anything, and certainly not for the simple reason that he'd told her to. Therefore, she was still pursuing her hunch about the Earl of Kingsfeld. She just wasn't telling him about it.

He brought the phaeton around to join the crush of vehicles, riders, and pedestrians meandering through the park. The ritual of afternoon socializing seemed absurd, particularly with the park so crowded that no one could possibly manage a meaningful conversation. It did have one benefit, though: it kept Victoria in his sight and out of trouble for at least an hour.

"I wrote to my friend Emma Grenville," she said unexpectedly, her gaze on the hordes filling the sun-dappled park. "Unfortunately, all she could tell me was that Lady Jane Netherby did not attend Miss Grenville's Academy."

"It was a good idea anyway," he replied, perfectly willing to encourage any harmless venues of investigation. "And now we know where she wasn't."

"Have you heard anything from Bates?"

Sinclair shook his head. "I don't expect him back for another few days. I hope he'll at least be able to tell me whether Lady Jane had any gentleman callers and who they might have been."

"My parents have invited us to dinner this evening."

"They have?"

"Yes. Apparently your pretending to be a gentleman has fooled them completely."

A touch of acid—finally. And though he scowled at the commentary, he actually felt more at ease. This Victoria, he knew how to deal with. "All right. What did I do now?"

She still wouldn't look at him. "Nothing. Shall I accept the invitation?"

"Not if you don't want to dine with them."

"I'll make our excuses, then. I just thought you might wish to interrogate them or something."

He narrowed his eyes. "Victoria, what's wrong?"

Vixen fidgeted for a moment, then sat back and faced him. "What are you going to do when this is over?"

"I'm going to meet with my solicitor, who thinks I'm a complete nodcock, and look over some of the estate books."

"I mean, what are you going to do once you've caught Thomas's killer?"

He held her gaze, trying to decipher the real question in her violet eyes. "I'm supposed to be a nobleman. We don't do much of anything, do we?"

The expression on her face didn't change, but she might as well have shouted her annoyance to the heavens. "Make what you will of your position, Sinclair. If you intend to sit and drink and wager all day, I . . ."

"You might have to find somewhere else to be," he finished for her. "I admire your confidence in your ability to change the world, but mankind is quite a bit more rotten than you realize."

"Just what did you see, Sinclair, that made you so cynical?"

He shrugged. "I'm not going to tell you."

"Why not?" she burst out, flushing. "I think I'm strong enough to take whatever ill news about my fellows you might have discovered."

"Shh," he murmured, unable to stop himself from reaching out to stroke her soft cheek with the back of his fingers. "It's not that."

"Then what?" Her slender fingers lifted and twined with his.

"I find a . . . peculiar comfort in your faith, Victoria."

"My faith?"

Sin nodded. "Your faith, and your compassion. I don't want to destroy that in you. It's . . . important to me."

For a moment she remained silent. "That's a very nice thing you just said," she finally whispered, teary-eyed and smiling.

"It's the truth. And since I'm making confessions,

when this is finished I suppose I'm going to manage Thomas's estates and business holdings and try not to make an ass of myself in Parliament."

"But they aren't your brother's estates any longer," she countered. "They're yours. And so is the seat in the House of Lords, and Grafton House, and . . ."

"And what?"

"And me."

His heart thudded. It made sense. She thought he'd married her so he could continue his investigation, and in part he had. Once the investigation was finished, the equation would change. Distracting her wouldn't work any longer, because he would have nothing to distract her from—except the realization that she'd married someone who only knew how to be a spy and a subversive thorn in an enemy government's side. With no enemy government to undermine, he could swiftly become very unpopular with his own.

"What do you want when this is finished?" he asked slowly.

She gave a small smile. "The same thing I've always wanted: to be useful."

"You're useful to me," he said, more because he hated that sad look in her eyes than because he wanted to make another attempt to explain how important she was becoming to him—how she centered and balanced him and managed to make him think he actually had a chance at being a passable Lord Althorpe.

Victoria wrinkled her nose. "While I'm happy to hear that, it's not precisely what I had in—"

"Seenclair! Mon amour!"

"Oh, good God," he muttered, yanking up on the reins to keep from running down the young blond woman who rose from the grass nearby and dashed out onto the pathway. "Miss L'Anjou. How are you?"

"Maintenant, je suis splendide!" she cooed, while her companions, seated on picnic blankets several yards from the riding trail, looked on with interest. Most were young men, of course; Sophie L'Anjou seemed to acquire a set of them wherever she traveled. *"Comment vas tu? Je t'manque, mon amour."*

He cleared his throat, not daring to look at Victoria, though he didn't need to see her face to sense her sudden keen fascination with the conversation. It would have been too much to hope that she didn't speak French. "I'm quite well, thank you, Miss L'Anjou."

"Qui est la femme?"

Victoria leaned closer to him. "She wants to know who I am, Sinclair," she murmured, her tone honeyed with deep humor.

At least the encounter amused her. But if he knew anything, it was that a man did not introduce his bride to his former mistress.

Neither, though, could he ignore her. Sophie would run after the phaeton, screeching and bellowing at the top of her opera-trained lungs, until he answered her. "Miss L'Anjou, Lady Althorpe. Victoria, Miss L'Anjou, a renowned opera singer in Paris."

"Good afternoon," the Vixen said politely. "We saw your performance the other evening. It was splendid— I envy you your talent."

Sophie looked up at Victoria on her high perch, then bobbed a curtsy. *"Merci,* my lady. My Seenclair often attends my performances, and he sends me flowers when he cannot."

Well, this was obviously going to get ugly. "I have

already explained to Lady Althorpe that you and I are old acquaintances."

Obviously not satisfied with that description, Sophie remained rooted by the phaeton, right where he would have to run her down if he attempted an escape. The line of vehicles behind them began to stack up, increasing the size of their audience.

"I am pleased to hear this," the singer continued in her halting, heavily accented English. "How do you know my Seen, Lady Althorpe?"

Before he could open his mouth, Victoria leaned forward to look past him at Sophie. "Sinclair is my husband," she said in a low voice.

Any attempt at subtlety was lost on Sophie. The blond woman's eyes widened. "What? Seen, you are married?"

"Only just," he replied, trying to make light of it.

"But this is not possible. You said you would never marry, Seenclair. *Jamais.*"

"Things change, Miss L'Anjou," he said, looking at her steadily. "People change, and circumstances change."

"You do not change. I know this. You are making a joke with me, *oui?*"

"No."

To his surprise, Victoria laid a hand on his arm. "Sinclair probably didn't have a chance to tell you. He unexpectedly inherited a title and some property, and his family insisted that he marry."

The lie was blatant, but even so the anger in Sophie's eyes lessened. That was his Victoria, helping the downtrodden and making them feel more comfortable, even at her own expense.

"I see," Sophie said stiffly, backing away. "How

unfortunate that you have lost your freedom, Seen—I know how important it was to you."

"I'm making do. If you'll excuse us, though, we are expected elsewhere."

"Perhaps I will see you in London again before I return to Paris."

Not if he could manage to avoid her. She knew too much about his black deeds on the Continent, and not enough about his motives for behaving as he had. There were some things about himself that he didn't want Victoria to know. "Perhaps we will," he said noncommittally and urged the team into a trot.

As soon as they were out of earshot, Victoria faced him. "So. Tell me, Seenclair, do you—"

"Victoria, I'm sorry," he interrupted. "I hope you weren't embarrassed."

"I'm not embarrassed. I just wanted to know whether you broke her heart on purpose."

"I didn't break her heart," he countered. "I don't doubt Sophie has one, but it's buried so far beneath her hunger for fame and notoriety and young, wealthy men, I doubt it has much room to beat."

"But you . . . were with her, weren't you?"

Sin scowled. "I needed her to trust me. There was nothing more to it than that."

"I'm sorry for that, then."

"For God's sake, what are *you* sorry for, Victoria?" he returned, with more heat than he intended.

"For what you had to go through. Returning to England under normal circumstances would have been difficult enough. Add to that a murder and inheriting a marquisdom, and it must—"

"I am not one of your lost lambs, Vixen. I chose to do what I did. Believe me, Thomas was ready to purchase me a captain's commission in the army if I'd wanted it. I didn't."

She searched his eyes, but if she was looking for a chink in his armor, he wished her luck. He didn't think he had any, any longer.

"You didn't kill him, you know," she said quietly.

Apparently he did have at least one chink remaining. And of course she'd shoved a sword right through it and into his heart. "No, I don't know that," he retorted. "If his murder had anything to do with that proposal you found, I might very well have had something to do with it. Thomas wanted the war prevented, and then he wanted it over with—because I was right in the middle of it."

Victoria didn't look the least bit put off by his fierceness. Instead, she adopted a thoughtful, serious look, which amused and annoyed him at the same time.

"Proceed," he prompted her. If she hadn't yet run out of pieces of wisdom to share with him, he could damned well use one or two at the moment.

"It's just that I didn't know your brother well, but he seemed like a very intelligent, thoughtful man. How can you be sure he wouldn't have done the exact same thing whether you joined the War Office or not?"

For a long moment, Sin just looked at her. Too many conflicting thoughts roiled around in his brain for him to sort out exactly what he wanted to say. Finally he let his breath out in a long, slow sigh. "Let me get something straight," he said. "I introduce you to one of my former mistresses, and you're more concerned that I feel guilty for my brother's death."

She cleared her throat. "Well, to be honest, I already suspected you knew Sophie L'Anjou better than you indicated. She wasn't much of a surprise."

Sin lifted an eyebrow. "She wasn't?"

"No. That night at the opera, you were blushing."

The phaeton stopped short. "I do *not* blush."

With a grin, she took the reins from his hands and flicked them at the team. "Well, I knew something was going on, didn't I?"

Good God. He hadn't realized he was so obvious. It was quite sad, really. And so was the way he'd come to rely on her for his humanity. For his sanity, it sometimes seemed.

He liked talking to her about things other than the murder—he liked her perception and her intelligence and her much warmer view of the world around them. Yet he still knew so little about her. It would take a lifetime to figure her out; he hoped she would give him the chance.

"What's your favorite thing to do?" he asked.

Victoria blinked. "What?"

"What do you like to do?"

"Why?"

Sinclair took a breath. He couldn't blame her for being suspicious; he never seemed to ask something without having some sort of ulterior motive. "Because I'm curious. I'm trying to behave like a husband, and learn about my wife."

Her expression became more thoughtful. "I'm not entirely sure that's what husbands do."

Aha. He'd surprised her. "We both know how lacking I am in husbanding skills."

Victoria chuckled, blushing prettily. "You're not so very lacking."

"My thanks. Now, indulge me: what do you like to do?"

"Oh, my," she whispered, and the carriage careened toward the shrubbery.

Sin snatched the reins back from her and returned the vehicle to the roadway. "Driving isn't one of your pastimes, is it?"

Victoria stuck her tongue out at him. "When I'm in the country I like to ride," she said, apparently becoming fascinated with the scenery again, as she did when she was embarrassed about something. "My mother always said I was a hoyden because I hated the broken-down old mare they kept trying to give me. I would make the groom ride her, and take his, instead."

He made a mental note to provide her with a spirited—but good-tempered—mount at Althorpe. If his Vixen wanted to ride, then she would ride. "What else?"

"My causes, of course," she continued, glancing sideways at him.

From her expression, she expected him to make fun, as he'd done during the first luncheon they'd attended together. "Have I mentioned that I tend to drool and say some very stupid things from time to time?"

"You don't drool." She folded her hands in her lap.

"Ah. I deserved that."

She chuckled. "That's all right. My very favorite pastime is chatting with my friends . . ." Victoria bit her bottom lip, her expression darkening.

"I owe you another apology, then. I've made all of your friends into suspects, haven't I?"

"No. It's not your fault. Some of them . . . I . . . I needed to see differently. They weren't really my friends. Better to realize that, than not."

Now she was being noble and making him feel like a complete cad. "Might I suggest we hold a dinner party, and that you invite the friends of your choice? No suspects allowed."

Victoria leaned over and kissed his cheek. Not about to be outflanked, he pursued her retreat and caught her lips with his own. After a second's surprise, she kissed him back. He dimly heard the tittering commentary of the pedestrians and riders around them, but ignored it. Victoria was his. And he wanted them all to know it.

"I agree, if you'll also invite the friends of your choice."

Sinclair straightened, immediately sensing a trap. "Damnation, Vixen. You want to force me to reveal my friends to your friends, don't you? Trust me or else?"

"Not everything is a war, you know," she retorted, scowling. "I want our friends to be friends. Invite them or not, Sinclair. I just hope *they* have a life to return to when this is finished."

Her violet eyes practically pleaded with him not to make an issue of a simple dinner party. Nothing, of course, was simple where murder and trust were concerned. He'd probably tortured her enough for a lifetime with that already, though. "I'll ask them," he grumbled.

"Thank you."

He'd made her happy for once, and a corresponding lightness touched what was left of his heart. That didn't last, though, as he realized he'd just announced his willingness to put his compatriots at risk in order to please his wife. And they would know it, too.

Lucy Havers fidgeted in her straight-backed chair while Pauline Jeffries and her mother, Lady Prentiss, prepared for Pauline's part in the afternoon's recital. The seat beside her stood empty, as Victoria chatted in the anteroom with Lady Kilcairn.

Marley leaned against a marble pillar at one side of the music room, watching. Recitals made his skin crawl, but as he'd managed to arrive late and intended to leave before Pauline began squeaking whatever tune her overbearing mother had decided on, he supposed he could stand it.

The intermission would run for another five minutes or so, and the Vixen, at least, seemed completely engrossed. With a last look toward the doorway, Marley pushed away from the pillar. Strolling over to the empty chair beside Lucy, he touched her shoulder.

"I see you're trapped as well," he murmured, sinking into the vacant chair.

She jumped. "Oh, my, you startled me. How in the world did you end up here? I thought you couldn't tolerate this nonsense."

"I lost a wager," he said in a low voice, glancing over his shoulder. "And you?"

"Vixen loves these things. And she went with me to Almack's the other night, so I had to come here."

"Vixen is here?" he asked, fixing a surprised look on his face.

"She's just in the other room. You didn't see her?"

"No," he lied, settling closer to her. "Althorpe isn't here, is he? I've heard more than enough of his gloating already this Season."

"What are you talking about?" she whispered. "Lord Althorpe seems very pleasant . . . though I wouldn't want to make him angry with me."

If anyone in the world was more gullible than Vixen Fontaine, it was Lucy Havers. "I'm sure he can be very pleasant," Marley agreed. "Most men can, when they want something. I worry about the rest of the time, though—especially with Vixen alone and helpless in his household."

Lucy wrinkled her brow. "He would never hurt her. I'm certain of it."

"Maybe not physically. But thank God I was there to silence him last week at White's, before he could do any permanent damage to her reputation."

"What was he doing?" she whispered, her blue eyes wide and concerned.

"He . . . suffice it to say that he said some things not fit for a young lady to hear."

"About Vixen?"

Marley nodded solemnly. "He was drunk, of course, which was the only reason we didn't come to blows." Movement in the doorway caught his attention, and he took Lucy's hand. "If you sense any danger for her, Lucy, please let me know at once. I worry about her. She is . . . a good friend to me."

"I should speak to her about this."

"Are you certain that's wise?"

She squeezed his fingers. "Yes. She should know what's going on. I'm sure there's a reasonable explanation."

"I only want to see her safe. And I miss the fun we all used to have together."

"She *has* been much more serious lately, now that I think about it," Lucy mused. "But don't worry, my lord. I'll keep my eyes open."

Pulling his fingers free, he rose. "Thank you, Lucy. I'll see you soon."

He made it back to the far side of the pillar as Vixen entered the room and reclaimed her chair. When Lucy leaned over to whisper something to her, Marley smiled. He felt like whistling as he strolled from the room. Married or not, Vixen Fontaine and her money would be much better off away from damned Sin Grafton and closer to him. And of course, he would be much better off as well.

"Sinclair, you don't have to do this."

Victoria stood squeezed against the windowsill as Sin and a small army of footmen rearranged the downstairs office. Her husband, coatless and with shirtsleeves rolled up to his elbows, hefted a corner of his late brother's mahogany desk.

"You said it gave you the shivers," he grunted. "Left, Henley. I can't say I'm terribly fond of the damned thing, myself."

"I know, but—oh, look out for the vase!" Leaping forward, she caught the tottering crystal before it toppled off the bookshelf.

"Good reflexes. Now, you still haven't said: do you want your desk beneath the window, or closer to the fireplace?"

Clutching the vase, Victoria returned to her tiny space by the window. "Grafton House has twenty rooms. You really don't have to stuff two desks in here."

By some miracle they shoved the mahogany behemoth into the hallway without bringing down the ceiling. A moment later, Sin leaned into the doorway. "Wait here." He vanished again. "Well, my lads, I think this calls for a glass of beer before we load this monstrosity onto the wagon. Milo, the kitchen."

"With pleasure, my lord."

The sound of cheers and backslapping faded down

the hall. Victoria set the vase back on the bookcase.
With the massive desk gone, the office looked much
larger and less formal. The carpet directly below
where the desk had stood was darker than the rest of
the expanse, though whether because of the sun or a
remaining bloodstain, she didn't want to speculate.

"Much better, don't you think?" Sinclair slapped at
the lingering dust on his trousers. His gaze went to the
dark patch of carpet as well, and he clenched his fist
and swallowed.

"Yes, it's much better," she said in her cheeriest
voice, "but it still isn't necessary."

"It's already done." He came forward, catching her
around the waist with a possessive confidence that left
her breathless. "I think we need to place you by the
window. The sunlight puts bronze in your hair."

"I have a desk in my study upstairs, you know."

Sin took her chin in his fingers and tilted her face
up toward him. "That tiny thing? That's for correspondence. The office is for business. If I'm to spend
half my damned life in here doing accounts, I would
at least like to be able to look up and see you."

He was talking about after—after he'd done his
duty by Thomas. It didn't sound as though he was
terribly excited by the prospect, but up until a few days
ago he'd never even mentioned it. Now, he had put
the future and Victoria together in the same sentence.
She took a steadying breath. "And what am I to do at
my office desk?"

"Business. Grandmama Augusta heads the volun-
tary London education committee."

"She—"

"You didn't know that, did you?"

The blatant surprise on her face must have been

easy to read. "No, I didn't. I know she's involved in several charitable organizations, but—"

"Public service has always had a high priority in my family—except for me, of course. It takes a great deal of Grandmama Augusta's time."

"I'd call risking your life for your country a public service," Victoria countered.

"Thank you," he murmured. "And anyway, my point was that Grandmama has expressed interest in reducing some of her duties. She needs a successor."

Victoria hugged him hard. "Thank you," she managed.

"Anything for you," he whispered almost too quietly for her to hear, rubbing his cheek along her hair.

And anything for you, she returned silently. She wanted that life he spoke of to begin, with a strength and a hunger she'd never felt before. It had never seemed possible she would ever find it before. Victoria loosened her grip and stepped back.

"If you don't mind," she said slowly, trying to select words that wouldn't make him suspicious, "I'm going out for luncheon with Lucy and Marguerite while you finish arranging. I have no wish to be crushed by my new desk."

Sin chuckled. "By all means. I've several things to look into this afternoon anyway." He leaned down and kissed her. "And I have several gentlemen to invite to a party."

Victoria hurried upstairs to change into her green flowered visiting gown. Green was Marley's favorite color. From his chat with Lucy yesterday, the viscount obviously wanted to see her about something, and she had a few questions for him herself. She was convinced the murderer was either Marley or Kingsfeld.

And before a real life with Sinclair could begin, she had to figure out which one it was.

Sin leaned back against his new desk. With a Persian carpet laid over the site of the old desk and the two smaller ones in place, it seemed a different room entirely. He liked it—Thomas's dark, conservative taste would never do in a household filled with Victoria and her lively menagerie. Part of him, though, felt as though he was removing memories of his brother. "I won't forget," he murmured.

His valet leaned into the doorway. "Very cozy."

He straightened. "Aren't you supposed to be keeping an eye on Victoria?"

"She's just leaving. You going to stay and play house all day?"

"Another crack like that, and I may lose my temper, Roman," Sinclair snapped. "Today's Thursday—Kingsfeld will be at the horse auctions. I'm going to forget that and call on him at home."

"You don't think it could be *him*," Roman exclaimed.

"Vixen does. A little reconnaissance might put both of us more at ease."

"Mind yourself, then."

"Go mind my wife," he retorted.

With a concerned scowl, Roman vanished back down the hallway.

Though they were used to working alone, Sinclair supposed he should have asked one of the lads at least to keep watch outside Astin's house while he was inside. The problem was, he wasn't willing to consider Thomas's friend a suspect—yet. And not solely because Victoria had suggested him as one. Sin knew what Crispin would have to say about that, and he didn't want to hear it.

He arrived at Hovarth House a little before noon, which would put Kingsfeld at the auctions for at least another hour. Suppressing a slight twinge of guilt at what he was about to do, and surprised that he still possessed the ability to feel guilty, Sin turned his stallion over to a groom and climbed the front steps. His knock reverberated into the house for several long seconds before the butler pulled open the door.

"Good afternoon, Geoffreys."

"Lord Althorpe. Lord Kingsfeld is not home at present."

Sin frowned. "Isn't he?" Pulling out his pocket watch, he flipped it open. "Damnation. He's still at the auctions, isn't he?"

"Yes, my lord. Is there—"

"Might I wait for him?" Sin cleared his throat. "When one storms out of the house, I don't believe one is supposed to return twenty minutes later."

The butler's expression didn't change. "My apologies, my lord, but the earl doesn't allow visitors when he is away from home."

Several alarm bells went off in Sinclair's head. While his first instinct was to push past the butler and invent another reason he had to be allowed inside, he needed a less obvious route. He still didn't know anything, and he wasn't about to ruin one of his few friendships over a fleeting hunch—or risk alerting Kingsfeld if Vixen turned out to be right.

"That figures," he drawled. "I'll go find him at the auctions. My thanks, Geoffreys."

"My lord." The door glided closed again.

Cursing under his breath, Sin collected Diable again

and headed for Covent Gardens and the horse auctions.

"I'll take this as a fortuitous coincidence," Marley said, hopping down from his phaeton.

As he joined her on the sidewalk, Victoria couldn't help glancing up and down Bond Street. Anyone who saw her in the middle of the shopping district with Lord Marley would be more than happy to share the news with the gossips. "How are you, Marley?"

"Better, now that you're here. Parrish insisted that we go to the Society Club last night, and we ended up tangled in a damned game of whist with Lord Spenser. Good God, what a bore."

Victoria chuckled. "It's good for you to learn patience."

Lady Munroe and Miss Pladden strolled by, and Victoria smiled and nodded as they passed. Blast. Lady Munroe made Mungo Park look like a Trappist monk parrot.

"Why is learning to accept interminable boredom considered a virtue? I intend to avoid it at every possible opportunity."

"I don't doubt it." Oh, this was ridiculous. She'd gone looking for him, for goodness' sake. And not only were her reasons for encountering Marley completely respectable, if somewhat—well, very—secretive, but she'd practically made an art form of being fodder for gossip for most of her adult life. But she knew the difference between accidental and intentional troublemaking, and she didn't want to hurt Sinclair.

"I have an idea," Marley said, grinning. "They've just opened a new monkey cage at the zoo. Come with me to see it, and I'll purchase you a lemon ice."

"Oh, I couldn't," she stammered, her cheeks warm. She'd wanted a chance encounter, not an entire afternoon spent with the man her husband most suspected.

"Nonsense," he drawled, taking her arm. "I've heard that one of the monkeys bears a striking resemblance to Prinny." When she hesitated, he smiled more broadly and twitched at her skirt. "Come on, Vixen. You're not married to a bishop. It'll be fun."

She wasn't married to a bishop, by any means, but Sinclair barely trusted her as it was. If she offended Marley or turned him down, though, she'd likely never be able to manage a private conversation with him again. "All right." She allowed him to lead her to his carriage. "But I can't stay long."

If he hadn't driven up in the open phaeton, she wouldn't have gone anywhere with him. She'd done it before, of course, ridden off with Marley to meet up with their friends at Vauxhall or some ball or other. In fact, her escapades with the viscount had been the reason her parents had kept her housebound until the Franton ball. But today, as they clattered down the street, she kept seeing the dark patch of carpet in the office. Victoria had never been an idiot about taking chances, and hopefully she wasn't being one now.

"I've heard that Lady Franton now begins every conversation with, 'Well, you know, the catastrophe happened in my very garden,' " he drawled.

"So it's 'the catastrophe,' is it?" she said, unsurprised. Her own perspective had altered over the past few weeks.

"For the entire male population of Mayfair, it's a catastrophe," he replied, glancing away from the busy street to look at her. "For me, it is."

Victoria forced a smile. "We both know my reckless

ways couldn't have continued much longer. My parents would have bustled me off to a nunnery."

"If you'd lasted until you reached your inheritance, you could have carried on however you wanted for the rest of your life."

"But it would have gotten dull, don't you think?"

Marley shrugged. "We always had fun."

For her, most of the mindless meandering had ceased to be fun a long time ago. He didn't need to know that, though. It certainly wouldn't do any good—and the friendlier they were, the more likely he was to talk to her. "Yes, we did."

He chuckled. "Do you remember when Lord Edward and I stole those fireworks from the stash at Vauxhall?"

"Yes. You two nearly burned down the Tower Bridge trying to set the silly things off."

Without warning, Marley leaned across and kissed her. Victoria jumped, clutching her hands together to fight the urge to push him away. "Marley!" She sent up a quick prayer that no one had been looking in their direction. "I'm married!"

"That doesn't have to change anything," he said in a low, urgent voice quite unlike his usual drawling tone. "Your damned husband's probably doing the same thing somewhere else right now. I heard Sophie L'Anjou was his mistress in Paris. How odd that she would come to London so soon after he arrived. Do you really think that's a coincidence?"

The coincidence hadn't even occurred to her until he mentioned it. But she didn't believe it for a moment. Sin would never do such a thing. "Oh, my, do you think so?" she asked anyway. This must be another of the compromises of conscience her husband had mentioned. Compromising her new feelings about Sinclair, though, was even more difficult than luring her friends in for interrogation.

"I wouldn't put it past him. You have to look out for your own interests, Vix. You used to like it when I kissed you, and that was only a few weeks ago. It doesn't have to change."

It had already changed. She didn't want anyone but Sinclair to kiss her or to hold her. He was the one who made her pulse fly. More importantly, he was the only man who seemed to like the person she liked to be.

"I don't know," she hedged. "Perhaps it might make a difference if you could tell me why you dislike Althorpe so much."

Marley gave a bitter laugh. "You mean besides the fact that he stole you away?"

"You didn't like him that night at the Frantons', and that was before any of this . . . mess happened."

He frowned. "It's not something you'd be interested in."

Victoria's heart lurched. The Vixen he knew wouldn't be overly suspicious, and neither would she be afraid of Marley, so before she could think better of it, she whacked him on the arm. "Of course I'm interested. I'm living in the same house with him, and you're my dearest friend. I value your opinion."

Flattering Marley had always been easy, though in the past she'd thought of it as humoring him to avoid any sticky conflicts and arguments. Now, though, she recognized it for what it was—her way of persuading him to do exactly what she wanted with as little fuss as possible.

And it worked as well as it always did. "I wish you'd valued my opinion enough not to go off dancing with him in the first place," he said, edging closer to her on the narrow seat.

"I'll listen to you the next time," she promised.

"You mean there'll be a next time, Vix?"

"That depends on how good your reasons for my avoiding Althorpe are." She was amazed her voice even remained steady, much less that it sounded amused and natural.

"I don't trust him," Marley said flatly. "His brother cuts him off, yet he manages to live well enough in France that he doesn't bother returning home when he inherits a sizeable fortune—not for two years."

"He was cut off?"

The viscount nodded. "Everyone knows. Althorpe—the former Althorpe—wanted to purchase him a commission in the army. Sin wouldn't have anything to do with it. I think he knew he could make his fortune elsewhere, and with much less worry over getting his head blown off."

Sinclair probably had heard the popular view of why he'd left England; he might even have encouraged the tale. Indignant anger rose in Victoria's throat, though, and she forced it back down. Her husband didn't want anyone to know why he'd been in Europe during the war.

"If he made his fortune in France," she said slowly, her frown real, "he isn't the only one to do so."

Marley shook his head. "No. But he was the only one with a brother so vehemently opposed to trade with France that he threw a case of damned fine French champagne on the floor of the House of Lords."

Victoria gaped at him; she couldn't help herself. "You think Sinclair killed Thomas?"

"I wouldn't put it past him. Thomas could barely bring himself to speak of his brother."

She knew the reason for that, thank goodness. "I didn't know you were so well acquainted with Lord Althorpe. You never said."

They reached the zoo, and Marley guided the phaeton into the long stand of vehicles on one side of the roadway. He tied off the ribbons and jumped to the ground, then came around the back of the carriage to hand her down.

"We were friends, until he became so rabid about everyone divesting themselves of French property that he wouldn't even sit at the same table with any of us any longer. I have to admit, I miss his fine brandy more than I miss him."

He hadn't done it. Abruptly, she was certain of it. Ever self-absorbed, Marley hadn't cared for Thomas's politics, but he had tolerated them because he liked Lord Althorpe's brandy stock. His comment could be an incredibly clever ploy, but the whole thing would entail Marley accomplishing something very intricate and difficult and not taking credit for it.

"I think I may be ill," she said unsteadily, clutching her middle and putting a wan expression on her face. "Sinclair Grafton a murderer? Why didn't you tell me this before I danced with him?"

Fanning at her with his free hand, Marley led her through the gated entrance. "Actually," he murmured, "I've been thinking about this. As long as Lord Sin is carrying on with his opera singer, there's no reason we can't continue having our own fun."

"Could we?" she gasped, beginning to feel like a stage actress. How had she ever considered Marley a friend?

"Why not? And even better, until you come into your fortune, we could . . . convince Althorpe that it would be worth, say, five thousand quid a year for us to keep our suspicions about him to ourselves."

She wanted to laugh at him for his complete and utter idiocy. "Yes, but I'm living under the same roof as he is. What if he decided to silence me as well?"

"He wouldn't dare," Marley said easily as they strolled past the bird cages. "Everyone would know that he did it, and then they'd know he did the other murder, too."

"Which wouldn't be much of a comfort to me," she said dryly.

He looked at her quizzically, and she realized she wasn't helping things by making fun of him. To cover her error, she became absorbed in studying the large enclosure of bright-colored South American parrots.

"I need you, Vixen," he said quietly.

Almost as much as he needed her money. She looked up at him. "Give me time to think about all of this," she said and smiled. "It's quite a lot for me to absorb in one afternoon."

"Of course it is," he soothed. "But you must trust me. You know I'm better for you than Sin Grafton ever could be."

If she were a betting woman, she would have wagered a million pounds that he was dead wrong about that.

Chapter 14

A stin Hovarth reined in his bay gelding and watched from behind the shelter of a bulky mail coach as Sin Grafton returned to his own horse and trotted off in the direction of the horse auctions. The earl's smile deepened. The gentleman he was following seemed to be following him.

He debated whether to catch up to Sin and hand over the new bit of evidence he'd uncovered about Lord Marley, but he quickly discarded the idea. The clue wasn't much; a torn bit of a letter used to mark a page in a book. Better that he be reserved and cautious about relinquishing it, perhaps over a glass of port tonight. After all, he was helping to amass evidence that might very well get a man hanged.

This entire exercise was a damned nuisance. As far as Augusta and Kit were concerned, Thomas was dead, and that was the end of it. If he'd realized finding the killer would be so necessary, he would have arranged for one to be discovered at the time of the murder. Digging backward for a murderer two years after the fact was time-consuming and very tricky. After all, if he'd had perfect clues, the killer would already have been brought to justice.

After another few moments to be certain Sin didn't reappear, Astin turned his bay toward Bolton Street. Since the new Marquis of Althorpe insisted on dredging up the past, he was going to have to take steps to be certain that a few specific parts of it remained buried. Damn Thomas Grafton anyway, for not revealing what his scapegrace brother had been doing in Europe. They had been friends; he might have mentioned that blasted Sin was working for the bloody War Office. A spy, of all things.

Of course, if he'd known that back then, killing Thomas might have been avoidable. With Sin dead, the former Lord Althorpe would have lost both his urgent need to halt the war and his damned impractical patriotism.

Lady Jane Netherby wasn't likely to voice any suspicions, if the pretty, overaged doll even had any. Still, with Sinclair sniffing about, he needed to be sure. As for Sin's lovely little trollop of a wife, she'd best learn to keep her mouth shut. If the Vixen didn't, he would have to unearth a bit of evidence concerning her so-called friendship with Thomas, or with Marley. That would certainly distract Sin—at least long enough for Astin to finish encouraging Lord Marley's guilt. He smiled again. Wouldn't Marley be surprised.

In keeping with her supposedly clandestine relationship with Marley, Victoria asked him to stop his phaeton at the corner of Bruton Street and Berkeley Place and let her off there. He'd tried to kiss her again—twice—but she'd managed to deflect his lips, if not his attentions.

As she walked the half block to Grafton House, she considered ways she could tell Sinclair what she'd discovered without making him angry at her methods. Telling him that she'd spent half the afternoon with Marley was out of the question, especially if she followed that news with a statement about the viscount's innocence.

She hated the prevarications and half-truths that had come to be part of this investigation. Even more troubling than telling lies was the knowledge that Sinclair was more skilled at dancing around the truth than she ever could be.

Milo opened the front door just as she reached it. "Good afternoon, my lady."

"Good afternoon. Has Lord Althorpe returned?"

The butler took her shawl and bonnet. "Not yet, my lady. Shall I set out some tea for you?"

Victoria had been gone for nearly four hours. As far as she knew, Sinclair's only task for the day had been to invite his three mysterious friends to their dinner party. A small worry tugged at her insides. If anyone was capable of taking care of himself, it was Sinclair Grafton, but she still didn't like the idea of not knowing where he was. If the murderer wasn't Marley, Kingsfeld was the best suspect. And Sin would hardly be on his guard around his supposed friend; they might even be together right now.

With a shudder Victoria snatched back her bonnet from Milo's surprised fingers. "No tea today," she said briskly, retying the ribbons beneath her chin. "I have another errand to run. Please fetch Roman for me."

The butler's sallow expression darkened. "I have not seen that person all day, Lady Althorpe. I could not venture to guess where he might be."

"They didn't go anywhere together?"

"Not that I'm aware. Is something amiss?"

"Hm? No."

She knew Sinclair's friends were lodging somewhere on Weigh House Street. If she couldn't get Sin to listen to her, perhaps she could convince them.

"Lady Althorpe?"

"Milo, did anyone ever deliver any letters to a Lady Stanton?"

He flushed. "My lady, I have no idea of Lord Althorpe's private . . . correspondence. I—"

"Never mind that. Who delivered Sinclair's letters to her?"

"Ah, that would be Hilson, my lady. He's a good lad, if a bit—"

"I would like to speak to him," she interrupted. "At once." She tried to rein in her growing nervousness. With both Sinclair and Roman gone, she was the only one in the household with any idea that something might be wrong.

The butler inclined his head and hurried off toward the kitchen. "At once, my lady."

A few moments later young Hilson appeared, shuffling and nervous. "My lady?" he stammered, tugging at his neckcloth.

She smiled, attempting to look her most nonthreatening. "Hilson, do you know the address of Lady Stanton?"

"I . . ."

Milo nudged him in the back.

"Yes, my lady."

"Good. Please take me there."

The boy blanched. "Now? I mean, now, my lady?"

At some point she would have to tell Sinclair how

concerned the servants were over her delicate sensibilities—or, rather, over his dalliances. If she hadn't known the identity of Lady Stanton, she would have been quite annoyed. As it was, nervousness pushed against her sense of humor until she was ready to start shaking people.

"Yes, now. You don't drive, I suppose? Milo, hire us a hack."

"A *hack*, Lady Althorpe?"

Victoria closed her eyes and counted to three. "If you please, Milo."

The butler straightened his lanky form. "Of course, my lady. I will see to it immediately."

"Thank you."

Victoria and Hilson waited on the front steps for what felt like an hour but must have been no more than five minutes. Finally, with Milo practically hanging on to the poor horse by its ear and dragging it along, a dilapidated hack turned up the shallow drive.

"Are you certain, my lady?" he pleaded. "I can have Orser rig out Lord Althorpe's coach in ten minutes."

"I'm certain. Hilson, sit with the driver and direct him," Victoria instructed, clambering unaided into the small, smelly coach.

Milo appeared at the door. "Lady Althorpe, what do you wish me to tell the marquis if he should return?"

"Tell him I have gone to visit Lady Stanton, and I shall return soon."

He stepped back as the coach clattered into the street. "Very good, my lady."

She hoped the butler had a chance to get her into trouble.

At Miss Grenville's Academy, she'd learned that a proper lady was always patient, calm, and collected.

As Victoria fidgeted in the hack, looking out one window and then the other, she decided those lessons couldn't possibly apply to new brides whose husbands were former spies looking for murderers. If anything had happened to Sinclair . . .

It made her ill just to think about it. Of course he was all right. He'd survived for five years in an enemy country. This was nothing compared with that. Just because the killer was probably one of his brother's closest friends, it didn't mean he was in any more danger than he had been a week ago—or so she hoped with all her heart.

Just as she was about to lean outside and ask Hilson if he'd become lost, the coach rattled to a stop. Victoria was already on her feet as the door opened.

"We're here, my lady," Hilson said, helping her to the ground.

She handed him some change from her reticule and hurried in the direction of the small house he indicated. "Send the hack away and wait for me here."

"But—"

Without waiting to hear whatever Hilson's protest might be, Victoria swung the heavy knocker against the door. At least she'd learned something from Sinclair: strange carriages caused suspicion, especially when they stopped in front of a supposed lady's residence.

The door opened, and she released a breath she hadn't realized she'd been holding. At least someone was home. "I need to see . . ." she began, then trailed off. "You're Wally."

The portly, balding man blinked. "I used to be," he muttered, glancing past her at the street and Hilson. "Now I'm just a dead man."

"May I come in?"

"You might as well," he replied and stepped aside. "Is Sinclair here?"

He closed the door. "I don't know anything."

Footsteps emerged from a room to her left. "Well, this is interesting."

She recognized the soft Scottish accent from the foggy night in Hyde Park. "Mr. Harding," she said, turning to face the tall, sandy-haired Scotsman. "I'm looking for Sinclair."

Folding his arms, he leaned against the door frame. "He isn't here. How come you to know where t'find us, Lady Althorpe?"

"I brought along Hilson—the footman who delivers Sinclair's messages to Lady Stanton."

"Ah. Anyone else? Your maid, or one of your pretty little friends?"

"Crispin," Wally muttered.

She remembered that Mr. Harding hadn't seemed to like her very much at their first official meeting. "No, just me. Despite popular rumor, I'm not a complete idiot. Now, do you have any idea where Sinclair might be, or do I need to go looking for him myself?"

"Seems to me, where Sin's gone is his own affair."

If she were a man, she would have begun punching people by now. Obviously, though, these two men could withstand any pummeling she could possibly deliver. Therefore, she needed another way of gaining their assistance. And she'd been dealing with men who thought they were tough and heartless for a long time.

"Yes, you're right, of course." Victoria sighed. "It's just that I don't know where else to go. You are Sinclair's dearest friends, and I can't imagine that he would . . . vanish without at least telling you."

Crispin squinted one eye. "How long has he been gone?" he muttered with obvious reluctance.

"Hours. He said he was coming to see you. Did he . . . did he at least get this far?"

"Crispin's been here all afternoon," Wally supplied, "plotting times and alibis. You didn't see him, did you, Crispin?"

The big Scot's frown deepened. "Nae. Wallace, have cook brew up some tea for Lady Althorpe."

"Right." Wally hurried off into the depths of the house.

"Thank you. I just didn't know what else to do."

"Mm-hm. Follow me if you please, my lady." Pushing back upright, Crispin vanished back into the room from which he'd emerged.

He didn't sound very convinced, but all she needed to do was to get him to listen for two minutes. Squaring her shoulders, Victoria followed him—and stopped again in the doorway.

Though the huge table in the middle of the floor showed this to be the dining room, the house's inhabitants clearly took their meals elsewhere. Scattered papers covered one end of the oak surface, while the rest of the table held a ramshackle collection of small wooden boxes and chess pieces, all with little flags decorating them. Intrigued, she stepped closer to view the flag attached to a black pawn. "Lord Keeling, 8–8:08 P.M.," she read aloud. Victoria looked up at the Scot. "This is Mayfair, isn't it?"

"Aye."

She leaned in closer. "And the box in the middle would be Grafton House." Slowly she circled the table. "I've never seen anything like this. You've been placing people in locations they were seen on the night of Thomas's murder."

He nodded, his gaze following her. "Sin was right about you."

"In what way?"

"He said you were bright as a diamond in sunlight."

Victoria blushed. "Oh. Ah, why go to all this trouble to map out the streets?"

"It's easier than doing it on a piece of paper. If we get new information, we just move the citizens around."

"Might I ask you a question, Mr. Harding?"

"Isn't that why you're here?" he returned, not moving from his post by the wall.

"Partially. Where ... where have you placed Lord Marley?"

"I haven't."

She scowled. "What do you mean?"

"I mean we placed him at White's until just after eight that evenin'. We don't know where he went after that. No one we've talked to seems t'have seen him until he left home in his coach, headed for parts unknown, just before dawn the next morning."

"And what about Lord Kingsfeld?"

Crispin shifted a little. "Kingsfeld?"

A flash of anger went through Victoria. Obviously Sinclair hadn't seen fit to inform his fellows about her suspicions concerning Astin Hovarth. "Oh, yes, that's right—he was a friend," she bit out. "We mustn't suspect anyone known to be Thomas's friend three years before the murder."

"I detect a small bit of sarcasm," Crispin said dryly. Surprisingly, he looked more intrigued than annoyed. "Sin doesn't agree with you."

"No, he doesn't. And I don't want to see him hurt because he refuses to listen to me." Her voice broke, and she tried to cover it by clearing her throat. "He won't even look in that direction."

"Sin's not usually wrong. If he was, we would all have been dead a long time ago."

"I know that. But how can he be so stub—"

"The pleasant thing about having partners," the Scot interrupted, "is that even when you're lookin' in one direction, somebody else is watching your back."

She had to take that to mean he would look into Kingsfeld himself. A relieved tear ran down her cheek. She was becoming such a watering pot these days. "Thank you, Mr. Harding."

"Aye. Now you'd best go home. I don't relish the thought o' having to explain to Sin what you're doing here."

"Neither do I." Even so, she hesitated. "Mr. Harding?"

"Aye?"

She strode forward and stuck out her hand. "I do think we want the same thing."

Slowly he reached out and gripped her fingers. "I hope so. For all our sakes."

By the end of the afternoon, Sin was three-quarters of the way toward wishing he'd knocked Geoffreys over the head and gone in to search Kingsfeld's home, after all. The earl hadn't been at the horse auctions, nor at any of his clubs, nor indulging in an afternoon ride in Hyde Park.

As Sin trudged wearily into the house, Milo greeted him with his usual polite nod and silence. Sin wasn't in much of a mood to talk, so for once he didn't mind the stodgy fellow's manner. Upstairs the conservatory door was closed, and after a moment's hesitation he continued on to his own rooms.

"Roman," he said, pulling off his coat as he entered the bedchamber, "a glass of port, if you please."

The valet emerged from the dressing room. "I think you'll want something stronger than that, Sin."

"Why? What happened?"

Growling something under his breath, Roman went to the liquor stand and poured him a glass of whiskey. He continued his unintelligible litany as he crossed the room to hand the glass to Sin.

"Speak up," Sinclair demanded.

"I lost track of your wife," the valet grumbled, backing away.

"You *what*?"

"It wasn't my fault. How was I to know she'd climb into a carriage and—"

Sin set the whiskey down hard enough that half of it spilled onto his dressing table. "I don't want to hear any damned excuses, Roman. Where is she?" Fear stabbed through him. They were getting closer to finding the killer. If the killer knew that . . . "Talk to me. Now."

"All right, all right. She went walking toward Miss Lucy's house, but then she changed direction toward Bond Street. Ten minutes later Marley stops next to her and climbs out of his phaeton, and a minute after that, she climbs back in with him. By the time I got a hack to stop for me, they were out of sight. I looked—"

"Shut up," Sin growled. "Just shut up. I need to think." He strode to the window and back again, while

Roman wisely stayed out of his way. "You're certain it was Marley."

"Of course I'm certain. What kind of spy—"

"I think you're the kind of spy who lost track of my wife!" Sinclair bellowed.

"Sin—"

He whirled back on the diminutive valet. "You're *certain* she didn't return here while you were bumbling about?"

"I asked Milo, but he just glared at me, like he always does."

"Milo!" Sinclair stomped back to the door and flung it open. Good God, she had to be all right. He'd warned her about Marley. Why, in Lucifer's name, had she climbed into a damned carriage with him? Why would she do that?

"Yes, my lord?" The butler emerged at the top of the staircase.

"Have you seen my wife this afternoon?" Sin asked, his jaw clenched.

Milo looked beyond him at Roman, standing with a condemned man's stare in the depths of the bedchamber. "Yes, my lord," he answered slowly.

"When and where?"

"Why the hell didn't you tell me, you bloody Mr. Highboo—"

"Roman, enough! Milo, talk."

"She and ah, Hilson, went to see ... Lady Stanton, my lord. She said she would return soon."

Sin closed his eyes, sudden relief making him almost dizzy. "Thank God," he whispered. "Thank God."

"Is something amiss, my—"

Grabbing the butler by the lapels, Sinclair jerked

him into the bedchamber. "Enough is enough," he
growled. "This little game of yours ends right now.
Not liking one another is one thing, but you may not
compromise the safety of my wife. You two stay in
here until you either make amends or one of you is
dead. I don't care which." He stalked into the hallway
and slammed the door shut.

Damn! Victoria Fontaine-Grafton was out of control. Her spying adventures had just come to an abrupt,
inglorious end. He started for the stairs.

Vixen was climbing the last step as he reached
them. "Did I hear you bellowing at someone?"

He wanted to grab hold of her and shake her. With
his entire strength of will, he kept his hands at his
sides and watched her approach. His jaw was clenched
so tightly that he couldn't have uttered a word if he'd
known what to say to her. This deep, frightened anger
was new to him—and damned hard to control.

Victoria reached up to cup his cheek. "I was worried
about you," she said softly, searching his face with her
violet gaze.

"You . . . were . . . worried . . . about me?" he repeated in a growl.

Her hand dropped. "Yes."

"And just where did *you* go today?"

For another moment she held his gaze, and then she
blinked and looked toward the open library door. "I
think we need to talk. In private."

He nodded with effort. Angry as he was, bellowing
at her in front of the servants would reveal too many
things he wanted to keep hidden. "After you."

He followed her into the library and slammed the
door. Victoria jumped at the sound, and he ruthlessly
stifled the thought that he was going to bully her into

behaving, just because he could. It was for her own good. She had to be safe.

"Tell me about your luncheon with Lucy and Marguerite."

Victoria stopped beneath the window. "I'll be happy to," she said, folding her arms across her bosom, "if you'll tell me whether your friends will be attending our dinner party or not."

"So that's how you want it to be?" he asked tightly. "I'm delayed from doing something, and you use that to justify riding off with Marley all afternoon?"

Her face paled. "How did you know I went anywhere with Marley?"

"Roman saw you. And don't try to pretend it wasn't you."

"I'm not pretending anything. You have Roman spying on me, don't you? Do you really trust me that little, Sinclair?"

"Don't try to put me on the defensive. You're the one who went off with him—after you told me you were going to luncheon with your friends."

"And you weren't where you were supposed to be either!" she shot back. "I went to find you, and you weren't there!"

Something besides anger began to sift into Sin's brain. Victoria might be reckless, but she wasn't stupid. "Why did you go to find me?"

"Ha! I don't even want to tell you now, you big ape." She glared at him for another moment, then turned her back. "You won't believe me, anyway. You never do."

Sin realized he'd lost the argument the moment he'd let her open her mouth. With a deep breath, he relaxed his tense combat stance and dropped onto the couch. "Try me."

Her long fingers whitened, her fists were clenched so tightly. "Marley approached Lucy the other day to have her warn me about you, and to tell her how worried he was about me. I knew you would never approve, but I made arrangements to encounter him today, to find out what he really wanted."

"You're right," he said grimly. "I would never have approved. Good God, Victoria. You might have been . . ." It took him two tries to even get the rest of the sentence out. "You might have been hurt."

"I made certain we stayed in public. Anyway, he tried to convince me that you were having an affair with Sophie L'Anjou, and that I should therefore have an affair with him."

Without realizing how he got there, Sinclair was on his feet again, halfway to the window. "And your answer was what?"

She gave him a sideways glance. "I asked him why I should avoid you. He said he was almost certain you'd killed your brother, and that was a damned shame, because Thomas always kept a good supply of brandy. In fact, we could blackmail you with the murder insinuation to get you to fund our affair." Slowly she faced him again, her hands clasped in front of her. "I don't know how I can convince you, Sinclair, but Marley did not kill your brother. He . . . he doesn't feel deeply enough to go to the trouble."

For a long moment Sin just looked at her. "The evidence still points to him."

"Whose evidence? Kingsfeld's?"

"Not just Astin's. Why did you go to see Lady Stanton?"

"Because you weren't here when I returned, and I kept thinking you might have gone to see Kingsfeld, and that you might . . . be in trouble. But your men said you hadn't been there at all."

"I meant to go," he said slowly. "I went looking for Astin first, and ended up spending most of the day racketing around London trying to find him."

She lifted her chin. "Why?"

"Because I wanted to ask him to show me the rest of that paper he and Thomas were working on. The one with the brandy stain."

"You believe me," she whispered.

The relief in her eyes crumpled the remainder of his anger. "I said you had a good point. When I couldn't find him, I stopped by to see Kilcairn. He doesn't recall any proposal like the one you found in Thomas's office being presented in Parliament."

She took a step closer to him. "Which means?"

"Which means you may have found the key. But I still can't be certain yet who pulled the trigger. We know that Marley had motive. I don't know yet about Kingsfeld." Sin closed his eyes. "But I will find out."

Her arms slid around his waist. He opened his eyes again as she tucked her cheek against his chest. "Whatever the outcome," she murmured, "you're very close. I know it. Just please be careful."

Sin wanted to ask her why she'd been worried about him, why she wanted him to be careful. With the way he'd treated her and used her, though, he wasn't certain enough of the answer to ask the question.

"I'll be careful if you'll be careful," he said instead. "No more going off alone with Marley."

"I won't—if you'll stop sending Roman out to spy on me. I don't like that, Sinclair."

"Fair enough. I'll call off Roman." He'd make certain Wally took over the valet's assignment, but she didn't need to know that—not until everything was over with and she was safe.

He slowly wrapped his arms around her, and she sighed. "Now. Who were you yelling at before?" she murmured.

"Roman and Milo. I told them to make friends or kill one another."

She chuckled. "I'll put five pounds on Roman."

"I don't know. Milo's fairly scrappy, and he's definitely got a longer reach."

"What if they do one another in?"

"It'll save me the trouble." Slowly and reluctantly he released her. "Have you seen the office?"

"No." Victoria twined her fingers with his. "Show me."

The old Sinclair would have pulled every last bit of information out of Vixen regarding her conversation with Marley. Every word and every nuance would have been revealed and analyzed and categorized. Crispin would say he was losing his edge. This Sinclair, though, trusted that Victoria had told him what he needed to know. This Sinclair wanted to know if his wife liked her new desk.

His bedchamber door remained closed, but he heard only silence. Either the two men were having a civil discussion, or they were both unconscious.

"What do you think?" Victoria whispered.

"Too soon to tell. If they don't appear by dusk, I'll go look in on them."

"Why were you so angry with them, anyway?"

He tightened his grip on her hand, reminded of how

worried he'd been. "Their reluctance to communicate compromised your safety."

Victoria stopped, looking up at him. "I had the same concern—about you."

"You actually do worry about me, don't you?" he asked wonderingly. She seemed so strong and so fragile at the same time; an enigma who needed protection, but who seemed equally determined to keep him from harm.

"Of course I do. You're my husband, Sinclair Grafton. You're . . . important to me."

Sin leaned down to capture her mouth with his own. Sweet Lucifer, she was tempting. This life was so tempting. He wanted it, and he wanted her in it. But one damned thing stood in the way; and if he couldn't resolve it, the chasm it would leave in their lives would keep them apart forever.

With the master bedchamber occupied, Victoria lured Sinclair into her private sitting room. Lord Baggles vacated the couch just in time to avoid getting squished, and as Sin slipped her out of her walking dress with his usual efficiency, Victoria hoped that Mungo Park was elsewhere in the house. That silly bird was acquiring quite a vocabulary.

Whatever worries or concerns he might have, Sinclair had the unique and delightful ability to make her feel safe and loved and secure. By the time they emerged, her hair loosely tied with a ribbon because he couldn't manage anything else, it was dinnertime.

"Stop fiddling with it," she said, slapping his hands away from her hair.

He chuckled, drawing her back into his arms. "You

should always wear it like that. You look like a fairy princess."

"Oh, yes, I can see myself walking into Almack's with my hair down. They'd think I was a complete savage."

Sin ran his fingers through the long tresses, then kissed the nape of her neck. "Then wear it like this at home. I *know* you're a savage."

Stifling an attack of the giggles, and relieved that his tense, worried mood had lifted, she patted his cheek. "Oh, dear. You've gone completely insane."

"Good evening, my lord, my lady."

Milo stood at his usual post in the dining room doorway. His left eye was bruised and swollen nearly shut, but he seemed cheery enough.

"Good evening, Milo. Are you all right?" Victoria asked.

"Splendid, Lady Althorpe."

Sinclair stepped around her. "And how is Roman?"

"You would have to ask him, my lord." His lips twitched. "He seems to be a very . . . resilient fellow. As you requested, there will be no more miscommunications."

"Glad to hear it."

As Sinclair held her chair out for her, Victoria leaned up and kissed him on the cheek. "If you can make those two get along, I really think you can accomplish anything."

He smiled at her, his amber eyes dancing. "Thank you. I'm almost beginning to believe you."

Chapter 15

Lord Kingsfeld was about to go out for the evening and make his call on Sinclair Grafton when Sin himself knocked on the front door.

"Show him in," Astin instructed Geoffreys, as he settled into a chair in the library and opened a book of poetry.

Sin appeared on the butler's heels. "Astin," he said, coming forward and extending his hand. "I'm glad to find you at home."

"What can I do for you, my boy? Have a seat."

The new Lord Althorpe sank into the chair on the opposite side of the hearth. "I was wondering. That proposal—the one Marley spilled brandy on—do you have the rest of it?"

Astin blew out his breath. "I suppose I've got bits and pieces of it somewhere. Thomas was actually writing the treatise; I was just making notes."

"Was it ever put before the House?"

He'd been wise to produce a supposed part of the proposal; if Sin had found any of it on his own, the questions would have been much stickier. "Sadly, no. It wasn't complete enough, and without Thomas . . .

well, I'm afraid I didn't have the heart to finish it on my own."

Sin's expression darkened. "Don't blame yourself. But whatever you've got would be helpful."

"I'll go through my papers, then." He paused, letting Sin notice that he was hesitating, then set his book aside. "I did find . . . something else, quite by accident. I don't know if it's relevant, but I thought I should at least mention it to you, and let you decide its merits."

"You have my attention."

Fumbling as though he'd forgotten which pocket he'd deposited it into, Astin curled his fingers around the piece of torn note and pulled it free. "I'd been using it as a bookmark," he said apologetically. "Thank goodness I decided to reread my Homer."

Sin took the torn page and turned toward the firelight. Watching the younger man's countenance as he read the fragment, Astin allowed himself a brief smile of satisfaction. Poor Marley. At the moment he'd give the viscount equal odds between being hanged and being shot dead by Sinclair.

"It's Marley's handwriting," Sin murmured. "What was it, a letter?"

"Yes. As I recall, we laughed about it at the time." He drew his face into a frown. "It doesn't seem so amusing now."

"Even with most of it missing, it's clearly a threat."

"It seemed like one—but tempers were so short at the time, nearly everyone was writing nasty notes to one another. It may well be nothing."

"Or it may be something."

Sinking back again, Astin shook his head. "It's so odd. At the time I would never have suspected Marley. Once you mentioned your concerns about him to me, though, all the strange little bits seemed to fall into place."

Sinclair turned the scrap of paper over and back again. "This nearly does it. I'll be going to the magistrate on Monday. When this is over, Astin, I will owe you a great debt."

"Your brother was my dearest friend, Sin. You don't owe me anything."

Young Althorpe was so grateful about the new evidence that he completely forgot about the proposal he'd come looking for. After Sin left, Astin poured himself a brandy. With only two days left before Monday and Marley's arrest, this nonsense was nearly over with. And he had a nice party at Grafton House to look forward to on Saturday. It looked to be a lovely weekend, indeed.

"He was trying to distract me." Sinclair paced around the dining table at Kerston House on Weigh House Street. "Vixen was right; he doesn't have any damned copies of the damned proposal, because as far as he's concerned, he's destroyed all of them."

Crispin, seated at the table, continued studying the new scrap of paper. "But what's your evidence? You've got nearly enough to convict Marley, but I don't see how you can even touch Kingsfeld."

"I know." Sin continued his pacing. "It's the damnedest thing. A month ago, with this evidence, I would have gone to Marley's home and shot him dead myself."

"What does your Vixen know, and what does she *think* she knows? You can't give all of her opinions equal weight, Sin, and you can't let her suspicions sway you. You'll go insane from spinning so fast."

"She knows Marley." Sin snatched the paper back, even though he'd already memorized the few scattered half words and warnings. "She said he didn't have enough depth of feeling to murder someone."

"It doesn't take depth of feeling. All it takes is greed or fear."

"I've already had this argument with myself, Crispin. Tell me something new."

"The murder's two years old, Sin. There isn't anything new. That's the problem."

Nodding, Sinclair resumed his circuit around the room. He *knew* something was wrong. After two years of cold trails and cursing, suddenly every clue Astin Hovarth came up with pointed to Marley. "Astin said he would never have suspected Marley until after I mentioned my concerns about him. I might very well have fed John Madsen to him."

"*If* the earl is up t'something." With a heavy sigh, Crispin leaned over the table and nudged one of the chess pieces into the middle of the makeshift street. "Kingsfeld was at White's that night, till at least ten o'clock."

"And after that?"

"I don't know. We didn't look into it very closely. And if he was cozed up with some lady, we'll never find out—unless he's kind enough to tell us."

"I find that very interesting, my lads," Wally said, leaning into the doorway.

Sinclair hadn't even heard him come in. He was tired and he was frustrated, and growing more so by the moment. Crispin was right; if he continued to allow himself to become distracted, he was going to miss something that might get one or all of them killed. "What's so interesting, Wally?" he asked.

"I know of one lady Kingsfeld wasn't cozed up with that night." Wally approached their table map of Mayfair and picked up one of the chess pieces standing to one side. "Lady Jane Netherby left London the day before the murder and didn't return for the rest of the Season."

Sin stopped in his tracks. "And?"

"And according to her lovely maid, Violet, she wore black and wept for a solid month."

"That's not so odd. If she and Thomas were close, I don't see why she wouldn't have—"

"They went straight to her grandmama's in Scotland. According to Violet, Lady Jane didn't receive the *London Times* telling about your brother's murder until they'd been at McKairn Castle for over a week."

A cold dread ran through Sinclair. If she had known about Thomas's death before she had read about it, then she had another source of information. "I think I need to pay a call on Lady Jane Netherby," he said slowly, clenching his jaw. "Would anyone care to accompany me?"

"You're a few days from seeing Marley in chains," Crispin murmured in his soft brogue. "Are you certain you want to begin a whole new trail? Ye might just thank Lady Vixen for her suggestion, but tell her she's wrong."

Sin stopped halfway to the door. "You think I would pursue Kingsfeld just to appease Victoria?"

Wally cleared his throat. "You have to admit, Sin, since you got married you've spent less and less time turning over evidence, and more time . . . turning over in bed."

"What?" Deep hurt and anger cut through Sinclair's chest.

"Well, you are just marr—"

"What was I supposed to do here in London?" Sin snarled. "Do you think I like playing friendly with these bloated, self-important asses? Do you think I like going to their parties and dancing with their daughters when I know one of them killed my brother?"

"But you married one of their daughters."

Sin strode around the table toward Wally. It wasn't enough that he asked himself those same questions and had those same doubts every day—now his closest friends were throwing them in his face as well. "Why don't you repeat that, Wally?" he growled.

His face pale, Wally shuffled closer to Crispin. "I think I'll just keep my damned mouth shut from now on."

"Good idea," Crispin agreed, eyeing him balefully. "If I ever need help stabbing myself, I'll come to see you first, Wallace."

The spy scowled and flung his arms up in surrender. "That's fine—you lot go ahead and make me the villain. I was just agreeing with you, Crispin."

"I'll stand on my own feet, thank you."

"Then stand on your feet," Sin demanded, "and tell me what you did mean, Harding. I thought Wally's translation sounded fairly accurate."

Crispin did stand, but only to pull his coat off the back of his chair and shrug into it. "We've stood back to back for five years, Sin. We knew we couldn't trust anyone but ourselves." He shrugged. "It was a safe way to live."

"What the hell are you talk—"

"Will ye shut up for a moment?" the Scot snapped, jabbing a finger into Sin's chest.

Surprised, Sinclair subsided. "I'm listening."

"Thank you." A half dozen candles lit the tabletop neighborhood, and one by one Crispin snuffed them out. "All I meant, really, was that maybe you're looking for a way to extend the way things are."

"I'm stalling."

"Maybe," Crispin said. "Three days from the end, you decide to turn around 'n chase somebody else."

"I'm not stalling," Sin argued, realizing what his large companion was hinting at. "I'm making sure. If there's a *chance* Kingsfeld's involved, I am not going to miss looking into it. And at the moment, I happen to think there's more than a chance."

With a sigh, Crispin motioned him toward the front of the house. "Then let's be sure."

Sin put out an arm and stopped him. "I happen to . . . like Victoria Fontaine. If you're jealous of that, I'm sorry. But don't expect me to give her up." He wouldn't do that for his friends, or anyone. "Believe me, the idea of having this over with terrifies me— but there are things beyond this mess that I would like to try."

After a long moment Crispin nodded at him. "As I said, let's go talk with Lady Jane Netherby."

They headed for the front door, Wally on their heels. "Will someone please explain to me what we were just talking about?" he complained.

"Aye." The Scot held open the door for them to pass. "We just established that our Sinclair is in love with his wife, and that he wants this investigation finished so he can become domestic and work on making babies."

"Oh. That's what I thought."

"Ye did not, ye big clod."

As the three of them made their way through the

darkness to the stable, Sinclair slowed. They'd had arguments before, and he knew Crispin and Wally's banter was merely their way of apologizing. Crispin was right, though.

He *did* want this over and done with, because Victoria Fontaine-Grafton had shown him that something important lay beyond seeing justice done. For two years he had planned toward one point, one goal, and damned everything that got in the way. Now, suddenly, those barricades and distractions were looking more important than he'd ever imagined possible—nearly as important as finding out who had killed Thomas.

"Sin, you coming?" Wally called softly.

He started, and then went to collect Diable, who was waiting patiently in the deep shadows. "Let's go," he said, swinging into the saddle.

They quickly made their way to Bolton Street.

"How d'ye want to play this, Sin?" Crispin murmured as Sinclair climbed the narrow front steps.

"Right in her face," he answered, and rapped the knocker against the door. "She knew Thomas, and by God, I have a right to ask her about him."

"This is new," Wally whispered, so low that Sin obviously wasn't supposed to overhear.

"Aye. The front door approach. I like it."

"You would."

The door opened.

"May I help you?" An elderly woman, no doubt the housekeeper, stood in the doorway blinking at them.

For a heartbeat Sinclair wondered how late it was; he hadn't thought to check. "I have an urgent matter to discuss with the mistress of the house. Please tell

Lady Jane that Lord Althorpe needs to speak with her."

He used the title deliberately and was rewarded by seeing the old housekeeper flinch. At the same time, though, it felt right.

"Wait here, if you please," the housekeeper stammered, and closed the door.

"That was rude," Wally complained. "She won't even show us into the parlor."

"I wouldn't either," Sinclair said in a low voice. "We don't look very friendly."

The door opened a second time. "This way, my lord," the old woman said, gesturing. "But your ... friends will have to leave."

"They'll stay out here."

She hesitated for only a second before she nodded and stepped back to let him enter. "Up the stairs, my lord. First door on the right."

"Thank you."

He entered the drawing room and stopped just inside the doorway, all of his senses alert. A single lamp in one corner served as the room's only illumination, while the room's lone occupant sat in a chair as far from the light as she could manage. The setting seemed almost absurdly dramatic; if she'd been wearing flowing white robes instead of a conservative blue gown, he would almost have thought he'd stumbled into the middle of an opera. The fear in her eyes, though, was real.

"Lord Althorpe," she said in her low, melodic voice. "What brings you here, of all places?"

"I have several questions. I thought you might be able to help me find the answers to some of them."

"I ... don't know what you could want from me.

I'm actually quite busy tonight. My grandmother is suddenly ill, and I leave tomorrow for Scotland to tend her."

Sinclair kept his expression calm and aloof even as his mind leapt forward. "I'm sorry to hear that. Was your grandmother the reason you left London two years ago, right before my brother was killed?"

She gasped, her already pale skin turning gray. "I do not wish to speak of such sad things."

"But I do. Tell me, Lady Jane, how you learned of Thomas's death."

Clutching a hand to her breast, she stood. "You should leave. I will not be interrogated in my own home. And certainly not by you."

"I think you know who killed Thomas," he continued, ignoring her protest. "If I leave, you won't have to answer only *my* questions. You'll be telling your tale to a judge and a horde of solicitors, as well."

Abruptly she sank back onto the couch, as though she'd lost all strength in her legs. "I have no proof," she whispered, "and he will deny everything. He told me that again today."

His heart thudding, Sinclair took a slow step forward. "Lord Kingsfeld is well respected, but he is not invincible."

She gave a brittle laugh. "Ha. That's what you think. I know better."

"You owe Thomas the truth."

"Thomas is dead," she said flatly. "And he should have known better."

For a brief moment Sin closed his eyes. "Better than what?"

"Better than to make so many peers angry. Now go. I'm not going to say anything else—except to tell you that if he knew you suspected him, you couldn't run far enough or fast enough to escape."

She had begun shaking, her eyes staring and withdrawn. He knew that he would never get a straight answer out of her—she was more frightened of the unnamed murderer than she was of him. Still, she had given him something.

"Thank you, Lady Jane. Convey my best wishes to your grandmother."

Her gaze darted in his direction and back to the shadows again. "Go."

He did as she asked, and showed himself from the house. "Let's go," he told his friends, walking past them.

"What did she say?" Wally asked.

"She said that she wouldn't tell me anything. Someone's got her frightened half out of her wits, and whoever it was called on her today to remind her of that. I worked Kingsfeld into the conversation, and she didn't contradict me."

Crispin scowled. "That's not much help."

"It is, actually. I happen to know that Marley spent most of the day with my wife, and wasn't available to make threats against frightened, lonely women."

"Sinclair, you aren't going to go do something rash, are you?" Crispin asked. When his friend declined to answer, the Scot clamped an iron hand over his shoulder. "Sin?"

He shrugged free. "With what proof?" he snapped. His brain still refused to accept the idea that Astin Hovarth had shot Thomas. They had been friends, for God's sake. *Friends.*

"Your Vixen will be happy to know she was right."

Keeping a wary eye on Sin, Wally circled around to his horse.

"Vixen," Sinclair repeated, his chest tightening for the second time that night. "I can't tell her."

"Why not?"

"Because she's Vixen." They looked at him blankly while he uttered a few choice curses. Victoria's heart shone in her eyes, and she could no more lie than she could turn away her menagerie. Astin would know the instant he set eyes on her that they suspected him. "Kingsfeld is going to be at my house tomorrow night. And so are you, and Victoria's friends. If she *knew* . . . I can't risk her giving us away. Kingsfeld killed his closest friend; I won't risk making him suspicious by telling Victoria."

"In a way, this could be handy. Why don't I miss the party and go calling on Hovarth House during his lordship's absence?" Crispin suggested.

Sinclair shook his head. "I promised you would be there. I could explain Bates missing the soiree even if he returns in time, but not you two." He caught their quick exchange of looks and frowned. "What's done is done. Go back to Kerston House and see if you can find anything to help us with Kingsfeld."

"And where are you going?"

"Home—to lie to my wife again." And to pray that she would forgive him for it later.

"They agreed to come?" Victoria repeated, smiling widely.

Sinclair didn't seem quite as pleased as she, but she put it to his more cautious nature. No one needed to know his friends were spies, but they could at least all become acquainted with one another.

"I don't think Bates will be back in time, but Wally and Crispin will be here," he confirmed. "And I need—"

Milo entered the open morning room, three china plates of varying patterns held out for display. "These were the three with green in them, my lady."

"Which one looks the friendliest, do you think?"

Her husband looked at her. "Friendliest?"

"Tonight is important. I want it to go well."

He smiled, though the light in his amber eyes wasn't quite as joyous. "So do I. All of the settings look quite friendly. I doubt any of them would misbehave."

Victoria leaned forward on the couch to smack his knee. "Rogue. Milo, I like the one with the roses."

"They seem friendly to me, my lady. I shall have them put out at once." With an awkward bow, the butler restacked the plates and exited.

Victoria sat back again to look at the guest list. For once it didn't really matter where anyone sat, because most of the guests were friends already. "Would your Crispin mind sitting across from Lucien?" she asked, "or would that be too much like bear baiting?"

He didn't answer. When she looked up, he was gazing at her, his expression the sheepish one of a schoolboy who'd put a frog in the teapot.

"What is it?"

"I . . . oh, damnation." Sinclair sat next to her and pulled her hand over to play with her wedding ring. "I know you don't like him, and I know you're suspicious, but—"

"—but you invited Lord Kingsfeld, didn't you?" She looked back down at her list so he wouldn't see how hurt she was. "You said no suspects, Sinclair. I know how important this investigation is to you, but

I wanted . . . I wanted tonight to be for us."

His lips brushed her knuckles. "Whatever you think of him, I couldn't exclude him without a reasonable explanation." He kissed the inside of her wrist. "I won't do any spying tonight."

Victoria knew why he was kissing her, yet knowing he was attempting to distract her didn't make it any less stimulating. She watched, mesmerized and shivering, as his mouth slowly trailed up the inside of her arm.

"Do you still believe me?" she whispered shakily. "Do you still believe it might be Kingsfeld?"

"What I believe," he returned in a low, seductive voice, "is that I'm going to make love to my wife." He removed the clips from her hair.

"The door is open," she enunciated, trying very hard to keep a grip on her sensibilities. "And you didn't answer my question."

His lips favored her throat with feather-light kisses, which followed along her jaw and up to the corner of her mouth. "Victoria," he whispered, "kiss me."

"But . . . don't you—oh, my, that feels good—don't you care that the man who killed . . . your brother may be dining at your table tonight?"

Sinclair captured her lips in a deep, hungry kiss. Fire spun though her as she slid her hands slowly up his chest and around his broad shoulders. He knew so much of the world, and she kept waiting for the moment when he would tire of her and her unending silliness; kept watching for any sign that he wanted to return to the exciting life he'd pursued for the past five years. All of her thrilled to his every touch and every soft-spoken word murmured in her ear. If tonight—now—he wanted to forget the spying and the hunting to be with her, she would be a fool to remind him of it again.

He pressed her down on the couch, his lean body stretched half on top of her. His mouth continued to plunder and explore hers until she could barely breathe, much less think.

"Sin, do you—"

They both started. Roman stood with his well-muscled arms stretched to either side of the doorway as he leaned into the room. His ruddy face darkened further as he spied them prone on the couch.

"Ah. Never mind me," he grunted and grabbed the door handle to shut it soundly.

"I knew he was good for something," Sinclair murmured, and slid lower to caress her bosom with his warm, soft lips.

Victoria tangled her fingers into his dark hair, arching up against him as he swept his arms under her and swiftly loosened the fastenings of her morning dress. As she lay back again he tugged it down to her waist and resumed kissing her bare breasts.

Shifting sideways, he allowed her to remove his coat and waistcoat and his cravat, now hopelessly crushed and wrinkled. His shirt proved more difficult, because he didn't seem to want to stop kissing her and caressing her skin with his long, knowing fingers.

"Sinclair," she finally protested, and yanked the shirt off over his head when he paused to look down at her.

"I want to be inside you," he murmured, and took her breast into his mouth.

She moaned in helpless lust, wriggling her hips as he pulled the gown the rest of the way down. He went up on his knees, batting her hands away as she reached

up to help him undo his breeches. She loved it when
he was like this; she loved the way he seemed to want
her so much he could barely keep his hands steady.

As soon as he freed himself, he nudged her knees
apart and sank down again, entering her as he did so.
She moaned again, this time in satisfaction. Keeping
most of his weight on his elbows, he leaned down to
kiss her again, open-mouthed, his tongue moving inside her with the same rhythm as the heated thrusts of
his hips. Victoria dug her fingers into his strong back,
relishing the sensation of him moving so strongly and
deeply inside her.

Her body knew his now, and she began to pulse as
she felt him moving close to release. He lifted his head
and looked down at her, his eyes dark with passion
and desire, as he came with a last deep thrust and she
joined him in ecstasy.

"We've crushed your guest list," he noted breathlessly, tugging it from beneath her.

Chuckling, Victoria brushed dark hair from his eyes
and pulled his face down to kiss him again. "No harm
done."

He hoped that was true. It was small comfort that
he hadn't quite lied to her about Kingsfeld; he'd simply avoided answering her questions, and counted
himself lucky to have gotten away with it. How long
he could keep up the deception, he had no idea. She'd
managed to uncover his other secrets without much
difficulty.

She sighed, sliding her arms around his waist. "All
right, Sinclair. Since you've gone to this much trouble
to persuade me, I suppose I can tolerate Kingsfeld for
one evening."

"Thank you. I'll keep him as far from you as possible." *At gunpoint, if necessary.*

"No, you won't. You don't want to make anyone suspicious of anything. We're all supposed to be a herd of happy, scandalous hedonists, aren't we?"

"Some happier than others," he whispered, kissing her ear. Slowly and regretfully he sat up, wondering whether he would ever feel sure enough about her safety to tell her how much he was coming to care for her. Soon, he told himself. As soon as he had Kingsfeld. As soon as he'd fulfilled his duty to Thomas and could be reasonably assured of staying alive long enough to begin his duties to her. "You are very understanding."

"And you are very persuasive."

He brushed a finger against her soft, smooth cheek. "I'm glad you think so. Now, I do have one errand to run today."

Victoria sat up beside him, her violet gaze serious. She opened her mouth to say something, then obviously changed her mind. "Just promise me you'll be careful."

So she still wasn't sure what he was up to. "Would you miss me?" he asked softly, kissing her again.

"Yes. And it would ruin my seating arrangements."

With a chuckle, Sinclair leaned down to gather his scattered clothes. "We can't have that."

Once they'd managed to return to some semblance of decorum, Sinclair rode to the House of Lords, where one of Thomas's fine bottles of brandy convinced the clerk to produce five boxes of rejected proposals and treatises from the regular session of Parliament two years earlier. Though Sinclair suspected Thomas's paper wouldn't be among them, it took two hours of searching to confirm it. Thomas had authored several unsuccessful treatises, but none of them was as direct and defiant and as threatening to noble purses as the draft Victoria had found.

Waiting until the clerk became tired of the dust and bored with hovering about, Sinclair slipped into another room to search for a second set of records. This time he wasn't making a random exploration in the hopes of stumbling across something. He knew precisely what he was looking for, and it took only a short time for him to find it.

The Earl of Kingsfeld had indeed divested himself of several minor shares of stock in minor companies with ties to France. What he had kept, though, was ownership of a company located a few miles outside of Paris—a company that manufactured parts for gas streetlamps.

Sinclair cursed. No wonder Kingsfeld had kept silent about his ownership of such an innocent, progress-minded business. Sin knew of the factory; he'd even visited it in the company of one of Bonaparte's generals. And though pipes and fittings for streetlamps had been visibly stacked in a corner, he doubted even one single lamp had been constructed during the war. The factory had been too busy with its secondary task—making muskets. Muskets that had armed Bonaparte's soldiers at Waterloo.

Swiftly Sin returned everything to its place, puttered in the storage room for another few minutes, thanked the clerk, and left. The angry, sick feeling in the pit of his stomach grew. He'd seen death and betrayal; he'd even participated, when the task had called for it. But he'd considered the earl a friend. He'd *trusted* him. And tonight the bastard would sit at his table—

the table that used to belong to Thomas—and laugh and smile, and Sinclair would have to laugh and smile with him, because although he *knew* Kingsfeld had murdered Thomas, he still had no proof. He would find that proof, though, and soon—even if it killed him.

Something was terribly wrong. Victoria perched on the arm of the couch to chat with Lucy and Lionel, but most of her attention was on the laughing conversation at the other end of the room. Sinclair and Kit stood with Kingsfeld, all of them acting as though nothing untoward was going on at all. Kit, she could believe, but not the other two.

". . . and of course, after Almack's exploded, no one wanted to tell Lady Jersey about it."

Victoria blinked and looked at Mr. Parrish. "What?"

"You were right," Lucy said, sighing heavily and unsuccessfully hiding a grin. "She wasn't listening at all."

"I am so sorry." Victoria clasped her friend's hand. "You have my undivided attention."

The girl giggled. "It's all right. If I had a husband as splendid looking as Sinclair Grafton, I would spend all my time gazing at him, too."

Lionel lifted an eyebrow. "I think I might be offended."

Lucy blushed. "Oh, Lionel. It's not—"

He put up his hand. "No. I will not be mollified. In fact, tomorrow I am going to speak to your father about it."

"What?"

With a fond grin he kissed Lucy's cheek. "Now who's going to be ogling whom?" he asked, and strolled over to join another cluster of guests.

"Oh, my," Lucy whispered, and burst into delighted laughter.

Victoria hugged her. "That's splendid," she said, chuckling. "And if he's teasing, I will never forgive him."

"Neither will I." Lucy laughed again, tears welling in her eyes. "I will torture him terribly tomorrow. But tonight do you think I might ask Marguerite to play?"

Victoria took her arm. "I think that is a splendid idea." She glanced toward her husband's group again, though her gaze wasn't on Sinclair. "I should love to dance."

Her husband had promised he wouldn't do any spying tonight, but she hadn't made any such agreement. The Earl of Kingsfeld would eventually make a mistake. Waiting for it to happen, though, meant worrying about Sinclair every time he vanished for an hour, and fearing for the safety of Augusta and Christopher at every moment of the day and night. Perhaps, she could encourage Astin Hovarth into giving away something—anything—that would prove his guilt to Sinclair.

Convincing Marguerite to play was easy enough, especially when Kit volunteered to turn the pages for her. Deciding how to partner with Kingsfeld for a waltz presented more of a problem—until she remembered that she was, after all, Vixen Fontaine, who would say or do practically anything.

Squaring her shoulders, she swept up to the group of men. "Lord Kingsfeld," she said, ignoring Sinclair's abrupt step toward her, "I have decided to give you another opportunity to charm me."

He smiled. "It would be my pleasure."

Marguerite had already begun the waltz, so she allowed him to lead her into the middle of the room and slip his hand around her waist. She suppressed a shudder as she placed her hand in his. With a light pressure, he swung her into the dance. This was for Sinclair, she reminded herself as she looked up into Kingsfeld's cool brown eyes. This was for them.

"We seem to disagree whenever we begin a conversation," he said, returning her gaze evenly. "Perhaps we should refrain from any discussion at all."

Victoria laughed. "I had considered the same thing, and I decided on a topic for which we both have admiration: Thomas Grafton."

He didn't flinch or look the least bit guilty. "But not his . . . drawings, of course."

Reminding herself that she'd pretended to be charmed and flattered a thousand times, she nodded. "Not his drawings. Only the man himself."

"Very well. And how shall we begin this pleasant conversation?"

"I shall say that in the short time I knew him, I never saw him dance. Both of his brothers, though, seem quite skilled. Do you know if he had a reason for not stepping onto the dance floor?"

"Well, my dear, I believe Thomas thought the waltz too forward. You and your friends undoubtedly didn't attend the staid gatherings where more formal dances were favored."

"That's true," she mused. "But you waltz, and very handsomely."

"I'm not quite as conservative as Thomas was."

She chuckled, glancing across the room as they twirled, to see Sinclair conversing with Lucien and his tall friend Crispin, and apparently not noticing her at all. "Sinclair has said Thomas was the most conservative man he ever knew. I wonder how the two of you remained such close friends."

"Why do you wonder?"

It might have been her imagination, but she thought his hand tightened a little around hers. His expression didn't change, but if he'd escaped suspicion for a murder, he wasn't likely to panic over something she said. "It's only that your tastes seem so much more . . . liberal. I would have thought you and Sinclair would have been the ones to become friends."

"Sinclair wasn't liberal; he was reckless. I find no appeal in that." Kingsfeld must have seen something in her eyes, because he smiled. "Thankfully he has become more wise as he's gotten older."

Finally, an opening. "You must have thought his adventures in Europe very reckless indeed." The last stanza of the waltz began, and she realized she was swiftly running out of time. "I know I did, until he told me his reasons."

"And now?"

In her imaginings, drawing him into a confession had been much easier. "And now, I'm pleased you're assisting him in his hunt to find Thomas's murderer." Stifling her desire to vomit, she leaned closer. "I admit, though, that I have my doubts about Marley's guilt."

"Do you?"

"Yes. I think the killer must really have been someone quite stupid, because he left some papers behind. Marley is much more clever than that."

She'd made him angry; she could see it in his eyes, and in the cold turn of his thin lips. Victoria held her breath, hoping with all her might that Marguerite would want to show off for Kit and repeat the last stanza with her famous flourish.

"The killer has evaded detection for two years, my dear. These . . . papers you refer to couldn't have been much of anything, or they would have been used to bring the murderer to justice already."

"Oh, I think they are the key," she whispered in a conspiratorial tone. "I only just found them, though. Sinclair hasn't even seen them yet. I was going to show him in the morning, as a surprise."

Kingsfeld opened his mouth, and then closed it again. "I pray you're right," he finally murmured, "though you shouldn't get your hopes—or Sin's—up needlessly. Perhaps you should show these papers to me first. You wouldn't want Sinclair to think you were silly, or merely trying to protect Marley."

If her husband knew what she was doing, he would think her worse than silly. "I have no reason to protect Marley, my lord."

"Of course you do. Sin told me he only went to ruin you that night in order to draw Marley out. Imagine his surprise when it didn't succeed, and he had to take more drastic action."

The waltz ended. Victoria was sure her heart stopped beating in the same moment. Everything inside her went cold and still and dead. "You are mistaken," she managed, her mouth dry.

"Oh, I don't think so," the earl continued in a low, intimate tone. "Now, why don't you show me those papers?"

A hand grasped her elbow from behind, and she jumped.

"Apologies, Vixen," Alexandra said in her humor-touched voice, "but you look as though you could use some air."

"Yes, I could," she blurted, grabbing Lex's arm. She wasn't about to show Kingsfeld anything. And even though he'd only been trying to fluster her, she still needed to think. If what he'd told her was true—

"Come on, my dear, you're white as a sheet."

As Marguerite began another tune, Victoria allowed Alexandra to lead her out of the drawing room and down the hallway into her animal-filled conservatory. They opened the tall glass doors, and the cool evening breeze flooded the room.

"Oh, that's better," Victoria said, sinking into a chair. Lord Baggles jumped onto her lap with his usual good timing, and she buried her face in his soft fur.

"You're not just worn out." Alexandra sat on the arm of the chair beside her. "What's wrong?"

"Nothing. I was just warm."

"Mm-hm. I should have realized. You've never been able to tolerate more than one dance in an evening, delicate and shy as you are."

"Just be quiet, Lex. I need to think."

"Do you want us all to leave? Lucien can clear out a room in less than a minute. Believe me. I've seen him do it."

Victoria grabbed her friend's hand. "Don't go."

"All right. But you have to tell me what's upset you so much."

Mungo Park flapped over and perched on the back of the chair. " 'Kiss me again, Vixen,' " he squawked in his impression of Sinclair's deep voice.

Victoria burst into tears.

"Uh-oh. What happened?"

She shouldn't say anything. But she was so tired of

all the secrets—especially if there wasn't any point in her trying so hard to close this chapter of Sin's life. "I think Sinclair only married me to spite Marley," she sobbed.

"What? Did Kingsfeld tell you that?"

"Yes. And . . . and I know Sinclair hates Marley, and it would be very like him to do something so sneaky . . . but I . . ."

"But you love him," Lex finished.

"No, I don't. I would be stupid to fall in love with him if he didn't mean anything by marrying me."

"Of course he meant something by marrying you," her friend soothed, squeezing her hand. "Why would Kingsfeld say something so awful? And why would Sinclair hate Marley?"

"I can't tell you!"

"All right. But tell me this: who do you trust more—Kingsfeld or Sinclair?"

Wiping her eyes, Victoria straightened. "Sinclair," she whispered.

"Then what's the difficulty? Come, now. Take deep breaths. It's not good for you to be so upset."

Alexandra seemed rather keen on the subject of her health, which was somewhat odd. As Victoria's thoughts cleared a little, she looked up at her friend. "Since when are you so worried over my health? I used to go riding in the rain, you know."

For a long moment Alexandra looked at her with her calm, aquamarine gaze. "Perhaps I'm wrong, then."

Victoria scowled and swiped at her damp cheeks again. "Wrong about what?"

Her friend sighed, humor touching her eyes. "To put

it delicately, dear, when was the last time you . . . had your monthly courses?"

"Not since I've been married, of course."

Alexandra's smile deepened.

"What? I . . . I thought they stopped once you were . . . intimate."

"Well, goose, then you don't know as much as you think you do. They stop, Victoria, when you're with child."

Chapter 16

❧

Dark, worried anger coursed through Sinclair at the sight of his Victoria in that bastard's arms. Whatever the cause, however important it was, he didn't want her anywhere near Kingsfeld. Wally said something, but he barely noted the comment, or his own reply. He wasn't jealous; this was hotter, more pure than that. He was terrified—that something might snatch Victoria away from him. They were so close to the end, but if it meant losing her, it wasn't worth it. Not any longer.

Sin took a step away from his companions. He had loved Thomas, but his brother was gone. Victoria, vibrant and warm and beautiful, was alive, and she was placing herself in danger—for him. He'd been wrong when he'd claimed he would do anything for the mission. If it came down to a choice between finding a killer and being with Victoria, he knew the answer. He didn't just admire Vixen; he *loved* her with every bit of his heart, and he would do anything—*anything*—to keep her from harm.

A hand clamped down on his shoulder. "What are you doing?" Crispin murmured.

"Getting my wife away from that—"

"He's not going to do anything here. Just wait."

"I don't want to wait."

"You don't want to make a mistake now, either, Sinclair."

Crispin was right. His jaw clenched, Sin watched them dance about the room, his willpower stretched to the breaking point. Only when he saw they'd fallen into their familiar pattern of arguing did his heart lurch and begin beating again. As Alexandra escorted Vixen from the room, he shook himself and returned to his conversation. *She was safe*, he kept telling himself. All he needed to do was keep her that way.

He concentrated on returning his breathing to normal as Kingsfeld strolled over to rejoin them.

"Your wife is a splendid dancer," he said, accepting a glass of port from a footman.

"You acquitted yourself well also, Astin," Kit said, grinning. "I didn't see you step on her toes once."

With a quick glance toward the door through which Victoria had vanished, Kingsfeld put his hand on Sinclair's shoulder. "Might I have a quick word with you, Sin?"

Sinclair forced himself to answer in a normal tone. "Of course. Excuse me a moment. And don't wager anything with Kit, Wally. You'll lose."

"Damnation, Sin. Stop warning my victims."

Astin strolled across the room to the far windows, and with growing worry, Sin followed him. They obviously weren't supposed to be overheard, whatever it was the earl was up to. He blinked, trying to pull himself together. She was safe, and he had very nearly caught a killer. Well, then, Vixen would just have to understand if he ended up doing a little spying this evening, after all.

"I hesitate to say anything," Kingsfeld began in a low voice, "because I don't know how deeply you've permitted Vixen to become involved, but I thought this was important."

At the mention of Victoria's name, Sinclair's tension rose another notch, and he wondered whether Kingsfeld knew how close he was to dying, proof of his guilt forthcoming or not. "What is it?"

"I know you wanted your investigation kept quiet. While we were dancing, though, your wife kept chattering on and on about Marley not being the killer, and about mysterious documents which only she knew about which would prove the identity of the murderer. Needless to say, I was quite concerned, Sin. If it hadn't been me she spoke to, or if she has spoken to anyone else in the same fashion, she might have destroyed all of your hard work—and endangered you and your family."

Sin couldn't breathe. A frightened fury unlike anything he'd ever felt jolted through him, cold and hot and dreadful. He clenched his fists to keep from throttling Kingsfeld right in the middle of his drawing room: the bloody blackguard was so damned self-confident that he'd actually dared to threaten all of them to Sin's face. An equal part of Sinclair's anger, though, was directed at Vixen—for putting herself so squarely in the path of danger.

"I'll speak to her at once," he hissed, "the silly chit." The last comment was for Kingsfeld's benefit; his own choice of vocabulary over Victoria's reckless behavior was much stronger. Not daring to say anything else, he strode from the room.

She wasn't in her sitting room, or her bedchamber, and without bothering to knock he slammed open the conservatory door. Victoria sat in a chair, sobbing, while Alexandra Balfour rubbed her back. They both jumped as he charged into the room.

"Lady Kilcairn," he growled, "I require a word in private with my wife."

The taller woman straightened. "Vixen is over-wrought at the moment, my lord. Can this wait?"

"No. It can't."

"It's all right, Lex," Victoria managed, her voice breaking.

Giving him a warning look, Alexandra released her friend's hand and left, shutting the door softly behind her. Sin wanted to stomp up and down the room to vent some of his anger, but the floor was covered with kittens, puppies, squirrels, and rabbits, all gathered around their weeping mistress.

"I would like to know," he said, his voice tight and barely controlled, "what in God's name you thought you were doing, gossiping about all of your suspicions to Kingsfeld?"

She gazed at him, teary-eyed. "I was helping," she sniffed. "And I wasn't gos—"

"Helping? *Helping?* Do you have any idea how much . . . trouble you might have caused?" He'd almost blurted that she'd put herself in danger, but that would have meant admitting that he'd lied to her again, this time about his suspicions regarding Kingsfeld. If she knew how close she was to the truth, she would never back off.

Victoria wiped at her eyes. "Is it true," she whispered, "that you married me just to spite Marley?"

He blanched, his brain stumbling over the topic. He

hadn't expected it, and he had no lies—or truths—at hand with which to comfort her. "Who . . ."

"Kingsfeld told me. Is it true?"

Astin Hovarth had certainly learned his Roman military history; he'd managed to divide them in the space of a four-minute waltz; all that was left was the conquering part. The earl had left him with no time to make explanations, or even to protest his love for her. She wouldn't believe it now. "I want you, and Grandmama Augusta and Kit, in a coach headed to Althorpe first thing in the morning. If you—"

"No! I won't g—"

"If you," he hammered over her outburst, "are going to say . . . stupid things to people just to provoke them, then I . . . can't have you here. I can't watch you play games and attempt to catch a murderer at the same time."

Standing there and watching the hurt and bewilderment and disappointed anger in her eyes was the hardest thing he'd ever done. With every fiber in his body, he wanted to take her into his arms and tell her that she'd put herself in so much danger that he didn't dare allow her to remain anywhere near London and Kingsfeld. Just as he realized he couldn't stand to lose her, he needed to make her angry enough—he needed to hurt her enough—that she would leave.

Her ploy was indeed likely to flush the earl out—but just far enough to kill her. It was brilliant, but he wasn't about to put her at such risk. "You are leaving in the morning," he repeated harshly. "Is that clear?"

Another tear ran down her cheek. "Yes. Perfectly."

"Good." He turned on his heel and left the room.

Sinclair didn't attempt to disguise the fact that he and Vixen had had a terrible argument. It would put

Kingsfeld more at ease, and it would explain why Victoria left London in the morning. Just in case it didn't quite convince the earl, though, he wanted Augusta and Christopher out of harm's way, as well. If he lost any of them . . . He couldn't even think about it without breaking into a cold sweat.

Once their guests left for the evening, Sin posted Milo in the upstairs hallway to make certain both that Victoria stayed put and that no one else attempted to get in to see her. Even so, he didn't want to be out of earshot of the house while she was there, so he gathered his lads in the dark stable.

"What in damnation happened?" Wally asked as Sinclair slipped in through the door.

Another, less familiar voice spoke from the near darkness. "My wife wants to strangle you," Lucien Balfour said calmly.

"I hope she has a chance to do so," Sin replied. "Thank you for joining us."

"Let's just say you've piqued my curiosity."

Sin decided he'd worry about that later. "Crispin, what did Kingsfeld do when I left the room?"

"He went over t'chat with your grandmama," the Scot said. "Nothing important; just comparing social calendars for the rest of the week."

Cold dread jolted through Sinclair again, but he managed a grim smile. "I'm glad you didn't listen when I said no spying tonight. He thinks Victoria knows something the rest of us don't about the murder. He's checking to see where everyone's going to be for the next few days."

Lord Kilcairn's dark form stirred. "Then no one should be where he expects."

"I'm sending them away tomorrow."

"It's none of my affair," the earl continued in his low, dry voice, "but how are you making Vixen leave?"

"I deliberately made her angry. She'll go."

"Where d'ye want us, then?"

Sinclair took a deep breath. "Kilcairn, if you could help a few rumors along that Vixen has left me and I've spent the night getting very drunk, I would appreciate it."

"Easy enough. I take it you'll be absent from Parliament tomorrow, then?"

"I'll make an appearance, just to make sure Kingsfeld's there. It won't be pretty when I leave."

"Are we going into Hovarth House?" Roman asked, the light of battle gleaming in his eyes.

"You're not. I want you with my family."

The valet looked at him skeptically. "And how are you going to explain that?"

"Vixen's the only one who knows who you are. Be a groom. Just watch over them."

"Your Vixen's the one I'm worried about."

For a moment Sinclair closed his eyes. After this, if he had to beg for Victoria's forgiveness every day for the rest of his life, he would consider it a small price to pay. "I don't think she'll be paying much attention to what's around her," he said slowly. "Stay out of her view if you can."

"This is not going to go well," the valet muttered.

Wally patted Roman on the shoulder. "And Hovarth House?"

That was going to be the tricky part. Too subtle, and they would be wasting their time. Too bold, and they would alert Kingsfeld. The earl, though, had already been alerted.

"He won't have kept anything to tie him to the murder," Sin decided, "but I want him good and rattled."

Harding cursed. "Sin—"

"Crispin, Wally," Sinclair interrupted, "don't let anyone see you, but I want to be damned certain he knows someone was in his house, looking through his things."

"No. With you vanished from Parliament, he'll think it was you," Crispin countered, shaking his head. "Setting yourself up to be dead won't solve the murder—and it won't keep your loved ones safe."

"That's not the plan," Sinclair countered. "Not yet, anyway."

"Where will you be, then?"

"Seeing Marley arrested."

Lucien chuckled in the shadows. "I'm somewhat relieved we've become allies, Althorpe."

"Kingsfeld will have to come to me to find out what's going on. We'll see what kind of tale I can spin."

"It'd better be a damned good one, Sin, or he'll kill you."

"Not if I kill him first."

"But—"

"He should feel relieved with Marley arrested and me drunk. Tearing up his study will unsettle him."

"It unsettles me," Wally muttered.

"And it'll coax him here to find out why," Sin continued. "I'm going to have to ask for one more key piece of evidence in order to assure Marley's conviction. The rest of that letter, I think, since he made it fairly clear that he had nothing else of it left. Don't take it, if you find it. When he produces it, that'll be when we take him."

"Jasus," Crispin muttered. "I hope Bates gets back before the fun's over."

"So do I. I need to send him back into the Parliamentary records to make sure a few items there don't disappear. I'll get you a list of what I need."

Crispin looked at him. "We'd best go, then. Me 'n Wallace have a few things to do before morning."

"As do I," Kilcairn said, and offered his hand. "Good luck, Althorpe."

"I'll see you tomorrow."

Victoria wondered whether, fairy tales aside, anyone had ever actually died of a broken heart. All night long she'd sat in the conservatory, wondering what she could do, what she might have done, to fix things. If he had never cared for her, though, there was nothing to fix. She'd finally lost her heart, apparently to a man who knew nothing of love.

But he had to feel something for her; her mind refused to accept that every kind thing he'd said, every gentle, pleasurable touch, had been a lie. And now she wasn't the only one affected by her stupid faith and trust. Now she carried his child. Yesterday she would have wept with delight at the news. Today, she just wanted to weep.

"My lady?" Jenny said softly, opening the door from the sitting room. "His lordship told me to pack some things for you."

"Yes. Please do."

"But . . . how long will we be gone?"

She stirred, lifting the sleeping Lord Baggles down from her lap. "I don't know, Jenny." After Sinclair finished his investigation, he wouldn't need her at all. It was entirely possible that he would abandon her at

Althorpe or one of his smaller estates where she would become a hopeless recluse.

Finally she rose to go change out of her evening gown, putting on something suitable for traveling. She could stomp her feet and make a scene and refuse to leave, but if he didn't love her, it seemed pointless. Part of her, too, was angry—angry for falling in love with him when she knew better, and angry that his few, cutting, uncaring words had so completely up-ended her world.

"What about your babies, my lady?" Jenny asked, as she laid out a light traveling cloak.

Victoria started, giving the maid a sharp look. "My—"

"I'll have Milo look after them."

Sinclair stood just inside the bedchamber doorway. Unlike her, he looked composed and calm, and not at all upset at the prospect of her leaving. But then, he hadn't wanted her there in the first place.

Shaking herself, Victoria stood. "I would like to leave now," she stated.

He gave a small, abrupt nod. "The coach is wait-ing."

At his signal several footmen hurried into the room to collect her luggage. Sinclair remained by the door, looking at her, though she didn't know what he ex-pected to see. Defiant anger swirled through her veins. She certainly wasn't going to weep again—not in front of him, anyway.

She followed her things out the door. At the top of the stairs Sinclair offered her his arm. "I would sooner break my neck," she murmured, and descended on her own. It wasn't true, of course, but if he touched her she was entirely likely to do something stupid and humiliating like clinging to him and begging to be allowed to stay.

"This is for your own good."

"This is for *your* convenience. Don't pretend otherwise."

Ignoring his hand again, she allowed Milo to help her into the coach. Jenny joined her luggage in the second vehicle. She knew she should tell him about their child, but now was certainly not the time. It would just sound as though she was asking to stay, or even worse, trying to gain his sympathy.

"Augusta and Kit are waiting for you at Drewsbury House. From London it's an easy two days to Althorpe." Sinclair reached out his hand as though to touch her cheek, then lowered it again. "This will be over soon, Victoria."

"Yes, I imagine so. Now you won't have anything to distract you from what's important."

With another stiff nod he softly closed the door. A moment later, the coach rocked into motion. Belatedly Victoria realized that with the way he seemed determined to ignore her advice and suspicions, she very well might never see him again. She sat back and wept.

Sinclair Grafton, you are going to Hades for this. He watched the coach out of sight, part of him wishing Victoria would come out of her doldrums enough to stop the coach, stalk back up to him, and punch him. He would have let her do it. Obviously, though, he'd done such a fine job of angering and humiliating her that he'd be damned lucky if he could convince her to return at all.

"Damnation," he muttered and turned back to the

house. Milo and the footmen stood glaring at him, more balefully than they had when he'd first returned to London to claim the title.

Going to Parliament drunk would have been easy, because he wanted a stiff whiskey almost as much as he wanted Victoria back in his arms. The best, swiftest way to achieve that, though, was to finish this and arrest—or preferably shoot—the Earl of Kingsfeld.

"Will there be anything else this morning, my lord?" Milo asked stiffly.

"Yes. I'm going to the House of Lords this morning, but I expect to return here for luncheon." In case Kingsfeld came looking for him, he wanted to be easy to find.

"Very good, my lord."

With a last look down the street in the direction his Victoria had vanished, Sinclair went back inside the house. It was time for the final act to begin.

He arrived at the House of Lords precisely twenty-seven minutes late. As he staggered through the tall old doors into the main chamber, he noted that both Kilcairn and Kingsfeld were present. As he'd expected, after he'd purposely excluded Marley from their party last night, the viscount hadn't made an appearance.

"Good morning, gentlemen," he drawled, and with liberal handholds on shoulders and coats, made it to the vacant seat beside Kingsfeld. The annoyed looks from his peers were knowing rather than surprised, so Kilcairn had been tending to his task.

"Did I miss anything?" he asked Kingsfeld, and was immediately shushed by his nearest seatmates.

"Only a taxation speech," Kingsfeld murmured. "What happened to you, Sin?"

"Well, thanks to you, Vixen thinks I only married her because of Marley," he whispered back, real anger touching his voice. The story helped his ruse, but his fingers still curled with the desire to hit Astin. The earl had already destroyed his past with Thomas, and now was ruining any chance he had at a happy future—because that future had to include Victoria. He didn't want a future without her.

"Oh, dear. We were only jesting. I didn't think she would take me seriously."

"Well, she did, and now she's gone."

"Shh!"

"Gone? Gone where?"

Sinclair blew out his lips. "Who knows? I told her I was going to finish this today, but she just glared at me and said she was leaving." He leaned closer. "You haven't seen Marley, have you?"

"No. You have no idea where your wife ran off to?"

Sweet Lucifer, Kingsfeld really *did* intend her harm. Sinclair clenched his jaw and fixed a perturbed look on his face. "She didn't say, and I didn't ask. I really don't wish to discuss it."

"I understand, lad. Of course. So you're going ahead with Marley's arrest?"

"I'm certainly not going to leave that bastard on the loose when I don't know where my wife is." Despite his barely checked fury, the conversation was going well; better than he'd anticipated. With a quick breath he decided to continue: they couldn't count on Kingsfeld following him home for luncheon. "I meant to ask you last night," he continued, making certain the earl got a good whiff of the whiskey liberally soaked into his cravat, "you don't have the rest of that letter somewhere, do you? With just a few words here and there,

I don't want any damned solicitor saying it's really a letter to Marley's dear sick aunt."

"I don't know where it would be, if I did," Kingsfeld whispered back. "But I did find the first piece. Perhaps I used the rest of it in the library, as well."

"It would be very helpful."

"Lord Althorpe!"

With a start, Sinclair looked down at the floor of the House. The Earl of Liverpool stood glaring at him, hands on his hips and his lips pressed thinly together in obvious annoyance. "My lord?"

The prime minister took a step closer. "We are discussing matters of taxation. Do you have anything of importance to add to the debate?"

No one had spoken to him like that since he was a schoolboy. As Crispin pointed out on numerous occasions, though, he would do anything for the sake of the mission. He gave a lopsided grin. "That depends. What are we taxing? Oh, let me guess. Whatever it is, it's meant to pay off more of Prinny's debts."

A low, rumbling roar began at the more conservative end of the House, and by the time it reached those around Sinclair, it had become a full-blown shouting match. Liverpool was yelling at him, but in the din it took a moment for him to decipher what the prime minister was saying.

"We will not tolerate your drunken interruptions here! This is a serious place of law, not a brothel!"

Sinclair stood. "You could have fooled me," he said and stumbled back down the risers. "Good day, gentlemen," he said, grinning, and strolled for the door. As he left, he glanced back to see Kingsfeld looking at his pocket watch, and, farther down the row, Lord

Kilcairn apparently taking a nap, despite the glinting slit of a gaze aimed in his direction.

That was one step taken care of. And now for Marley.

"All right. For the sake of argument, let's say Sin is sending you away because you quarreled." Kit sat on the backward-facing side of the coach, his scowl growing deeper with each passing mile. "If that's true, though, why did the big oaf insist that Grandmama and I go with you? We didn't argue with him."

Victoria leaned her cheek against the windowsill, trying to catch some air on her face. She hadn't meant to discuss her departure at all, but Christopher had his brother's persistence. Neither of her companions knew precisely what was going on, and she didn't want to be the one to enlighten them. On the other hand, her limited tolerance for lying had several hours ago reached its fill.

"He's just trying to protect you," she said, shutting her eyes and then quickly opening them again when the rocking of the coach threatened to make her ill.

"Protect us from what?" Kit retorted. "The London Season? I was supposed to go on a picnic with Miss Porter tomorrow."

"My, Hampshire is such lovely country," Augusta broke in. "I have always been very fond of it."

Hampshire. Victoria straightened. "Where in Hampshire are we?"

"The road passes through the southeast section on its way toward Althorpe." Christopher's scowl darkened further. "I really would like to know what Sin thinks we need protecting for. This is ridiculous. I haven't—we haven't—seen him for five years, and now he decides he's had enough of us?"

She heard and understood the hurt in his voice; she felt it herself. It would be so much easier if Sinclair didn't blame himself for what had happened to Thomas; he felt so responsible that it seemed he would rather risk losing the love and understanding of his family than even consider them being hurt.

Victoria blinked. He was willing to risk everything. Did that include her?

She sat up very straight. Things had fallen rather conveniently into place yesterday. Circumstances in Sinclair's vicinity seemed to have a way of doing that. And she'd fallen right in with his plans. Sending Kingsfeld to insult her seemed far-fetched, but Sin wasn't likely to explain things, or to let an opportunity go by unused. She was not some timid miss to be banished to the country at her husband's convenience, however. Not without getting some answers first.

"Stop the coach," she said, grabbing onto the windowsill.

"We're just a mile or two from the next inn," Augusta said. "We can rest there."

"No. Stop it now, or I'm going to be ill."

"Damnation." Kit lurched to his feet. "Driver, stop the coach!" he bellowed, knocking on the roof with his fist.

Slowly they rolled to a halt. Kit flung open the door and vaulted to the ground so he could hand Victoria down. As soon as her feet touched the rutted track her stomach settled, but her mind continued careening in every direction.

For several minutes she strode up and down the road while Christopher kept pace beside her and Augusta leaned out the coach's doorway to watch them. Soon the second carriage with their servants and luggage came up behind them and stopped.

"Better?" Kit asked.

"I think so." For appearance sake she continued to clutch her stomach and make occasional groaning sounds. How much of what Sinclair had said to her had been lies, and how much had been the truth? Was he trying to protect her, or did he really, truly wish to be rid of her?

"Are you ready to continue?" Kit asked.

She couldn't keep tramping along the roadside forever. With a nod, Victoria turned back to the coach again—and stopped so quickly that Christopher ran into her from behind.

"Damn," he mumbled, grabbing her elbow. "My apologies. You're not going to faint, are you?"

"I might."

The coach's driver sat facing away from her, a big, crooked hand blocking his countenance from her view. The hand, though, was as recognizable as the face, as was the driver's short stature. For a brief moment Victoria wanted to burst into song. Just as quickly, though, she stifled the urge. Simply because Sinclair had sent Roman to drive them all to Althorpe didn't mean he'd had motives other than the one he'd stated for sending her away.

"Driver," she called, "I require a word with you."

Roman jumped, glancing at her, and then faced away again.

"Driver!"

"Yes, my lady," he muttered, climbing slowly and reluctantly to the ground.

"Vixen, do you—"

"Excuse me, Kit," she interrupted. "I'll just be a

moment." She stalked up to Roman. "What are you doing here?" she demanded.

"I'm driving the coach, my lady. And if you would be so kind as to return to your seat, we'll continue on to the Red Lion Inn, just up the road."

The Red Lion. A plan began forming in her mind. First, though, she had a few more questions. "If Sinclair was tired of my presence, why didn't he send me to my parents' house?"

The valet cleared his throat. "I wouldn't know, my lady."

"And why did he banish his family along with me, and place us under your protection?"

"I wouldn't—"

"I'm going back. Turn the coach around."

It was a bold move, but it paid off. Roman blanched—which comforted her more than all of his stumbling denials. Something was going on; and the most important realization was that perhaps Sinclair *hadn't* tired of her after all.

"I'm not taking you back to London," he said firmly. "I have my orders."

Victoria rubbed her chin, surveying the pretty countryside. Augusta and Christopher complicated the plot; if she returned to London, they would go with her. She couldn't place them in danger, not just because she had a hunch, and not when Sinclair had gone to such efforts to remove them all from harm.

Taking a deep breath, Victoria made her decision. She couldn't allow Sinclair to decide her life, or her place in his. A night of sleepless tension and stress made bursting into tears easy. Sobbing, she returned to the carriage.

"Whatever is wrong, my dear?" Augusta exclaimed, helping her up into the vehicle.

"Nothing, really. I'm just . . . I'm just so tired."

"Of course you are."

"You know, we're very close to my old finishing school."

"Miss Grenville's Academy?" A slight furrow appeared between Augusta's eyebrows.

"Yes. My . . . my good friend Emma is headmistress there." She clutched Augusta's hand, not having to pretend the worry and tension running through her. "I would really like to visit her for a few days, if you . . . don't mind. I'll follow you to Althorpe at the end of the week."

"Absolutely not, child! If you wish to visit your friend, we'll all go."

Leaning into the coach from his position on the bottom step, Kit nodded his agreement. "We're not going to abandon you—especially after Sin was such a cad."

Real tears coursed down Victoria's cheeks. Nothing was going to happen to these people. *Nothing.* "Thank you, but it's not like that. Really. I just need a day or two . . . alone." At Kit's hurt look, she smiled. "Besides, it's a girls' school. No men allowed."

Augusta looked at her for a long moment. "I hope this isn't because of Sinclair's behavior," she finally said in a low voice. "I think he cares very much for you."

Victoria sniffled. "I hope so."

"Very well. Christopher, inform the driver that he is to take us to Miss Grenville's Academy at once."

"Yes, Grandmama."

*   *   *

Tracking down Marley took longer than Sinclair anticipated. After questioning the viscount's butler and then searching half the gentlemen's clubs along Pall Mall, he reasoned that his quarry might very well have departed London for his estate in the country.

And if he couldn't arrest Marley, then Kingsfeld would have no reason to feel easier about his own involvement, and Vixen would continue to remain in danger.

Just as Sinclair decided to return to Madsen House and pummel the butler until he gave up his employer's location, he spied Marley's bay gelding at the border of Hyde Park.

"Thank God," he murmured and kicked Diable into a gallop.

He'd wanted a public setting for the arrest, and it seemed he was going to get his wish. The afternoon crowds had already begun to fill the park's paths, while vendors offered flavored ice and pastries on the green.

Galloping in Hyde Park was strictly forbidden, in addition to being nearly impossible, but Sinclair wasn't about to risk losing sight of Marley now. Touching his heels to Diable's ribs, he sent the black soaring over a park bench and around a crowd of picnickers.

Ignoring the resulting chorus of "You there" and "It's that damned Althorpe," he closed the distance between himself and Marley. After this was over he was going to owe the viscount one hell of an apology, but he'd do his best to make Marley come out a hero. As for himself, he didn't care as long as he didn't lose Victoria.

"Marley!" he bellowed as he pulled even.

The viscount gave him a startled look and had time for nothing else as Sinclair launched off Diable at him. They both tumbled to the ground in a whirling leaf-and-grass-covered pile. Sinclair got to his feet first and yanked Marley up by his lapels.

"What . . . is the meaning of this?" Marley sputtered, jerking himself free and shoving Sinclair backward.

"You really didn't think you'd get away with killing my brother, did you?" Sinclair spat and pulled out his pistol.

"I don't know what you're talking about!"

"Don't you?" Grabbing the viscount again, Sinclair elbowed him hard in the ribs. Marley doubled over, and Sin leaned down beside him. "Go along with this," he hissed. "I'll explain later."

"I will not!" Marley sputtered.

Sin jammed the pistol in his ear. "I wasn't asking."

"You're . . . you're mad, Althorpe!" the viscount sputtered, his expression of fear unmistakably real.

"We'll see about that, you murderer!"

"What's all this?" shouted a voice.

Finally! A group of Bow Street Runners pounded up the path toward them, their own weapons drawn. Sinclair waited until they were close enough to intercept Marley if he tried to flee, then lowered his pistol.

"This man killed my brother," he stated. "I want him arrested."

"You're mad! I didn't kill anyone!"

"We'll sort this out soon enough," the largest of the Runners grunted, pulling Marley back upright. "Both of you gentlemen will have to come to Old Bailey with us to swear out a statement," their captain said, urging Marley back toward his horse.

"You're insane, Althorpe! I didn't kill your brother!" Whether Marley was acting or not, he was doing a damned fine job.

A very small part of Sinclair regretted putting the viscount through this, but Marley *had* attempted to convince Victoria to begin an affair.

"Save your denials for someone who'll believe them," Sin retorted, noting the rapt attention of the gathered crowd. Kingsfeld should hear about this in no time at all. "Justice will be done," he added for good measure.

"He's drunk!" Marley pleaded with the Runners on his either side. "You can smell the whiskey from here!"

"We'll see this straightened out soon enough, my lord. Come along, now."

Still breathing hard, Sinclair reclaimed Diable and swung up onto the stallion's back. The captain stood about for another minute, informing the crowd that there was nothing to see. With a grim smile, Sin turned to follow the parade of Runners. He would have to agree with the captain; the real fun would begin when he and Kingsfeld next met.

Chapter 17

❦❦❦

"Vixen?" With a warm, delighted smile, Emma Grenville swooped into her office and pulled Victoria into a tight hug. "You are the very last person I expected to see in Hampshire. What are you doing here?"

In response, Victoria burst into tears for the sixth or seventh time that day. She'd become such a watering pot that she'd lost count. "I need your assistance," she blurted.

Emma gestured her to a chair and sat in the one opposite her. "You have it," she stated in her usual comforting, practical tone. "I'm just sorry I was away earlier and you had to wait so long."

"That's all right. I needed time to think."

The headmistress gazed at her. "Molly said you arrived in the company of a young gentleman and an older lady, but they left without you."

"Yes, Sinclair's relations. They continued on to Althorpe."

"Without you, and with your Lord Althorpe nowhere to be seen, apparently."

Astuteness had never been something that Emma

348

had lacked. "It's a long story, and I'm not certain how much time I have to tell it."

"Then you'd best tell it quickly." Emma rose again, taking Victoria's hand and pulling her to her feet, as well. "Over dinner, I think. You're pale. My girls will enjoy meeting you, anyway. You're notorious, you know."

Victoria managed a chuckle. "You're just trying to make me feel better." She took a breath. As nice and comforting as it was to be able to pour her troubles out to practical Emma, solving hers and Sinclair's dilemma was more urgent. "I promise to tell you the entire tale soon, but right now I need a carriage, or a horse, or a hack. I'm going back to London."

Emma hesitated. "And why is that?"

"Sinclair and I quarreled, and he sent me away. I have been considering his motives, though, and I think he was concerned over my safety and wanted to remove me from danger."

"Danger," the headmistress repeated. "Then perhaps you should do as he says, Vixen."

Victoria shook her head. "I am concerned over *his* safety." Her voice shook, but at least she seemed to have run out of tears for the moment. "I will not abandon him just because he thinks he knows what's best for me. Ha. I don't even know what's best for me— but I do know it's not being sent away to the country so he can risk his own life."

Her bright hazel eyes sympathetic, Emma squeezed Victoria's fingers. "I would like to meet your Lord Sin some day," she said softly. "I never thought to see the Vixen lose her heart."

"Oh, Emma, I hope the same thing may happen to

you one day. When it's not the most awful thing on earth, it's quite . . . wonderful."

Laughing, Emma hugged her again. "Based on that recommendation, I think I'll stay a spinster, thank you very much. And you may borrow Pimpernel, of course, but I'm certainly not going to allow you to go galloping off in the dark."

Victoria scowled. "You sound like a headmistress. You're only three years older than I am."

"I am a headmistress. And you will have to set an example for my students. You may leave in the morning—which I hope will give you enough time to tell me your tale."

Despite her desire to leave immediately, Victoria knew Emma was right. Riding out in the dark would likely see her lost, or killed by highwaymen. She rubbed her still-flat stomach. And she had more than herself, and even Sinclair, to consider now.

Angry as she had been with Sinclair and furious as she still was with him over his presumption in sending her away, she missed him terribly. Her heart ached to see him again, to be held in his arms and finally have no secrets between them. It might be nothing more than a fairy tale, but she wanted to tell him they were going to have a child, and have him finally tell her that he loved her.

She sighed. "It all started one night in Lady Franton's garden."

Emma smiled. "This is going to take a while, isn't it?"

Victoria nodded. "And it doesn't even have an ending yet."

*   *   *

"So he didn't come by at all?"

"No, my lord."

Sinclair glared at Milo, willing the butler to alter his answer, but that seemed about as likely as Prince George taking up ballet. He'd missed luncheon, but Kingsfeld had had no way of knowing he hadn't been at home. The earl should have been eager to discover whether Marley had been arrested or not.

"Was there a note, then?"

"No, my lord. No visitors, and no correspondence."

"Damnation," Sinclair murmured. He hated this part of an investigation, when he'd done everything he could and had to wait for the target to walk into the trap. "I'll be in my office if anyone should call."

"Yes, my lord. Might I presume you are at home to receive correspondence, as well?"

Now Milo was just being insolent, but Sin could hardly blame him for it. "Yes. And any artworks, musical serenades, or dancing bears that might happen by. I want to see anything and anyone that comes calling."

Sinclair stalked down the hallway to the office. As soon as he stepped through the door, though, he realized it was a mistake. Victoria's desk, neat and bare, stood beneath the window in the pale afternoon sunlight.

He nearly turned around and left again, but that wouldn't have been much use. Everything in Grafton House reminded him of Victoria: every flower in every vase, every strip of wall covering, every patch of sunlight seemed colored by his thoughts of her.

After two years, he was about to apprehend Thomas's murderer. He should have been pleased, relieved that they'd come within sight of victory and justice.

Instead, he paced up and down the office missing his wife and wondering whether he'd hurt her too badly to earn her forgiveness, much less her love.

He was used to regrets, but never one that stabbed into his heart like sending her away had done. Victoria's parents had treated her like a child, distrusting her common sense and locking her away—sending her away—when that had become the easiest alternative. He'd just done the same thing, knowing it would hurt her enough to make her want to leave. He would never do it to her again.

For an hour he paced up and back along the carpet, until he thought he would go mad from waiting. Parliament would go on all afternoon, but he had thought Kingsfeld's curiosity would have sent him home early—to find his house ransacked and with Sinclair the most likely culprit. The front door finally opened, and at the sound of a female voice he strode to the entryway. To his surprise, Lady Kilcairn stood in the foyer, speaking to Milo.

"My lady?" he said, brushing past the butler. "What—"

She hit him in the jaw.

"Damnation," he grunted, staggering. The blow hadn't hurt, but it had bloody well startled him. "What was that for?"

"How could you let her leave?" Alexandra snapped, coiling her fist and looking as though she wanted to punch him again.

"That's none of your affair," he said stiffly. If he couldn't tell Victoria what was going on, he damned well wasn't going to tell her friends.

"Will you excuse us for a moment?" the countess said, glancing pointedly at Milo.

Sinclair took her arm and led her down the front steps to the graveled drive. "I apologize if I've offended you," he said, urging her toward her waiting carriage, "but I don't intend to stand about and argue with you about my wife. Not today."

"Very well, I'll go. I just wanted to let you know one more thing that isn't any of my affair."

He rubbed his jaw. "What might that be?"

"Your wife is carrying your child," she shot, her eyes flashing.

He blanched, the ground rolling beneath his feet so wildly that he had to sit on the bottom step. *"What?"*

She nodded. "Given the way you yelled at her, I didn't think she would tell you, but I also think that she deserves a chance at being happy. She thinks that chance lies with you, Lord Althorpe. I don't think you should disappoint her."

Gathering her skirt, she climbed into her carriage and instructed the driver to leave. Sinclair sat at the edge of the drive for a long time, staring at the ground without seeing anything at all. *His child.* That was why she'd been so upset. And he was an absolute blundering, blithering, idiotic boor. He was going to be a father, and he didn't deserve it—or her.

He'd definitely done the right thing, though, sending her away. At Althorpe she would be safe until he could go to her and apologize and tell her that he loved her. Slowly he rose and went back inside, barely noting Milo in the doorway as he walked past. He was going to be a father. Good God.

It was dusk when he finally heard the front door open and the low murmur of male voices. He seated himself behind his desk, his pistol in one hand. For a moment he wished he hadn't removed Thomas's massive desk from the office; putting a ball through Kingsfeld from that seat would have seemed poetic justice. This, though, would be enough.

The office door opened, and he curled his fingers around the pistol's ivory handle. The widening doorway, though, remained empty.

"Sin? It's Crispin. Don't blow my head off."

Sinclair cursed. "Get the bloody hell in here."

The tall Scot stepped inside, and Sinclair's breath stopped in his throat. Crispin's face was drawn and serious, and an even grimmer-looking Wally followed on his heels. When Bates appeared behind them, Sin stood so abruptly that his chair went over backward.

"What happened?" he snapped.

"We're not sure. We dumped Kingsfeld's desk drawers out and pulled half the books off his shelves in case he needed more convincing that he'd been ransacked." Crispin drew a breath, his expression becoming even more dour. "It's my fault. I rode straight here in case you needed assistance. Wallace stayed to keep an eye on Hovarth House."

"And?"

Wally cleared his throat. "Kingsfeld went home right on schedule. Not five minutes later he came running outside like a bat out of hell, grabbed his horse from the groom, and rode off." The stocky man shifted. "I thought he was heading here, so I went to see if Bates was back, to send him after the papers you wanted."

Slowly Sinclair sat on the corner of his desk. "So where did Kingsfeld go?" he asked, his jaw clenched so tightly that he could barely get the clipped words out. "I know he didn't come here."

"We don't know, Sin. By the time we realized he

wasn't here, he'd been missing for over an hour."

"His clubs," Sin snapped, rising and striding for the door. "We'll split up."

"Sin, we—"

"Damnation, Crispin! Why did you wait so long to tell me?" He whipped around, jabbing a finger into the Scotsman's chest. "Forget I said that. It's my own bloody fault, for trying to be so damned clever instead of just shooting the bastard."

"We checked the clubs already," Crispin countered. "And Gentlemen Jackson's and every shop on Bond Street."

Dread made Sinclair's blood run cold. "Check them again. I'm going to Hovarth House, and Geoffreys had best know where his employer went."

"Where d'you think he went?"

"Just find him," Sin said grimly, his chest tight, "because I don't want to think where else he might be."

Even without saying it, though, he knew. Kingsfeld hadn't evaded any hint of guilt for two years by being foolish. Victoria alone might have gone anywhere, but with Augusta and Kit leaving at the same time, the number of possible destinations narrowed considerably. In his anxiety to protect them, he might very well have left them vulnerable to a murderer. If anything happened he would never forgive himself.

"Sin?"

"We'll meet back here in an hour. If you see Kingsfeld, grab him. I don't care how."

Milo stood in the foyer as they exited, his expression a mixture of annoyance and bewilderment. The time had come, Sinclair decided, to stop slinking around in the shadows and trust a little.

"Milo, I need you to keep watch here for Lord Kingsfeld. Choose three footmen, and all of you arm yourselves."

"My . . . my lord?"

"It is my belief that Kingsfeld is the man who killed Thomas. I don't want him wandering around where he can hurt anyone else."

The butler drew himself up straighter. "If he comes here, my lord, he will not be leaving."

Sinclair nodded. "We'll all be back here in an hour. You can trust these men," he said, gesturing at his lads. "And Lord Kilcairn."

"Yes, my lord."

Most of the lights were off at Hovarth House, which Sin took as a bad sign. Kingsfeld hadn't returned, and the servants weren't expecting him back anytime soon. Sinclair pounded on the door.

It was nearly a minute before Geoffreys pulled it open. "Lord Althorpe? I'm afraid Lord Kingsfeld isn't home."

"Where is he, then?"

"I'm not at liberty to say, my lord."

"You had a break-in earlier, didn't you?"

The butler looked momentarily startled. "Yes, my lord. How did you—"

Sinclair shoved a hand into the man's chest, pushing him back into the foyer and following him inside. "I know because I did it," he snarled, slamming the door with his free hand. "Where is Kingsfeld?"

"My—I don't—please unhand me, my lord."

"I almost like you, Geoffreys. Don't make me loosen your teeth with my fist." He shoved the butler up against the hall table.

"This is highly irregular, my lord."

"Yes, it would seem to be. Answer my question. Now."

"I can't do that, my lord. Arthur! Marvin!"

Sinclair scowled. "That was stupid."

Two large footmen pounded into the hallway. "You'll have to let him go, my lord," the bigger one grumbled, moving toward them.

With his free hand, Sinclair pulled the pistol from his pocket and aimed it at Geoffreys' forehead. "Your so-called employer murdered my brother, Geoffreys. Don't think I won't return the favor. Now, for the last time, where is the damned Earl of Kingsfeld?"

The butler gasped. "I don't . . ." His eyes rolled back into his head, and with an oddly delicate-sounding groan, he fainted.

"Damn," Sinclair growled, taking Geoffreys' weight on his shoulder and letting him sag to the floor.

As he turned, the footmen hit him. He saw them coming and ducked beneath the first one, even as the second slammed into his legs, knocking them all to the floor on top of Geoffreys. With a curse, Sinclair rolled to his feet and caught the first man to rise across the forehead with the butt of his pistol. Flipping the weapon in his hand, he aimed it at the second one, who was just climbing to his knees.

"Which one are you?" he snapped, wiping blood from his lip.

"M . . . Marvin."

"Marvin, I am going to ask you one question. If you don't answer it, I am going to shoot you in the head, and then ask Arthur over there the same thing when he comes to. Do you understand?"

"Yes, my lord."

"Splendid. Where is Kingsfeld? An educated guess will suffice."

For a bare second he wasn't certain the large footman would answer him, and Sinclair tapped him none too gently in the forehead with the pistol barrel.

"Did I mention that I'm not joking?" he murmured, narrowing his eyes.

"Ouch! Bloody . . . he'll kill me!"

"So will I. Now or later, Marvin. Decide."

"He went to Althorpe."

Sinclair's heart stopped beating. "Alone?"

Marvin shook his head. "Wilkins and two others were to meet up with him on the road."

Wilkins was the head groom, Sinclair recalled, another large, unpleasant-looking man. "Did any of them say anything else?"

"Just that we were to say the earl had gone home to Kingsfeld on urgent business, and he would return shortly. Geoffreys didn't know any different."

"I'm glad I didn't have to kill him, then. I suggest you and your friend be here when I return," Sinclair said, "and that you be ready to repeat what you just told me, as many times as necessary. If you run, I will find you. Is that clear?"

"Yes, my lord."

Sin backed toward the front door. He doubted any of Kingsfeld's servants would remain in London by dawn, but he couldn't take the time to tie them all up and make certain there was no one else in the house to free them later. Unless . . .

"I've changed my mind. Come with me."

"But—"

"Now, dammit!"

His hands carefully away from his sides, Marvin

reluctantly followed Sin outside. Sin gestured his captive toward the street and pocketed the pistol as soon as the footman's back was turned. "Hail a hack," he ordered.

Cursing under his breath, Marvin did as he was told. Sinclair freed Diable's reins from the bush where he'd flung them and swung up into the saddle. The generally calm black seemed to sense his tension, because it sidestepped nervously and snorted.

"Easy," he murmured and urged the horse up to the side of the hack. Marvin climbed in, and Sinclair kicked the door closed. "What's your name?" he asked the driver.

"Gibben. What's it to you?"

"Gibben," he said, pulling a hundred-pound note from his pocket and lifting it so the man could see it, "if you take this man to Grafton House and turn him safely over to the butler there, you will receive two more of these. How does that sound?"

"Like angels singing, m'lord," the man answered, grinning.

Sinclair handed him the money. "The butler's name is Milo. Tell him I've gone to Althorpe, and that he'll find your fee in the bottom left drawer of my desk."

"Aye, m'lord."

"If you arrive there without this man, I will hear about it, Gibben."

The driver gave a grim smile, leaning forward to stuff the money into the top of his boot. "Oh, he'll get there, m'lord. May be a bit banged up, though."

"Just make sure he's alive."

Gibben tipped his hat and snapped the reins over his team. The hack lurched back out into the street at a rather frightening speed for such a dilapidated vehicle. Sin almost felt sorry for the footman inside.

Taking a deep breath, Sinclair turned Diable toward the southwest and kicked the stallion in the ribs. Crispin and the lads would follow, but he wasn't going to wait. They had a long distance to go tonight—and he didn't intend to stop until he reached Althorpe. He wouldn't rest until he held Victoria safe in his arms. And after this, if she would forgive him, he was never letting her go again.

"I don't like you riding off alone. It's hours to London, and there are highwaymen everywhere."

Victoria kissed Emma on the cheek. "I used to ride alone all the time. And there's no one else to ride with me."

"I could get John, the gardener. Or one of Lord Haverly's grooms. He's just down the road."

"I'll be fine. I need to do this, Em. I'll send for Jenny in a few days."

The headmistress scowled. "And just what do you think you'll do if you make it to London alive? I should think that Lord Althorpe knows precisely what he's doing."

"He may be a fine spy," Victoria returned, stepping up onto the mounting block and sliding onto Pimpernel's broad back, "but he hasn't a clue how to be a husband. I am going to educate him. And I'm not leaving him to face Kingsfeld alone."

She'd barely slept again last night, worried that Sinclair would be so angry with her that he would refuse to believe in Kingsfeld's guilt, after all. If the earl hurt him, or killed him, she would die, too. She'd never find anyone else who accepted her silly, flighty ways as easily as Sinclair, and she knew she would never meet anyone else in whose arms she would feel so happy. If he didn't love her, she would convince him to do so. There had to be *something* she could do.

"All right, Galahad," Emma said, her face still concerned. "I know I can't stop you. But *please* be careful, Vixen. Don't let your heart make you do foolish things."

Victoria smiled. "Goose. That's what hearts are for."

She tapped Pimpernel in the ribs, and the sorrel mare obediently trotted toward the front gates of Miss Grenville's Academy. Little girls' noses were pressed against the upstairs windows of the converted monastery, and she briefly wondered which one of them would be the next Vixen. And she wondered whether her own daughter would attend the Academy one day.

That made her think of Sinclair again, and how badly she wanted to box his ears and tell him to stop being so stubborn about protecting her. He might very well protect her right into a box, and then there would be no room for the two of them.

About two miles east of the Academy, Victoria stopped at the top of a rise. The winding road looked clear and untraveled as far as she could see, and she took a deep, steadying breath. If they kept a good pace and the weather didn't turn, she could be in London by nightfall. Her back didn't relish the thought of riding sidesaddle all day, but neither could she stand the thought of being away from Sinclair and not knowing whether he was safe.

"Well, let's go, Pimper—" Four riders came over the far hill, and her heart chilled. It was ridiculous, of course. As Emma had said, the school lay on Lord Haverly's land, and the riders could be his men, or visitors, or travelers, or any number of things. They were too far away to make out more than their dark clothes, but something about the lead rider seemed very familiar.

Abruptly she realized what it was. One of Thomas Grafton's sketches had been of Lord Kingsfeld on horseback. The horse looked the same, and so did the way the rider held himself. Her heart skidded and thudded against her ribs as ice-cold dread ran through her. If Kingsfeld was here, something had happened to Sinclair.

"Oh, no," she whispered, all the blood draining from her face and leaving her feeling cold and dreadful and dizzy.

The riders didn't pause at the distant crossroads but continued northwest along the rutted trail. The logical part of her mind acknowledged that they were heading for Althorpe, no doubt looking for her.

Cursing, Victoria wheeled Pimpernel and headed back down the rise in the opposite direction. She might not be at Althorpe, but Augusta and Christopher were—and they had no idea who Kingsfeld really was. Sinclair had lost his brother; it would kill him to lose anyone else. She wasn't going to let that happen.

Since she was north of the meandering road, she and Pimpernel had a three or four mile lead on the horsemen. With luck, she could reach Althorpe ahead of them. Victoria kicked the mare into a dead run. She had to make it. She wasn't going to let Sinclair, or herself, down.

Chapter 18

It was only because of Thomas's sketches that Victoria knew when she'd arrived at Althorpe. The lake, the birch and pine trees, and the rolling fields seemed so familiar that she could almost believe she'd been there before.

Althorpe itself, white and sprawling and magnificent, was larger even than her father's estate at Stiveton. She had little time to admire it, though, as she galloped up the wide front drive. "Hello!" she called, belatedly remembering they would only have opened the house yesterday and that very few servants might even be in residence. "Hello!"

The front door opened, and Roman strode out onto the steps. "Lady Vixen! What in God's name—"

"Kingsfeld is right behind me," she panted.

"Sweet Lucifer." The valet hurried forward and helped her down from Pimpernel. "Is he alone?"

"No. I saw three men with him. Where are Augusta and Kit?"

"Inside, having luncheon. Did they see you, my lady?"

"I don't think so, but I'm not certain. There are some long, flat stretches of road."

"Aye. Let's get you inside."

She leaned on his arm, her legs wobbly and cramped. "How many servants are here?"

"Only half a dozen, including the cook and the upstairs maid. Not enough to hold off four armed men."

"Do you think they're armed?"

"I would wager so."

Kit met her in the dining room doorway, his expression even more astonished than Roman's had been. "Vixen! I thought—"

"Please listen," she said, limping into the dining room. "Lord Kingsfeld is on his way here, with three men."

"Astin?" Kit repeated. "Why is he—"

"My God," Augusta whispered, her face going white.

"Your brother and I believe he may have been the one who killed Thomas," Victoria said quietly, wishing she had time to break the news to them more gently.

"*What?* No! I don't believe it!"

"Christopher," his grandmother said, "for the moment we will take what Victoria says as fact. What are we to do?"

"Are there any neighboring estates where we might find help?"

Kit shook his head. "Not during the Season. They're all closed for the summer."

"I'll get the coach, and we'll go," Roman said grimly, turning for the door.

"No," she countered, putting a hand on his arm.

"Even on tired horses, they'd catch us. Out in the open, we'd have no chance."

"Do you really think he means to harm us?" Kit asked, his face a mixture of anger and hurt confusion. She couldn't blame him; five minutes ago, Astin Hovarth had been a dear friend.

"I can't think why else he would be out here. Augusta?"

Lady Drewsbury slowly shook her head. "Neither can I." She stood. "This is a very large house. I suggest we hide."

"Hide? From the man who murdered my brother? I think not!"

"Lady Drewsbury's right," Roman broke in. "If they separate to find you, I'll have a better chance against them."

"And who in damnation are you, sir?" Kit demanded.

"He's a former spy for the War Office. Like Sinclair."

"A former . . . Good God, I'm losing my mind."

"Lose it later, Christopher," Augusta said crisply. "For now, see if you can find us some weapons."

The distant sound of clattering hooves on gravel came to them through the half-open window. "They're here," Victoria said, panic pushing at her. "Upstairs, everyone. Now."

Roman produced a pistol from his pocket. "I'll go say hello," he said grimly.

"You will do no such thing. You will protect Augusta and Christopher. Is that clear?"

"And who's going to protect you, my lady?"

She gazed at him, daring the valet to contradict her obvious lie. "I am."

He cursed, then grabbed her arm and pushed her toward the hall. "I'll protect everyone," he growled. "Upstairs."

Althorpe looked quiet and deserted as Astin Hovarth pounded into the courtyard. A sorrel mare stood to one side of the doorway, her chest lathered in sweat. Whoever had arrived ahead of them was going to have no more luck than the rest of Sinclair's family—especially his bitch of a wife, who had aimed all this mess in his direction in the first place.

"Don't kill anyone until we have them all," he ordered, swinging down from his bay. "Unless you have to, of course."

"Aye, my lord."

The front door was half open. Leaning into the entry, Astin nudged it wider. The foyer stood empty. He gestured his three employees inside, following them and closing the door after them. If anyone tried to leave, he wanted to hear it.

As soon as he'd learned that not only the Vixen but also Augusta and Kit had gone missing, he'd known. Sinclair thought he was so clever, asking for more clues about Marley when he was really looking to trap his late brother's dearest friend. Marley's arrest had surprised him momentarily, until the condition of his office had made it clear that Sinclair was only playing another game and trying to lure him into making a false step. It was an arrogant ploy, and it had almost worked.

Once he'd realized that Augusta, Kit, and that damned female must have headed to Althorpe, though, he knew what needed to be done. Sinclair still had no real evidence against him, or he would have made the arrest already. A tragic house fire would take care of his troublesome wife and would sufficiently distract Sin long enough for Astin to ensure that all remaining evidence against Marley was safely in place.

If he worked it well enough, he might even be able to suggest that the fire itself was Sin's doing. The lad had been clearly distraught over his wife's departure, and the *ton* already considered him a rather unbalanced menace. Astin allowed himself a brief smile. Yes, that would be a fine way to conclude this business.

"No one in the front rooms, my lord," Wilkins said, returning to his side.

"They seem to have known we were coming. That will complicate things, but not by much. Find them. We'll gather the household in the kitchen."

"The kitchen, my lord?"

"That is where most fires start, is it not?"

Victoria had never been so frightened in her life. At the same time, though, growing anger coursed through her veins. This was *her* house, by God, and those men downstairs didn't have any right to be here. The people cowering with her in the connected bedchambers were *her* relations, and *her* servants, and protecting them was her responsibility. Hers and Sinclair's.

He wasn't here, and so it fell to her to keep his servants and his loved ones safe. Her heart beat cold and empty at the thought that something might have happened to him, but she couldn't think about that right now. She would weep and mourn later. At the moment, she had a battle to plan.

"Roman," she whispered.

The diminutive valet crept around the wardrobe to

her side. "My lady, don't be frightened. I won't let those bastards near you."

"Shh," she murmured. "We need to capture them alive."

Both of his thick brows lifted. "Alive?"

"We can't be sure that Sinclair has all of the evidence he needs to convict Kingsfeld."

"Begging your pardon, but I really don't give a hang about that right now. He told me to take care of you, whatever the cost."

"He did?" My goodness, she loved him. "And I intend to take care of him, whatever the cost. He doesn't just want revenge, Roman. He wants justice."

"He wants you to be safe."

She scowled. "Don't argue with me, Roman. I need your help."

The valet sighed. "I hope Sin has the chance to kill me for this. What's your plan?"

"I told you—we need to capture them alive."

With a brief chuckle, Roman shook his head. "We need a bit more than that."

"Well, I'm new to this. You're the expert—what do you think?"

The adjoining door creaked open. Victoria gasped, clutching her chest. When a white handkerchief fluttered low in the opening, she could have fainted from relief. Kit's head followed. "I want in on this," he muttered, crawling across the short expanse of floor toward them.

"You heard us?"

"No, but I know you're planning something. I owe Kingsfeld as much as Sin does. More, even. Right after the funeral, he told me he knew he could never replace my brother, but with Sin gone as well, he would be honored to substitute as best he could. I took him at his word. I let that bastard write me a letter of recommendation to Oxford."

"All right," Victoria murmured, taking his hand and squeezing his fingers. "You may help us. As long as you're careful."

Kit smiled grimly. "Fair enough."

"Just a damned minute," Roman protested. "I am not going to allow—"

"You have two options, Roman. We can either get in your way, or we can assist you," Victoria snapped.

"Bloody hell," the valet said. "If we want them alive, we need to get hold of them one at a time."

"Alive?" Kit repeated, scowling.

"Evidence," Victoria whispered.

Sinclair's brother nodded. "Oh. Right."

By the time Augusta joined them and they had explained everything yet again, footsteps had begun creeping up the near staircase. Victoria didn't feel easy about including Sinclair's grandmother or Kit in the venture, but she wasn't about to tell them they couldn't participate. She knew all too well how that hurt.

The bedchamber in which they had positioned themselves lay seven or eight doors distant from the top of the stairs, with the rest of the household at the far end of the hallway. As she heard the fifth door softly open and bootheels slowly tapping down the hall, Victoria wished she'd been in the first room. She could barely stand waiting ten minutes. But Sinclair had waited and watched and listened for over two years.

"Ready?" Roman mouthed from behind the door.

She nodded, her mouth dry. This was for Sinclair

as much as it was for her. She couldn't make a mistake. There would be no second chances today.

The door handle slowly began to turn. Victoria held her breath. She was seated on the bed, and if Roman didn't pounce quickly enough, she would have nowhere to run. The door inched open. A large, stocky man stepped into the room, a pistol in his hand.

"What the . . . ," he said, as his gaze found Victoria.

"Hello," she said softly, smiling. "I've been waiting for you."

He took another step forward, the pistol lifting in her direction. One more small step, and they would have him.

"You're the Vixen, ain't you?"

"Yes, I am. Would you like to know why they call me that?"

"Sweet—"

A stout fagot of firewood came down on the back of his head, and with a grunt he dropped heavily to the floor.

"They call her that because she's smart as a fox," Roman muttered, taking one limp arm while Kit emerged from beneath the bed to grab the other and pull the man away from the door. Augusta slipped out of the wardrobe and gently closed the door again.

"One out, three to go," Kit said grimly, using the curtain pull cords to bind the man's arms behind his back.

Roman examined their attacker's pistol and turned to Kit. "You know how to use this, Master Kit?"

"Of course." Kit pocketed the weapon. "Do we just wait here for the next one to come by? It could be hours."

The door slammed open.

Shrieking, Victoria dove sideways off the bed as Kingsfeld launched himself at her. His hand closed viselike around her ankle, and she kicked hard with her other foot. He grabbed that leg too, and yanked her back onto the bed, her skirts sliding up above her knees.

"That's enough, Vixen!" he snarled and slapped her hard across the face.

She fell backward onto the bed, stunned by the blow. When he pulled her upright again, her hair loose and falling into her eyes, she caught sight of a second man in the doorway, his pistol aimed at Kit and Roman.

"All right! We surrender!" she screamed.

"You heard the lady," Kingsfeld growled. "Drop your weapons."

"Astin! What is the meaning of this?" Augusta stood beside the window, a vase gripped in her hands. Seeing the steely anger in the woman's eyes, Victoria realized where Sinclair got his strength of character.

"The meaning of this, my dear Augusta, is that your grandson has become a raving lunatic, leaving me with no choice but to set things right again. Put that down. Now."

Reluctantly Augusta dropped the vase onto the bed. "And just how do you intend to set things right, you murderer?"

"By cleaning up the mess I seem to have left." He smiled grimly. Grabbing Victoria by the hair, he hauled her to her feet. "This way, everyone."

Victoria was the first out the door into the hallway. She stumbled as the earl shoved her toward the stairs—and then froze. Sinclair stood there, his eyes dark with fury. For a moment she thought she must be hallucinating, until he uttered one quiet word.

"Duck."

She dropped, and his fist shot out, catching Kingsfeld flush on the jaw. As the earl pitched sideways, she ran back into the room, throwing herself on the second gunman before he could do more than open his mouth. Kit hit him low in the legs, and with her weight on his back, he toppled forward, knocking Kit's head hard against the nightstand.

The thug threw her off, and she smashed into the wardrobe, wrenching her arm. Shoving the dazed Kit aside, the man crawled toward her, snarling. At the last second Augusta stepped in front of her and slammed the vase down on his head. He collapsed amid the sounds of breaking porcelain.

"Splendid shot, Grandmama," Kit complimented, unsteady as he picked himself off the floor.

"Thank you, dear."

A shot rang out, the ball whizzing past them to imbed itself in the far wall. With a gasp, Victoria ducked again. Sinclair slammed the spent pistol out of Kingsfeld's hand.

"You are done with hurting my family," he snarled, and hit the earl again hard.

They both went down, and Victoria crawled to the bedchamber doorway as they crashed down the hallway toward the stairs. Sin caught a fist in the face, and blood trickled from a cut lip. He didn't even seem to feel the blow as he continued hammering at the stockier Kingsfeld.

Victoria wanted to shout at him to be careful, but she didn't dare risk distracting him. Then the earl pulled a knife from his boot. "Sinclair!" she shrieked.

"I hope you know how to use that," Sin snarled, dodging backward as Kingsfeld struck at him.

"Well enough to put you and the rest of your family out of my misery." The earl lunged at him again.

At the last second Sinclair ducked and heaved upward, throwing the earl over his shoulder. With a cut-off shriek, Kingsfeld went down the first flight of stairs headfirst and collapsed on the landing. Sinclair was down beside him in what seemed like one leap, kicking the knife from the earl's limp fingers.

Kingsfeld's head lay along his shoulder at an impossible angle. Sinclair rolled backward on his haunches and sat, bone-crunching weariness and relief flooding through him. He'd been in time, thank God—or whichever deity looked after fools like him.

"Is he dead?" Kit asked shakily from the railing, rubbing at an ugly knot on his forehead.

"Yes."

"There's one more, Sin."

"No. I found him in the drawing room; he won't be going anywhere for a while."

"Good."

Slowly Sinclair got to his feet again, his body and mind exhausted. Victoria stood at the top of the stairs, gazing at him, her hair disheveled but her expression for once unreadable.

Part of him had thought he would never see her again, sure that he was never to be allowed the happiness Victoria gave him. Even now, he wasn't sure. He'd lied to her and insulted her and manipulated her too many times. She couldn't possibly forgive him.

He climbed the stairs anyway. "Victoria," he said softly.

She flung herself into his arms. "Sinclair," she

sobbed, digging her hands into the back of his coat as though she never intended to let go. "Are you all right? Tell me you're all right."

Sinclair closed his eyes, burying his face in her hair. "Victoria, I'm so sorry," he murmured. "I'm so sorry."

"Don't you *ever* lie to me again," she said fiercely.

"Again?" he repeated, pulling her away from his chest so he could look into her violet eyes. "You mean you're giving me another chance?"

"Of course I am. I love you."

He stared at her. The dark, distrustful armor protecting his hurt, cynical insides melted away as though it had never been there. "You love me?" he whispered wonderingly, reaching out to tuck a straying strand of her midnight hair behind her ear. "Me?"

A tear coursed down one soft, smooth cheek. "Yes. I borrowed a horse from the Academy. I was going back to London to find you, but then I saw Kingsfeld heading here, so I turned around to warn—"

"You . . . you put yourself in danger. On purpose."

"So did you," she murmured.

Slowly he drew her into his arms again. "I love you," he said into her hair.

She lifted her face to him, and he kissed her fiercely. Victoria Fontaine was *his*. Finally. For whatever reason, she wanted to stay with him, and he wasn't about to question her wisdom.

"Sinclair," she whispered, "I need to tell you something."

"I already know."

Victoria looked at him. "You *knew*, and you still sent me away?"

"No, no, no," he said quickly, keeping tight hold of

her in case she attempted an escape. "Alexandra told me last night."

"Alexandra?"

"She punched me and then told me about the baby," he said, kissing her again.

Her violet eyes began to dance. "Lex punched you? She's never even punched Lucien."

He nodded. "I had the distinct impression that she was rather angry at me. Furious might be a better word. Sweet Lucifer, Victoria. You rode all the way from the Academy to Althorpe? Are you certain you're all right?"

"I am now."

He kissed her again. "You have every right to punch me yourself, you know. Or worse. I know you were hurt and angry."

"I was—until I figured you out."

"Again," he said with a soft chuckle.

"What finally convinced you about Kingsfeld?" She glanced over his shoulder toward the landing, but he turned her away.

"You don't need to see that. We're finally finished with him—thanks to you. *You* convinced me. And then I discovered that he owned a lamp factory in Paris."

"He killed Thomas because of *lamps*?"

"No. I happened to have visited it once, when one of Bonaparte's generals lost a wager to me. He owed me a rifle, and since we were both drunk and he therefore wasn't exercising the soundest judgment, he took me to a munitions factory. I didn't discover until the other day that it had the same name as the lamp factory Astin owned."

"Then he deserved to die," she whispered fiercely. "Do you think Thomas found out?"

"I think Astin was concerned he would. Apparently he meant to read a list consisting of every peer with French holdings when he presented his treatise before the House."

"He suspected Astin already, or he wouldn't have hidden those papers."

Sinclair nodded, looking up as Christopher and his grandmother approached. "I'm sorry I couldn't tell you. It was too dangerous."

"You should have told us anyway, you big oaf," Kit said heatedly.

The double doors downstairs slammed open. "Sin?"

"Upstairs. We're all right."

Victoria smiled at him. "Yes, we are."

Crispin thundered up the stairs, pausing for only a moment to look down at Kingsfeld's body. "Thank God. We heard a shot as we came over the hill."

A few seconds later, Wally and Bates joined them. "I'm getting too damned old for this," Wally rasped, bending over and panting.

"No matter," Sinclair said, hugging his wife as tightly as he dared. "I've just retired."

"Um, Sin, just so ye recall, we have one more matter to tend to back in London," Crispin countered.

Sinclair looked at him blankly for a moment. He was finished with this; finished with spying, finished with avenging Thomas, and finished with lying. Now he could finally look forward, instead of back over his shoulder. And he had something to look forward to: life with Victoria, and children, and whatever animal she decided rescuing next. He didn't think he'd mind if she *did* end up finding an orphaned elephant.

"What's left?" Victoria asked, resting her head against his chest.

"Marley," Wally prompted.

"Marley?" she repeated, frowning. "He didn't do anything—did he?"

"Damnation," he muttered. "No, except try to steal you away from me."

"He never had a chance, Sinclair."

"I had him arrested, though, to fool Kingsfeld. We have to get back to London before they decide to hang him."

Her lips twitched. "Poor Marley."

Sinclair kissed her smiling mouth. "Yes. I'll have to be the one who gets you into trouble from now on, I suppose."

Laughing, Victoria hugged him. "Is that a promise?"

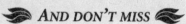